"Don't think."

"I can't afford—" She pressed her cheek against his. "I like you too much."

"That's a bad thing?"

"It could be. I don't know what you're up to."

"I don't mean to cause you any trouble at all." He squeezed her hand, and she turned to him, eyes bright with her willingness to taste more trouble. All he wanted was another taste of her, which was no trouble. Not for him, anyway. Not unless thinking made it so.

"Oh, Del, you..." She dropped her head back and laughed. "You have no idea."

A Cowboy's Best Friend

New York Times Bestselling Author

Kathleen Eagle

&

Cathy Gillen Thacker

Previously published as *Never Trust a Cowboy*
and *The Long, Hot Texas Summer*

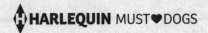

 HARLEQUIN® MUST♥DOGS

Recycling programs for this product may not exist in your area.

ISBN-13: 978-1-335-08016-5

A Cowboy's Best Friend

Copyright © 2020 by Harlequin Books S.A.

Never Trust a Cowboy
First published in 2014. This edition published in 2020.
Copyright © 2014 by Kathleen Eagle

The Long, Hot Texas Summer
First published in 2013. This edition published in 2020.
Copyright © 2013 by Cathy Gillen Thacker

This edition published by arrangement with Harlequin Books S.A.

For questions and comments about the quality of this book, please contact us at CustomerService@Harlequin.com.

Harlequin Enterprises ULC
22 Adelaide St. West, 40th Floor
Toronto, Ontario M5H 4E3, Canada
www.Harlequin.com

Printed in U.S.A.

CONTENTS

Books by Kathleen Eagle

Harlequin Special Edition

Wild Horse Sanctuary

Visit the Author Profile page
at Harlequin.com for more titles.

NEVER TRUST A COWBOY

Kathleen Eagle

In loving memory of Phyllis Eagle McKee

Chapter 1

Delano Fox enjoyed watching a smooth heist in progress the way any skilled player might be entertained by another's performance. Sadly, under the starlit South Dakota sky on the flat plain below his vantage point the only real skill on display belonged to a blue heeler, and even he was a little slow. Del was going to have to forget everything he knew about rustling cattle if he was going to fit in with this bunch. Otherwise he'd find himself itching to take over, which wasn't the best way to get in thick with thieves. Even rank amateurs had their pride.

One by one, six head of black baldy steers stumbled into a stock trailer, each one springing away from the business end of a cattle prod or kicking out at the biting end of the dog. There was no ramp, but a jolt of fear helped the first two clear the trailer's threshold.

When the third one tried to make a break for it, Ol' Shep lunged, crowding the animal against the trailer door. The guy manning the door cussed out both critters, while the one handling the prod added injury to insult by missing the steer and connecting with the dog. It would've been funny if he'd stung the other man with a volt or two, but Del instantly set his jaw at the sound of the yelping dog. Inexperience was curable, but carelessness could be a fatal flaw, and lack of consideration for man's best friend was just plain intolerable. The best cowhand of the lot—the one with paws—jumped into the bed of the jumbo pickup, where he shared space with the gooseneck hitch.

Two shadowy figures climbed into the growling workhorse of a pickup that was hitched to the stock trailer, while the third—the prod handler—hopped into a smaller vehicle—a showy short box with an emblem on the door—parked on the shoulder of the two-lane country road. He would be Del's mark. One of them anyway. He would be local, and he would be connected. Rustlers were high-tech these days, and they used every resource, did their research, found their inside man.

Del didn't go in much for high tech. He did his research on the down low, and he had already had a private, persuasive conversation with a man he knew to be one of the two hauling the stolen stock. The job he himself was looking for would soon be his.

He chuckled when he passed the sign welcoming him to the town of Short Straw, South Dakota, promising, You'll Be Glad You Drew It.

Maybe, but there was bound to be somebody in the area who wouldn't be. Del knew how to handle the short straw. He'd drawn it many times.

He followed the sawed-off pickup at a distance, which he kept as he watched the driver pull up in front of a windowless storefront emblazoned in green neon with what would have been Bucky's Place if the *P* were lit up. The *B* flickered, trying mightily to hang on to its dignity, but it was *ucky* that cast a steady glow above the hat of Del's mark, the man who had just helped steal six head of cattle. Del could see enough of the guy's face now to add a few pieces to those he'd already collected. He could now read the Flynn Ranch emblem on the pickup door. So far, so good. The driver wasn't much more than a kid, early twenties, maybe. The steers might well belong to his father. Wouldn't be the first time the heir decided to help himself to his inheritance a little early. Del just hoped Junior had the power to hire and fire ranch hands.

It took Del all of thirty seconds to disable a taillight on Junior's pickup.

A typical edge-of-town watering hole, Bucky's was shades of brown inside and out. Customers were lean and green or grizzled and gray, but they were all on the same page at Bucky's. They were winding down. Two guys sat side by side at one end of the bar, a third sat alone at the other, a man and a woman exchanged stares across the table in a booth and pool balls clicked against each other under the only bright light at the far end of the establishment.

"I'm looking for the owner of the Chevy short box parked outside." Del was looking at the bartender, but he was talking to anyone who'd noticed his entrance. Which would be everyone.

"That'd be me." The kid who'd wielded the cattle prod waved a finger in the air and then turned, beer bottle in hand. He wore a new straw cowboy hat and sported a pale, skimpy mustache. "What's up?"

"The name's Delano Fox." Del offered a handshake. "If you're with the Flynn ranch, I was told you might be hiring."

Junior admitted nothing, but he accepted the handshake. "Who told you that?"

"Ran into a guy who said he'd just quit. Told me to look for a red short box with a taillight out. Your taillight's out."

Junior frowned. "You been following me?"

"More like following up on a tip. Not too much traffic around here. Hard to miss a single taillight."

"When did he say he'd quit?"

"Maybe he said he was *about to* quit. I don't remember exactly how he put it, but if you're not short one hand, you soon will be. You hire me, you won't need anybody else. I'd get rid of the other guys."

The bartender chuckled.

"Only got one hand. *Had*, sounds like. Where did you run into him?"

"Couldn't say. Somewhere along the road." Del tucked his thumbs into the front pockets of his jeans and gave an easy smile. The way to play the game was to keep the questions coming and the answers on the spare side. "After a while they all look alike. Faces and places and roads in between."

Junior nodded toward the empty stool beside him.

"Did he mention his name?" Junior asked as Del swung his leg over the stool. "Or mine?"

"Flynn was all he gave me. Said he was helping move a few steers and that the guy driving the red pickup might be hiring. That last part was all that interested me."

"Brad Benson. Tell me why I should hire you."

So this wasn't Junior. One missed guess, but it was a small one. As long as the kid could hire a new hand, he would be hiring Del.

"I'll put in a full day every day." Del sealed the deal with a sly smile. "Or a full night. Whatever you need."

Benson took a pull on his beer, took his time setting it down and finally glanced sideways at Del. "How about both?"

"A guy's gotta sleep sometime. But yeah, calving time, I'm there. Workin' on a night move once in a while? I can do that, too."

Benson didn't bite. "Where have you worked before?"

"Just finished a four-month job on a place west of Denver. The Ten High. Foreman's name is Harlan Walsh." Walsh was his standard reference. Harlan knew the drill. Del had actually worked at the Ten High, just not recently.

"If Thompson don't show up tomorrow—"

"Pretty sure he won't." *Damn sure he won't.* Thompson had been most cooperative once Del had ruled out all other options.

"If he don't, then we'll try you out. The Flynn place is sixteen miles outside of town on County… Well, I guess you already know the road. We pay thirty a day to start, six days a week. You'll have the bunkhouse to yourself, and you'll get board with the family." The grin was boyish. "Bored, too. Get it?"

"Either way, as long you've got a good cook in the family."

"You can always get yourself a microwave," Benson said, tipping the beer bottle in Del's direction. "Oh,

yeah, and you answer to me. It's my stepdad's operation, but he's getting on, and we're trying to get him
to take it easy."

"Understood."

"And if it turns out you're more skilled than most,
more…specialized…" Benson's lips drew down in the
shape of his mustache. "You could bump up your income, put it that way."

"Like all good cowboys, I'm a jack-of-all-trades." Del
tapped his knuckles on the bar as he dismounted from
the stool. "With resourcefulness to spare."

"Just to show your appreciation, spare some on buying the second round."

Del chuckled. There hadn't been a first round. "My
employer always gets the better end of the deal. I'd suggest the other way around if I wasn't dog tired. I've been
on the road awhile."

"And I'd show you to your room, but I ain't ready
to hit the road."

"I'll be there by eight."

"Breakfast's at six."

Del glanced at the shot the bartender set down next
to Benson's beer, and then gave his new boss a slight
smile. "I'll be there by eight."

The Flynn Ranch sign hung high above the grav-
eled approach five miles south of the scene of the previous night's crime. Del's first thought was how easy it
would be to alter the Double F brand that adorned the
intersection of the gateposts and the crossbar on both
sides of the entrance. A seasoned rustler would have it
done by now even if he was hungover. Del was betting
Benson was fairly new to the game and that last night's

haul still carried the Double F. He doubted Benson had any authority to recruit new thieves. A man new to the game only stole his own cattle for show, to convince family, friends and FBI that he was among the victims. And by peeling off some skin and dropping it into the game, he bought himself some street cred. But he'd have to keep up appearances on both sides. Del looked forward to seeing whether Benson was any more serious about his acting than his rustling.

The red Chevy pickup was parked kitty-whompus beside an old two-story farmhouse that probably had been a local showplace in its day. The right front tire had crushed a bed of pretty blue-and-white flowers. Some of the once-white paint on the house was peeling, and some had been scraped. The covered porch looked as though it had recently been painted.

Del mounted the steps to the sprawling porch and rapped on the screen door. He heard movement, peered through the screen and saw a pair of chunky rubber flip-flops—neon green, if he wasn't mistaken—sitting on a rag rug in the dim alcove.

The bare feet that belonged to the shoes appeared at the top of the stairs beyond the alcove, paused and then ran down like water bouncing over rocks. Del was fascinated by the quickness of the flow and the lightness of the feet. He'd never seen prettier. He watched them slip into the rubber thongs, pink toenails vying for his attention with bright green straps. The colors spoke volumes about the woman who came to the door.

He wasn't sure why he wanted to hold off on looking up. The colors were cheerful, the feet were pretty and their owner probably belonged to his new boss. But for some reason he wanted to take her in bit by stirring bit.

She wore jeans that ended partway between her knees and her curvaceous ankles—Del admired a well-turned ankle—with a sleeveless white top over a willowy body. Her neck was pale and slender, chin held high, lips lush and moist, dark hair pulled back, and her big blue eyes stared at him as if he were some kind of a rare bird. Maybe he was looking at her the same way. He couldn't tell.

"Mornin'." Del recovered his game face and touched the front edge of his hat brim. "I'm looking for Brad Benson."

He watched her shut down any interest he'd sparked. "You came to the wrong door."

"If you wouldn't mind pointing me to the right one…" He smiled. "Sorry. Del Fox. I'm your new hired man."

"I don't have an *old* hired man. Or a man of any kind behind any of my doors. And if I did, it wouldn't be Brad Benson."

"My mistake. I saw his pickup out here." He was pretty sure she hadn't meant to be funny, but he had to work at keeping a straight face. His new boss was clearly in trouble. He stepped back and nodded toward the side of the house. "Looks like his pickup anyway."

She pushed the screen door open and ventured across the threshold, took a look and planted her hands on her hips. "It does, doesn't it?"

"Same plates and everything. Must be around some-where. You wanna tell him I'm here?"

"I want to tell him to get his pickup out of my flower bed. Or maybe you'd tell him for me when you find him."

"Should I try the doghouse?"

"I don't have one. My dog…" She stepped past him and surveyed the yard. Her tone shifted, the wind dropping from its sails. "Should be chewing on the seat of your jeans right about now."

"Guess he ain't hungry. Maybe he got a piece of Benson."

She gave her head a quick shake, banishing some momentary doubt that had nothing to do with him or with Benson. "Maybe you should check the pickup." She nodded toward the dirt road. "It's another mile and a half to the new house, and you can be sure Brad didn't walk. How drunk was he when he hired you?"

"Couldn't say."

"And you wouldn't if you could." She lifted a lightly tanned shoulder. "It really means nothing to me, but it might make a difference to you."

"I'll check the pickup." He touched two fingers to his hat brim and stepped back. "Sorry to bother you. Sign says Flynn Ranch, and Benson wasn't clear on where the house would be."

"I'm Lila Flynn," she said quickly. "Brad is my stepbrother. He lives down the road with his mother and my father."

"In the *new* house." He smiled, grabbing the chance to start over. "You get the home place."

"And you'll get the bunkhouse out back if Brad remembers hiring you." Suddenly retreating, she cast a backward glance. "Like I said, check the pickup."

Before the screen door slapped shut, Del caught the edge of a smile, the flash of blue eyes. Slim chance, he thought, but the door to making a second first impression had been left ajar.

Driveway gravel rattled under Del's boot heels as

he approached the red short box pickup. Benson's chin rode his collarbone as his head lolled from one side to the other.

"Good morning."

Benson opened his eyes halfway, squeezed the right one shut again and squinted the left one against the sunlight until Del's shadow fell across his face.

"Remember me?"

"Yeah, I remember." Brad waved a fly away from his face as he slid his spine up the back of the pickup seat. "You said you had all the experience I might be looking for. You haven't seen Thompson around, have you? The guy you're replacing?"

"Not since last night. Your sister's the only person I've run into since I got here."

"*Step*sister. She sure can be a bitch, that one." Brad draped one hand over the steering wheel and rubbed his eyes with the other, muttering, "The kind you wanna bring to heel."

"She said I could have the bunkhouse out back."

Brad dragged his hand down over his face. "She did, huh?"

"She did, but it's up to you. Like you said, you're the boss."

"You just said the magic words. What's the name again?"

"Del Fox. Do I need a key?" No answer. "You got anything you want me to do before I stow my gear?"

"What time is it? You probably missed breakfast."

"I had breakfast."

"That's right. You got yourself hired and called it a night. Showed up on time, too. Maybe we'll keep you around." He fired up the pickup. "Make yourself at home. Fox? It's Fox, right? Sorry, I'll be more hospitable after I've had some coffee." He pointed to the cabin fifty yards or so behind the house, not far from an old red barn with a lofty arch roof. "That'll be your home sweet home. We've got another barn down at the new house, but that's the only bunkhouse. Who needs two bunkhouses these days, right? Or two hired hands."

"One of each is more than most places have." And having a cozy log cabin to himself was a vast improvement over his usual accommodations.

"Everybody around here is downsizing. Either that or diversifying."

Del glanced to one side and noticed a fenced area close behind the house with a swing set, a little playhouse, a sandbox and more kid stuff. For some reason he was surprised, and he turned quickly back to Brad. "Which is it for you?"

"You'll have to ask Frank. My stepdad. Can't seem to make up his mind." Brad shifted into gear. "Take your time. I'll be getting a slow start today. If Thompson shows up, tell him to come find me."

Del dropped his duffel bag just inside the bunkhouse door and drew a deep breath. Pine pitch and dust. Pine was fine, but dust— He grinned—busting dust was a must. He opened the window between the two single beds and heard someone whistling—warbling, more like—and then calling out for Bingo. From the window he had a view of distant tabletop buttes and black whiteface cows grazing on buffalo grass. A meadowlark sang out, and a chorus of grasshoppers responded. He liked the sights and sounds, most of the smells, and he decided he wouldn't be living out of a suitcase for a while. He liked the idea of hanging up his shirts and putting his toothbrush on a shelf.

He was wrestling with the drawers in a broken-down dresser when the warbler tapped on the door.

"It's open."

The woman with the big blue eyes, Lila, peered inside. "It's always open, but you can have a lock on it if you want."

"I don't use locks. You knock, I'll answer." *Gladly.* No man in his right mind would lock her out. She was a pretty woman trying to pass for plain, and it wasn't happening. The world owed women like her a clue. She'd get noticed no matter what. "You need any help?"

She pushed open the door with the edge of a straw laundry basket. "I brought you some bedding. I have a feeling you won't see Brad before suppertime, and I don't know what's here."

"Somebody's clothes. If anyone comes looking, they're in that box on the bench outside the door." He nodded toward the floor in front of the dresser, where he'd tossed the sheets he'd stripped off the beds. "I wasn't sure what I was gonna do with those."

"I'll take care of them." She peeked into the bathroom. Her hair was clipped up on the back of her head in a jaunty ponytail. "I guess I could spare you some towels. Doesn't look like the last guy…" She turned and handed him the neatly folded bedding. It smelled like early morning. "I still can't find my dog," she said quietly as he set the laundry on the bed.

"I didn't see anything on the highway."

"You weren't really looking."

"You want me to? I've got nothing else to do. As far as I'm concerned, I've been on the payroll for about an hour now."

"He's pretty old. Doesn't usually go far from the house."

"You probably don't want your kids to find him first. How old are they?"

"My kids?" She gave him a funny look, as if maybe he'd been reading her mail. And then the light went on. "Oh, the play yard. I do some day care. *Other* people's kids."

"Maybe other people's kids took your dog."

"The kids aren't here on the weekend. Bingo. Little black terrier. If you see him…" She wagged her finger and chirped, "Bingo is his name-o."

"Ain't much of a singer, but I'm a hell of a whistler." He reproduced her warble perfectly. "Like that?"

"He won't be able to tell us apart." She smiled. "I'm not a hell of a whistler."

He smiled back. "You're a singer. You can have my whistle for a song. I'll drive out to the highway and walk the ditches. How's that?"

"As you said, you're on the payroll, but you don't work for me." She started for the open door, did an about-face on the threshold and came back. "But it's a generous offer, and I'll take you up on it. In return I'll—" she grabbed the laundry basket by one handle and lifted her shoulder "—owe you one."

"Two." He presented as many fingers. "If one good turn deserves another, I'll take two towels. If you're sure you can spare them."

"I'll even throw in a washcloth."

He came back empty-handed and genuinely relieved. He liked dogs and didn't want to see her lose hers. He was good at turning on the charm for people no matter what he was feeling, but there was no pretense when it came to dogs. He'd lived with them, worked with them, learned to respect them without exception. Lila Flynn was a dog person. He could be himself with her on that score.

Plus, she'd brought him clean sheets without him even asking.

He parked his pickup near the bunkhouse, taking care not to block the view from the door or either of the windows. He had to smile when he noticed the broom and mop leaning against the bench on the little plank porch, along with a bottle of Pine-Sol. His favorite.

His return didn't distract her from pinning laundry to the clothesline in her backyard. He watched her from his new front yard, a little below the level of hers. Another nice view. The summer breeze batted blue denim and white cotton around and toyed with Lila's hair. He enjoyed watching. But if she was still feeling friendly toward him, he would enjoy shooting the breeze with her even more.

Especially if she'd found her dog.

"Any luck?" he asked when he reached the clothesline. She shook her head. "I didn't find anything on the highway." She paused for a moment. "Guess that *is* lucky, when you think about it." He ducked under an assortment of socks and turned so he could see her face. "Maybe he's off huntin' rabbits."

She didn't look at him, but she smiled a little.

Try again, he told himself. "I haven't been around too many terriers. Maybe not big enough to take down a rabbit."

"Size doesn't matter. Not to a terrier. They'll take on all comers." She snapped a wet shirt straight. "So to speak."

He was pretty sure she meant to be funny, but her face wasn't showing it.

He smiled big. "A little confidence buys a lot of respect. From most comers anyway."

"Thanks for your help." She slid her empty basket across the grass and touch tested a sheet. "Oh, right. Towels." She headed for another line. "Let me fold these sheets and then I'll see if they're dry."

He stepped forward to help, and they fell naturally into the two-person task of taking down sheets and folding them, meeting corner to corner, brushing hand to hand.

"So your dad's kicking back and letting Brad take over?" Del asked.

"Take over what?"

"The cattle operation. Sounds like your brother's stepping up."

"*Step*brother."

"Stepping on toes, is he?" He surrendered a smooth sheet to her charge. "Kinda feelin' my way here. You hire on with a family operation, you like to get a feel for the pecking order before you step into the coop. Don't wanna slip on anything the first day."

She bent to the laundry basket. "You'll be on the bottom."

"And you?"

"I'm not part of the order. There's no pecking in my coop."

"Good to know." He unpinned a stiff towel. "Is the bunkhouse part of the peck-free zone?"

"That's up to you. Do you have any terrier blood in you?"

He laughed. "I can sure tell you do."

"Here you go." She selected a pair of blue towels, started to turn them over but paused for a quick nuzzling. "Mmm. Don't you just love the smell of air-dried laundry?"

"Mine usually comes from the Laundromat."

She straightened suddenly, her attention drawn to something just outside the play yard. "Bingo!" She dropped the towels in the basket, ducked under the clothesline and took off toward a mass of conspicuous greenery. "Bingo?"

A telltale hiss prompted Del to follow her. The woman could sure move.

"Lila, back off," he shouted, and she froze at the edge of the vegetable garden. "Step back real slow. That's not Bingo."

The critter sprang a good two feet above an orderly row of bush beans. It was a badger.

"He's got something cornered," Del said quietly.

"Bingo!"

He grabbed her from behind, pulled her to his chest and clamped his arms around her. "Good Lord, woman."

He held her close and still, and they watched the badger disappear and a rattlesnake spring forth. Snake down, badger up, like squeezing a long balloon, alternating ends. It might have looked funny if desperation hadn't been alternating with brutality.

"Damn. We're not even on their radar."

"I've never seen anything like it," Lila whispered, mesmerized by the hopping and hissing. "Good thing Bingo isn't around. He'd be right in the thick of it."

"You were close." And he wasn't letting her go.

They were close. She turned her head and looked up at him, and for a moment he was as deep into her as the

snake was into the badger. Just as surprised. Just as engaged. Her eyes were crystalline, as blue as the sky, and
damn if they weren't almost as big. They had power.

It wasn't until she turned back to the combatants
that he was able to draw breath. He loosened his arms
reluctantly but didn't let go, and she seemed a little re-
luctant to be let loose. An even match, neither could
gain without yielding. It was too late to compromise,
too soon to take prisoners.

Too late for a handshake; too soon for a kiss.

"I can't tell who's winning," she whispered.

He chuckled. All things considered, he'd made gains.

"No, really," she insisted. "Can you?"

"I think they're both hurtin'. Probably both wishing
they'd never met."

Finally the two animals jumped apart as though
someone had blown a whistle, then turned tail and took
off in opposite directions.

"What do you s'pose that was all about?"

"Home." His arms were a little lazy about letting her
go. "Some dank hole in the ground. Had to be. They
sure as hell weren't fighting over the same female."

"As long as it wasn't about my dog."

"I didn't hear either one call out, 'Bingo!'"

"You're funny." Her little smile settled the urge to
apologize. "I like that."

"You really love your dog. *I* like *that*." He grinned.
"How about going to supper with me?"

"You're expected at the other house."

"That's what I mean. How about going with me?"
He shoved his thumbs into his front pockets. "When I
get my first paycheck I'll take you to the best café in
Short Straw."

"I thought you'd been to Short Straw."

"I've been to Bucky's Place. Had a sausage-and-egg sandwich there this morning. Fresh out of the microwave."

"I can make you some lunch."

"My stomach's still working on that sandwich. Iron gut chippin' on a rock."

"It doesn't get much better in Short Straw. As for Flynn ranch fare…" She glanced past him, nodded toward the road to the other house. "Here comes your boss. Do you have much experience working cattle?"

"I'm a good hand, yeah."

"Don't let Brad get to you. He likes to give orders."

The red Chevy short box turned off the road and sped across the grass in their direction. Brad leaned out the window. "Hey, Fox, you ready to get to work?"

"Been ready."

"Hop in and I'll show you around." He pulled on the brim of his straw hat. "What's up, Lila?"

"Have you seen Bingo?"

"What, that old dog? You lost him?"

"I can't find him."

"Then he must be dead somewhere. I guarantee you, nobody would steal him." Brad caught Del's eye, expecting an ally. "Good for nothing, that dog. Except making a lot of noise."

"Only when you come around," Lila said.

"Recognition of the alpha. One thing about dogs, they know their place." He stroked his scraggly mustache with thumb and forefinger, then grinned, basking in the perfection of his observations. "I'll keep my eyes peeled. If I see hide or hair, you want me to bag it up for you?"

"If you find him, I'd like to have him back. Del's already searched the right-of-way."

"*Del*, huh? Just remember he works for *me*, Lila." He watched Del slide into the passenger seat. "Don't let her boss you around, man. She likes to give orders."

"Just something to do while I was waiting on the boss."

Del's smiling eyes connected with Lila's as he propped his elbow on the open window and gave her a conspiratorial wink.

Chapter 2

Lila wasn't taking the new hand seriously. She'd known he was kidding when he asked her to go down to her father's house with him for supper. She had managed not to look out her kitchen window more than once or twice, checking for signs of life at the bunkhouse. She told herself she was only parking her horse in Dad's corral now because it was time to check in. She hadn't seen her father in more than a week, and she was suddenly missing him.

She stuck her socks in her boots and left them in the elaborate mudroom June had added to the plans for the new house, padded through a kitchen filled with the smell of beef and fresh bread—interesting, since she'd never known June to bake bread—past the kitchen table normally used for meals and ventured into the dining room.

"Well, look who's here," Brad said. "There's an

empty chair next to me and one beside our new hired hand. Take your pick."

"Your new hired hand asked me to go to supper with him." Del almost managed to get out of his seat and pull out the chair before she claimed it herself. Lila tamped down a smile. "So I choose him."

"You should've told me you had a date, Del. We could've picked her up." Brad peered across the table at Lila. "How'd you get here? Don't tell me you finally decided to put the crazy woman in the closet and get behind the wheel of a car again."

She eyed him right back. "The horse I rode in on is helping himself to your hay."

Frank laughed. "My daughter is no crazier than I am, son. I'm taking up bread making. Watched one of them videos and got the recipe off the internet. How'd I do?"

"I knew he'd find it relaxing," June said. Her red hair looked freshly styled, the color skillfully revived. Dar's Downhome Dos had done it again. "It's very good, my darling. And you notice, the baker in the video was a man. The best chefs are men. So it doesn't surprise me that this bread is delicious. No more store-bought for us." She flashed Frank a doting smile. "No surprise, he especially enjoyed kneading the dough."

"What else has he been kneading?" Brad pulled a fake double take. "Never mind. We probably don't want to go there with our parents. Right, Lila? I mean, we're eating."

Once begun, half done, Lila reminded herself.

"He experimented with the dough hooks that came with that new mixer I got him, but that didn't do it for him. Right, Frank? I'd say mission accomplished, technique perfected. What do you think, Del?"

Del brandished the buttered heel he'd just torn into. "Great bread."

"There's more in the kitchen," Frank said.

"Just for you," June told Del. "When Brad said he'd hired a new hand, Frank was all about welcoming you with a good meal."

Frank gestured with the point of his table knife. "If you're as good as Brad claims, I'd like to keep you around for a while. Guess Thompson took off without saying too much. I never thought much of him, tell you the truth. Brad says he called a guy you worked for, what? Couple of years, right? Said you're a top hand." He turned to Brad. "Where'd you say that was? Colorado somewhere?"

"Denver," Brad said.

"So you came along at the right time. You mind puttin' up hay?"

"It was a four-month job," Del said quietly. "This last time. But I've worked for Walsh before. And I guess I wouldn't be much of a ranch hand if I minded putting up hay."

"I used to hate that part of the business, but nowadays, with the new equipment we've got, I can just—"

Brad's knife clattered to his plate. "I'll make sure Del has plenty to do, Dad. I drove him around all afternoon, so he knows what he's in for. He's like you. Says his cowboy ass ain't sittin' on no ATV. Right, Del?"

"Brad fixed me up with a good mount." Del glanced at Lila, an I'm-on-your-side look in his eyes. "Nice big buckskin."

"Hombre," Brad told Frank. "Figured you wouldn't mind."

"Best horse on the place." Frank grinned. "He should be ridden, and by somebody who knows how."

Between her father's grin and the look in the hired hand's eyes, Lila suddenly took heart.

"Sounds like something I've heard before," Brad said.

"That's what Rhett Butler said to Scarlett," June put in.

"Kissed." Lila attended to buttering her bread. Attention with a secret smile. "He said she should be *kissed* often."

"I don't get to many movies," Del said. "This Butler, is he a cowboy? You got a horse needs ridin' or a woman needs kissin', you find yourself a real cowboy. Ain't many of us left."

"Probably just as well," Lila said. "Hollywood isn't making many Westerns these days."

"R-e-a-l," Del instructed. "Not *r-e-e-l.* The world is full of actors."

Lila flashed him a richly deserved smile.

"You like that?" His answering smile lit a true twinkle in his nearly black eyes.

"I do."

"What's going on here?" Brad said. "If I didn't know better…"

"You'd think I was rackin' up points with the boss's daughter. But I can already tell she doesn't give out easy points. I'm just trying to keep up with the conversation." Del glanced around the table. "Lila and I witnessed a rare sight this morning." He nodded at her. "You tell it."

"We watched a fight between a badger and a rattlesnake. They tore up my garden."

"I thought *I* tore up your garden," Brad said.

"You ran over a flower bed." She took Del's cue and kept going. "It was amazing. They really kept at it for, I don't know, five minutes, maybe… They just kept at it." She turned to Del. "Didn't they?"

A loaded look accompanied Del's nod. "Time stood still."

"In fact…" *Damn*, he was good-looking. Nearly black hair, chiseled cheekbones, angular jaw and no white-above-the-eyebrows farmer tan on this cowboy's face. Unless she was mistaken, he'd be head-to-toe brown. Lakota, probably. It took her a moment to turn her attention to her father. "Del caught me before I walked right into the fray."

"How awful. I hate snakes of any kind." June gave a tight end-of-story smile. "And I really hope you'll start joining us for supper regularly, Lila."

"I didn't have any kids today. Del helped me look for Bingo. I've been searching on horseback, still haven't found him." She lifted one shoulder. "So I was…in the neighborhood."

"I haven't seen the pup at all lately." Frank turned to his wife. "Have you? You've been out quite a bit getting groceries and whatnot."

"I thought he always stayed around your yard," June said, turning to Lila.

Lila nodded. "That's why—"

"Bingo is the first dog we've had around here since Lila left for college," June explained, apparently for Del's information. "I'm not a dog person. Kind of allergic." She turned to Lila. "I think that's why you decided to move into the old place when you came back, isn't it?"

"That's my house," Lila said.

"I know, but it's as old as the pyramids, all dark and depressing. We'd like to see more of you. That's all I'm saying."

"I'm not far away, June. You have to drive past my house to get to the highway. We see each other all the time." Lila welcomed the mental distance that slid over her like a cool cloud. "And your hired hands are always perfectly positioned to keep an eye on me."

"That happens to be where the bunkhouse is," Brad said. "The men don't give you any trouble, do they? You tell me if they do. I never hire anybody without checking him out. And I don't tell them to keep an eye on you." He turned to Del. "I never told you to spy on her, did I?"

Del shook his head. "This was a fine meal." He tucked his napkin under the edge of his plate and slid his chair back from the table. "It's been a long time since I had any homemade bread. Sure was good."

"Now, listen, you tell her I never said anything about—"

Del chuckled. "In my line of work you quickly learn when to hold 'em and when to fold 'em. Hold your tongue, fold your napkin and leave the table." Which he did, all but the tongue-holding part. His calm, cool parting shot was aimed at Brad. "I can handle most any chore, but spyin' ain't one of 'em." He nodded at June. "Thank you, ma'am."

Lila found Del in the barn currying the buckskin. He'd had time to saddle up after making that break for it, killing the time she'd allowed to pass before she left the house. Nothing further had been said on the subject after he left. Maybe they all felt ridiculous. *Keep an eye on her.* If Brad had asked—and she had her doubts about that—Del would have refused. She'd only been around him for a few hours, but she'd learned a lot, and she had no doubt he would have said no.

"So that was awkward, huh?" She ducked under one of the cross ties and scratched Hombre's throatlatch. "I'm sorry."

"Forget it. Whatever that was about, it's for you guys to deal with."

"But we put you in an uncomfortable spot, and I'm—"

"Don't apologize. It had nothing to do with me." He glanced at her. "Unless you think otherwise?"

"I don't. I know you wouldn't go along with anything like that." She smiled. "I realize we just met, but I'm a pretty good judge of character. Brad can't push you into doing anything you don't want to. I'm surprised you're still here."

"I'm here to work, and I've been at this kind of work long enough to know when to excuse myself from the table." He ran his hand down the horse's back and patted his rump. "I'm the one who owes an apology. I asked you to come with me for supper, and then I didn't show up."

"You were working."

"I don't know what I was thinking. Should've taken my own pickup instead of getting in with Brad. But now that I've got this guy…" He lifted a familiar black saddle onto the buckskin's back. "Brad didn't tell me he was Frank's. You think he minds?"

"I think he's glad to have you ride him."

"Is he a good judge of character, too?"

"Sometimes. He's already taken a shine to you."

"So…" He gave the saddle cinch a firm tug. "Would you like some company on the ride back to your ancient digs?"

She smiled. "Would you like a tour of the ruins when we get there?"

"You got any mummies?"

"I had one, but she died when I was twelve. Now I just have a stepmummy." She gave a shy smile. She knew she was being too cute by half. She was far afield of her comfort zone. "You?"

"Mine's dead, too. So's my dad. Been a while, so, uh…" He lowered the stirrup. "We should cover new ground on the way back. I didn't get much chance to look close, flying around the pasture in Brad's pickup— hey, that man sure has a lead foot—but I tried to be on the lookout. You know, for…any kind of sign."

"See what I mean? You're obviously a nice man."

"You want me to throw a saddle on that pretty black?"

"I pull out my own chair and saddle my own horse." She smiled. "But thanks for the thought."

"Yes, ma'am." He touched his hat brim. "Always thinking."

The sun hovered above the sawtooth horizon and the air was still, leaving the horses to stir the grass and offering the crickets a quiet setting for their serenade. Lila had covered the side of the road before supper, so they took the south side, zigzagging separately, cutting across a wide swath. She knew the odds of finding anything weren't great, but every search was a chance, and she wouldn't rest until she knew for sure. She'd adopted

Bingo from a shelter in Rapid City, and he'd seen her through some lonely times.

"Was he sick or anything?"

Lila looked up and saw Del staring at something on the ground. His dismount was as fluid as any she'd ever seen. Reins in hand, he squatted on his heels, picked something up and sniffed it.

"C'mon, Jackpot." She trotted her horse in his direction. "Anything?"

"Too old." He stood up and tossed his discovery. "A piece of something hairy, but all dried up."

"Why do I have a feeling you haven't always been a cowboy?"

"I don't know." He used the horn as a fulcrum and swung back into the saddle without benefit of a stirrup. Grinning like the boy who'd taken a run and jumped all the way over the creek, he adjusted his hat. "Maybe I started out as a trick rider."

She narrowed her eyes, considering, and shook her head. "What else you got?"

"I like to work my way up, one surprise at a time. Keeps 'em guessing." He braced his forearm over the horn and took a turn studying her. "Where'd you go to college?"

"Minneapolis." He'd started moving. She nudged her gelding to catch up. "Were you ever a cop?"

He gave her an incredulous look, caught himself and laughed. "How did you come up with that?"

"The way you examined the evidence."

"Too many detective movies and not enough Westerns, college girl. What did you study?"

"Art history, music, British history, literature—"

He whistled appreciatively.

"—business, library science."

"That's a lot of studying."

"I didn't quite finish," she said quietly.

A meadowlark answered Del's whistle.

"I'm listening," he prompted after a moment had passed.

"I had a bad car accident."

He let the words have their due. The grass swished, crickets buzzed, the sun settled on the sharp point of a hill.

"Hurt bad?"

"I wasn't. The person I hit… She was." She cleared her throat. "I don't drive anymore."

"Not at all?"

"Not at all."

More grass sound filled in.

"She okay now?"

"Were you ever a reporter?" she retorted stiffly.

He said nothing. He'd gone one step too far. Game over.

"Put it this way," she amended. "You don't strike me as the kind of man who usually asks a lot of questions."

"I'm not the kind who'd strike you at all. I'm the kind who'd do his job, tip his hat when you walk past him and keep his thoughts to himself."

"Sounds like we're two of a kind. Or *were*, until you took an interest in helping me find my dog."

"You'd do the same, right? It's all about the dog."

"We were talking about ancient history before," she reminded him. "Mummies and all like that. Been a while, you said. For me, too. And the passage of time helps. I know it does. It takes the edge off regrets, shuts down the what-ifs." They were riding slowly now, the search all but set aside. "She recovered, but it took a long time, and it changed her life. Don't ask me how it happened. It doesn't matter."

He nodded.

She knew she didn't have to tell him not to discuss it with anyone. It wouldn't kill her if he did, but somehow she knew he wouldn't. They had things in common, spoken and unspoken things. What things they were didn't matter as much as how they felt about them. They could move on without exchanging details.

"I have to find Bingo, no matter what. I have to bring him home."

"Do you have a picture of him?"

"You'll know him when you see him. He's the only little black terrier around. This isn't exactly terrier country."

"What's the cell phone reception like around here?"

"Terrible. You have to go up on a hill, and even then it's hit or miss. You're welcome to use my old reliable landline anytime."

"I was thinking if I find the dog and he won't come to me…"

"He loves cheese." She tucked her hand in her back pocket, pulled out a chunk of it wrapped in brown paper and reached between horses to hand it to him. "He won't care if it's a little squashed."

"Funny dog."

She smiled. "You two will hit it off just fine."

At breakfast the next morning Del was assigned his first official chore. No surprise, he was to ride the fence and check for breaks.

"Neighbor called and told Dad there's been cattle

disappearing again. I'm gonna head down to the south pasture and start counting."

"If I find anything, you want me to fix it right away?" Since he knew where to look, he was going to help himself to a second cup of coffee. He gestured with the pot, and Frank offered up his cup for a refill.

"Well, *yeah*," Brad said. "That's one job you can be sure gets delegated."

"Just wanted to make sure."

"If we're missing cows and we don't find them, we'll let the sheriff in on all the details."

Frank took no notice. Either he didn't hear, didn't want to hear or his agreement went without saying. In any case, nobody was too concerned about preserving a possible crime scene.

Del took his time riding the fence along the dirt road that separated two Flynn Ranch pastures. He knew he would find the wire down less than a mile off the blacktop, but along the way there was a chance he might run across Lila's dog. He found himself hoping otherwise. This far from the house, it was bound to be a sad discovery.

A faint set of tire tracks in the dry ground led to the hole in the fence. Three loose strands of barbed wire curled away from the steel post in three different directions. A qualified lawman would be able to get a clue or two, and fixing the fence wouldn't make too much difference. But it would make some. Not to Del, of course. He'd been a witness. Now he had to figure out where Frank fit in, and he knew better than to ask questions he didn't know the answers to.

He fixed the wire, and then he followed the fence line until it took a right turn at the highway. There he saw the grass stir. It could've been a snake or a grouse, but it wasn't. He knew before he reached the spot that he'd found the little black dog.

Not quite what he'd expected, but it was small and male and black. Who else could it be? And he was alive, which was a whole lot better news than he'd expected. Del whistled. The paper crinkled as he unveiled the chunk of cheddar.

"Got some cheese for you, Bingo. Come and get it, boy." He sank to his knees, and the pup bounded through the grass and pounced on the cheese. Del's left knee cracked in protest as he stood with his arms full of wiggly, scrawny, finger-licking dog. "I thought you'd be fuzzier. How'd you get this far from home on such short legs, huh?" The dog seemed a little young, but maybe that was because he was scared and hungry. He rooted around Del's shirt, struggled to get his nose in Del's scratching hand. "That's all I've got, boy, sorry. We'll go get you some more. Lila sure is gonna be happy to see you."

But she wasn't.

She petted the pup's head, but she wouldn't take him in her arms. "He's cute enough, but he's not my dog."

"What do you mean, he's not your dog?" Del put the dog on the ground, let him check out the furniture legs on Lila's front porch. "I found him not three miles from here, nobody else around. He fits your description. He's— You're pullin' my leg, right?" The dog sniffed Lila's bare toes. "He likes you."

Then he abandoned bare toes for black boot.

"Hee-yah!" Del ordered, and the dog looked up and cocked his head as though he needed a translation. And, of course, he did. Forgetting himself—more like forget-

ting his cover—Del had spoken in Lakota, his father's first language. "No. Don't you dare."

The dog wagged and whined.

Lila laughed. "He likes you even more."

"Only because I fed him. Hell, he loves cheese, just like you said." He jerked his thumb toward the porch steps and told the dog, "Show her you know where to pee."

Lila folded her arms imperiously. "He's not Bingo. He's too young, and he's not even a terrier."

"He's a little black dog. Bingo?" The wagging speed doubled. Del had to reward such obvious name recognition by picking him up again. "Yeah, Bingo. She's messin' with me, ain't she?"

"He'd wag his tail for you if you called him Stupid. He's not my dog."

"Damn." Del lifted the dog's muzzle and looked him in the eye. "You sure?"

"I've never seen him before. I'll ask my kids' parents when they drop them off, but my guess is, you've found yourself a dog."

"What do you mean, *myself*? I've been looking all over hell for *your* dog."

"He doesn't have a collar. Either somebody dropped him off or…" Lila scratched the furry head. "Are you lost? Did you run away? Speak."

"Ruff!"

"Aw." Del put the pup down and offered a hand. "Shake." Paw plopped into hand. Del flashed Lila a grin. "And you can just tell he's housebroken, too."

"Lucky for you," she said. "Because I'm not looking for *a* dog. I'm looking for *my* dog. Unless somebody comes looking for him, the finders-keepers rule applies."

"I like dogs, but there's no way."

"Yes, there is. I see the will in your eyes." She glanced at the dog. "And thirst in his." She retrieved a pan of water from the other end of the porch and set it down. They watched him go for it. "Bingo... When he comes back, Bingo will let him stay with you, but not with me. So you'll have to take care of him, and you might as well start now."

"No, I can't..." Del slid the pup a sympathetic glance. "Somebody's been teaching this dog tricks. That somebody's looking for him as we speak."

"And if that somebody comes to call, you're in luck. Or out of it, which would be—" Lila levered an eyebrow and growled *"—ruff."*

"I'm bettin' somewhere there's a kid crying over this dog." The eyebrow arched again, and he groaned. "You got some food for him?"

"I have all kinds of stuff you'll need for him. I'll drop it off in the bunkhouse. And I have kids coming this afternoon. I promise I'll ask about him."

"They'll love him." And they'd all play with him, give him a name.

"If nobody comes looking for him, you'll have to get him vaccinated before he can be around my day care kids." She patted his arm. "I'm holding out for Bingo."

"I looked all over, Lila. This little guy needs—"

"All over? You've only been here a couple of days. This place is a lot of all over." She watched the pup for a moment, stepped back and shook her head. "It was an honest mistake. I don't want to keep you from your job."

"You're not. I was on my way to find Brad." The

little black dog was right behind Del when he left. He turned, looked down at the wagging tail, the expectancy in a pair of big brown eyes, and he chuckled. "Yeah, you can come along."

"Wait!" she called after him. "I'm…" He stopped, but he didn't turn around. "I'll get you some dog food."

"Leave it in the bunkhouse."

Del walked away muttering, "The hell with her," to the dog. If she was interested, the woman heard him. If she wasn't, a little curse didn't matter to her anyway. But he was pretty sure he still had her attention, pretty damn sure he was getting under her skin right now.

"And we both know there's more'n one way to skin a cat," he whispered to his new companion. "Ain't that right?" Then he laughed at himself for conjuring an image of peeling Lila's T-shirt over her head. "Skin the cat" was one of his dad's crazy sayings.

"The hell with her" was not.

Del found Frank cleaning a saddle in the new barn. One wall of the tack room was lined with racks stocked with saddles and hooks heaped with bridles, all in beautiful condition. Frank was a true horseman.

"Brad back yet?"

"Haven't seen him." Frank tapped the lid on a can of saddle soap. "He took his pickup. I don't think he was too serious about checking cows. Not from a pickup."

"The fence was down about a mile off the highway on the cut-across. All three strands cut."

Frank dropped the can into a rubber tub. "Could be kids."

"There were tire tracks. I don't know why kids would go to all that trouble, though. Not the best place for a party. Nothing left behind. No cans, no bottles, no butts."

"Did you fix it?"

"For now. Should be replaced."

"You rode the fence line on horseback?" The older man's face lit up. "There's wire out in the shop. We'll load some up, drive over and do it right."

"I can take care of it now. Just say the word."

"I did. It's *we*. We'll go out and stretch some wire." He slid his stool up against the wall, lifted his John Deere cap, raked his fingers through thinning gray hair and then settled the cap back in place as though they were heading for town. "I think I'm gonna like you, Del. Seems like you're here to work."

"I've worked for guys who want me to wade right in and do what needs doing and guys who want me to wait for orders. I'm good either way."

Frank clapped a sturdy hand on Del's shoulder. "Then you'll be good loading up the wire in case my wife looks out the window. I'll bring the pickup around."

"Guess I'm done waiting."

The chance to spend quality time with Frank fit nicely into Del's plan, and considering the way things were working around the Flynn place, it had come sooner than expected. It was a good sign, he thought, and then he dismissed the idea. He was looking to connect the dots. From his perspective they were neither good nor bad. They were just dots. The connections were all that counted.

"I didn't mean to bother you with this," he told Frank as they approached the stretch of fence he'd patched earlier. He pointed, and Frank pulled over. "Retirement must be nice."

"Brad says I'm retired?" Frank chuckled. "Don't worry. You can answer truthfully. It won't get back to him."

"I guess what he said was, he's trying to get you to take it easy."

"In my old age?"

"Now, he didn't *say* that. You've got a real nice place here, Frank. Probably been building it up acre by acre for…"

"Most of my life." Frank pushed his door open, but he wasn't in any hurry to get out. He was taking in the view. Grass and sky. "Belonged to my wife's family, my first wife. I own half the land. Lila's grandmother left her the other half, along with the home place." He turned to Del, as though he was about to deliver news that deserved special treatment. "My first wife died."

"When Lila was twelve."

Frank raised his brow. "Brad told you?"

"Lila did. My mother died young, too."

Frank gave a tight-lipped nod. Del read the message in his eyes. Tough break all around.

"Lila's never forgiven me for getting married again. She should've outgrown that by now. A man doesn't stop living just because his wife dies. Especially not if he has a young child. Your dad remarry?"

Del shook his head. "Never did."

"Is that some kind of tradition?

"You mean for Indians?" Del shook his head. "My mother was white. My dad was Lakota. I'm sure he had his reasons for not getting married again, but being Lakota wasn't one of them."

"It's hard, losing your wife sudden like that. Or your mother. Leaves a big hole right through your chest. The wind—" he gestured with a shivery hand "—whistles right through."

Del showed Frank the tire tracks, which, interestingly enough, didn't elicit much reaction. Del had to fish for it.

"Brad said neighbors have been losing cattle."

"Could be rustlers, I guess. There's been some rustling now and again lately, but it's mostly been tribal cattle. I don't lease any tribal land, so I stay out of their business, but I've heard rumors about the tribe being short quite a few cows." Frank turned his attention to the fence, but he kept talking as he examined Del's fix. "They say the ranch manager is a suspect. Old fella named Stan Chasing Elk. His daughter and mine were real close."

"Who's accusing him?"

"Mostly the tribal police, but I guess the tribal council is getting down on him. Anyway, that's what I've heard. As long as it's just the tribe's cattle, it's none of my business."

"Could be it's your business. You callin' the law on this?"

"If we're missing cows, you damn betcha. You did a nice job here, but we'll string up new wire." His tone shifted, as though he'd been asked to testify. "It ain't Stan. We go way back. Good man, Stan." He turned his attention to a passing cloud. "Stan the Man. Remember the baseball player?"

Del glanced at the cloud, half expecting to see a Stan or two up there, acknowledging Frank's memory with a thumbs-up.

Frank snapped out of his reverie with a chuckle. "Course not. That was a long time ago."

"Stan the Man Musial. One for the books, and I do

read some. Musial said, 'When the pitcher's throwing a spitball, just—'"

"'—hit it on the dry side,'" they quoted in unison, and then they both laughed as Frank clapped a hand on Del's shoulder.

"I played baseball in high school. First base. Pretty good hitter." Del read approval in Frank's face, and he figured the old man had faced more spitballs over the years than he had. "Your sport, too?"

"Was. Never had time to play much, but..." He looked down at the tire tracks and shook his head. "Yeah, I think we might've lost some cows. We'll see what Brad comes up with. I keep my books on paper. He's got this computer thing going, and we don't always match up."

"I'm not much of a computer guy myself."

"Glad I'm not the only one. Guess we need to get with the program, buddy." Chuckling, he laid his hand on Del's shoulder. "They say everybody's replaceable these days. Even cowboys."

"Yeah, that horse is out of the barn."

"Come to think of it, they haven't made the computer yet that can chase that horse down and run him back in."

"Or string wire," Del said. "So I guess I'm not completely replaceable."

"Brad either chose well or lucked out this time." Frank smiled. "I admire a man who knows the value of a good horse. Still the best way to herd cows."

Del tried two hills before he found a piece of high ground where his phone quit cutting out. Truth be told, he was one hell of a space-age cowboy. While truth telling wasn't part of his job description, he made an effort to keep mental tabs on it, and taking his smartphone in hand and tapping out a couple of texts allowed him to get in touch with reality even as he was keeping his head in the game. The message that came back was unsatisfying, but at least it was a contact.

Follow Benson. Get a line on Chasing Elk. Move up the line ASAP.

ASAP wasn't Del's preferred approach to a job. Space-age aside, a dyed-in-the-hide cowboy didn't do ASAP. If the question was "Fast or good?" his answer was always "The best you've ever had."

Which made him think of Lila.

"I like her," he told the dog in the passenger seat. He gave the animal's head a vigorous scratching, the velvety drop ears a floppy workout. The pup lifted his head, eyes closed in pure bliss. "Okay, so she rejected you for now, but it's not personal. She can't give up too soon. It would be like saying out with the old, in with the new. That's hard for a woman like her. She's got no ASAP button. Give her time."

The dog whined.

"No? Sorry, buddy, we got no choice. We gotta let her come to us. Okay?" He patted the dog's back. "Meanwhile, I'm here for you."

Chapter 3

"I think we're missing six head of steers," Brad reported. He glanced at Del as though he might have something to with it. Then he turned his attention to Frank, but he didn't look him in the eye. He dug his boot heel into the pulverized corral dirt like a kid who was having trouble making stuff up as he told his father how he'd done exactly what he was supposed to do. "Unless they got in with the cows. I mean, I drove across the south pasture and didn't see any steers in with the cows there. That's the only place..." He jerked up his chin suddenly. "You say there's tire tracks?" he asked Del. "What kind?"

"Sixteen and a half inch, probably a GM, maybe a Ford—big one-ton sucker—towing a gooseneck trailer."

"What color?" Frank asked, straight-faced as hell.

"The pickup or the gooseneck?"

"Either one," Frank allowed. "Hell, both."

Del's expression matched the old man's. "Black. Had to be a matched set."

Brad was speechless, waiting for something to drop— a shoe, a net, something. Del purely enjoyed the seconds that passed before Frank tapped his shoulder with the back of his hand, signaling it was time for a good laugh.

"I can read tracks, but not quite that good," Del said.

"Ground's too dry," Frank said. "You were doing real good finding any tracks at all." He turned to Brad. "You sure we're missing six? You got ear-tag numbers?"

"Dad, they're *missing.*"

"You get the numbers that are there," Frank explained with exaggerated patience. "The ones that aren't there are the ones we're looking for."

Brad glared briefly at Frank and then at the fence wire in the back of Frank's pickup. "You know, I told Del to get that fence fixed." He turned to Del. "You didn't need to go to my dad for help."

"He didn't," Frank said. "He was looking for you. I went out there with him because I needed to get out of the damn house."

"Well, good. That's good." Nodding, Brad slid Del a cold glance. "I'll give the sheriff a call, tell him where to meet up so he can see what's going on out there." He turned back to Del. "You go get the tag numbers off those steers out where I showed you yesterday. You remember how to get there?"

"You don't want him to show you where he found the tire tracks?" Frank asked.

"You said the cut-across, right? How far off the highway?"

"Little less than a mile. I marked the fence with a

red flag. You can tell where it was cut. Anyway, Sheriff Hartley can tell." Frank turned to Del. "I'll get us the list of tag numbers. We'll go out and check them off, see what's missing."

"You're not thinking about getting on a horse," Brad challenged.

"I think about it all the time."

"Don't tell Mom that. She's thinking all the time, too. About that trip you promised her after you get your other new knee." Brad sidled up to Frank. "Let me take care of this, Dad. We'll check the ear tags and figure out what's what. You get hold of Hartley. Better you than me." He looked over at Del and went back to being boss. "Mount up. Dad knows best."

Del let his horse drop back to a trot when he heard the roar of the pickup at his back. He didn't need help with taking ear-tag inventory—he could easily handle Frank's metal clipboard himself—and he doubted he would get much. But making waves didn't suit his purpose. Neither did ignoring Brad, as much as he wanted to. They both knew how many steers were missing. Brad didn't know or care which ones they were. But Frank cared, and that was another good sign.

Sign. Just a piece of information. *Connections, Fox. That's all you're looking for.*

"This works out better," Brad called out from the pickup.

Del slowed to a walk. "What does?"

"Letting Frank be the one to deal with the sheriff. I had a few run-ins with Hartley back when I was a kid, young and dumb. But I've stayed away from him since then. I need to keep it that way."

"I hear you." And hearing was enough. He kept his eyes on the view. Clear blue sky and rolling hills. The grand scheme. "Cops have tunnel vision. Out of sight, out of mind."

"You know it. I didn't count, but I figure there was probably a hundred head of steers in that pasture. Frank won't be satisfied until he has ear-tag numbers. There's no way around it."

"Don't worry about it. I'll take care of it."

"That's what I like to hear."

Brad came to a stop and toyed with the accelerator. Power. Play. Del spun his horse and let him prance a little in response.

"But you can't fake it," Brad warned. "He still keeps records."

"He seems pretty sharp."

"He's slipping. A year or two ago he wouldn't trust me to count the eggs in the fridge. So you got this?"

Del spun again, enjoying the buckskin's responsiveness, but a hint of something black lying in the shade of a chokecherry bush caught his eye. He urged his mount to trot ahead.

Brad shouted out to him and then followed, but he had to slow down for rutted terrain. By the time he reached the copse of bushes, Del had dismounted, dropped a knee to the ground and greeted the little corpse by name. Only the soft black hair moved, ruffled by the breeze.

"You got something I can wrap him up in?" Del asked when the sound of footsteps interrupted his thoughts. This wasn't the way you wanted to find the friend of a friend.

"Just leave him. I'll tell her there wasn't much left."

Del got up and craned his neck for a look in the pickup

bed. "A plastic bag or something? When we get back to the barn I'll find something better to put him in."

"It's a dead dog, for God's sake. Coyotes should've made short work of the thing by now."

"They didn't." Del pulled his hat brim down to block out the sun. Or, far more irritating, the sight of Brad Benson. "She said she wants him back no matter what. It's a small thing to ask."

"Throw it in the back of the pickup. What's the use of having coyotes around if they don't do their part?" Brad gave him a look, half suspicious, half mocking. "Fox, huh? Maybe you're the coyote."

"Yeah, maybe."

It bothered him all afternoon. He worked around the steers as quickly as he could, taking care not to disturb them too much while he took inventory, but he thought about that dog the whole time. Thought about Lila. Thought about the fact that her damn stepbrother had no respect for anything that mattered, and that her affection for her dog mattered in a way that not much else in Del's own world did.

Except the job. His *real* job. Starting out, the job had meant freedom. It had meant reporting only to one person instead of a dozen. It had meant eating what he wanted, going to bed when he felt like it. It had meant out with the old and in with the new. He wasn't going to miss any of the old, and the new was yet to be discovered. But affection hadn't figured in anywhere. His father was gone, and Del couldn't help but think he'd died of a broken heart, that his affection for his son had become such a heavy burden that his big heart had cracked. And with his father's death a chunk of Del's own life had been removed, like some kind of surgical amputation. What he had—what there was for him to build on—was a strange and unexpected job.

Which had nothing to do with putting the lid on the small pine box he'd fashioned, hoping it would bring some kind of comfort to the woman who was going to miss the old dog he'd put inside.

"Wondered where you were."

Del closed his eyes and stifled a groan.

"You missed supper. What's… You got that dog in there?" Brad came too close for Del's comfort to the two sawhorses that supported the little casket like a crude catafalque. "Nice box. Where'd you find it?"

"I made it."

"That quick? You're a man of many talents, Fox." Brad ran his hand over the unfinished pine. "Where'd the wood come from?"

"Frank said I could help myself to the scrap pile."

"When I hired you, did I mention you'd be working for me?"

"You did." If Brad got a splinter, it would be Bingo's revenge. He'd treated the dog's body like roadkill.

"You got a question, I want you to come to me with it."

"You got work you want done, I want you to tell me." He smiled. He liked the way Brad had to look up to meet his eyes. "I didn't ask. He offered."

"You didn't seem like such a charmer when you hired on, but it sure didn't take you long to get all up in my family business." Brad pointed a finger. "You report to me, and I report to Frank." He came dangerously close to poking that finger into Del's chest. "And Lila's off-limits." Then he came to his senses and lowered his ridiculously soft hand.

"You tell me what you want done, I'll put in a full day's work and then some. You tell me who I can and can't talk to, I'll be leaving before the day's over." Del raised a brow. "And we both know you need me more than I need this job."

"Hey," Brad said quietly, palms raised in surrender. "Let's just, you know, step back from the edge here. I can tell you're a good hand. I see that already. And yeah, like they say, good help is hard to find." He leaned on the casket. "I'm a little touchy about my family. I've got a lot on my plate these days."

"Try taking smaller helpings." Del cast a disapproving look at the hand on the box.

"Yeah, you're right. I take on too much." Brad quickly folded his arms. "Now that you're on board, I'm gonna leave the haying up to Frank. He likes to run the machinery, but we gotta make sure he doesn't do much more than that. He won't even use the AC in the John Deere." He shrugged, as if to say, *What're ya gonna do?* "So why don't you go check in with Frank. Tell him as long as he's puttin' up hay, breakfast to dinner you're all his." Brad picked up the box. "While I deliver this little gift to Lila."

Del watched his "boss" walk out of the barn with the small casket under his arm. He told himself Brad was right. He needed to leave Lila alone. He knew better than to confuse himself for anybody's friend. What he'd just done had crossed the line.

"Like this."

Lila demonstrated the fingering on her plastic recorder for the umpteenth time. And for the umpteenth time little Denise jumped in and played the tune start to finish before Rocky could get two notes in edgewise.

"Let's try it this way," Lila said. "Rocky plays the first three notes by himself." Lila demonstrated. "And then Denise has the next three notes by herself. They're just the same at the first three. So it's…" No sooner had Lila put the instrument to her lips than Denise started tweedling. "A little too fast," Lila said.

"But it's right."

"The notes are right, but you're going too quickly. It's, 'Hot cross buns. Hot cross buns,'" Lila sang, demonstrating the tempo. "And then the next part—" The four-year-old beat her teacher to the tweeter once again. "That's good, a little closer than the first time, but not quite—"

All heads turned as Brad's pickup interrupted the front porch music lesson.

"He's driving across the yard again," Denise complained. "He shouldn't be doing that."

Lila shook her head slightly as the red short box pulled up only a few feet from the porch steps. Brad liked to make an entrance, and she had a feeling this one was part of some production she could do without. He got out, whacked the door shut, adjusted his jeans and strode around the front of the pickup as though he was there on official business.

"I wanna swing," Rocky said quietly.

"Lila doesn't like you driving across the yard," Denise called out.

"Sorry, I forgot." Brad propped his booted foot on the second porch step. "You got a minute?" he asked Lila.

"This one is taken." She smiled. She was nothing if

not a good role model. "I should have one soon. What do you need?"

"I brought you something." He glanced at the kids. "It's after six. Where are the parents?"

"On their way."

"I wanna swing," Rocky repeated.

"I'm with you." Brad gave Rocky a thumbs-up. "Why don't you let them jump on the swings?"

"Go ahead." She held out her hand. "I'll take care of the recorders. We'll get it down pat tomorrow so we can put on our show next week." The two children couldn't drop their recorders and take off fast enough.

Lila set the plastic instruments aside and approached the pickup. She could see the kids from there.

She could also see the small box in the short box. "It's Bingo, isn't it?"

"'Fraid so. I found him in the south pasture, tucked up under a chokecherry bush."

She already had lowered the tailgate and pulled the box onto it. The lid was tied on with a length of soft cotton rope. She reached for one of the ends.

"You don't wanna do that."

"No, I don't." She slipped the half hitch. "But I have to make sure."

"You don't believe me?"

She didn't care about him. Her best friend lay still in a wooden box, cushioned on folded, well-worn denim within a nest of fresh hay.

"Hoo-wee!" Brad yowled. "Hard to get past the smell. That's why I said—"

"It's okay," Lila said. Alfalfa brought the scent of summer, and the smell of pine attested to newly sawn wood. She touched her friend's soft fur and discovered dampness. She couldn't tell whether there had been blood or bites or broken bones. Her friend might have been asleep except for the fact that he didn't lift his head and greet her hand with his wet nose and smooth tongue. She pulled the clip from her hair, making sure a few strands came with it. She liked it because it was shaped like a Milk-Bone. "And Bingo was his name-o," she whispered as she placed the clip inside the box.

"Damn," Brad said softly. "Hey, I'm sorry, Lila."

She looked up, puzzled.

"Really. I know how much he meant to you."

He didn't know, but he was trying to, at least for the moment. She would give him that. She didn't believe Brad had found him, picked him up and brought him back home, and there was no way he'd prepared the dog for burial.

"I'd dig a hole for him, but I'm supposed to be some-place right now." He looked up the road. "Here come the Vermillions."

Lila couldn't laugh any more than she could cry right now, and she wasn't sure which way she would go if her brain hadn't gone numb. But it was either very funny or awfully sad that her stepbrother had no idea how transparent he was.

"Denise's mom." Quickly she put the lid back on the box and grabbed the loose ends of rope. "I'm going to put him in the library for now. Would you…?"

"Yeah. Glad to." He waved to the oncoming car, and then turned and made a megaphone of his hands. "Hey, kids! Somebody's mom is here."

Del found the nameless black pup waiting for him when he opened the door. He could tell his bed had been appro-priated by a small body with black hair, but otherwise a double dose of scratching with a hearty "good dog" was in order. After the day he'd had, he welcomed the feel of the living, breathing, squirming dog in his hands. He figured Brad had helped Lila bury her own dog—why else would he hijack the remains?—and she probably wasn't in the mood for a canine visitor just yet. But on his very first off-leash walk, Not Bingo took off. Sure enough, he followed his nose for excitement and discovered Lila digging a hole smack in the middle of her garden.

Damn Benson for not taking care of that for her.

"Can I help you with that?" Del called out. The pup was already sniffing around the dirt pile, looking to answer the question for himself.

"I'm almost finished." She tossed a shovelful of South Dakota clay past the peak of the pile, and Not Bingo chased it.

Del eyed the box—somebody had retied his knot—and then peered into the hole. "That's pretty deep."

"I know." She leaned on the shovel, brushed away a strand of hair with the back of her other hand. "I have a plan."

"You're gonna plant something over him?" He took hold of her free arm by the wrist and turned it palm up. Two blisters were blooming there. "Where are your gloves?"

"I wasn't thinking about my hands except…" She curled her fingers over her palm as though he'd caught her red-handed. "I don't like to wear gloves when I work in the garden. I like the feel of the dirt."

He reached for the shovel, and she released it to him. He dropped the blade into the hole and pushed hard on the handle.

"Thank you," she whispered. He glanced over his shoulder. From the sound of her voice he expected tears, but there were none. Sad eyes, wistful smile. She glanced at the pup—big help, digging in the dirt pile—and her face brightened a bit. But only momentarily, as she turned her attention back to the small pine box. "He looks comfortable in there. Like he just curled up and went to sleep. Could you tell what happened?"

"Just what you said. He found a shady spot, laid his tired body down and went to sleep."

"Why did you clean him up?"

He added dirt to the pile. "Figured you'd open up the box to say your goodbyes and he'd want to be looking his best."

"You're the one who found him, aren't you?"

"We were out checking for…" He paused in his digging so he could look her in the eye. She wanted details. He wanted to oblige. "Yeah, I found him." He drew a deep breath, trying to sort through the details and find words. "Didn't look like he'd been messed with at all. Not before or after. He looked peaceful."

She thought about it for a moment, as if she was forming a picture she wanted to keep. She looked him in the eye, nodded once and almost smiled. "I owe you a pair of jeans, don't I?"

"Nope. They were ready for retirement."

He dug until she told him to stop, squared up the bottom of the hole and they buried the box. She'd put up a good front until the hole was filled. Now she was making a point to turn her face without turning her back on him, but he could see her tears. The worst of it was she didn't make a sound. He wanted to do something, the right thing, the thing she needed, and he felt like putting his arms around her. But he knew she wasn't ready.

The pup knew it, too. He'd grabbed himself a cool

patch of grass and sat quietly, but he was tuned in, waiting for a signal. He was all eyes and ears. All the woman had to do was glance his way.

She knew it, just like the pup did, and just like the pup, she held back. "Have you named him?"

"Nope. Waiting for you."

"No, he's yours. He likes me all right, but he picked you. I called the vet. He'll be making a call at one of the neighbors on Monday, so he's going to stop by."

"I'll pay his bills and everything, but I don't..." Del sighed. It was a bunch of hooey. *He picked you.* Beggars couldn't be choosers, neither man nor beast. "He picked the wrong guy."

"I don't think so. They know." She brushed her hands together, winced a little, and that was his signal.

He took her hands in his, turned her palms up and made a sympathetic sound deep in his throat. "I've got something for this." He looked up and smiled, then let one hand go so he could brush a glittering tear from her cheek with the tip of a finger while he tucked her other hand against his chest. "I'm no stranger to blistered hands."

"No." She pressed her trembling lips together for a moment, and he expected to be turned away. The evening breeze lifted a hank of hair and wrapped it across her eyes. She tossed her head and gave him a sad smile. "No, you wouldn't be."

He put his arm around her shoulders, and they walked to the bunkhouse, where he threw his hat on the wooden chair as he ushered her to the bathroom. She stood in front of the sink and started to turn on the water, but he reached around her and beat her to the faucet handles. He stole a glance at the mirror. Her eyes were closed, lashes wet, cheeks shiny. His chest felt tight. He wished she'd just let go, let the dam bust wide-open. But it was her call.

He left the door open and the light off. The shadows gave her privacy. It was a small room, barely space for one, so he sat on the can, took Ivory soap in his hand and gently washed her blistered palms. Her hands were steady, but her shoulders shuddered, and her breath quivered almost imperceptibly. She was holding on by a thread, trusting him with her broken skin. He felt privileged.

He blotted her hands dry and took her to his bed, where he sat her down and squatted on his heels beside her knees so he wouldn't be on the bed with her. All the touching and caretaking was making him feel randy as hell.

He took a flat, round snuff can from the nightstand drawer. It was one of the cans his father had used for the all-purpose remedy that had gotten Del through blisters, burns and scrapes over the years. He'd never seen his father chew snuff, but he always had a stash of empty cans.

"This stuff is magic," he promised as he dipped his finger into the old can and dabbed the salve on her blisters. "My dad used to make it. He used it on any kind of wound, any kind of hide, skin, whatever living thing that could get hurt. I used to say, 'Dad, you're in the wrong business. You could sell this stuff and make a fortune.'"

"What...business?" She took a breath between words. Her voice was heavy.

"Cattle. Horses. Nothing like what you've got here, but we got by. Like most small..." She made an unrestrained sound. Finally. A little whimper that might've come from the pup. Del's heart raced, but his hands moved slowly, carefully applying the salve, and he kept his eyes on the road map laid out in the creases of her palms. "It only stings at first. Dad called it heals-quick. 'We'll put some heals-quick on it,' he'd say. And then he'd..." Del blew gently, filling her hands with the air he'd taken in. He wanted to be magic. It was a foolish thought, but he wanted to be—just for a moment—anyone but who he was. Undercover, he'd been playing an assigned role so long—an alter ego, maybe—that he didn't know who Delano Fox really was anymore. And until this moment he'd been fine with that.

In another moment he would be fine again.

Unless he did the stupid thing, which, of course, he did.

He looked up and got lost in her eyes.

Lila lifted her gaze from his rough and gentle hands to the lush black-brown hair that angled across his forehead. She wanted to touch it, but she didn't want to discourage him from tending to her hands. Funny. She was generally given to taking care of herself. She didn't like feeling needy.

But maybe that wasn't what she felt. His touch, his breath on her skin, his undivided attention, it was all good. It felt like kindness getting its arms around sadness. She willed him to look up and let her see this wondrous thing in his eyes. And when he did, the feeling came full circle. It was mutual. It was an electrical charge, a living spark. She smiled a little through unshed tears.

He smiled a lot. "Better?"

She nodded.

"Asap."

She questioned him with a crinkled brow. He opened his mouth to explain, but the dog startled them both by leaping onto the bed, tail wagging.

"How's that for a name? It just came to me. Him and me, we had a conversation about his situation. We got all philosophical about timing and possibilities."

"Asap," she echoed, nodding.

"It's one of those names that strikes you as smart-ass— me anyway—but when you think about it, there's two sides to the ASAP story. Soon, but not rushed. Good is possible, but so is not so good." His eyes held her gaze as he pressed the lid back on the can and tossed it past her onto the bed. "Did I mention my father was Lakota? Or had you figured that out?"

"Neither. You didn't, and I didn't, not exactly." She touched his chin with her fingertips, traced the angle of it, felt its surprising smoothness. "But I wondered. You're beautiful."

"So are you."

He slid his arm around her shoulders, nestled her nape in the crook of his elbow and drew her to him for a sweet kiss, a tender greeting eagerly met. With the touch of his tongue he bade her to part her lips and taste his beauty, let him taste hers, and she did, and he made her want more. If she took him in her arms she could have more. He nibbled her lips playfully, changed the angle of their kiss and made it harder and deeper and wetter, and then he made it soft and sweet again. A needy sound threatened to escape her throat, but she held it back. It was such a pathetic thing, it tucked its tail and mercifully retreated.

He knew. He touched his forehead to hers and whispered, "Not possible." And then he amended, "Or maybe just too soon."

Chapter 4

Bucky's Place was about the last place Del wanted to be, which was a sure sign he'd lost focus. The truth was, Bucky's was exactly where he needed to be. The atmosphere was right for getting his head back into the game. Meeting the locals was a necessity. He had to give most of the jokes at least a chuckle, drink no more than one beer for every three Brad was putting away—same for winning at pool, no more than one round out of three—match the names up with the attitude and file it all away. Some people just begged to get robbed. Others looked for times and places to oblige them.

Bucky's was the right place for the confluence of the first with the second.

"Looks like them rustlers are back," a voice at the end of the bar announced. Taylor Rhoades. Del had him in the "comedian" file. "The Blaylocks just lost a dozen head."

"Yeah, we lost six," Brad said. "Steers," he added. "Was it cows they took from Blaylock or steers?"

"Pretty sure he said steers. Cow-calf operations, they're probably safe this time of year. Steers are a helluva lot easier to move."

"You heard about Stan Chasing Elk, didn't you?" Carl Schrock offered. Carl's input was worthy of a mental file. His wife was the hometown hairdresser, which made him privy to all kinds of local lore. Whether it was thirdhand, secondhand or straight from the horse's mouth, talk was news in a town like Short Straw.

"He selling off tribal cattle again?"

"They never proved that," Carl reminded anyone listening. "You ask me, it was Chet Klein. After they fired him from that ag program at the college, suddenly the whole rustling epidemic kinda died down."

"Sounds like it's flared back up again," Taylor said.

"Maybe never really died, you know?" Brad speculated. "If a guy's got any kind of insurance…"

"They don't pay out until every last form is filled out and all the official noses have smelled every armpit in the county." Taylor wasn't speaking from experience. He drove truck for the Short Straw Co-Op.

"Who's going to the VFW shindig this weekend?" Brad asked. "I hear they're bringing in a live band. All the way from Pierre is what I hear."

"Could be a line from their theme song. 'They got a band from Pierre, that's what I hear,'" Taylor crooned.

Carl groaned. "Taylor used be in the church choir till they kicked him out for singing."

"All he really wanted was the robe," Brad said with a grin.

"And I never gave it back, neither."

"They didn't want it back after they found out you wore it on Halloween, buck naked underneath."

"How'd they find out?" Del asked.

"He flashed the choir director." Carl flipped open his denim jacket as he spun his bar stool full circle.

"Mooned," Taylor protested above the whoops and whistles. "And she told my ol' lady, which is why we don't go to dances no more. I keep telling her, ain't no way we'd run into that woman at a dance."

"You going, Carl?" Del asked.

"You damn betcha. They've got my wife selling tickets to her hair customers. Those old soldiers know how to round up the troops. Just give every woman a book of tickets and tell her it's all for charity."

And so went the boys' night out.

Mental notes neatly filed, Del figured on calling his badge-carrying contact on his way back to the Flynn place, but Brad jumped into the passenger seat just as he threw the truck into Reverse. "You'll have to bring me back for my pickup in the morning." Brad nodded toward Main Street. "Sheriff just drove past. You don't drink much, do you?"

Del draped his arm over the back of the bench seat and looked over his shoulder. Story of his life. "I can take it or leave it."

Brad slid down in the seat. "I sure hit the jackpot when I hired you."

"You going to this dance?"

"Not if I don't have to. And since I'm not married or otherwise tied down, I don't have to. I might stop in and check it out, but if the band sucks I'll find another party." He glanced sideways. "You?"

"Lila doesn't seem to get out much."

"She doesn't want to." Brad chortled. "Go ahead and ask her. See what she says. Bet you fifty bucks she says no."

"Ain't much of a bettin' man."

"He don't drink, and he don't gamble. With so damn much to recommend you, it's funny you're not married, Fox. Women love cowboys."

"That's because we're lovable. You want marriageable, you're looking for a whole different breed."

The lights were on in the old schoolhouse that stood within a few yards of Lila's place. As late as it was, Del figured he ought to check out the place, see what was going on, make sure she was okay. *Quietly*, if he could manage it. The heavy door threatened to give him away, but he kept the squeak to a minimum and slipped into the entry, clearly once a mudroom. A list headed Library Rules was posted above a row of metal coat hooks. "Honor the honor system. Sign the guest book. Book donations welcome."

She called those rules?

Lila was sitting on the floor, back to the door, hunched over whatever she was working on. If the pup was studying for guard duty, he was asleep on the job.

"Are you—"

They yelped and jumped, woman and dog both, like a pair of jack-in-the-boxes.

"—open?" Del squatted, butt to boot heels. "Get over here, Asap. The idea is to jump up *before* the dirty crook makes you look." He scratched the wiggly pup's chest. "Dog ears never sleep, Ace."

"Oh, look what you made me do." She'd dripped black paint on her work in progress. "Made me more than look, you dirty crook."

"Sorry about that. I figured this time of night it might be an actual crook. What are you making? A sign?" Pretty obvious—it said Free Library—and she told him as much with a wide-eyed glance. "I thought maybe this place was for the kids. Where you teach them, or whatever you do in day care. Isn't it like nursery school?"

"*Nursery school?* What rock have you been living under? My day care is like preschool, only we don't have preschool around here, so people think of me as a babysitter. Which is okay, but I do teach. Even though I'm not certified, I sneak it in anyway.

"But this—" she gestured expansively, and with no shortage of pride "—is for everybody. Including sneaky crooks and hired hands. And kids, of course. I'm still working on it. People are beginning to stop in. The county used to have a bookmobile, but the funding was cut."

He surveyed the shelves. Most of them came up to his waist. He would have to crawl around on the floor to find a book. But he said, "This is great."

"My dad bought the schoolhouse for a dollar after they built the district school, the one I went to."

"He moved it here?"

"He did. Before I was born, so it's been here all my life. Dad said he bought it for storage, but he actually went to school here. One room for all the elementary grades. Don't you just love it?"

He meant merely to indulge her by taking a quick

look around, but she was right. The place was enchant-
ment in the making. The practical rancher had storage
in mind, but his daughter had a better idea.

Del took a close look at the woodstove in the back of
the room. "Is this original to the building?"

"Dad put that in when I started playing here. I
claimed it by coming in here all the time, bringing
toys in and leaving them here, putting my marks on
the walls."

"Little squatter," he said with a smile.

"See those desks?" She pointed to a motley collection of old student desks in the back corner. "Whenever we ran into one on sale somewhere, Dad would
buy it for me."

"Sounds like you were Daddy's girl."

"I always was, I guess. And for a while after my
mother died, it was just us."

"Yeah," he said. "I know what that's like."

But she'd done better than he had. She'd made good,
and the schoolhouse was only one example of the good
things she'd put her mind to. It reminded him of a little
town he'd visited on a school trip a very long time ago.
It was a place out of time, a retreat.

A library.

There were two tall bookcases against one wall,
each shelf partially filled with books, and two waist-
high shelving units in the middle of the open space that
were crammed with what looked to be children's books.
Each wall had its own color—red around the windows
on the east wall opposed by solid black behind the old
slate blackboard on the west, yellow surrounding the
metal bookcases on the south and white backing the
mudroom. Clearly, she knew something about his fa-

ther's people besides the fact that they produced good-looking sons.

For the Lakota, the four directions were more than ritual symbols. They looked to the East for the rising red sun, which brought light, the mark of wisdom. West was black—the end of day, darkness and death—but it was also the home of Thunderbird, who brought rain to sustain life. Cold white North brought hard times, but it also offered cleansing, and yellow South's warm winds prompted growth and promoted life.

Del thought of Stan Chasing Elk, the man some suspected of stealing cattle. He hadn't met the man yet, but standing within four walls painted the colors of the four directions, he felt the need to clear him, lay all suspicions to rest. Strange feeling, since he wasn't a religious man, not the way his father had once been.

Hearing Lila talk about her father had him looking around for some kind of connection to his own. Hell, it was just paint.

"This used to be my playhouse," she was saying. "Play school, play castle, play store. Now it's my community contribution after we lost the bookmobile." She nodded toward the dog and questioned him with a silly frown. "Ace?"

Del shrugged.

"I know what you're up to," she said. "But an Ace doesn't replace a Bingo."

He laughed. "You're giving me way too much credit, woman. I'm not that clever." He signaled the pup. "Get over here, Asap." He flashed Lila a bright-eyed wink. "See how that works? Wagging his tail behind him."

"Hmm. Too cute by half. Both of you." She turned to her artwork, and he peered over her shoulder. She'd messed up the dot over the *i* in *Library*. "Now what am I going to do?"

"I got this." He took a knee, braced his left forearm and gestured for the brush. "Turn it into something else."

"No smiley faces," she warned.

"Not your style." He considered his options for a moment, then dipped the brush into the black paint and deftly turned the stray marks into an open book. "How 'bout that?"

"It's perfect." She turned a genuinely smiling face to him. "You have a good eye and a steady hand."

"Which make me the designated driver."

"For Brad and his buddies?"

"Just Brad. The man in charge."

"Do you really think so?"

"I went out in the field with Frank today. He tested me out on the mower before he let me run it. Then I got to knock down a patch of alfalfa while he raked the crested wheat he'd cut the other day. I love the smell of newly mown alfalfa. Frank says he's had trouble around it lately. Gets all stuffy."

Lila shook her head. "Brad is useless."

"He's the one who hired me, so I gotta say he has his good points. But Frank's the cattleman in this outfit."

"It's *his* outfit."

"And yours, right?"

Her tone became guarded. "I have a lease agreement with my father for the use of my land. That's all. It's my father's operation. He manages everything, keeps it afloat, feeds and waters, buys and sells, and he writes the checks. It'll be his name on your check, not Brad's, and definitely not June's." She arched an eyebrow. "Not yet anyway."

"Brad doesn't do much without running it by Frank, huh?"

Both eyebrows. "He didn't run you by Frank."

"But?"

"But maybe we got lucky. For once Brad was in the right place at the right time and hired, yes, maybe the right man." She studied his artwork. "Saturday night at Bucky's Place, right? You stopped in for what? Directions?"

He offered half a smile. "A little more than that."

"What more?"

"I wanted a drink. I *needed* a job."

"And there was Brad." She raised an eyebrow. "Fate works in mysterious ways."

"Sure does." He handed her the paintbrush and turned to the tall bookcases. "So what've we got here? You willing to trust me with a book?"

"I trust everyone with a book. I'm not always here, but the door's always open. So far I've found that the honor system brings out the best in people."

He chuckled, and he ran his finger along a row of book spines. "If I wasn't honor bound before you said that, I sure am now. Help me pick out a good Western."

"Check this box." She scooted a big carton across the floor. "The word's gotten out, and the donations have been pouring in. I'm running out of shelving."

"I can help you with that. There's plenty of good lumber in what your dad calls the scrap pile."

"You're a good carpenter," she said quietly.

"It won't be fancy. I'm a pretty good *rough* carpenter."

"I'll make you supper. It won't be fancy, but it'll

stick to your…" She trailed off as he reached for her hands, turned them over and checked for signs of healing. "Ribs. It helped."

His gaze met hers. "What did?"

"Your dad's medicine. You." She smiled. "You helped."

"Dad and me. We'll take you up on your offer. We could both stand to put some meat on our ribs, but especially Dad. Bony as hell, that guy." Poor Lila looked stricken. He indicated the walls with a gesture. "You've honored the colors of the four directions here. You know about sharing your food with the *wanagi*, don't you? Feed the spirits?"

"I thought you were supposed to honor the dead." She chided him with a look. "Bony as hell?"

"Graveyard humor." He shrugged. "Closely related to Indian humor. But feeding the spirits is no joke."

"Okay."

He smiled. "I'd like to come for supper. But there's something I'd like more." He tucked his thumbs in his belt. "I'd like to take you to the dance this weekend."

"Dance?" Stricken again.

"At the VFW." He put her hands on his shoulders, slipped his arms around her waist. "I get to hold you like this. You get to hold me. We get to sway to the music. Don't know what kind—some band from Pierre."

"A live band?"

"So they tell me. Fund-raiser for the VFW. Support our troops." He drew her hips close to his and swayed slightly, slowly, side to side. "Dance with me," he whispered.

She lifted her chin, he lowered his and they met halfway. He kissed her eagerly, licking her lips apart, seeking her tongue, stealing her breath, and she held nothing back. She pressed her fingers into his shoulders, kneaded him there, made him imagine her working him over, shoulders to soles and all points in between. He made a promise to himself in that moment that they would get there, and he lowered his head to deliver his promise to her slender neck and her velvety earlobe. She trembled in his arms.

Del rocked her, hip to hip, and, oh, yeah, there was music playing inside his head. He glanced down at the floor behind her and realized they were being watched. Asap tipped his head to one side, all big eyes and cocked ears. Del laughed.

"I'm not much of a dancer," Lila said. She started to pull away, but he was having none of that. "Because I tend to stiffen up," she added quickly.

She wasn't the only one.

"Got a radio?" He nuzzled her hair. "We could use a little easy-does-it music."

"Even without music, you move like the ocean," she whispered.

"Because I'm not thinking about it." He slid his hands down, spread them high on her bottom. Her jeans felt loose enough that he was sure he could slip his hands under the waistband and fill them with her tight little ass. "Don't think."

"I can't afford—" She pressed her cheek against his. "I like you too much."

"That's a bad thing?"

"It could be. I don't know what you're up to."

"I'm trying to get a date for the dance. I asked. I tried out, didn't step on any toes." He backed off gradually and looked her in the eye. "Did I?"

She smiled and shook her head.

"You move like a natural woman. You didn't stiffen up at all."

She gave him a naughty smile. "*You* did."

"I'm a natural man." He sat on the desk, took her hands in his and drew her to stand between his spraddled legs. "A man who's wondering what it's gonna take to get an answer."

"That kiss is still working on me."

"Here comes its reinforcement." A tug on her hands brought her lips within reach of his.

This time their kiss was like frosting on the cake— smooth and playful, topping off a welcome temptation.

He opened his eyes slowly and found her licking her sweet bottom lip. "Yes?"

"Yes. And the bookshelves…" She took a seat beside him and surveyed the empty wall space. "You don't have to do that. That's extra work, and I can't…" She gave her head a tight shake. "Thanks, but the truth is, I'm just glad you're here to help Dad. Lately we've had some hired men who were more trouble than they were worth."

"I don't mean to cause you any trouble at all." He squeezed her hand, and she turned to him, eyes bright with her willingness to taste more trouble. All he wanted was another taste of her, which was no trouble. Not for him anyway. Not unless thinking made it so.

"Oh, Del, you…" She dropped her head back and laughed. "You have no idea."

"I don't know about that." He carried their clasped hands to his mouth and kissed the back of hers. "Do you have any ideas?"

"Call it a night before the sun beats us to it?" She raised an eyebrow. "Maybe get some sleep."

"Mmm, let's just sit here together and watch the paint dry."

She laughed.

"As soon as it's light out, I'll put the new sign up for you and take some measurements for the shelves. You got a tape measure?" She lifted her shoulder and he frowned, touched his fingertips to her temple and then slid them through the soft hair pulled back from her face. He imagined releasing the clip and unfurling her hair. "I'm not looking for anything in return. I'm donating. The sign says donations welcome."

"*Book* donations."

"I have a few paperbacks I can throw in." He eyed the existing bookcases and pictured them replaced with others of his construction. "How tall do you want them? They should all be the same. All wood. We can paint them, and I can bolt them to the wall." He caught her dubious look. "I like to keep busy."

"Brad will keep you busy."

He shook his head. "Give me a break. Bucky's Place is gonna get old real fast."

"I don't know what your agreement is, but don't let Brad tell you his hands work overtime. Most of them turn out to be next to useless."

"I won't. I'll do you proud on the shelving. I learned a lot helping my dad. Life skills, you know? Best father-to-son legacy there is. I'm a hands-on kind of a guy." He smiled and gave her hand a quick squeeze. "Trade-wise."

"But you like to read."

"I do now. Hated school when I was a kid. Hated

being cooped up." He gave a dry chuckle. "I had no idea. Guess you're right. Ideas aren't my strong suit."

"I'm not gonna touch that one," she said with a smile.

"Aw, c'mon. Disagree with me." He stood and drew her to her feet. "Here's a simple one. How 'bout I walk you to your door? Unless you'd rather get complicated and walk me to mine."

"You can drop me off. Ace will see you the rest of the way. He's *your* dog. And it looks like he needs water." She glanced at the dog, whose tongue was lolling. "By the way, I fed him."

"So did I. Looks like he's working both sides." Del wagged his finger at Asap. "You've got us figured out, don't you?"

The pup jumped up and wagged his tail in response.

"I wish *I* did," Lila said as they walked to the door.

"You're trying too hard. Just go with the flow." They stepped out onto the plank platform that served as a stoop. "Would you look at that," Del said softly. Morning's first blush colored the horizon. "Here's an idea. Feed me, and I'll repay you with a few bookshelves."

Lila nodded toward the sawtooth silhouette underpinning the spread of an orange-red splash and the slow rise of gold rays. "After this." She turned to him as a flurry of birdcalls hastened sunrise, and he took her in his arms and kissed her thoroughly.

Chapter 5

With his phone to his ear, Del sat on his patient mount and watched a small herd of Double F cows graze the grassy draw below. He never knew where he might be able to get a cell signal, and he was apt to lose a signal as unexpectedly as he found it. He had to make the minutes count.

"My guess is Saturday night," he told his contact. "There's gonna be a big charity event, and most people will be in town. Benson's not too subtle about checking on the neighbors' plans. Could be he's just feeding information to whoever's calling the shots. If he makes a move, I'll play my next card. If not…"

"Have you run into Standing Elk yet?"

"Soon. He's a friend of a friend. That's the best way to gain access here. I know what I'm doing."

The sound of his own words suddenly hit him hard. He was telling the kind of loaded truth that always left a prickly feeling in his mouth. He'd been working both sides of Rustler Street for so long he knew every sign and every shortcut better than the residents—ranchers on one side, rustlers on the other. He was some of each—a trickster and a true mixed breed—which made him the right man for a job that rendered him the wrong man to be doing anything but that job. He was bound to it, and for good reason. He'd dug himself a hole, and the job was his lifeline. But it was a tightrope, a one-man wire. He could easily find himself back at the bottom of the hole. A good man would stay clear of anyone he felt tempted to get close to in a good way. If he took a fall, he could easily take her with him.

But instead of staying clear, he was taking her to a damn dance. He tried to tell himself that it just fit too perfectly into his plans and, really, as long as he didn't try to take it any further, what could it hurt? Besides, he'd just gotten his hair trimmed, bought a new shirt, shined up his boots—the whole nine yards.

So much for turning a trickster into a good man.

"Dad was really surprised when I told him I was going to the dance," Lila told Del as they headed onto the highway on date night. Midsummer's early-evening light was still bright, but it had gone nice and soft. "I thought he might decide to go, too, but June said no."

"She doesn't strike me as the stay-at-home type."

"She likes to go places, but she's not interested in Short Straw. It's drab. It's dull. The people are twenty years behind times. Harkin's Grocery doesn't sell her brand of yogurt. She'll drive all the way to Pierre for a loaf of bread." Lila leaned her head on the rest and turned toward him. He could feel the warmth of her easy attitude. They were friends now. "Dad isn't quite as old as he looks, and June isn't as young as she thinks she is."

"Your dad looks like a man who's worked hard all his life. I wouldn't want to guess how many years that's been. June seems like she's got one foot out the door. Kinda temporary."

"Like you?"

"I'm here for the job. A hired hand is always temporary. But while I'm here, I need to be part of the operation. Otherwise, why keep me on?"

"You are one wise cowboy. Is Brad going to this thing tonight?"

"He said he might check it out."

"Without his hired man? That's a surprise. Brad likes to show up with a sidekick. Makes him look important."

Del smiled at the road ahead. "Lots of surprises, and the night's still young."

Lila wished she had worn jeans. This was, after all, the Short Straw Activity Center, and a woman in a dress was a rarity. Blouses were ruffled or sheer or scoop neck—maybe all three—but there were no skirts. Tight jeans tucked into a pretty pair of boots was considered female finery.

There wasn't an unfamiliar face in the whole place, and she sorely wished they'd stop looking at her as though she'd just walked into the wrong bathroom. She tugged on the skirt of her silky soft-blue dress—it felt as though it was twisted somewhere—and looked up at Del when she felt his hand on the small of her back. He smiled, and nothing felt twisted anymore.

Which didn't stop the neck twisting their presence seemed to be causing. Unlike her stepbrother, Lila didn't want to get noticed, especially not as the unexpected guest, the woman who never left home. If people talked about her, speculated about her or, worst of all, pitied her, she didn't want to know about it.

"Lila!"

Oh, for Pete's sake, had Connie Vermillion forgotten seeing her just yesterday when she'd picked Denise up from day care? She hurried in Lila's direction, giving a window-washer wave.

"Lila, you're here. Good for you, honey. Jeez, I almost called to see if I could get you to take the kids tonight. Grandma isn't feeling well. But Jeanie decided to stay home tonight, so…" Connie sneaked a quick peek at Del and added, "Jeanie's my sister."

Lila introduced Del to her friend, who stared at him as though he was made of chocolate. "He's working for Dad," Lila supplied.

"I'm… My daughter goes to Lila's for… You're not from around here, are you?"

Del smiled and said he wasn't, and Lila thought surely Connie's gesturing and sputtering had to be uncomfortable for him, but it didn't show. Because he must get this kind of reaction all the time. He was the best-looking man in the room. And she was with him.

"Is the rest of the family here?" Connie asked, and it took Lila a moment to tune in.

"I'm, uh, I'm here with Del." And he was patiently carrying a big Tupperware bowl. She relieved him of it quickly. "Where should I put this? Just potato salad."

"I'll take it. You can never have too much potato salad." Connie took the bowl, turned and then re-turned. "It's good to see you, Lila. I mean, I just saw you, but it's good to see you *here*, out for a…" Her smile was outrageously wide. For Del. "Good chance to meet people."

"I've met a few." He scanned the room. "I see some familiar faces."

"You two have fun, okay?" Connie was blushing as she looked at Del, and she looked quickly away. "I like your dress, Lila. You look great."

"I should've worn jeans," Lila muttered as she watched pretty, petite Connie walk away.

"You kidding? You're turning heads."

"I know. And it's not the dress." She laughed. He was wonderful. "You'd think I didn't socialize. Ever." And maybe she didn't, but she used to. It wasn't as though she'd been in storage. She was disgusted with herself for feeling self-conscious. It wasn't fair to her date. They were on her home turf. She should be introducing him around.

But she wasn't ready. "Let's get a table."

"You see anyone you want to sit with?"

"Yes." She grabbed his hand and met his eyes. "Right here."

"How about that corner—"

"Perfect." Not a corner table, but the very end of a long table in the far corner of the room. Glasses of tasseled wheat served as decorations "Let's grab it."

"What would you like to drink?" he asked.

"I don't know. I haven't eaten much today."

"Then we'll get you something to eat. Where's the kitchen?"

"Oh, no. I'm fine. I should've sampled more potato salad. Are we early? These things never start on time. I'm just—" she hunched up her shoulders, gave a tight smile and told a little white lie "—ready to start dancing."

"Let's." He slipped his hand around hers. "How can I make this easier?"

She drew a deep breath, blew it out, looked up at him and smiled. "I'm good."

"Hey, Del, are those seats taken?" A friendly little guy with a firm paunch and farmer tan, Carl Schrock gestured with the Stetson he gripped by the point in the crease of the crown. Del waved him on over. "Good to see you, Lila." Carl toasted her with his hat before he clapped it on his head and pulled a slim, curly-haired blonde to his side. "Del, this is my wife, Darlene."

"We've met. Paid a visit to Dar's Downhome Dos today." Del took off his hat and plowed his fingers through his hair. "You did such a nice job, Dar, I should've left the hat off. Now I'm sportin' hat hair."

"Del bought my last pair of tickets, too," Darlene said. "Like I told him, he sure works fast. New to Short Straw, and already he's dating the homecoming queen."

Lila questioned Del with a look, and he lifted one shoulder. "She asked me who the other ticket was for. Royalty, huh? If I'd known that, I might not've had the nerve to ask." He turned back to Darlene. "Lila owed me a favor after I helped her with a sign for the library."

"No woman can resist doing a little charity," Carl said. "Right, Dar? Dar won the prize for selling the most tickets. What did we get, darlin'?"

"We got a flagpole. Last year I won the flag. First thing tomorrow we're going to get it all set up."

"We?" Carl poked his wife's arm as though checking for doneness. "Will you be digging the hole or mixing up the cement?"

"The library gets a sign, and my shop gets a flag. We're calling out to the people on the highway." Darlene used her hands to describe her plan. "We'll change our colors. We'll make a barber pole for the house and put up a new sign by the gate. Red, white and blue."

"We." Carl turned to Del and rolled his eyes.

"A theme," Darlene enthused. "I'll change the shop name from Downhome to All-American. Dar's All-American Dos." She turned to Lila. "Do you have the phone number on the library sign? You might get more customers if you put the phone number right on the sign."

"The library's free. I don't get customers. I wanted a sign on the schoolhouse so people would stop coming to the house."

"My shop's in the house. The basement. A barber pole to show where the door is, Carl. We have to put in a separate door anyway. I got another warning notice."

"See there. The damn hair police'll be coming for us. You don't need any more attention, Dar. You've got enough customers." Carl grabbed a stalk of wheat from the table arrangement and held it like a pencil. "I priced it out. You know what an outside door into the basement would cost me? Even if I did it myself, it would—"

"We could hire Del," Darlene suggested. "He made the library sign."

"I made the library sign," Lila said. "He just—"

"We could hire Lila," Carl said with a grin.

"Lila has her own home business with a separate door. Right, Lila?"

"Yes, but I don't have a flag."

"You need a flag," Darlene said.

"Dar…" Carl said.

"It's a *library*." She slapped her husband's arm. "Lila definitely needs a flag."

"Sounds like you're in good with the VFW, Darlene.

Maybe you can talk them out of another flag for Lila,"
Del suggested. "And maybe persuade them to get this
party started."

"This is what they call the social hour," Darlene said.
"Buy your drink tickets now, you get peanuts and pretzels—all you can eat."

"We gotta play short straw to see who's buying." Carl
snatched several more stalks of wheat from the vase and
snapped off the grain. "See, Del, this is always the table
decoration in Short Straw. Built-in entertainment." He
snapped one straw in half. "Who wants to draw first?"

Del reached across the table, but Lila slipped her
hand over his elbow.

"You don't have to buy any—"

"I got paid today." He patted her hand. "Relax, okay?"

"Will you look who's here," Darlene whispered to the
group. "Paula Rhoades. Taylor got to come to a dance.
Whatever you guys do, if he starts acting crazy, don't
egg him on."

The band started to play before the food was served.
A few pretzels took the edge off Lila's hunger and a
glass of white wine eased her nerves. After about half
a glass the stuff actually tasted pretty good. The second half loosened her up for dancing. Del seemed to
be nursing his beer, but he didn't need much loosening
up. He had ball bearings in his hips, and his boots were
made for dancing. Food was soon the furthest thing
from Lila's mind. Somehow he made her body swing
and sway, made her feet go the right way, and when she
tripped herself up, he covered for her. He was a good
time, and she was having it.

Until Brad showed up.

"You got her to come." He made a show of shoving a congratulatory hand in the direction of Del's gut. "What did we say? Fifty?"

Laughing, Del managed to avoid the handshake by countering with a friendly hand on Brad's shoulder. "Whatever you said, man, I wasn't listening. No harm, no foul, no debt."

"That's right. You had the inside track, and you passed it up." Brad eyed another couple on the dance floor. "Looks like Carl Schrock is having himself a fine time."

"His wife is this year's ticket-sales champion," Lila said as she linked arms with Del. He was her date. She was there with him, and yes, she wanted everyone to know it.

"Won the grand prize," Del added. "Seem like good people, the Schrocks."

"I like Carl." Brad watched for a moment, and then he turned away muttering, "Good man."

Del was having himself a damn good time. It was fun to watch Lila come out of her shell. They exchanged quips and shared laughs with the others who stood in line for the buffet. He had almost forgotten why he was really there—or maybe he'd almost changed his mind about it—when he noticed Brad was leaving.

"I'll be right back. Okay? Right back." He took a plate from the serving table and put it in Lila's hands. "Be sure you get enough to eat. We've got more dancing ahead of us."

He could feel her eyes boring into his back as he pushed open the door. She hadn't asked earlier, hadn't said a word, just looked at him, all big blue eyes filled with confusion. He would explain. The moment would come, and he would tell her what he could and hope it was enough. But for now he had to take care of business.

There was no need to keep Brad's taillights in view. Del knew where he was headed. Only a few hours ago he'd gotten his hair cut there, and he'd noticed how many steers were grazing the pasture north of the house. Two miles down the road he found the hole cut in the fence.

They'd picked the right spot, the one he would have chosen himself. Clear, black velvet sky, moonless night, the draw was hidden from the road and there was a little hill for good measure. He used the good measure for his own cover. As a bonus, it afforded a cell phone signal.

"Could be the same outfit, but they brought a bigger trailer," Del reported. "Looks like twenty head. They've got good dogs. I'll give 'em that."

They'd brought in two dogs this time. Del was pretty sure the one they'd had with them last time around was the younger of the two. The older dog would be the one in the lead, the one getting right after those bovine back legs without making a fuss. The younger one was doing more barking than you'd want, but you still shouldn't go swatting him the way the numbskull with a quirt was doing.

Use the quirt on the cattle, you idiot. The dog is your partner.

"You're always judging rustlers by their dogs."

"I judge them by the way they treat their dogs. A good rustler takes care of his dog." If he could get his hands on that quirt right now, he knew what he'd do with it. "I'm bettin' Benson set Schrock up."

"Is he there?"

"He got out ahead of me, but it looks like his pickup is here."

"Why didn't you go with him?"

"Wasn't invited. Next time."

"You don't have a lot of time."

"When have I failed to deliver? Hell, by now I know what I'm doing, and *you* know that."

He felt as though he was watching a very long snake loop its body around its prey and haul it in, but it wasn't the body he was tasked with finding. It was the head. He had a role to play, and the reason he'd never failed was that he omitted nothing. He played his part, delivered his lines precisely.

But now there was Lila.

Except she was gone when he got back to the Short Straw Activity Center.

"Darlene took her home," Carl told him "Had to. She was looking for a ride, and she wasn't about to wait around." He clapped his hand on Del's back and peered up at him with eyes several beers' worth of serious. "Not a great start if you're trying to court the boss's daughter, my friend. And make no mistake about who's the boss of the Flynn Ranch. Brad Benson talks big, but he don't know a road apple from a cow pie." He glanced toward the door and his tone tempered. "Dar's back."

"What's wrong with you men?" she demanded.

"Us men? Don't lump me in with those bastards, honey."

She poked Del in the chest with a sharp red fingernail. "Barely get that woman to hop on the party boat, and then you leave her high and dry."

"I left her with you," he reminded her.

"And I took her home, which is where you'll find her if you've got a sincere apology on you somewhere."

"I wasn't gone *that* long."

"Long enough."

* * *

The bunkhouse was empty. Del expected a tail-wagging welcome, and the stillness was a disturbing disappointment. He was looking for rustlers. He didn't need to be complicating his assignment by looking for company. Even more disturbing was the too-tempting thought of finding the pup hanging out with more company he longed to keep. It was okay to enjoy their company, but he didn't need to be wanting it the way he did. Not a good sign for a committed loner.

But Asap had taken up residence with him, and a young roommate couldn't be allowed to go missing. And Lila deserved an apology.

The pup greeted him at the bottom of the porch steps. "Good boy." He didn't mind going down on one knee for a guy who didn't care where he'd been or what he'd done. He didn't much like feeling guilty. Guilt had been dogging him too damn long.

Lila's voice floated forth from the shadows. "He wouldn't come out of the bunkhouse at first."

He looked up, and there she was, standing at the top of the steps, still wearing that pretty blue dress. She descended on bare feet, sat down, tugged at her skirt so that it draped way down over her knees. Seated, she was forced to look up. He didn't want that. He took a seat beside her.

"I'm sorry, Lila. I didn't expect to get held up that long."

"You got held up?" She tipped her head sideways. He couldn't see light in her eyes, but there was a hint of it in her tone. "Was it a gang, or just one masked man?"

"What do you consider a gang?"

"I don't give much thought to gangs, not way out

here. But I have to consider that you might be wearing a mask." She reached out and touched his cheek. "A very attractive mask, but still…"

"I'm really sorry. I got back as soon as I could."

"It doesn't matter." She took her hand away, but the warmth of her touch lingered. "I'd been there long enough. I'm not much of a party girl."

"Yeah, me, neither." They looked at each other. He tried out a sheepish smile, but she wasn't buying it. "I wanted to take you out, and Short Straw doesn't offer many options."

"No excuses?"

"Excuses only weaken the apology."

"Explanation?"

"You said it didn't matter."

"That's right, I did." She stacked her hands on her knees and rested her chin on them. "And it doesn't. It's done."

He scratched Asap's ears, then between his shoulders, the base of his spine, ruffling fur until the dog was ready to turn cartwheels for him. His dad had often told him that you could tell a lot about a man by a dog's first impression of him. *An animal doesn't care what you're wearing.* Lila was right about the mask, but it didn't bother Asap. And that was worth hanging on to.

"I have some land, too." Which had nothing to do with anything except that it was personal. It was a piece of him, a peace offering. "Along the Grand River, up by Mobridge. It's on the reservation. My dad left it to me. It's real pretty there, especially this time of year."

"You said your father was a rancher?"

"Cows and horses." He stretched one leg to a lower step and braced his forearm across the other knee, leaving a niche for Asap. "It wasn't a big operation, but the calf check paid the bills with a little left over, and the horses... Paints... Dad was known for his Paints. He didn't worry about registering them or anything like that. A Dan Fox Paint was worth more for how he was put together and what he could do than for any list of names on a piece of paper." He rubbed his thumb over the pup's soft ear. "That's what kept him going after my mother died."

"How old were you when she died?"

"I was five. Car accident. My father was driving." He gave that bit of information its due. A quiet moment. And then he launched into a torrent of detail. "Bad weather, bad roads, bad visibility, bad tires, all kinds of bad luck coming together in an instant. You can change a lot of things in life, but death ain't one of them."

"I know that. I do." A piece of her, a piece of him, something in common. No explanation could match that. "What happened to your father?"

"He put it behind him. The accident, not my mother's death. He never talked about any of it—it happened, she was gone, no use looking back—but he never stopped missing her. We were real tight, my dad and me. We didn't need anyone else. Oh, my aunts helped out, but mostly it was just us. We had a nice little calf crop every year, raised Paints, sold some beautiful saddle horses." He turned his head toward her. "I can put a real nice handle on a horse if you have a need. Do it for you in my spare time, just for the pleasure."

"I might take you up on that offer. But, of course, I'd pay for—"

"I said for the pleasure. And for you." He smiled. "Actions speak louder than explanations."

"You don't owe me anything, Del."

He turned his attention to the sky full of stars. "I learned a lot from my father. Pick yourself up. Cowboys don't cry. Put the past behind you. Pretty soon you've stacked up this big wall behind you, so there's no turning back. And that's good, as long as you can move day to day. As long as you can find some kind of a way ahead.

"We lost the cattle first. We had a bad winter—everyone lost some cattle—and then a bunch got stolen. Never recovered. When my father started talking about selling broodmares, I told him I didn't need to be going to college, I could hire out. Hell, I was a pretty good bronc rider, good enough to bring in some extra cash. But I was seventeen, and things weren't falling into place fast enough to suit me. I was making new friends, trying a few new things. Got arrested a couple of times."

He could feel her stiffen up a bit, and he held his breath. She deserved a chance to ask the smart question. *For what?* And then he'd have to lie.

He was good at lying. It was all in a day's work, and he was good at his job. But he was telling her about his father, and it was all true so far. He didn't have a good lie on the tip of his tongue the way he always did when he was working a case.

But being with this woman didn't feel like part of the job. It should have, but it didn't. He wanted to pour everything out to her right here and now and see if she'd still be sitting beside him when he was done. He wanted to, but he didn't. And she kept quiet, too. Damn, but this was one patient woman.

"I gotta say, the court went pretty easy on me at first." He wasn't thinking to give her another opening, but his tongue thickened up for a moment.

And still she let him tell it his way.

"By then it was all about me. The cows were gone, horses were gone and my father took it hard, all of it. No turning back, no way forward. He was slipping away, and I didn't see it. You ask me, he died of a broken heart. Worn-out, maybe. Too many cracks. First heart attack laid him low. Within a few days the second one put him away."

"I'm sorry," she whispered.

"I can hear him laughing. 'What the hell are you talking about, a broken heart? Sounds pitiful.'" He chuckled as he turned to her. "He was a strong, quiet man. You'd've liked him, Lila. He'd've liked you."

"From what I'm hearing, I know I'm seeing him in you. I don't know about quiet," she excepted with a smile. "But strong. Caring."

He nodded. "He taught me better manners than I showed tonight."

"You're a pretty good dancer." She waited moment. "Now you can tell me I am, too."

"I don't know how it looked from the outside, but it sure felt sweet on the inside." Smiling, he took her face in his hands. "We were good together."

He kissed her hungrily, and he wanted so much more than the forgiving kiss she returned. She'd withdrawn from him some, but not all the way. She could have taken everything back, and he would have understood. But he wouldn't have given up, not the way he was feeling about her now. And she was willing to give him what she could, even though she didn't understand.

"You have to take a step back sometimes," he whispered across her lips. "Catch your breath."

Chapter 6

Lila's invitation for supper had been left open. Del kept thinking she would surprise him, but he didn't see her at all the following day. His day off. Hers, too. Not that he was keeping track, but if she'd wanted to spend time with him, he'd been handy. Proximity-wise. Now he decided to *get* handy, project-wise. Not that he had anything to prove on that score, but he liked to keep busy.

He went to the library. The librarian wasn't there, but he wasn't looking for her, and he was carrying a measuring tape to prove it. He had to borrow pencil and paper—maybe he wasn't *totally* prepared—but he ended up with his head in his plan. He and Asap took the long way back to the bunkhouse. The gardener wasn't in the garden. The teacher wasn't on the playground. Not that he needed a glimpse of her, or a word, or even a wave.

The long way around was more scenic than the gravel driveway, that was all.

Well, that and it was filled with images of Lila.

By midnight he'd cut and sanded pieces for three bookcases. Frank had offered to help when he'd loaned him the tools, and Del had sensed some disappointment when he'd turned the old man down, but he made up for it by partnering with him in the hay fields early the next morning. Frank needed a hand, and Del hadn't been exaggerating when he'd declared himself to be a good one. He enjoyed the work. It reminded him of the years he'd had with his father. He hadn't been smart enough to value them at the time, but he valued his memories.

At midday he and Frank headed to the house for dinner. Del knew Lila wouldn't be there—didn't know why he even let the thought enter his mind—but he caught himself trying to think up reasons to call her, settled on "Would you mind taking Asap out?"

No answer.

Of course not. She had a life.

So did he, for crying out loud. He could damn sure take the time to take out his own dog.

His own dog. There. That was all he needed. A guy had a life if he had a job, a good pickup and his own dog.

"You left early this morning, Brad," June was saying. The sound of her voice prompted Del to look down at his plate and notice—halfway through the meal—that he was eating chicken and rice. Not much taste to it. "Did you take Lila to do her shopping?"

"She didn't say nothin' about shopping. If she needs a ride, she'll let me know." Brad reached for the salt. "Won't she, Del? Del got her to go to the VFW dance. You believe that?"

"*Del* did?" June frowned at Brad, and then turned a look of wide-eyed wonder on Del.

"It was Brad's suggestion," Del said. Getting his head back into the game. He had a life, he had a job and Brad was his mark. "He was a little worried about her after we found the dog."

"Yeah, she took it pretty hard," Brad said. As if he would know.

"She introduced me around," Del said. "We had a good time."

"So what did *you* do this morning?" June asked her son.

"What did I do so far today?" Brad tapped his chin. "Well, let's see. I took a turn around the north pasture. We're still down six steers—they haven't wandered back—but otherwise the numbers add up. More than you can say for Carl Schrock. Rustlers got to him next."

"Worse than coyotes," Frank grumbled. "They wait till the price goes up some, and then they swoop in, hit us from all directions. By the time the law draws a bead on them, they're gone. At least the coyotes belong here. They're *our* coyotes."

"A thief is a thief, Dad."

"Or a hunter," Del said quietly over a forkful of rice.

"Right." Frank poked his food around with his fork. "Coyotes have to hunt to eat. Otherwise they're just dogs. How many head did Schrock lose?"

"Twenty." Brad swallowed hard, glanced at Del and then settled back into himself with a shrug. "Or thereabouts. That's what I heard. He figured it happened while he was at the dance last night."

"Twenty head?" Frank glanced up from his plate.

"He tallied up his losses that quick? Must've gotten out there and taken a count right away."

"I don't know for sure. That's just what people were saying today." Brad tried a change of subject on his mother. "Did a little shopping myself this morning. I needed to pick up a few things at the Co-Op, ran into the usual coffee crew. Fenton, Creitzer, that whole bunch."

"That whole bunch is my *old* bunch." Frank chuckled. "Bunch of semis, like me. Semiretired but still fully equipped."

"You're not their age, Frank." June raised the coffeepot in Del's direction.

He shook his head, doubled up with a no-more gesture, but thanked her with a smile. June's coffee was tolerable in small doses if you liked it strong enough to make a spoon stand up straight in the middle of your cup. Who knew what a potion like that could do to an old man's equipment?

"George Fenton wasn't too far ahead of me in school," Frank was saying. "Believe me, boys, it's beer with your buddies at Bucky's one day, coffee with the old coots at the Co-Op the next."

Del glanced up and favored Frank's joke with a chuckle, but in his mind one old man was gradually morphing into *the* old man, the one who was supposed to be too tough to die.

But he wasn't. And Frank reminded him of his own father.

"A friendly guy like me can handle both the same day," Brad said. "Tell you what, Del, you make hay while the sun shines this afternoon, and when it goes down tonight I'll buy you a beer. You'll be thirsty, and you won't want to stay that way, my friend."

"You're on."

The table talk went on around him, but Del had withdrawn. Brad was on for more than a beer. He was in for the kind of trouble Del had known firsthand, the kind sure to dump distress on an old man's doorstep. And Del was about to help bring it on. Oh, sure, he knew Brad was the one about to land in some very deep, very hot water, but the ripples would hit the whole Flynn family.

And he also knew he was letting himself get too close.

Sundown did nothing to relieve the day's heat. Beer with the boys at Bucky's wasn't exactly Del's idea of a fun night, but he didn't keep time by the clock. Not in his line of work. Hanging out, nursing a beer, losing a game of pool he could easily win—sounded like a dream job. But closing the deal could be a killer.

"Two in the corner."

Click. Blue went down.

Del nodded. "You're good, Brad."

"Practice." Grinning, Brad chalked his cue. "Nobody wants to take me on anymore."

"It's like watching a game on TV. You start getting the itch to play, but your turn never comes."

"I don't mind stepping aside. You wanna break next time?"

"Yeah, it's time I caught a break. But you don't need to step aside." Del glanced over at the bar. Three guys at the far end were crooning along with Garth Brooks about friends in low places. And Brad missed his shot. "That was a nice piece of work out at Schrock's place. Bigger trailer, bigger haul."

Brad frowned as he lowered his cue. "You were there?"

"You and me, boss." Del motioned for the chalk. "We were both there."

"But you were with Lila."

"Yeah, she's not too happy with me for leaving her. She caught a ride with Darlene."

"Schrock?"

"Yeah, Darlene Schrock. The irony, huh?" Del blew chalk off the tip of his cue. "Look, I'm not here to make trouble. I want in."

"In what?"

Del offered a knowing smile.

"If you were there, you might've noticed I wasn't really involved."

"You're involved, my friend. A bit player, maybe, but your ass is branded." Del studied the table. "You're the inside man. They tell you what they're looking for and you supply all the information they need. You come up with the time and the place, best ways in and out, and you sell out your neighbors, maybe even your family. That's the way it works." He sighted along his cue. "Three in the side." The red ball rolled into the hole. "You don't have to say anything, Brad. I've got eyes. I've been out of the game for a while, but I know the drill. Got into it probably the same way you did. I wanted something for myself."

"Everybody loses a few head every year. One way or another, it's part of the business."

"Sure it is." Del described his next shot and then banked the purple ball into the corner. "Tax write-off, right? That's what you tell yourself. It won't hurt the Double F. Won't hurt the Schrocks. Some guys carry insurance, some don't, but you tell yourself they'll all recover. Some sooner than others, but you figure they'll come out okay in the end. Anybody who goes under from the loss of just a few head was already teetering on the edge. You did him a favor by nudging him over. He's better off working for wages."

"Look, I gave you a job. You want more money? I'll come up with more money." Brad stepped closer. "I don't know how to get you in. Like you said, I'm just a bit player."

Del smiled. "It's kind of a rush, isn't it?"

"Watching some guys load up a few cows?"

"It's like winning at poker on a bluff. You rake in the pot, now you're really a player. Hell, Benson, you're a cattle rustler." Del shrugged. "Hey, there's good money in it. But you gotta learn a few more skills, work your way up."

"I'm not goin' anywhere. When they move on, I'll have something to tide me over."

"So will I." Another shot, another hit. Del kept talking while he lined up his next move. "When you get your next call, tell them your hired hand's interested in trying out for a role. Tell them he's had some experience."

"Okay, I'll give it a shot."

"Thanks." Del racked his cue. "Maybe I'll see you in the morning."

"Where are you going?"

"I'm a workin' man, Brad. Gotta get to bed on time if I'm gonna keep up with Frank tomorrow." He chuckled. "That man is hell on tractor wheels."

The lights were on in the schoolhouse, and the dog was missing from the bunkhouse. The woman had left him a trail of bread crumbs, which he was sorely tempted to ignore.

No, he wasn't. Not sorely. Not even slightly. There wasn't a cell in Del's body willing to turn away from the light in those schoolhouse windows. Gravel crunched beneath his boot heels and crickets cheered him on as he topped the rise in the driveway that curved through the grass. A shadow flitted past the window, which then went dark. He stopped in his tracks. The door opened and shut, and two shadows approached—the small one loped along, the tall one glided and neither spoke to him.

Asap reached him first. He gave the pup's floppy ears a tousle. Lila's footsteps slowed, and Del's heart pounded so hard he was sure she could hear it. He reached for her, and she leaned into him, slid her arms around him and lifted her face to his. Their kiss was all consuming. Her throat vibrated with a needy moan, his chest with a hungry groan. He plunged his tongue past her lips, held her close, their bodies fully flush. She welcomed him entirely, moved with him mouth to mouth and hip to hip, and every fiber of his being, every filament of hers, was infused into the kiss they made together.

In the breathless moment that followed, they agreed without saying a word. She took his hand, and he knew where they were going. Her place. The room filled with Lila, where she felt secure enough to let him come to know her. And know her he would.

There was a storm coming. Lila had felt it, had known even before darkness had fallen, and now she squeezed his hand and lifted her face to the first dollops of rain. It would be hard and heavy, but it would relieve the heat and clear the air.

She'd been ready for this—for him—for hours. Days. Maybe her whole life. She laughed, and she would have quickened her steps, but she'd left her flip-flops in the schoolhouse. Del tugged on her hand, whirled her around the way he had when they'd danced together, but this time he swept her into his arms and somehow kissed her and carried her and climbed the front steps without the slightest hesitation. Later she would relive this night, and this part would have her smiling right from the start, but right now her body was eager to move past it.

He let her legs slip, her body slide over his, her feet find purchase on the porch as he kissed her from a different angle. She met his kiss with her own and happily gave it back. She grabbed the screen door, threw it open and pulled him in after her. He followed her up the stairs. It wasn't until they reached the top that the pup came bounding after them. Another time she would have laughed, but not now. She could hardly breathe, but somehow her chest swelled and her heart fluttered. Deep down she shivered and quivered and burned all at once.

She hadn't made her bed that morning, but she lacked the presence of mind to care as she fumbled with the snap on her jeans.

He pushed her hands aside and whispered, "This is for me to do."

He kissed her again, and before she could do more than nibble his generous lips he was sliding her jeans over her hips, dropping to his knees and one at a time lifting her feet clear of the rain-damp denim. He kissed her belly, then licked and play-bit while his thumbs slowly dragged her cotton panties below her hip bones. She plunged her fingers into his thick hair and pressed her nails into his scalp. She was wet now, and the rain could not be blamed.

He feathered his lips lower, dispatched her panties and then rubbed his chin back and forth, ruffling her tight curls as he gently slid his thumbs into the folds of her groin. So close. So tantalizingly close. She tried not to look, but she had to, and there were his smiling eyes, waiting for some signal. She answered yes with a slight shift of her hips, and he teased with a flickering tongue until her breath quivered and she shivered deep down.

She bit her bottom lip. Every part of her wanted to be touched. It almost hurt to stretch her fingers and let go of his hair, almost pained her to draw breath and feel her bra abrade her nipples, almost killed her when his hands left her even momentarily. He stood, took hold of her bottom, lifted her and pulled her to him, oh, yes, and rocked against her and kissed her, plunged his tongue in and out until she caught it, and yes, she sucked it as she tugged at his zipper, and yes, it gave way.

Her T-shirt came off, her bra slid away and she was on the bed, unsure of how she got there, unsure of anything except that she ached, everything tingled and ached, and when he touched her the tingling stung sweetly and the aching throbbed terribly. His incorrigible mouth made her nipples so tight they threatened to explode, while his maddeningly slow, deft touch between her legs, into her secret folds, around her most sensitive flesh, had her palpitating with such wild abandon that her whole body gave in to wave after wave of pure pleasure.

She couldn't stop, and he wouldn't let her. He drew her hand to his penis and whispered, "Touch me, Lila. That's all I need."

But *she* needed more. Much more. He gasped when she drew him inside her, lifted her hips and held him hard, then rocked him as only a woman's body could rock a man. She gave him no quarter, no option but to answer with the matching motion of his own hips. He stroked inside her until she called his name and shuddered blissfully, and he, marvelous man, swiftly withdrew and flooded her belly.

And for the first time that night she was aware of rain on the roof, wind rattling the trees and thunder rumbling in the night.

They held each other for a time neither measured, resting, caressing, listening to the rain, admiring each other's body when a flash of lightning filled the room.

"I was afraid you wouldn't come tonight," she said finally. Her voice sounded deeper than she remembered it from...when? An hour, a day, a lifetime ago?

"Didn't want to come too soon." He chuckled. "You knew that was coming."

"I should have." Lightning flashed, thunder rolled and a wet nose nudged her hand. "Ace! Have you been here all along? You bad boy." She wasn't sure why. It was Bingo who'd always seemed human, and Asap wasn't Bingo.

"That would be me. I'm the bad boy." He held up a hand. "No dogs on the bed, Asap. We've been over that." He curled his arm around Lila. "Only the alpha gets on the bed." He turned back to Lila. "And yes, you should've known I'd come."

"Why did it take you so long?"

"I was afraid you'd turn me away."

"I planned to." She snuggled against his shoulder. "I took my horse out for a long ride yesterday, visited a friend, a man I know you'd like. His daughter was my best friend growing up. I was gone all day."

"Mmm-hmm."

"You noticed?"

"Maybe."

"Well, I wasn't angry. It wasn't that important, our little date. But if you'd shown up last night, it was going to be…different."

"Because?"

"Because, because."

Senseless answer. She wanted to take it back before he took advantage with a quip or a quote, something smart. She had no answers, not even for herself.

But he kissed her temple—tenderness for a tender place—and whispered, "How did you know I was coming up the driveway?"

"Ace let me know you were out there."

She'd turned off the light, looked through the window and then she'd been on her way out the door, because he'd been there. Heart pounding, pulse racing, his name her only clear thought, she'd slid through the dark to be with him.

"I knew you were gone yesterday," he told her. "Last night I started making bookcases."

"You did?"

"They're just pieces so far. You can still make changes on anything but the size."

"Where? There's nothing…"

"Down in the shop. Frank let me use his tools." She felt him smile against her temple. "I told him I'd always wanted to build a library. He asked if I needed help, but I told him I wasn't sure exactly what I was going to do. I think he knew what I meant. I hope he did. I start with a plan, and then it's trial and error until I find the finished product. It's hard to work with somebody else when you're flying by the seat of your pants."

He was making bookcases. *For her.*

"And I borrowed a couple of books from the library. How long do I get to keep them out?"

"As long as you need to. What are you reading?"

"A Western. I've read it before, so I'll get through it quick."

"A comfort read, huh?"

"An old friend." His lips stirred her hair as he spoke.

The rain pattered steadily, and the wind still blew, but the thunder's rumble was distant now. Maybe the storm was going away.

"Tell me about your friend and his daughter."

"Crystal Chasing Elk and I started the day care business together after I came back from Minnesota."

He stilled for a moment, midbreath. "Chasing Elk?"

"Uh-huh. Her father is Stan. You know him?"

"No."

"I'll have to introduce you. Anyway, I didn't come back right away after the accident, but when I couldn't get myself together enough to make any sense of what I was doing, I left school. This house had been empty for years, so I asked Crystal to move in with me, and we fixed the place up. The day care was her idea. She'd been thinking about it, had some people interested, just didn't have a place. This was perfect.

"She was the driving force behind it, she… Well, she did all the driving. We had more kids then. I didn't know she was sick. I mean, I knew she was diabetic, but I didn't know she was having problems with her kidneys." She sighed. It was hard to admit she hadn't known how sick Crystal had been. If she had just pulled her head out of her butt sooner… "I couldn't even give her one of mine. We weren't compatible. We were *so* compatible, like sisters, in every other way. But my extra kidney was useless to her."

She laid her hand on Del's sturdy chest and felt the beat his heart. "I wish you could have met her. You really would have liked her."

"I could have been compatible."

"If you were, would you have…?"

"No question." He covered her hand with his. "Yeah, that's something I would do. That would be easy." He gave a dry chuckle. "Whether I liked her or not. I mean, they give you some kind of drugs, you go to sleep, you wake up, maybe there's a little scar, but otherwise you don't miss a kidney."

"You could." She kissed his shoulder. "If you're down to one."

"Last time I checked my birth certificate, there were no guarantees on parts, and the cost of repairs has gone through the roof. But if you can find a used kidney…" She thumped him. *"Oof!"*

His sense of humor was so much like Crystal's, it might have been a transplant. "She would have liked you. After you blew me off at the dance—"

"I what?"

"—she would've said, 'I told you, never trust a cowboy.' But those bookcases…"

"You don't have them yet."

"But I will. You strike me as a man who finishes

what he starts. Anyway, you did. You blew me off. But when I saw you outside tonight, I knew how I felt. I know you."

"Feeling and knowing are two different things."

"True. So tell me what else I should know."

"I could tell you anything right now, couldn't I? Think about that, Lila. Think about what your friend would tell you, what she'd tell you now."

"Crystal didn't—"

"You know, you shouldn't be saying her name, since she's dead. Lakota, right?"

"What difference does that make?"

"Speaking their names can hold them here," he said solemnly, and then he made a funny sound in his throat, like an uneasy chuckle. "That's what they say anyway. I don't know if I believe it, but just in case… It's not fair to hold them here, you know? Let them go free." He paused. "Does that sound crazy?"

"No." In fact, she liked the idea. She could picture her friend's release, an ethereal spirit with smiling eyes and no need for a name.

"Superstitious?"

"Not if it's what you believe."

"My dad believed it. I respect him. Always did. I don't know what I…" He drew a deep breath and sighed. "Lila, I had to go with Brad. I saw him leave, and I had to go right away. There was no time to discuss, explain, none of that."

"He really isn't your boss, Del."

"I know. Your dad writes the checks." He nuzzled her hair. "I like Frank. He's a good man."

"He's henpecked."

Del chuckled. "Must be why my dad didn't go for the

second wife. You notice I don't say his name. That's the part that ties a spirit down. That earth name."

"Would you like to meet Crystal's father?" He groaned. "I say her name a lot. I'm not Lakota."

"Like I said, I'm not too traditional. I just…" He shook his head. "Yeah, I'd like to meet Stan Chasing Elk."

"I'll take you there. We'll ride. Whenever you have time."

"I'll make time." He reached for the sheet, pulled it across their no-guarantees bodies, and they cuddled. "Man, that wind sounds strong."

"We should move to the basement," she said. Again he groaned. "I have a storm shelter down there. Food, water, blankets, flashlights. All the necessities. We put it together mostly for the kids." He didn't move. "There's a sofa."

"I like it here." He kissed her breast all around her nipple, which he then licked. "I'm blowing you off," he said, and he blew softly, steadily.

A rumble of thunder. A howling wind. Lightning split the darkness in two. Lila stiffened. Asap whined.

Del sighed. "Okay, honey, take me down."

He woke up during the night, confused at first about where he was. It was pitch-dark, and his ass was cold. But his arms were full of warm, soft, musk-scented woman, and he was stiff all over. But mostly where it counted.

She stirred in his arms, and he grew harder. He was going to have to do something about that. Either get up or something else. Something better.

"Is it morning?" she asked.

"Feels like it."

"Do you think that was a tornado that came through?"

He smiled against the dark. "I got hit pretty hard by something. How about you?"

"Want some breakfast?"

The chance for something better was going to slip away if he didn't make something happen fast. "After we take a shower."

"You shower while I make breakfast." She started to climb over him.

He stopped her midway, took a thigh in each hand and made her straddle him. "One false move and you're ready for the grill, darlin'. Chick on a stick."

"You really are a bad boy."

"Fire or water? Your call. You take a shower with me. I'll fix breakfast for you."

"Save the fire for February. What do you want to fix? I might not have everything you need."

"You do, my pretty." He bounced her once and unleashed a mock evil laugh. "Everything."

She ran for the stairs wrapped in a blanket. Del brought up the rear, and his was buck naked. He tried to snatch the blanket, but she shrieked and then tripped on the damn thing, and he felt like a real dog. An indignant yip from the real dog at the foot of the stairs made him slow down. He might have made up for his bone-headed play by scooping Lila up and carrying her the rest of the way, but the stairs were narrow, and falling down them bare assed would have spoiled what was left of the mood.

Instead he steadied himself on the railing with one hand and slid the other around her waist. "You okay? I'm…" Oh, God, she was shaking. "Lila? Where does it—"

"Let go of me, please."

He stepped down slowly and dropped his arm to his side.

The blanket dropped over his head, and he heard feet pounding up the steps.

"Damn it, woman!"

By the time he reached the bathroom she was stepping into the shower, laughing like a little girl. He barreled in after her, backed her under the water and kissed her until they both nearly drowned.

"You scared me, you know that?" he said.

Of course she did. She was still giggling, hair plastered to her head, eyelashes all spiky and her eyes sparkling like Christmas morning. She looked so perfect that he was almost afraid to touch her. He grabbed a bar of wet soap and started rolling it between his hands.

"You were chasing me."

"Did you get hurt?" He set the soap aside and sudsed up her shoulders. "It was the damn blanket that tripped you up, not me. What were you trying to cover up?"

"I was running up the stairs. And I was jiggling!"

"So you covered up?" He laughed. "I was jiggling, too."

She spared his erection a quick glance. "That's basically one, well…" She cupped her breasts. "I have two of these, and they're boneless." She reached around back. "And this jiggles, too, and I'm just not the jiggling type."

"You're a funny girl." He drew her hand away from her body and claimed it for himself, tucking it between his legs. "I don't think too much about how things look." He slid his hands up her torso. It was his turn to cup her breasts. He smiled as he thumbed her nipples. "Boneless and beautiful. Tasty, too."

She closed her eyes. "Don't stop." Her hand intensified her persuasiveness.

He rested his forehead on hers, and they brought each other to heavenly heights without giving another thought to jiggling.

Lila stood looking out the bathroom window, a white towel wrapped around her chest. Del ruffled his hair with the towel he'd used to dry himself. "Something wrong?" he asked as he tucked it around his waist.

"The storm. There's a lot of debris, looks like a lot of damage. The fence, the play yard, the garden…" She leaned to one side. "The barn looks okay, but I can't see it all, can't see the corral. The horses…"

"They'll be in the barn. I'll go."

"And the schoolhouse. I can't tell from here."

She turned to him, and she looked scared. Scared for her animals, her fruits and flowers, her sanctuary. And that schoolhouse, with its memories, mysteries, history… It meant more to her than the typical bygone-era castoff that thrifty farmers bought for a song and parked behind the barn for just in case. Lila was more builder than collector, and she built dreams. She was bringing new life to that old schoolhouse.

And whatever was out there now, whatever the condition, he wanted to see it before she did.

"Wait for me, Del."

"I'm gonna grab my pants and take the dog out real quick." He looked back and nodded. "Let me go first."

Chapter 7

Eager to run off the night's jitters, the two horses charged past Del and into their little pasture as soon as he opened the gate. Other than a little roof damage, the outbuildings below the hill had fared well. It was a relief to report good news when Lila met him at the kitchen door. And it was a pleasure to smell coffee and bacon.

"No injuries to the livestock, all the buildings are still standing and my job is secure."

"The new house came through fine. I called. Dad said the wind lifted a few shingles, but nothing major." She handed him a cup of hot coffee. "Your job is to keep him off the roof."

"I'm the hired hand. My job is to be handy."

"I didn't hire you." She gestured toward the kitchen table with the gray Formica top and stainless-steel trim. He'd grown up with one almost like it. "But I'll feed you, even though I *did* share the shower." She set a plate in front of him. "I hope you like your eggs scrambled. I know every inch of your body, but I have no idea what you like for breakfast."

"Anything jiggly and boneless." He flashed her a wink, and he picked up his fork. "I'll work it out with Frank and fix what needs fixing. It's mostly the yard. There's a little water damage inside the schoolhouse. Lots of shingling to be done, but I'm good with heights."

"I want to go over and check on Stan. I called, but there was no answer." She joined Del at the table. "I turned on the news. No tornado touchdown was reported, but some places lost power. Do you have time to give me a ride? It's not far. It won't take long."

"Over to Stan Chasing Elk's? Sure. The man's had his share of troubles lately."

She gave him a funny look. "I thought you didn't know him."

"I know *of* him. Last night you told me he's your friend, your friend's father. That's all the endorsement I need."

"What do you mean?" She frowned. "Did Brad accuse him of something? Because if he did…" She shook her head. "We don't need Twitter around here. We've got Brad Benson. He has a habit of repeating rumor as fact."

"I can generally tell the difference."

She was quiet for a moment. Then defensive, as though someone had accused *her* of something. "There is no way he stole any cattle."

He lifted one shoulder. *Back on the job.* "When there's a lot of talk, you reach for the salt."

"It's beer talk. Bar stool babble." She pushed her

chair back from the table. "I need a ride over there. You can just drop me off."

"You said I could meet your friend. I can do that now if I can talk your dad into staying off the roof until I get back."

Stanley Chasing Elk lived a small house flanked by a cottonwood and chokecherry shelter that stood beside a creek fed by runoff from a cluster of rolling hills a few miles away. His pole barn was twice as big as his house, and he seemed to be running more chickens than cows these days.

He was standing on the front step when they drove into the yard. He was a tall man who cut an imposing figure in his crisp plaid Western shirt, cowboy boots and the graying braids gracing his shoulders. He would have seen their pickup turn off the blacktop highway onto his rutted approach from more than a mile away. He lived alone now, and his once-thriving ranch saw few visitors.

Lila greeted him with the embrace of a daughter for her father. "I tried to call, but you didn't answer. I was worried."

"The storm passed by me. Thunderbird decided I'd had enough trouble lately."

Lila slid Del a glance. He was staring at the ground, waiting his turn.

"Who's this you brought?" Stan asked.

Del stepped up quickly and introduced himself with a traditional slight-grip handshake.

"Fox? Some Foxes up by New Town." Stan turned to Lila. "I just made coffee." She nodded and went into the house, pleased to be treated like a daughter.

She knew the Chasing Elk kitchen as well as her own. When she returned with coffee and cups, she knew that little had been said in her absence. Stan stood with his arms folded across his chest, Del with thumbs hooked into the front pockets of his jeans, both staring past Stan's empty corral, seemingly watching cloud shadows slide across the waving prairie grass. They were either waiting for her or the coffee to get the visit started.

Del took two cups from her and handed one to Stan, who nodded toward the redwood picnic table beneath the rustic round "shade" made of stripped poles and thatched with cottonwood branches.

"But you're not from Fort Berthold," Stan said, as though he had last spoken only thirty seconds ago.

"Hell no. I'm Lakota. My father was from Standing Rock." Del waited until Lila and Stan were seated across from each other before he took his place beside her on the bench.

"Don't know any Foxes up there. But I don't know everybody." Stan sipped his coffee. "Small world, Indian country. You get to be as old as I am, you think you know everybody. But you don't." He lifted his chin and gave Del a considering look. "I can tell you're from Standing Rock. You've got that look, like you've been out in the sun too long."

"You talk like my father." Del nodded. "I haven't been this far south that much. I thought you'd be a lot shorter."

Stan nodded back at Del, then turned to Lila with a broad grin. "Good man. Where did you find him, my girl?"

Del couldn't help feeling warmed by the old man's praise, but he kept his face impassive.

"Brad hired him. But you mustn't hold that against him, Stan. He's making me bookcases."

"For the library? Good man, good man. Be sure the children can reach their books on their own. We want them to find books without being told."

"Stan built the children's shelves for us. That was back when we were fixing it up just for day care. It was all about making everything child-size, and I wanted it all 'One Little, Two Little, Three Little Indians' at first, but I was told to get real." She flashed a smile Stan's way.

"Not by me. They're little Indian kids. There's nothing wrong with counting them."

"She'd hated the song ever since she was in preschool because it was only about boys. 'What about us girls?' she said."

"That was my daughter," Stan said to Del. "Always wanted everything just so. Just like this one." He nodded at Lila. "They were like sisters. They'd butt heads over something one day, go off not speaking, next day they've got it figured out."

"So we decided on the colors of the four directions, and each color was a station for stories and singing and snacking and sleeping."

"My kind of school," Del said.

"We'd barely gotten started," Lila said. "We had so many more ideas. She was a bundle of energy."

"She was that." Stan patted Lila's hand. "So are you. And I know it was hard on you when she died."

"Hard on *me*?" Lila put her other hand over the old man's. "I should have seen it coming. She was young and strong, and when she came back from her clinic appointments and I asked, 'How's it going?' and she said, 'Good,' that was all I wanted to hear. And then she was gone.

"I'm a wimp, Stan. I almost went back into the shell that Crys—that your daughter pried me out of. If it wasn't for you…" She turned to Del. "It took me too long to reopen. I lost most of the kids."

"But then they came back, some of them," Stan said. "Isn't that so, my girl?"

"Yes, because you talked me up with the parents. They weren't sure I'd stick with the program on my own. They came for…" She glanced at Del. "I didn't know I wasn't supposed to be saying her name."

"You told her that?" Stan asked Del.

"Well, yeah." He shrugged. "Wasn't I supposed to?"

"It don't matter. The *wanagi* only hear *us*."

"My mistake." Del flashed Lila a sly wink. "Guess you don't count with the Lakota spirits."

"Really?"

He squeezed her shoulder. "Don't take it personal." And then he grinned at Stan, and they both chuckled.

"Is it true or not?" Lila insisted.

"It is until we find out different," Stan said.

"Which I'm not planning to do any time soon," Del added.

"You two must be related," Lila grumbled good-naturedly. "Indian humor. I never know how to react until you say *just kidding*."

"Did you say it?" Del asked Stan. "I know I didn't say it."

"Well, I know I'm not taking any chances," Lila said. "I don't need to speak her name. I have much more to remember her by."

Stan patted her hand again. She offered a misty smile

and then cleared her throat. "Dad lost some steers. He thinks they were stolen. Well, Brad thinks they were stolen, and Darrell Hartley—"

"Sheriff Hartley probably thinks I stole them. I had a visit from the tribal police."

Lila frowned. "They don't really think you stole them, do they?"

"They think maybe I know something about it." Stan wrapped his big, leathery hands around his cup. "I pastured tribal cattle until most of them disappeared a while back," he told Del. "They had all kinds of cops out here looking for some way to prove I was in on the disappearance, but they couldn't come up with anything.

"Lost some of my own cattle, too, so I'm not in the cattle business anymore. Sold all but twenty head when I lost my lease. They'll have to dig around in somebody else's backyard. Maybe that big shot from the college, that Klein."

"Didn't they fire him?" Lila asked.

"Yeah, because he bought a bunch of equipment for the ag program and took it to his own place."

"Did they get the equipment back?" Del asked.

Stan lifted one shoulder. "They got a tractor back that was five years older than the one he *borrowed*, a busted backhoe and I don't know what all else."

"There should've been paperwork on the equipment," Del said.

"Should've." Stan gave a humorless smile. "Turned out Professor Klein wasn't too good with paperwork. He could've *sworn* everything was in those files."

"Could've or did?" Del had heard stories like this before.

"All I know is he had a lawyer." Stan shook his head

in disgust. "Tribal colleges get themselves into a bind over contracts like everyone else. The tribe had to pay him to be rid of him. Nobody paid me, but I'm not in prison, so that's something."

Lila laid her hand on the old man's plaid sleeve. "You were never charged with anything, Stan."

"Ninety-six head," Stan said angrily. "Somebody got away as slick as bear grease with ninety-six head."

"Looks like somebody's back for more," Del said.

"It wouldn't be the same outfit, would it? They wouldn't try hitting the same place again. That wouldn't be too smart." Stan scowled. "Course the tribe's cattle aren't in the same place." His face broke into a sly smile. "I hope it *is* the same damn bunch of thieves. Hell, they'll get caught this time for sure."

"How many head does the tribe have left?"

"I wouldn't know. None on my land. I check mine pretty often, and I know what's here. I can count to twenty pretty easy."

"If you need anything…" Lila said quietly.

"Don't you start now. I've got all I need except something to do." The old man glanced at Del. "Maybe you'd let me help out with those bookcases."

"We got broken swings, busted fence and some water damage in the library. Plenty to do whenever you wanna jump in," Del said.

Stan looked at Lila. "I'm hearin' a lotta *we*. Who did you say this man's workin' for?"

Del smiled. "I'm like you, Stan. I like to keep busy."

On the way back to the Double F, Del waited for Lila to tell him what she needed first. The air in the little space they shared was filled with frustration, and she didn't know the half of it. But the half she knew was heavy enough.

She'd gotten herself mixed up with a man she didn't know much about, and what she did know couldn't be sitting too well with her. The old man she did know well was suspected of something she knew he couldn't have done. Maybe the problem she was sitting with was also the *man* she was sitting with. If she asked him straight-out, he had to be ready with a lie or some kind of half-truth—*same as a lie, Fox, be honest in your own head, at least*—and he didn't know if he could come up with anything right now.

What kind of help could he offer? What did she need?

"Do you still have a driver's license?" he asked finally.

"I do. It's handy for identification. I don't have a car, though."

"How about insurance?"

"I had good insurance. Everything was covered."

Ah, the accident. That wasn't where he'd been going with his questions, but he was more than willing to follow her lead.

"There was a child, wasn't there?"

She said nothing, and the moment drew out. It was up to her.

"Yes. A child."

"And it wasn't your fault." He was no therapist, but some things were obvious, and it couldn't hurt to say them. As long as it wasn't about him.

"It wasn't the little girl's fault. It wasn't her father's fault."

"Her father?"

"The poor guy. He tried to…" She drew a deep, unsteady breath. "I don't want to talk about this, Del. I've made my peace with it. At least I think I have. And every time I say that, I think, who am I to make peace? And then the dreams come back."

"Yeah, I know about dreams." Not like she did. There were no children in his dreams. Everyone he'd ever hit had been a man who'd been begging Del to slam a fist into his gut. Those were the good dreams.

"I was driving, but I wasn't charged with anything. Officially, it was nobody's fault." Her voice dropped. He had to strain to catch every word. "It was bad. It doesn't matter how it came about. It's *what* came about that matters. Talking about it changes nothing."

"I know. I was just thinking, if you ever feel like you want to try driving again, maybe I could help you."

"I'm doing just fine. I know how to drive. I choose not to."

"Okay. What do you want me to hit first?"

"Hit?"

He smiled. "The fence? The swings? Maybe the schoolhouse roof in case we get more rain, but I'd have to get shingles."

"You don't work for me, Del."

"I'm gonna go down and talk to Frank. Meanwhile, you make a general plan."

Again she was quiet, and he thought he'd lost her. But then she perked up some, smiled wistfully. "I get to be the general?"

"How about the queen?" he offered. "I wouldn't make it as a soldier."

He was gone longer than he'd thought he would be. He and Frank checked the hay field and agreed that it was too wet to work it, but a full day of sun would make all the difference. Frank seemed happy with Del's concern for the damage at the home place and his assurance that he could fix it all, and Brad readily agreed to check cows after he picked up Del's list of building materials. Del exchanged a look with Frank. They both knew what Brad's idea of checking cows was. Kill a little time driving around in his pickup, come back for dinner and report that everything was looking good.

Lila had piled up some debris in front of the schoolhouse and the edge of the play yard, and she was working on the garden, tossing ruined plants into a wheelbarrow, muttering as she worked. "Damn storm." Golf ball–size green tomatoes rattled as they hit. "Damn badger. Damn rattler. Damn, damn—"

Del walked up to the wheelbarrow and offered her his gloves. "Either put these on or take a seat on the throne." She glowered at him, and he smiled. "I'm yours for the rest of the day." He snapped the gloves. "What's the plan?"

"I have gloves."

"And blisters."

"They're almost…" She turned her hands and they both saw the traces of blood mixed with dirt. "All right. You're right. I was just going to clear away some of it so I could see if there's anything left, and the more I cleared—"

"The more you cussed."

"Waste of breath, right?" She wiped her forehead with the back of her hand as she surveyed the jumbled garden. "There won't be many tomatoes."

"This should cheer you up. Brad's gonna go get us some shingles."

"Brad is?"

"And some woven wire. And some posts. Glass for the window. I'll have to take that sucker apart. Can you think of anything else? I'll add it to the order."

"And I have you for the day? How did you manage that?"

"Hey, your dear stepbrother just wants to help out."

"What*ever*."

"He knows they dodged a bullet down at the new house, and you caught one up here. Everybody pitches in." He grinned. "Don't look a gift horse in the mouth, woman."

"Is that what you are?"

"Could be." He reached for her hand. "After we clean you up again, is this where you want to start?"

"I want to save as much of the garden as I can. I'm going to put a raised bed over Bingo. I'll grow special things there, like herbs and healing plants." She took another wistful look. "I started a lot of this from seed. Even the tomatoes."

"Tell me what you want me to do," he said as they walked back to the house.

"Let's clean up the garden, then the schoolhouse and then the fence. Or the play yard. We'll need the…" She looked up at him and smiled. She seemed happy to have him. "Let's work together. I'll try not to cuss."

"Me, too."

Once he was satisfied that her hands were protected, they made short work of the garden cleanup. He claimed the rake and garden fork, and she was allowed to judge each plant's chances for recovery. He had her joking about the powers of royalty. But he was the one who kept coming up with ideas for improvements on top of repairs.

"Hey, how about putting rocks around these flower beds?" he asked as they rounded the corner of the house pushing a wheelbarrow full of discards toward the appropriate pile. "Nobody's gonna drive over rocks, and there's a whole pile of them behind the bunkhouse."

"I love that idea. I'll put it on my list."

"Put it on *my* list." He upended the wheelbarrow. "I'll have to replace that broken window out in the schoolhouse, but I should be able to use the old frame. I don't suppose you'd want to upgrade those windows? What do you do for heat in the winter?"

"In the library I burn wood and wear a coat. We were saving up to put in propane heat, but we didn't get that far, so I made it a library. I mean, we needed a library. The kids like to come in here until it gets too cold, and then we stay in the house a lot. If I get more kids…" She turned and appeared to be speaking to the schoolhouse when she asked, "How long are you going to stay?"

He couldn't give his usual answer. *Couldn't say.* "All I know is I get paid by the month."

"How long do you usually stay?"

"As long as the job lasts." He was glad to see some activity at the Double F gate. "Here comes our delivery truck." Briefly getting him off the hook.

A clacking noise below her bedroom window pulled Lila to the surface of sleep. It was still dark. The middle of the night, said the bright numbers on her bedside clock. She peeked outside and saw Del's pickup. He was standing in the bed, heaving huge rocks over the side.

"Hey." He dropped to the ground and shed his leather

work gloves as she approached, harsh words dissolving on her tongue when she saw his beautiful face close up in the moonlight. "I couldn't sleep. Couldn't stop thinking about moving these rocks."

She smiled. "It's a lovely night for moving rocks."

"Great night for it."

"As hard as you worked today, you should be sleeping like a baby."

"How do babies sleep? Don't they wake up every few hours?" He sat down on the pickup tailgate and beckoned her with a gesture. "I wake up sometimes and feel like the walls are closing in. I have to go outside and get some air."

"It's a wonder you were able to sleep down in the basement."

"I was with you." He reached for her and drew her between his knees. "I slept like a baby. Face between your breasts."

"Want to try that again? Upstairs this time."

"I do. Upstairs, downstairs, under the stairs, I'd sleep with you anywhere, darlin'. Right now..." He nodded toward a patch of once-tall coneflowers and bushy Shasta daisies, some lying low, some still standing. "Once I get started on something, I like to get it to the point where it starts to look like what I pictured. Then I know I'll finish it. Until then, I won't be able to sleep."

"I couldn't really sleep, either."

"Did I wake you up?" He chucked her chin. "Did you miss me?"

"I'm afraid I will. Who will I have to talk to besides four-year-olds and the wolf at the door?"

"Don't let him in, honey. He can't replace the Fox."

She boosted herself up to join him on the tailgate. He

slipped his arm around her, and she put her head on his shoulder. She could get used to this. The sex was surprising and risky and amazing, but this quiet comfort... It surprised her almost as much. She had come by it without seeking it, like hunting for wild turnips and discovering a pasqueflower blooming out of season.

"The child I hit was only five," she told him. Unplanned, unrehearsed, the story simply rolled off her tongue into the cool night air. "It was winter. Dusk. She came shooting out of a driveway on a little blue plastic sled. It happened so fast. I heard a terrible scream. I didn't even know what I'd hit until I got out of the car. It was her father who screamed, not the child. He'd had her out on the sled, and he'd pulled her up the driveway. I can still hear him saying he'd only turned his back for a second. I looked at him and knew it was true. Having the kids here now, I understand even better. A second. A fraction of a second. They're so quick, those little ones." She shook her head. "It was a good thing it was so cold, they said. It slowed the bleeding."

He gave her shoulder a quick squeeze. "She came through, though. That's the important thing."

"She was so small, so still. They said I called 911. I don't remember that. Or covering her with my coat, I don't remember *that*, either. I remember how she looked and the way her father screamed, and how another man—a neighbor—kept him from moving her." She swallowed nothing. Her throat was dry. "She lost a leg. She was lucky, they said. She almost lost...a lot more. Her father had a hard time with it. Blamed himself."

"She's doing okay now?"

"She hates the prosthetic. She outgrows them so fast. But she's doing well in school. Plays the violin."

"So you keep in touch."

"It's a nice family. They've been through so much. I've almost been able to separate the child lying so still in the snow from the voice on the phone who tells me about her part in the school play."

"Almost?"

"It's the dreams."

He nodded. "Something bad happened. You can't change that. Sounds like that nice family has made their peace with it while you keep telling yourself you don't have the right. Why are you hangin' on to that child lying in the snow?"

"I'm not."

"That child lived and grew. She isn't the two-legged kid she might have been, true. She's the one who has a life and tells you about it."

"I know," she whispered, dry-eyed, her throat prickling. "I know. I'm glad she does. I don't want to think about that day. I try not to. There's a lot I don't even remember."

"I'm no psychiatrist, that's for sure. But I know something about self-inflicted wounds. They're twice as painful as any other kind."

She looked up at him. "Where's yours?"

"Same place as yours. In my head."

"And you don't like to talk about it either, do you?"

"I can't. I wish I could." He nodded toward the bunkhouse. "There's a bigger rock back there. Petrified wood, I think. Real pretty. I can't lift it, but I could drag it behind the pickup. It would look real nice out here in the yard somewhere."

"I know the one you mean." She patted his knee, an unconscious imitation of the woman who came immediately to mind. "Grandma used to call my grandfather the rock man. He brought them home from all over the place. That one is South Dakota petrified wood. There's more of it around. He was going to make something with his collection." She sighed. "I hardly remember him. We used to sit at the kitchen table and see who could eat the most ice cream. He scared me once when he caught me trying to open the chute on the grain bin. He told me never, never try to get into the grain bin. I was just trying to get some oats so I could get my pony to come to me."

"Yeah, I got in trouble for messing around in the shed where my dad stored oats. It looked like a mountain of stuff that was perfect for jumping into. There was a ladder—"

"Oh, God."

"He caught me in time." He smiled. "My father did. My father who art in heaven with your grandfather. Right?"

"He died when I was five."

"What was his name?"

She raised an eyebrow. "Are you testing me?"

"Checking for Lakota blood." He smiled. "You think about where you want that rock, I'll move it for you."

They sat together without speaking as a long moment passed. "You offered to make repairs, but it sounds as though I'll be getting some real improvements," she said at last. "That storm must've been heaven-sent."

"Aren't they always?"

"I think I could sleep now. Will you come to bed with me?"

"No." He covered her hand with his. "I want you in *my* bed."

"It's a single bed. There's only room for one."

"Or two trying to be one." He kissed her forehead, and then his lips feathered his promise against her skin. "I'll let you sleep. I'll just hold you."

He felt bone tired but muscle revived when he came out of the shower. He slipped into a pair of jeans, and she greeted him with a hand on his hip when he lay down beside her.

"Do you often sleep in your clothes?"

"No. But it'll be hard to just hold you if I'm not wearing anything."

"That was *your* plan." She snuggled against his chest. "I'm ready for that two-becoming-one trick."

"No tricks. I never want to trick you or deceive you about…" He drew a deep breath. "There's something you should know about me."

"I know all I need to." She knew all she *wanted* to. "You are—" she traced the shape of his flat areola with her finger "—a kind and gentle man. A cowboy. Granted, mothers always warn their daughters about cowboys, and I've always stayed away from them, but you…"

"I'm an ex-con." Her hand stilled. "Remember I told you I got arrested a couple of times?"

"You said the courts went easy on you."

"At first." He covered her hand with his as though he expected her to take it away. "I did time in the state pen for grand theft."

She swallowed hard. "How old were you?"

"Old enough. I wasn't a kid. I knew what I was doing. You wanna talk about guilt? That's what killed my father. Watching his son go to prison. I was gonna get everything back for him. That's what I told him anyway. I told him I was doing it for him. Worst lie I ever told in my life." His voice dropped to a low, secret register. Del had never spoken to anyone else about his crimes or the real reason he'd committed them.

He hated excuses. It was time for them to end. "I did it for myself. It made me feel like a big man. I was good at it, better than anybody I knew. That ain't sayin' much, of course, since they were all small-time thieves."

"Were you a big-time thief?" she asked quietly, and he stared at her. *Was she joking?* "Well, isn't that what grand theft is?"

"If it involves livestock, it's grand theft felony in this state." He paused. She was dead serious, and he had to give her all the truth he could. "I stole cattle."

"Oh." He could almost hear her processing the news. "How long ago?"

"I've been out for almost seven years."

"The ranchers you work for…don't know."

"When I was on probation, they knew. I had to report to a probation officer. Since then, well, nobody's asked."

"My father…"

He shook his head. "What do you think he'd say?"

"That you're a good hand."

"You think he'd trust me?"

She released a quick sigh. "He'd give you the benefit of the doubt."

"How about you? Do *you* trust me?" Her silence nearly killed him. "Lila?"

"As much as I did before. Maybe even more, since you get points for telling me. It's funny, isn't it? If I were going to hire you, I'd probably do a background check. But here I am, in bed with you. And I don't just do the two-trying-to-become-one thing with... I mean, I'm not easily impressed, and I don't let people... But you're very..."

"Kind and gentle?"

"Yes. Kind and gentle. And I feel like being kind and gentle back. Listening the way you do. Telling you secrets. Touching you. Being touched by you and no one else." She pressed her cheek against him. "Does that scare you?"

"No." He groaned. "Yeah, a little. I've never met anyone like you. I'm a big risk for you, and that scares me. I want to keep you safe." He pulled her into a twofer embrace. "I want to keep you, Lila. With me."

Chapter 8

Del had a job to do. It was his real job, the one that really paid off, the one he enjoyed. He knew when he was closing in on something big. Brad had no idea what kind of deal they were mixed up in, but Del did. They were gofers at the bottom of a network of tunnels. Brad was anyway.

Del was a mole.

Brad was pumped when he pulled Del off the schoolhouse roof. It was twilight. Del had already decided to knock off at the end of the current row of shingles. He'd repaired the swings, fenced in the play yard, and he was bone tired. He didn't need a smashed thumb.

Brad's eyes glittered once he had Del riding shotgun in his pickup. They were going to hit tribal cattle, he said. They had a man inside, and the pickings were fat. Adrenaline had turned Brad's mouth into a fountain of information.

"They won't *all* be tribal cattle," he said, as though he wanted to head off some imagined offense. "They've got a couple of places picked out. Indian ranchers running steers for big operations out of state. Gotta figure they won't miss a few head. Part of the cost of doing business. As for the tribe's cattle, hell, they get their stock on the government's dime anyway, right? Maybe some casino profits?"

"Yeah. Always have," Del said dismissively, but what he thought was, *Typical*. What Brad had bothered to learn about the federal government's association with tribal land—what was left of it—and how the Lakota Nation survived would fit on the head of a finish nail. "How long have you lived in Indian country, Brad?"

"Most of my life. But not on the reservation, of course. I mean, we butt right up to it, but they've got their land and we've got ours." Brad spared a glance toward the passenger seat. "You're from one of the reservations up north, right? Not that it matters. This is a good deal, and you're smart enough to cut yourself in."

"Absolutely." Del stared at the road ahead. Not that *what* mattered? His willingness to steal from his cousins? His stomach churned, reminding him of the time when he had been.

"This outfit we're hooked up with, it's big. But they'll get in and get out. A couple more jobs and they'll disappear for a while. But they'll be back, and we'll be here."

"How did you get in with them?"

"Chet Klein hooked me up. You know Chet?"

"Heard the name," Del said, thinking back to his visit with Stan Chasing Elk. He had a mental file on Klein and he was ready to add to it.

"Yeah, you hear it a lot. If there's money to be had,

Klein's got his hand out. Tribal college got a big grant for that agriculture program, and there was Chet, offering his services." Brad chuckled. "Made out like a bandit."

"Yeah? How'd he do that?" *Tell me more about this bandit than I already know.*

"You might say he's a facilitator. I took a couple of classes from him—my mother's idea, you know, impress Frank—and I got to know him pretty well. I'm not a tribal member, and neither is he, so when he'd 'borrow' stuff, I was the one he got to help run it out to his place. He told me right out to forget where we put it. Said nobody would ever ask me—tribal cops don't mess with white guys—but if anybody did, I should play dumb and then let him know." He shrugged. "Nobody ever asked me. No surprise, he got fired. I don't know what he did with all the stuff he took."

"How long have you been rustling? How many raids?"

"They just started working our area. I've set up a couple now, but there's a lot more to it. I know they find an isolated place where they can meet another truck, but I've never seen how they set up a rendezvous, change the brands and all that."

"If they're good, they'll be in and out in the time it takes to pitch a round of horseshoes." Del smiled. They might come close, but no matter how good they were, he was better. "You pitch horseshoes?"

"No. Frank does, though. He's pretty good."

"You'll have to try it."

Close counted in horseshoes.

It was dark in the isolated draw several miles from the sign marking the reservation boundary. They were a little late to the party. If Brad was planning on rising in the ranks, he was off to a bad start. Rustlers kept a schedule. Timing was everything, and everybody was expected to be on time. In and out, like clockwork. Del figured Brad was hearing about it from the hauler while he stood back waiting for his cue. The hauler was the driver, which put him in charge of the move. It was the hauler who signaled for Del to step up.

"Name's Chip," the hauler said as he handed Del a cattle prod.

Del nodded. "Fox."

"You know how to use this?"

"I do."

"You stand up there," Chip told Brad as he nodded toward a patch of prickly pear. "You let any get past you, you're done."

Del moved toward the trailer, where the cattle prod would come in most handy, but he watched the dog handler out of the corner of his eye. The same dogs were working this job as the last one. If the dogs were any indication, the outfit was making money somewhere. But if the man in charge could see the way the wrangler miscued his professionally trained herding dogs, it would be the man hitting the road. Not the dogs. The younger dog was barking his head off again because the stupid man didn't know how to use hand signals.

"Let me try." Del approached the handler when he could no longer stand to watch. He gestured for the bait.

"Don't I know you?" The man—yeah, he did seem familiar, Del thought—handed him a plastic sandwich bag containing dog treats.

Brad hung back the way he always did when there was work to be done, but he caught the man's question and edged closer. At this point it didn't matter. Let the word leak out. It proved Del's honor among thieves.

"Last name's Fox, right?" the guy said, his eyes lighting up. "I remember you now. We worked a few jobs together up in Missouri Breaks country, remember?" He patted his own chest. "Joe Clumer."

"Joe Clueless?" Del grinned. The nickname still fit. It wasn't often he ran into a guy who recognized him— the attrition rate was pretty high in the rustling business—but it happened.

"Damn. Heard you got sent up for, I don't know, was it rustling?" Clumer laughed. "What, you didn't get rehabbed?"

"Hard-core, I guess." Del whistled and gave a hand signal. The pair of blue heelers split up and double-teamed the recalcitrant steer threatening to cut loose. Between the snarling dogs and the trailer ramp, the choice for the steer was abundantly clear.

"You always was real good with the dogs. How long you been working for Pacer?"

"Just started." And just added a new mental file tabbed *Pacer*. Who was Pacer? Del knew he was being sized up. Brad had permission to bring him along. The rest was up to him, and he'd already made the right impression. He was the elusive Fox.

"We got a hell of an operation. You should see how fast we work the stock when we meet up."

Del stepped closer to his former compadre. "Can you get me in the truck?"

"Pacer likes to keep locals working the roundup side, but your friend's—"

As clueless as you are.

"I'm not local. Only been working at Benson's stepfather's place a couple weeks. I'm looking for something that pays better."

"I don't make any decisions around here. Word is Benson's got the same idea as you. Let me see what I can do. If I tell them I've seen you in action…"

"Whatever it takes to get me on."

Once the selected steers were loaded into the stock trailer, Clumer tried to get a cell phone signal. He finally had to take to higher ground, but he returned victorious.

"You're golden, Fox. Is there such thing? Red fox, gray fox. Is there such a thing as a golden fox?"

Del gave half a smile. "Like you said, you're lookin' at him."

"We're making one more haul this week. Pacer wants to fill the big trailer with Flynn's steers. Fifty head." Clumer clapped a beefy hand on Del's shoulder. It made him feel crawly. "You in?"

"What do I get out of it?"

"If you want in, that's what you get. *In*."

Del nodded. "Why Double F steers?"

"Because they're ripe for picking. Benson's setting it up. It's gonna be fun. With a haul like that, we'll fix the brands right on-site." Clumer grinned. "These locals get us to the basket so we can score."

"When?"

"As soon as we take care of this load. Be ready."

Del motioned for Brad to vacate the driver's seat, and the hell with the fact that it was the little bastard's own pickup. He wanted to fill his hands with the steering wheel. Otherwise he'd be tempted to cold cock the kid before they got out on the highway. Brad complied without a word.

"What are you doing?" Del demanded. "The Double F has already been hit. Why risk a second raid? You're above suspicion."

He was also flying high on something. Del saw it in his eyes. He could only hope it was just adrenaline.

"You know that coulee in the corner of the north pasture?" Brad said. "About seven miles off the highway, so it's isolated, but there's easy access from the cut-across. They can set up right there on the cut-across. You move the steers into that coulee. It's perfect."

"You don't need to bring them into your backyard again. That's where you live, man. That's where you eat, where your family sleeps. What are you thinking?"

"Bigger haul and a bigger cut for us, man. You said it best. Thinking about getting something for myself. Nobody's gonna get hurt. They say the big man will probably be there, the one they call Pacer." Brad shifted in his seat, angling toward Del. "You're thinking about getting a little something from pretty Miss Lila, aren't you, Fox? Hey, can't blame a guy for tryin'. I'd sure tap that." He chuckled. "If I had the time."

Time? Del set his jaw, put his tongue on lockdown and stared at the road ahead. *A hundred years wouldn't even get you close.* That thought and a long, deep breath kept him steady.

"All right, Brad. We'll play in your backyard."

Though *playing* wasn't exactly what he had in mind.

Del was already working the hay field at sunrise. He would have the storm-soaked windrows turned by dinnertime. An afternoon of hot Dakota sun would go a long way toward preparing the field for the baler. Frank showed up a little while later with the same idea, but Del had beaten the old man to the punch, which Frank acknowledged with a wave of approval before heading out to finish mowing. Del wished he could be around to help bale up the hay. For the moment he was exactly the man he'd claimed to be—a good hand—and he liked it. For the moment.

He worked all morning, then skipped dinner at the Flynn house. He didn't feel like talking. The rocks he'd carted up to Lila's flower bed beckoned. The sun was merciless, which was fine. He wasn't looking for mercy. He wanted cleansing heat. Fire power. He could hear children's voices, and he knew there was shade in the play yard he'd repaired for them. He smiled when Lila's voice mixed with theirs in song as they played an age-old game. He had a circle forming around the flower bed, and he imagined the little circle she was making with the kids. He glanced over at the patch of shade behind the corner of the house where Asap lay watching his human bake himself in the summer sun. Was that pity in those puppy eyes? Or prudence?

More likely common canine sense.

It made little human sense for Del to imagine what his bookcases would look like finished and filled with books, or how the old schoolhouse windows would hardly look any different once he'd weatherized them. He could bring that sweet old building up to anybody's code, even his father's. The old man would be pleased to know how much his son had learned from him, how eager he was to put that handed-down know-how to use. *You might not care, Delano, but someday your wife will.* Del had turned his teenage nose up at the idea of a someday wife or a future home. But it turned out that some part of him had tuned in.

And for today that meant something. He was building a rock garden for the first woman he'd ever imagined as his wife. For today he was simply her father's hired hand—a good man aspiring to become a better one, dreaming of building a life with the boss's daughter. Unlikely as it sounded, it was a possibility today. Tomorrow—or maybe the next day—it would not be. How could it? He would be facilitating a theft at the Double F. A net would be cast, and people were going to get caught. As always, the net would yield some surprises.

The pup stirred from his spot in the lengthening shade.

"What are you two up to, Ace?"

"Stay there," Del called out at the sound of Lila's voice. She stood at the far corner of the house, where she could still keep an eye on the kids, fists resting on her sweet hips.

"Me or the dog?"

"Both. *Stay.*" He laughed as he mopped his face with the bandanna he'd tucked in his back pocket and started toward her. "I'll come to you. This isn't ready for your inspection."

"Inspection? Oh, how exciting" She glanced over her shoulder, checking the play yard. "You have a surprise for me, don't you? The kids and I are going in pretty soon for cookies and lemonade. Would you care to join us?" She started baby talking Asap. "You, too, Ace. You want some water?" She reached down to pet him, and the dog's tail started spinning like a pinwheel. "You want a cookie? I have a cookie for you. Oh, yes, I do."

"We're good. We both have water."

"But you don't have cookies," she chirped as she turned toward the play yard again. She'd left the gate open, and her tone shifted from birdsong to drill sergeant. "Rocky, put your tennis shoes back on."

"I have to warn you, I took out the plants that looked dead," Del said as he strode from sun to shade at the back of the house. "Which was most of them."

"I know. Between Brad's pickup and the storm…"

"The good news is you can put new stuff in. It's shaped a little different. You'll probably want different stuff." God, he wanted to greet her properly. Even a quick kiss would go a long way toward twilight, when he planned to walk with her. Simply stroll hand in hand the way lovers were supposed to. "I don't know much about flowers. I know my rocks, but flowers are a woman's special…thing."

"Will you have supper with me tonight?" She smiled, her eyes twinkling. "I think you'll like my special recipe for 'Trail Rider's Hot Dish.'"

"I can't wait."

"I can't, either. But I guess we'll—"

"Lila, Rocky won't…"

They turned quickly like two guilty kids. And there stood the third kid.

Little Denise. "Is this your boyfriend, Lila?"

"How did you guess?"

"By the way you're looking at each other." Denise gave Del an imperial once-over. "Are you supposed to be here? Because my sister has a boyfriend, and he isn't supposed to come around my sister when she's working."

"Question is, where are *you* supposed to be?" Del

softened the challenge with a wink and a smile. "Cut us a little slack, huh? We work, too."

"Del built the new fence and fixed the swings after the storm knocked them down."

"And now I'm fixing up the flower bed on the side of the house." Del flashed Lila a smile. "And my boss just told me it's almost time for cookies and lemonade."

"You're her boyfriend and she's your boss?"

"I'm nobody's boss but mine." Lila folded her arms. "And that's the way I like it."

"But Rocky won't stop—ouch!" A small green tomato bounced off the back of Denise's head. She whirled, stomped her foot and shook her finger. "Rocky Rhoades, you stop throwing stuff."

"Rocky Rhoades?" Del slid Lila a *seriously?* look, and she confirmed with a smile.

"You're not the boss of me!" Denise told Rocky vehemently.

"Whoa, Rocky," Del said, grinning.

"I'm nobody's boss but mine, and you are not my boyfriend!" Denise shouted.

"Hey," Del said. "I've got the perfect job for you, my man. You wanna help me? No girls, no bosses." He glanced up at Lila. "Call us when you've got the cookies ready." He took the little boy's hand and headed toward the corner of the house. "Is Taylor Rhoades your dad?"

"Yeah. You know my dad?"

"I do. Quite a sense of humor he's got."

"What do you mean, sense of humor?"

"He tells great stories. My dad was like that, too. Told some whoppers, my dad did."

"Is he still, like…"

"Still with me? He sure is. I don't say his name, but

I tell his stories." He tapped his hand against his thigh. "Come with the boys, Ace."

"Why don't you say his name?"

"Because…"

When Paula Rhoades arrived, Rocky grabbed her hand, made a beeline toward the driveway, took a sudden right-angle turn and skidded to a halt beside the garden he'd helped build. He was pointing out the rocks he liked best, reporting how he'd helped Del switch this one with that one because they were too heavy for one person, and where Lila was going to put the special flowers for the butterflies. Del enjoyed the whole spiel, partly for the kid's enthusiasm and partly for the smile on Lila's face as they caught up to mother and child.

"And nobody better try to run over these rocks. Anybody who does has got rocks in their head, 'cuz Del and me worked really hard." Rocky pointed to a pinkish boulder. "That's granite. When we washed everything, some of them sparkled. I get to help water the plants, and Denise doesn't."

"You get to show the others how to water," Lila reminded him.

"Yeah, and Denise doesn't get to boss me."

"Sounds like you had a good day." Paula nodded at Del. "I didn't get a chance to meet you at the dance. I'm Taylor's wife. He's talked you up, too. Wanted me to meet you, but seems like you left early."

Del nodded toward Rocky. "You've got the makings of a good landscaper here."

"He's just like his father—all boy. He sure likes Lila." She smiled at her son. For Del she had a more purposeful look. "We all do."

"She got hit hard by the storm," Del said. "Tore up the kids' play yard pretty bad, but we fixed it up."

"Well, good," Paula said. "You sure made a nice flower bed here."

"*We* did it, Mom. It's called Rocky's Rockery."

"Thanks. I just...wanted to say how nice it was to see—" she grabbed Rocky's hand "—Lila get to go to the dance."

"It was nice to see *you* there, too, Paula. It's been a while for me," Lila said. "I'm such a homebody."

"That's me, too. Once you get to a party like that, you never know what'll happen."

"Mom," Rocky piped up. "Lila has a boyfriend, and you know who it is? It's Del."

"Rocky! That's none of your... Who said that? Your dad?"

"Denise guessed, and Lila said how did she guess."

Paula looked surprised when Lila laughed. "I'd better get him home," she said.

Lila turned to Del as the last car of the day sped toward the highway, dust trail fluttering from the bumper like rust-colored sheets flapping on the line.

"I'll bet you think that was weird."

"No, I don't. I know her husband."

"You think I'm a little weird, too, huh?"

Del smiled. "No, I don't. I know your boyfriend." She laughed, and he added, "And I know small towns. People see things, they think they know things and they talk. I didn't mean to embarrass you."

"I don't get embarrassed."

"I didn't mean to hurt you. I don't ever want to cause you trouble, Lila. That's the last thing I want. The last..."

He took her shoulders in his hands and pulled her closer for a kiss thorough enough to erase the word *last* from his mind, at least for a while. He came away smiling.

That night he stuck with his plan. After a delicious supper—damn, that woman could cook—they watched the sun set and walked through tall buffalo grass along the pasture fence line during the magic hour, the time when daylight was softened by coming nightfall, meadowlarks tweedled in the grass and crickets let it be known that they would be taking over now. Del surprised Lila with a pallet of blankets and South Dakota sage, fresh cut and pungent, which made for especially sweet lovemaking. They were surrounded by a black velvet sky overrun with stars that brightened when they touched each other and danced with them when they soared together.

Spent and content, they held each other and marveled at the way they had shifted the heavens and moved the stars. They whispered back and forth, back and forth, like water softly lapping earth's still body, while the smell of sage helped the night breeze chase mosquitoes away.

"Have you ever been in love before?" she asked because she dared, because she must have known his answer would not, *could* not, detract from what they were feeling.

"Not like this."

"Not like what?"

"Not like I am now. With you." He nuzzled her hair. He hated lying, and this was one thing he wouldn't lie about. When she found out what he was up to, she would never believe him again, but right now, in this moment, he wanted her to know the deepest, brightest, most important truth he had in him. "I'm not a boy who's crazy over a girl or a piece of a man looking for a way to get through the night. I'm a whole man in love with a whole woman."

"Wow." Her face, washed in starlight, was open and innocent of color. "You take me by surprise at every turn." She smiled. "In a good way."

"Not always."

It wouldn't feel like a good way, not for long. If she loved him back, she wasn't going to enjoy the surprise he had waiting for her. It was already in place, right around the next turn. If she loved him, it was going to hit her hard.

She gave him an odd glance, then went on. "But you know what really surprises me? I can handle that. You know? Take a chance, Lila," she instructed herself. "Life isn't always any particular thing. It comes with surprises." She touched the tip of her nose to his cheek and whispered, "I've never been in love before, and I never expected to be."

"You didn't expect me. And I sure as hell didn't expect you." He pressed his lips against the top of her ear and ran the tip of his tongue inside the delicate curve. She giggled, and he felt her joy deep in his gut. It hurt. He closed his eyes, rested his forehead on her crown and whispered, "You're the right woman at the wrong time."

"How can there be a wrong time to love the right woman?"

He groaned. "It's complicated."

"Of course it is. You're complicated. Fortunately, I'm not. So lay it on me." She popped up suddenly, propping herself on her elbow. "Wait. Are you married? Because if that's your next surprise, you won't like the way I handle it."

He laughed. "You're a pistol, you know that?"

"I'm not, and I don't have one. But I can get one in a hurry."

"I'm not married, and I never have been." He rubbed her bottom lip with the pad of his finger. "Everything I've told you about myself is true. But there's one more thing. And I can't get into that with you. I just…can't."

She lay down again—flopped back a little too hard, sounded like—folded her arms and stared at the sky for a moment.

"Now what do we do?" She wasn't whispering anymore. "Play Twenty Questions?"

"Now you trust me. Or you don't." He had to take back something he'd once said to her. A long time ago, seemed like. A different life. "Actions can be deceiving. Sometimes explanations *do* matter, but I can't give you one yet."

"You haven't gone back to your former profession, have you?"

"I'm not a thief." He took her chin in his hand and turned her to face him. "Believe that, okay? No matter what."

"Do *you* have a pistol? Because if you were convicted and went to prison…"

One corner of his mouth rose. "The only thing that stops a bad man with a gun is a good man with—"

"Which one *are* you, Del?"

"Some of each, I guess. But without a gun. I never pack a gun."

"Because…"

"Because I don't wanna get killed." He sealed that big truth with a kiss and then added another equally big truth. "Even more important, I don't want you to get hurt."

"This is—"

"No more questions. Trust me." He touched her bottom lip again, this time with his thumb. "You're not sleeping with the enemy, Lila. I promise."

He took her in his arms and blessed her moment of silence.

Short-lived though it was.

"I can't sleep. Will you answer just one question?"

"If I can."

"What's your name?"

"Delano Fox. I guess it was Takes The Fox, but they changed it somewhere along the line." He chuckled. "Maybe it was Steals The Fox. Maybe I come from a long line of thieves."

"You were a thief, but you aren't anymore, and your name really is Del."

He kissed her eyes closed, one at a time. "When we make love, do you think I want you callin' out a name that ain't mine?"

Chapter 9

Del wondered if Asap thought he'd treed some kind of prey. If sawdust could be called a tree and a chirping cricket qualified as prey, then the pup was a true hunter. He turned off the table saw, brushed tree shavings from the smooth plank and examined his cut.

"These are gonna be real nice, Del." Frank had come out to see if he wanted supper and stayed to check out the first bookcase as though he was thinking about buying it. "You've got a knack for woodwork. I can handle the basics, but when you want a nice finish 'cuz you want to be able to put something inside the house, I'm not your man. I bought all those tools. Whenever I come across a deal on a tool I don't have, I put it in the cart."

"But some of them you've never used."

"I was always gonna get around to it when I got caught up. But you never get caught up in this business.

Maybe not in this life. When you're young, there's always something else you want. You get old, there's a lot more you want to do." Frank leaned his butt against the workbench, adjusted his Short Straw Co-Op cap by the bill and folded his arms over his barrel chest. "What do *you* want, Del?"

"I'm gettin' along pretty good with what I've got. All I was missing were woodworking tools, and now…" His sweeping gesture took in Frank's table saw, jigsaw, sanders and more.

"You seem to be getting along pretty good with my daughter."

Del wasn't about to touch that one.

"I'm glad." Frank drew a deep breath. "Not that it's any of my business. I mean, I don't meddle. Lila keeps to herself. I think I told you, she owns half the ranch. The land anyway."

He wasn't going to touch that one, either.

"It's hard work, and it's a roller-coaster business. But you know that."

"I know the work. The business side is the boss's worry."

"Brad for sure ain't cut out for it."

Del stacked the plank with three others just like it. He hoped he would have time to sand that last edge.

"I know you haven't been around this family too long, but long enough. A man like you, you figured us out pretty quick."

Us? He had Benson figured out pretty quick, but *us?*

No. Not possible. He *had* been around this family long enough, and it was Benson. Just Benson.

But Frank was standing there with a look in his eyes

that said he had something on his mind and he was trying to decide whether it was time to let Del in on it.

Ordinarily he would be all ears. He wouldn't look
the man in the eye, but he would nod at the right time,
maybe offer a word or two of encouragement, get him
to keep it coming. Times had been tough, money was
tight, all he had to do was look the other way while the
boy, the mother, the wife...

But this wasn't his usual assignment. When had he
ruled Frank out? Right about now Del wished he wore
a hearing aid with a mute button. He eyed the power
saw longingly, but it would be rude to turn it on now,
and there was nothing to cut anyway.

"I ain't ready to quit," Frank was saying. "Sure, I've
had a few medical problems, but I'm not that damn
feeble. All I need is a good hand to help out. Guys like
you are hard to find. Hell, that last bum Brad hired was
useless. You could just tell he wasn't gonna be around
long." Frank shifted his weight, switched the way he'd
had his ankles crossed. "Are you?"

"Am I what?"

Frank cleared his throat and then allowed a precious
moment of silence to pass. "My wife wants me to turn
the place over to Brad."

"And you're not ready."

"I'll never be ready. He'd run it into the ground so
fast..." He shook his head and blew a deep sigh. "I don't
want to go live in Florida, but I could take her on that
boat ride or whatever kind of trip she's so anxious to
take if I had somebody here I knew I could depend on."
Another firm adjustment of the cap. "No, sir, Brad's not
gettin' this place."

Was it time to breathe a sigh of relief?

"If you're asking me what his plans might be, I can't—"

"I don't care what his plans are. I don't think he has any. I guess I'm asking you what *your* plans are."

Oh, jeez. Frank would know soon enough. Ordinarily Del would slip out the door, content with the knowledge that the bad people would get their day in court and their years behind bars, while the good people would... Okay, sure, they might be in for some rough days, depending on the circumstances, but they were good people, sturdy stock. They would put their lives back together and move on.

And so would he.

"I like my job here."

"And my daughter? You like *her*, too, don't you?"

He swallowed hard, nodded once. "I do."

"See, that's what I like about you, Del. There's no beating around the bush with you." This time the precious pause was pregnant. "So are you two, uh...?"

Speaking of boat trips, Del's hard glance was a shot across the bow. *Now's the time to chug off, Frank.*

"I just mean, with all the work you've been doing for her—and I appreciate it, because I offer, and she says she can handle it herself, but you're putting in extra time—hell, all that extra work, you must be—"

"I don't mind."

"So you're doing it for Lila."

"I went out and checked the alfalfa." It was the answer to the kind of question the boss actually had a right to ask. "The field's dried out pretty good."

"Like I said, you're a good hand. I'd like to keep you around. I think Lila would like that, too."

Del chuckled. "And you'd also like to keep *her* around."

"If it's what she wants, I'd like it very much if she stayed." Frank slowly shook his head. "I don't know what she wants. She keeps to herself. She had that accident— I mean, I know it was bad, but she never talks to us about it. Scared her so bad she stopped driving. I know that. I know it wasn't her fault. No charges or anything. But I *don't* know…" He looked at Del. It was the look of a man who cared enough to swallow his pride. "She tell *you* about it?"

"Some."

"She stayed up there in Minnesota for months after it happened. We thought she'd finished college. Found out later she didn't. I was pretty damn pissed about that, but she never explained herself. Not to me anyway. Maybe to the Chasing Elks." He lifted one shoulder. "Yeah, probably."

"She didn't have to explain herself to them. Or to me."

"Tell you what, when I was growing up, I sure as hell had to explain *my*self. If I'da had the chance to go to college, and if I'da got so far and then walked away…"

Frank slapped his palm on the workbench. Del wasn't sure what that meant, but he *was* sure he wasn't going to ask.

"Did you go to college?" Frank asked finally.

"Hard Knocks U," Del said.

"Now, there's a degree that can open doors or close 'em."

"It does both. Gives you some options."

"That's why Lila went away, I guess. Looking for

options. This place is all I have, and she owns half of it. It's not a bad option."

Del nodded, but he had nothing of his own to add to the conversation, and he wasn't about to contribute anything that belonged to Lila.

"I shouldn't be butting into her business," Frank said.

Del raised his brow and agreed with a nod.

Frank chuckled. "When I was younger I had all kinds of plans for this place, for Lila, maybe even for Brad, if he'd been interested in learning something. I'm running the School of Hard Work here."

Del smiled. "You've got a fine campus."

"Yeah." Frank beamed. "Yeah, I do. What is it they say about life happening while you're making other plans? It's true." He pushed away from the workbench. "I want my daughter to be happy. Whatever it takes, I'm all for it."

"Have you told her that?"

"She knows."

"I bet she'd like to hear you say it." Del shook his head and chuckled. "Now we're both acting like we know what Lila wants."

"Even when a woman tells you she wants something, she's only giving you one little corner of the picture. There's always more to it, but she expects you to get the big picture off that one corner."

"A cruise ship is big, Frank." Del grinned. Frank scowled. "Complete package," Del explained. "Total picture, nothing left out. And come on. June hasn't been too subtle about drawing it up for you."

"You been on a cruise?"

"Nope."

"Well, I want June to be happy, too, but I can't leave

this place in Brad's hands, not even for a week. And that's what she wants. She thinks Brad could take over the Double F." Frank folded his arms again. "What do you think?"

"That kind of thinking is above my pay grade, Frank."

"You've been to Bucky's with him a few times, haven't you? Hanging out with the local boys?" Frank cocked his head, trying to look into Del's eyes and draw a bead on the truth. "Anybody else ever come around? Anybody who's not from around here?"

"Besides me?"

"Yeah, besides you. Somebody who smells like stolen cattle."

"Sure seems like this area's been mapped out by prairie pirates." Del started hanging tools up on wall pegs. "Rustling's become a big problem everywhere. Nobody's safe."

"You talking about places you've worked?"

"Everywhere. But yeah, they caught some rustlers where I was working out in Colorado not long ago. They'd come up from Texas, but they had a young guy working with them who was local. Stealing from his neighbors."

"You make an insurance claim, they pay up eventually, but then they drop you. I hate dealing with insurance companies. It's a racket. But then, so's rustling." Frank cleared his throat. Seemed as if he had to be making some kind of noise when he was taking aim. "You never answered my question, Del. You don't seem like the kind of a man who'd cover for somebody."

"Cover for somebody?" Del flashed Frank an incredulous look. "That's not where I thought your questions were leading."

"Brad's always been one to test the limits, you know? He's gotten himself into a few tight spots. Took a car and drove it into a river when he was in high school."

"*Your* car?"

"Would've been a hell of a lot easier if it was. I had to pay for the car and call in some favors to keep him out of court. That wasn't the only time. He's the kind of kid who really needs to pay the price for a lesson, and I—" he rolled his eyes "—can't say no to his mother."

"You think Brad's rustling cattle?"

"I don't know. I hope not. Like I said, he doesn't have the makings of a rancher. He's all hat and no horse. He did a little baling this afternoon, spent most of his time and mine pulling out twine he'd screwed up when he tried to splice it. Can't even make a square knot, that kid. He's a jack of *no* trades, as far as I can tell. He'd no more build something like this in his spare time than peel a grape." Frank laid a beefy hand on one of the bookcases. "Has Lila seen this?"

"I wanted to have one finished before I showed her. This one's ready to be painted. Shelves are adjustable, see?" He lifted the top shelf to show off the support pegs. He'd become a pretty good carpenter at Hard Knocks U. "The other two are ready to be put together. Just look at this one to see how the pieces all fit."

A long moment passed.

"Are you leaving?"

"That wouldn't be my choice, Frank, but in my line of work, you never know."

"What *is* your line of work, Del?" Frank asked quietly.

"Jack of many trades, like most cowboys." Del ran his hand over the smooth shelf. "Brad hired me. I appreciate that." He looked Frank in the eye. "What's between Lila and me is personal, but right here you can see…" He stepped back and gave an openhanded gesture. "I'm all for books and libraries, but this isn't my contribution to any cause. I care for Lila. Whatever happens, I want you to know that. I want *her* to know that."

Whatever was about to happen. Wheels were turning, trucks were rolling and people were on their way. The Double F was about to be hit, and with any luck Del would meet the man behind the plan. He'd driven up on the hill he was beginning to think of as his personal phone booth, conferred and confirmed. Now he would wait for Brad to pick him up.

As he approached the bunkhouse, he stiffened. He couldn't have left the light on in his room. It had been midafternoon when he'd stopped in for his phone and his ID, both hidden in the old dresser with the swollen drawers, one of which he'd made impossible for anybody but him to open, and he hadn't been back since. There were times when he regretted not having a gun. A nice little .22 pistol would come in handy right about now.

Or not. The conceal part of conceal and carry could be damn tricky for a cowboy. A .22 was made for strapping into a holster.

So he took a peek in the window and scoffed at himself when his heartbeat tripped into overdrive. Oh, he had it bad for the woman sitting on the floor beside his bed. He could only see part of her face, but he would know those pretty feet and that sassy roostertail hairdo anywhere. He signaled Asap to stay back while he snuck around the corner and barged through the door. He barely got a squeak out of her, but Asap started yapping his head off and rushed to somebody's defense. Probably hadn't decided whose.

Lila shook her head and gave him that sweet look that made a man feel like a kid again—the look that had once made him try whatever trick he had in his repertoire just so he could coax it from a pretty girl. The look that said, *You're the one.*

She was sitting in the middle of the makings of her own major project.

"What's all this?"

"I ordered it from that Swedish furniture company. It's supposed to be good quality, and you put it together yourself, so you save money." She waved a piece of paper at him. Instructions, unless he missed his guess. He would have left those in the box. "It's a new dresser. I know the drawers on the old one are a real pain. The top one, especially."

"Did you get it open?" He was taking a mental inventory. The case file, photos. She couldn't have opened it, but she might have noticed that it wasn't just hard to open, it was impossible—impossible unless you knew where the shim was anyway.

"Why would I want to open your drawers?"

He smiled.

"The directions are just pictures. The first part went together pretty easily, but these drawers…"

He watched her take two pieces of blond wood in hand and put tongue to groove. It was going to be a tight fit. She held her breath and pressed, let go with a sigh and groaned, leaned back against the side of the bed and scowled at the resisting parts. Then she took them in hand again, clearly determined to make them fit together. She took a firm grip and growled at the stubborn joint while she pushed until her hands shook. On the next attempt she tried a high-pitched squeal.

"Does it help?"

She looked up from her struggle. "What?"

He was pretty sure his imitation of her growls and squeals was spot on, but she wasn't laughing. He found an empty patch of floor and squatted on his heels amid parts piled together by shape and size. She'd sorted bolts and screws by size and type in a muffin tin. As he scanned the inventory, he heard the two pieces snap together. He looked up and enjoyed her self-satisfied smile.

"The squeaky wheel gets the job done," she said.

He smiled back. "The squeaky wheel gets the grease is the way I heard it."

"And then gets the job done. It takes elbow grease. The grease primes the elbows, and then you…" She stuck her elbows out, butted her fists together and pushed, reprising her grunts and groans. At the edge of the sprawl sat Asap, whining as he cocked his head side to side. "Yes, boys, every woman is born with the knowledge that a little noise helps move things along."

"Don't be giving away too many female secrets so early in the game," Del warned as he seated himself on the floor and picked up the directions. Asap flopped in place.

"The proof is in the pudding."

"We don't have any pudding yet." He perused the drawing on the paper and glanced at the frame. "Looks to me like we've got upside-down cake. One side's upside down."

"No, the directions show…" She scooted up behind him, rested her chin on his shoulder and reached around him to point to the paper. "See, this little guy is holding side A? And his wife is facing him with side B, so if you imagine them side by side—"

"How do you know that's his wife?"

"The wife gets the wavy hair. The dresser is for their kid's bedroom, obviously, because it's not big enough for the parents, even though they wear the same clothes, same size and everything." She patted his denim-clad thigh. "Just like us. Anyway, I pretended I was her, and then I pretended I was him, and I figured out the way they're holding the boards, so you have to turn—"

"Honey, we're looking at it head-on." He held the paper up for comparison. She moved her hand to his belly. He smiled to himself. "Does that look like it's sitting level to you? Did you have to force it?"

"A little. I've never made anything from a kit before."

"I'm bettin' it's the left side that's upside down." He turned his head toward her and smiled. "If it doesn't fit, it ain't time to quit."

She slid her hand over his belt buckle and rested it on his fly. "Would you help me make it fit?"

He reached around back of her head, released the big clip, freed her hair and plunged his fingers into it as he drew her mouth to his. She rubbed him, squeezed him gently, made his jeans feel tight and his head feel light. He canted his head for a second approach, a slip of the tongue, and she took the opportunity to slide into his lap, barely disturbing their kiss as she straddled him.

"I'll help you," he whispered. "I'll take you and make you over. Hold you upside down, turn you inside out." He kissed her neck, took her bottom in his hands and pulled her in, dragging her along the aching ridge in his lap. "Make me fit. I want to live inside you, Lila. I want to build my home in you." She answered with tremulous breaths and undulating hips. "I'm in love with you," he said, desperate to be loved back.

"Oh, my God, Del. I don't dare."

"Dare. You're a brave woman. You said it once." He leaned back far enough to read her eyes, to show her the depth of his need. "Tell me again. Now. Tonight."

"I've loved you since…" She glanced at the ceiling and back again. "Since you brought Asap."

"But you didn't know it then."

"I felt it. Something I've never felt before, and it just keeps—" she rocked her hips, kissed him hard, rested her forehead against his "—growing."

He gripped her hips and rose to meet her, to kiss her and hold her against him and make her feel more.

And then came the unwelcome knock on the door.

"Hey in there, you decent?"

"Damn." He kissed her again, quickly, just one more kiss.

"Hey, Fox, it's time."

"I'll be out in a minute."

She'd slipped off his lap, and now she slid her hand down his arm and grabbed his hand. "Stay," she whispered.

"I can't."

"Why not? What's Brad talking about? Time for what?"

"Just… I said I'd go along."

"Along with what?" Suddenly wide-eyed with alarm she should have no reason to feel, she shook her head. "Don't go, Del. Stay with me."

"I can't. He hired me, Lila. If I'm gonna come back to you, I have to go now."

"You *don't* have to go with him. You've put in your day's work. This is our time, yours and mine." When he failed to speak, the look in her eyes cooled. "Choose."

"Take care of Asap, okay?" He touched his lips to her forehead and said softly, "I choose you, I swear. But I have to go."

"Hey, what's…?" The door opened, and there stood Brad, grinning as though he'd found his sister's diary. "Well, hey, Lila."

Del got to his feet and offered her a hand, which she ignored.

"You guys can finish your project later, huh?" Brad cocked a forefinger at Del. "We've got a party to go to."

"Do you have room for one more?"

Lila drew surprised looks from both men.

"Not this time," Brad said. "It's kind of a bachelor party, and we don't want to be late."

"Are you going to Bucky's?" she asked.

Del put his arm around her shoulders and drew her to him. She neither obliged nor resisted. "I want to take you somewhere nice, just the two of us," he whispered. She looked up at him as though she'd given up on making sense of him. "You make a plan, okay?" He leaned close to her ear. "Remember what I said."

Chapter 10

"She was dyin' to come with us, you could just tell," Brad said as they sped down the highway.

What was the guy's problem? Del wondered. Didn't he know silence was golden leading up to go time? If he had to be all hyped and chatty, he should have been talking about the job. But he was as dense as granite.

"She's like the icicle hanging on to the house. Look but don't touch. What'd you do to warm her up, man?"

None of your damn business.

"You got a call about tonight?"

"A text," Brad said. "Two, in fact. They're on their way, and they want us out there."

Now you're on the right track, kid.

"I took a run out there after I got the first text saying we should be ready," Brad said. "The steers you moved the other day are still in the coulee, right where we want them. Haven't budged, like they're waiting for their ride to show up. So I texted back." He chuckled. "Then I made a mess of the baler. Kept Frank busy all afternoon. You cut the fence on the west side?"

"Hell no. Turn to page one, Brad. You're making it too complicated. This is gonna be the biggest job you've seen yet, and it has to move fast."

"Yeah, but when it's all over, we'll still be here. It looks better if there's a fence down, doesn't it?"

"Just use the gate. It's down. We just fixed it but now it's down again. Damn beeves must've busted through again. Then the cops want to know, how long has it been like that? When was the last time you checked that pasture, Mr. Benson?"

Brad finally got the message. "We don't know when it happened. My hired hand regularly takes care of that, and I thought he was still on top of it, but I guess we got our signals crossed. Dad's had him putting up hay the last week or so, so it could've happened any time during the last week."

"Leave Frank out of it," Del said. "He's got nothing to do with it."

"He's about to lose fifty head. He'll have plenty to say about it. So will Lila. That's her land."

"I'll fix what's broken if you don't fire me for not doing my job."

"Fire you? Why would I do that? You're a valuable man, Mr. Fox. Living up to your name. I'm keeping you around." Brad laughed. "When this is over you can go steppin' out someplace nice with my stepsister. Just the two of you." He was so pleased with himself, he couldn't quit. "Doing your own little two-step."

* * *

Lila sat on the side of Del's bed, her heart pounding. The night was hot, and the air was heavy with bad energy. There was no point in cleaning up the mess she'd made in the bunkhouse. He wasn't coming back tonight. Maybe ever. Brad was up to something, which was nothing new. Either Del was in on it, or he was about to find himself neck deep in trouble. He'd wanted to hear her say the words, say them now, *tonight*, but he couldn't stay with her, had to go with Brad, had to go now, *tonight*. Stolen cattle, ex-con, former cattle rustler. *Ex. Former*. The pieces fit together too easily in her mind, but her heart kept pulling them apart.

He was walking into something, or he was already in on it. She had to know which it was.

The keys were in his pickup. She *had* to know, and this was the only way to find out. She opened the door with a trembling hand, and the dog jumped in ahead of her.

"Oh, no, Ace, you can't go. I'll probably start at the bar. You don't want to go there. Come on." She gave a noisy air kiss. She wasn't sure she what was going to happen after she turned the key, and she couldn't risk anybody's neck but her own. "Come. I'll put you…" The yard light put a gleam in the dog's black eyes as he cocked his head as if to say, *What are you waiting for, woman?*

"You should be buckled in," she muttered as she climbed behind the wheel. "I don't know what I'm doing. I don't drive anymore. I don't even remember how to…

"Of *course* I do. Stop being a ninny, woman. Just—" All it took was a turn of the key and a shift of the gears. Just like riding a bike. "Do it."

No traffic, no headlights except for hers. Del's. His pickup, his dog, his trouble. She was crazy for trying to follow. She wasn't sure where they were going, but she had a feeling it wasn't Bucky's Place. The population might be sparse, but the miles were many, the prairie nearly endless. Still, there was only one road to Short Straw. She might be on a fool's errand, but at least she wasn't sitting at home. There was a chance she would catch up, she told herself.

Keep your eyes open.

And suddenly, there it was—a state patrol car parked at the turn to the cut-across. It was as good a sign as any. She couldn't imagine who'd called or how they'd gotten there so fast, but this was the scene of the earlier crime. Did that make it ripe for another picking? Lila calculated nothing but the amount of room she would need to make her turn. "Hang on, Ace. We're going in."

She blew past the Statie and hit the dirt road with a furor. The siren she expected didn't materialize. Maybe they realized she was on her own land. She'd spent half her youth driving these rutted back roads and the other half bouncing along in the passenger seat.

"You might want to get down on the floor, Ace." She glanced in the side mirror. She was okay so far, as long as she didn't fishtail. She'd grown up driving these roads. She could do this.

Paws on the dash, nose to the windshield, Asap whined.

"Down!" The dog flopped flat on the seat. "Amazing. In no time at all he has a stray dog and a crazy woman eating out of his hand, doing tricks, chasing after him like two…"

She could see lights several miles down the road, especially bright since she'd turned hers off. Especially crazy since she was barreling through the dark. The sight was like a September scene, when big trucks and tractors might run all night to bring in the fall crop or ship cows, or haul hay.

Wrong season, though, she thought. Wrong rigs. Loose cattle, men darting around, pushing, shouting. The gate was down, so she plowed through, then slowed down so no one would hear her coming. She parked safely outside the ring of light but close enough to see what was going on. There was a big one-ton pickup parked beside a huge stock trailer. She could hear cattle bawling, the sound echoing within the metal confines, smell the familiar acrid odor of burning hide and hair.

Branding? In all this mess, had somebody been branding cattle?

She counted at least five cars, with another one closing in behind her. It was a crazy scene. Only a lunatic would get out of the pickup and become part of it. But she rolled down the driver's window partway, told Asap to stay put and marched into the thick of it, heading straight for a man getting himself handcuffed. She would know that silhouette anywhere.

"Jesus, Lila, what are you doing here?"

"That's a good question," said the cop with the cuffs.

"I had to see for myself."

"Who are you?" the cop demanded.

"She's the land owner," Del said without looking away from her. With his arms behind his back, his hat gone, his hair hanging practically to his eyes, he looked almost boyish. "Her father owns the steers. They have nothing to with this."

"The owners have everything to do with it, especially when they know when and where it's going down."

"She didn't." He tried to step closer to her, but the cop jerked him back. "What are you doing here, Lila?"

"What are *you* doing here? *Why*, Del? I thought this was all behind you."

"Remember what I said."

"What you *said*? What I *see* is my father's cattle, somebody else's trailer, a bunch of police cars on *my* land and you wearing handcuffs. That sort of negates everything you've *said*."

He glanced past her. "You drove my pickup." He allowed her a half smile. "Lila, you drove. Good for you."

"Good for... Are you serious?"

One of the stock dogs started snarling at one of the men—good man or bad, Lila couldn't tell at this point. Asap poked his head and paws through pickup window and launched a blistering protest.

"You brought Asap?"

"He insisted."

More snarling near the trailer.

"Hey!" Del shouted to anyone who would listen as he was jerked away from her and pushed in the opposite direction. "Don't anybody hurt the dogs!"

Lila glanced a few feet away and watched Brad slide into the backseat of a squad car. She hoped she would have time to tell her father so he could prepare his wife for the news. Brad had been in trouble before, so it probably wouldn't be a great shock. Or maybe it would. She had no idea what it was like to be a mother. Probably never would.

She was mesmerized by the activity. Men being frisked and cuffed—things she'd seen only on TV. Real cops and robbers probably didn't even use those words. One of the men being frisked and cuffed was her step-brother. And dammit, one was her lover. Both were would-be thieves, and that reminded her of a song. A hymn, she thought. *And I mean to be one, too.* Saint or sinner, whatever—whoever—Del Fox was, she knew him by the love he'd shown her, and she wanted to be with him.

I'm not a thief. Believe that, no matter what.

She was dreaming. She was high on something. She'd lost her mind. How could she stand here and watch and feel completely numb? "I know that man," she muttered to herself as she watched one man lead another to a car with caged backseat. "I think that's Chet Klein."

Del whistled. She would know that sound anywhere. The shepherd was no longer snarling. Another cop opened the door to another car, and Del—with two hands tied behind his back—was allowed to direct the herder into the backseat. Proof of one of many gifts that could not be faked. Oh, he was a remarkable man.

Remarkably deceitful.

"Somebody said you're the owner."

Lila turned toward the voice. No uniform, but the tone of a cop. "I own the land. My father owns the stock."

"How about Brad Benson? He says this is his place."

"It isn't. He lives here because his mother is married to my father."

"What brought you out here tonight?"

"I knew my brother and, um, the hired hand had to be up to something."

"That would be Delano Fox?"

"Yes." She stole a glance at the cars that were being

loaded up with thieves. Then she turned back to the cop. "Are you going to arrest me, too? Because if you are—"

"I would have told you."

"I have rights."

"Yes, you do. You have the right to go back home. And my partner and I have the right to go with you. We need to talk to your father."

"I was hoping I could tell him myself so he could break the news to June. Brad's mother."

"Benson is no juvenile."

"Not legally." And then, well, she couldn't help herself. "What's going to happen to Del?"

"He'll be charged with grand theft. That stock trailer is customized for rustling. There's a set of chutes that let them work the cattle right in there, alter the brands. They'd already started. Open and shut." He paused, tried to get a closer look at her. "You okay?"

"No. But I'll manage."

"I'm going to need you to ride with me. Would you like for my partner to drive your pickup?"

"It's Del's. I stole it. The keys are in it, and so is the dog. The dog goes with me."

It had been four days. Four long days filled with sadness for Lila, and for her father… Well, she hadn't been to the new house since that first night, but she could tell those days had been hell for him, too. They didn't talk about it at all. They weren't the kind to talk feelings and failures, sunken hopes and slim chances. They didn't think too much. They didn't run. They stayed put and worked. They met in Lila's kitchen and made a plan at the end of each day for what needed to be done the next. Dad wasn't going to let her sacrifice her business, and she wasn't going to let him give up his ranch. They could adjust.

It was the one good thing that had come of the incident. She had her father back. She had begun to realize that she might have seen more of him all along if she'd chosen to, instead of keeping to her own house, her own life, but she couldn't add another regret to the pile. She needed to focus on this one good thing while the days of sadness crept past. Healing took time.

Del had disappeared from her life as unexpectedly as he'd arrived, and sooner or later she would think back on the time in between. She would remember the beautiful things he'd said, sweet things he'd done, pleasure they'd shared, and the hurt would grow hazy. But she had to work through the sadness. She'd done it before, and she could do it again.

Work was a godsend. There was fence to be fixed. Between the cops and the robbers, more than a few fence posts had been upended. Returning to the scene of the crime wasn't as hard as she'd thought it would be. The sun made all the difference. That and the meadowlarks tweedling in the grass and the sweet pup that followed her everywhere.

It had been a long time since she had helped stretch wire. "How's that, Dad?" she asked on day four. "Tight enough?"

"For now," he said. Beneath the bill of his cap, his face looked tired. "Good enough for now."

"How's June?" she asked quietly as she watched her father's gloved hands release the tension on the ratcheted wire stretcher.

"I don't know. Haven't seen much of her. She stays

in the bedroom. Kinda blames me, I guess. Says I never treated Brad like a son."

"So he decided to become a cattle rustler?"

"I don't know if whether what I'm doing is right or wrong, but I know I'm not putting up bail. Like they say, been there, done that, got nothin' to show for it. His mother has resources she can tap into if she wants to." He tested the splice, playing the wire like a guitar string. "I'm guessin' it won't come cheap."

"I know it wasn't easy for you to come to that decision."

"It's time." One hand on his knee, he pushed himself up from the ground. "I ask myself, would I do anything different if he was my flesh and blood? Truth is, I would've put my foot down a long time ago. So I have to take some of the blame."

"Not now, you don't." Lila retrieved his canvas saddlebag from the fence post. "At his age, the responsibility is all his."

"What about Del?" Frank asked as he bent to gather his tools.

"I have nothing say about Del Fox. Nothing." And because he wasn't looking, she pressed her hand to her chest. "It hurts. I need to empty this out and fill it up fresh."

"I know how you feel." He loaded the wire stretcher into one canvas pouch and the big fencing pliers in the other, took the bag from her hands and draped it over his shoulder.

She suddenly remembered that she, too, had been carried on those shoulders.

"I don't know what's going on there," he said. "But that Del's the real deal. And by that I mean a good man."

"I thought so, too."

"Not perfect, mind you."

"Far from it."

"I'm not putting up bail for him, either. I'm no fool. And I'm telling you, that man's no thief." He waved a hand. "I know he said he'd done a little stealing, but—"

"He said he used to be a thief, but he wasn't now. And then he took off with Brad."

"Have you been in the shop lately?" She shook her head. He laid his arm over her shoulders and started waking her toward the pair of saddled horses grazing nearby. "Come down there with me, girl. I want to show you something he's been working on for you."

Lila wasn't the only one who was surprised by the pounding that sounded as though it was coming from the shop.

"Sounds like we've got company," Frank said as he closed the corral gate. They headed for the back door of the shop.

Del looked up from pounding support pegs into the frame of his second bookcase.

Del?

"What's going on?" Frank demanded, but he quickly tempered his tone. "They sprung ya, didn't they?"

Del smiled, but he only had eyes for Lila. "Given the chance, I like to finish what I start."

"You posted bail?" Frank asked.

"You escaped," Lila said. She could almost believe it.

Del flashed her a bright-eyed smile. "I told them they either had to give me a different job or let me go."

"Who's *them*?" Lila demanded at the same time Frank was asking, "What job?"

"I'm not a cop or a special agent, don't have a badge or a rank, but I work with people who do." He finished setting the peg and then laid the mallet aside, turning to Lila and Frank both. "I'm an ace in the law-enforcement hole. I help catch rustlers, and I'm good at it because I've been one. But that was a long time ago. I'm not a thief." He looked at Lila. "I told you that."

"My eyes deceived me, then."

"Hell, I knew there was more to it," Frank said quietly as he backed away and headed for the door. "Ha-*ha*! I knew it!"

Lila and Del stared at each other until they heard the door close. She silently cursed the tear that escaped the corner of her eye and slid down her cheek. She wanted to throw her arms around him. She wanted to punch him in the gut.

She was shaking inside, and she hoped it didn't show. "You told me a lot of things."

"More than I should have, but I knew I could trust you." He took a step closer. "Lying is part of the job, but given who I am and what I've been, I don't have to lie too much. I really am a hired hand, and a damn good one. But that's not all." Another step. "There were things I couldn't tell you, but everything I've told you is true."

"All this, all the lovely…" Her sweeping gesture took in the bookcases, both complete and still in pieces, the dog sniffing at a pile of sawdust. "You'd have to gain people's trust, right? Your suspects, your employers, whatever we were. Was I part of the plan in this whole undercover thing? You said I wasn't sleeping with the enemy, but I don't know who—"

He grabbed her by her shoulders and kissed her, fast and full.

And then he looked into her eyes. "You know me, Lila. I'm still the man who loves you. Your father's steers are still out there eating Double F grass. Most of them still wear the Double F brand, and I'll help him fix the ones that don't. If he wants me to. If *you* want me to."

"How did you become an undercover..." She frowned. "Who do you work for anyway?"

"Have I told you it's complicated?"

"That might have been one of many words you used to get me to back off the questions."

"Well, now you can ask all twenty."

"Who do you work for anyway?"

"You know how bad livestock rustling is nowadays. It's high-tech. You saw that tricked-out stock trailer. You slide a panel inside that makes it easy to run the cattle through one at a time, slap the iron over the brand, change the markings in the blink of an eye right there on-site. Then you can truck the animals directly to a sale barn, collect one hundred percent of the value of your stolen goods.

"Down in Texas and Oklahoma they've got special rangers who handle nothing but cattle theft. Up here we've got the FBI handling cases on federal land, but they cooperate with state and local law enforcement. So they came up with a special task force. When they hire somebody like me, they can sidestep inconvenient technicalities like a felony conviction. The task force has that authority."

"So you were recruited for your particular work experience right out of prison?"

He leaned against the workbench and beckoned her with a gesture. She had to comply, right? Otherwise she wouldn't get the rest of the story.

He took her hands in his.

"I was in prison. My dad went to a relative, asked if there was anything he could do to help me out. In Indian country relatives do that, you know? But this wasn't Indian country, and this relative wasn't Indian.

"I never heard much of anything about my mother's people. I never asked. I think she took me to see them once or twice, but my memories are pretty vague when it comes to my mother. Pretty sure her family blamed my father for her death. Anyway, her father—my grandfather—he was a lawyer, a mayor somewhere, a state legislator at one time. He had connections. But he told my dad there was nothing he could do. You do the crime, you do the time. It wasn't long after that when Dad died. And then, finally, my grandfather came to see me. Said he'd had a visit with the warden, and he was real pleased to hear what a good boy I'd been since I'd gone inside. My clean jacket would help him swing the deal of a lifetime."

"Jacket?"

"Prison file. Anyway, that's what he did. He swung a deal. I was officially transferred to another prison. Nobody knew where, so my rep was secure. I was unofficially, very quietly, put on probation. I agreed to do training and five years' service. I paid restitution, and after five years my record was expunged. And that never happens with a felony conviction."

"You said you've been out almost seven years."

"It's not a bad job." He squeezed her hands. "Until you have to steal from your girl's father and arrange for her brother's arrest."

"*Step*brother. He's been in so much trouble, and my father keeps bailing him out. But not this time. I really hope he learns his lesson this time."

"It's a hard way to learn."

"But you did. And you made up for your mistakes. By expunged, you mean erased?"

"It means it's not public. It's sealed, but it'll always be there." He drew a deep breath. "I don't pack a gun, but I do carry baggage. I didn't want to bring it into your house. I didn't mean to touch you with it. But I have, and I'm sorry."

"It was awful seeing you in handcuffs." Another tear slipped past her eyelid, and she could do nothing about it. Her hands were tied.

"You thought I got caught stealing cattle. I belonged in handcuffs."

"It was unreal, like a bad dream. I've watched you work with your hands, handle a horse, play with Asap. I've felt them—" she lifted his hand and tucked it against her chest "—touch me all over. It was the handcuffs that tore me up inside. Seeing you like that."

"I don't know how many times I've been arrested, and even though I know it's just part of the job now, I still haven't gotten used to it. You weren't mad at me?"

"That came later. I remembered some basic math facts. Put two and two together and realized feelings don't change the facts. And now I know that you came here to do a tricky job, and you used me."

"How?"

"To get information? I don't know. I'm the boss's daughter."

"Who was barely speaking to the rest of the family." He sighed and rolled his eyes. "Okay, you're right. I have to get in good with people so I can figure out what's going on and who might be involved. That's the way I operate. So maybe at first… Aw, hell, Lila, I liked you right off, and it wasn't all about your pretty face or your high-headed sass. You got into my head that first day, and after that I had to keep reminding myself why I was here."

"Why are you here now?"

"I want to finish these bookcases. Come here." He drew her by the hand over to the nearly finished bookcase he'd been working on earlier. "You can adjust the shelves for different size books. I can paint them any color you want or do a wood finish, bolt them to the wall so they can't topple over. I cut the pieces for two more, and they'll all fit together in that space you said…" He trailed off and took her shoulders in his hands. "You wanted me to stay. Now I can. Do you still want me to?"

"My father needs help, and he'd like nothing better than for you to stay on. But you're not really a ranch hand, so I can't see you—"

"Then you're not looking. I've fulfilled my commitment, but I need a reason to refuse the next assignment. And I never know when another one will come along. Maybe it's time I changed jobs." He raised his eyebrows. "What do you think? Maybe I could be an actor. Or a dog trainer. Or maybe just a damn good ranch hand."

He slid his arms around her shoulders and smiled. "Funny. Frank says *you* would like it if I stayed around. You say *he* wants me to stay on. After everything that's gone down, I need to know who wants what from me. What do *you* want, Lila?"

She slipped her arms around his waist. "I want colors. I've already picked them out from a brochure."

"From the Swedish furniture company?"

She laughed. "I still haven't figured out that dresser."

"We could do it together."

"We could do many things together."

"I need an answer, Lila. I have other questions for you, but first things first." He kissed her damp cheek. "I know you love me. Will you dare to trust me?"

"I want you to stay. Next question."

"I'm going to help your father and fix what needs fixing, build what needs building and marry the woman I love whenever she decides she'll have me." He glanced at Asap. "And my dog. He's part of the package."

"So what's the question?"

"No more questions," he whispered, and their kiss became the answer.

* * * * *

Cathy Gillen Thacker is married and a mother of three. She and her husband reside in North Carolina. Her mysteries, romantic comedies and heartwarming family stories have made numerous appearances on bestseller lists. A popular Harlequin author for many years, she loves telling passionate stories with happy endings and thinks nothing beats a good romance and a hot cup of tea! You can visit Cathy's website, cathygillenthacker.com, for information on her books, recipes and a list of her favorite things.

Books by Cathy Gillen Thacker

Harlequin Special Edition

Texas Legends: The McCabes

The Texas Cowboy's Quadruplets
His Baby Bargain
Their Inherited Triplets

Harlequin Western Romance

Texas Legends: The McCabes

The Texas Cowboy's Triplets
The Texas Cowboy's Baby Rescue

Texas Legacies: The Lockharts

A Texas Soldier's Family
A Texas Cowboy's Christmas
The Texas Valentine Twins
Wanted: Texas Daddy
A Texas Soldier's Christmas

Visit the Author Profile page
at Harlequin.com for more titles.

THE LONG, HOT TEXAS SUMMER

Cathy Gillen Thacker

Chapter 1

There were times for doingt things yourself and times for not. This, Justin McCabe thought grimly, survey-ing the damage he had just inflicted on a brand-new utility cabinet and the drywall behind it, was definitely one of the latter.

Frustrated, because there was little he *couldn't* do well, Justin shook his head in disgust. Then he swore heatedly at the blunder that further derailed his tight schedule and made it even harder to prove the skeptics wrong.

It was possible, of course, that this could be fixed without buying a whole new cabinet. *If* he knew what he was doing. Which he clearly did not—a fact that the five beloved ranch mutts, sitting quietly and cautiously watching his every move, seemed to realize, too.

A motor sounded in the lane, and he hoped it was the carpenter who'd been scheduled to arrive that morning and had yet to actually make an appearance. Justin set his hammer down. He stalked to the door of Bunk-house One just as a fancy red Silverado pickup truck stopped in front of the lodge. It had an elaborate sil-ver Airstream trailer attached to the back and a lone woman at the wheel.

"Great." Justin sighed as all the dogs darted out the open door of the partially finished bunkhouse and raced, barking their heads off, toward the vehicle.

The obviously lost tourist eased the window down and stuck her head out into the sweltering Texas heat. A straw hat with a sassy rolled brim was perched on her head. Sunglasses shaded her eyes. But there was no disguising her beautiful face and shapely bare arms. The young interloper was, without a doubt, the most exquisite female Justin had ever seen.

She smiled at the dogs, despite the fact that they were making a racket. "Hey, poochies," she said in a soft, melodic voice.

As entranced as he was, the dogs seemed more so. They'd stopped barking and had all sat down to stare at the stranger.

She opened her door and stepped out. All six feet of her.

Layered red and white tank tops showcased her nice, full breasts and slender waist. A short denim skirt clung to her hips and emphasized a pair of really fine legs.

She took off her hat and shook out a mane of butter-scotch-blond hair that fell in soft waves past her shoul-ders. After tossing the hat on the seat behind her, she reached down to pet the dogs. The pack was thoroughly besotted.

Justin completely understood.

If there was such a thing as love at first sight—which he knew there wasn't—he'd have been a goner.

The woman straightened and removed her sunglasses. "I'm Amanda," she said in the same voice that had magically quieted his dogs.

Justin stared into long-lashed, wide-set amber eyes that were every bit as mesmerizing as the rest of her. His brain seemed to have stopped working altogether. His body, on the other hand, was at full alert. "I'm Justin McCabe."

"This the Lost Pines?" Amanda asked, taking a moment to scan their surroundings.

Working to get the blood back in his brain where it belonged, Justin merely nodded.

"So," she said, still admiring the acres of unfenced grassland peppered with cedar and live oak, as well as the endless blue horizon and rolling hills in the distance. "Where do you want me to park my trailer?"

And then, all of a sudden, the fantasy ended. This gorgeous woman had not been dropped into his life like a karmic reward for all his hard work. Brought swiftly back to reality, he stopped her with a regretful lift of his palm. "You can't."

She pivoted back to him in a drift of citrusy perfume. Her eyes sparked with indignation and her delicate but surprisingly capable-looking hands landed on her hips. "I made it very clear to whomever I spoke. My camping out here is part of the deal."

What deal? "It can't be."

She came closer, her soft lips pursed in an unhappy frown. "Why not?"

Embarrassed that it had taken him this long to correct her misconception, Justin explained without rancor. "Because this isn't the Lost Pines you're looking for."

A flicker of indecipherable emotion flashed in those beautiful eyes. She regarded him skeptically, seeming to think he was trying to pull something over on her. "But how can that be? The sign above the gate said this is the Lost Pines Ranch."

"The sign's on the long list of things waiting to be changed." A new one had been ordered but wasn't coming in for another month. Which meant he would continue to have these mix-ups with nonlocals.

"Are you sure I'm not in the right place?" she asked with a frown. "Because…"

Justin shook his head, a little disappointed that this beautiful amazon would not be settling in for a long stay. He turned and pointed in the opposite direction. "What you want is the Lost Pines *Campground,* which is another three miles down the road, next to the Lake Laramie State Park. But…" What the heck, why not? Just this once he was going to go for what he wanted. Which was a little more—make that a *lot* more—time with this sun-kissed beauty. "Once you get set up there, Amanda, I'd be happy to take you to dinner."

This was, Amanda Bliss Johnson thought, the most bizarre encounter she'd ever had. Even if the tall rancher with the shaggy chestnut-brown hair and gorgeous blue eyes was the hottest guy she had ever come across in her life. From the massive shoulders and chest beneath that chambray shirt, to his long muscular legs, custom-boot-encased feet—and ringless left hand—everything about him broadcast Single and Available.

Which meant Strictly Off-Limits to her.

She wished she'd left her sunglasses on so he wouldn't see her dazzled expression. "First off," she told him crisply, "I don't date customers."

Now it was his turn to look shocked. "Customers! What are you talking about?"

Amanda pushed on. "You called for a carpenter, right? At least, Libby Lowell-McCabe, the CEO of the Lowell Foundation and chairwoman of the board for the Laramie Boys Ranch, did. She said it was an emergency. That your previous carpenter quit with no notice and you only have four weeks to get the bunkhouse ready for occupancy." She paused to draw a breath. "I emailed her back that I'd be willing to help y'all out, but only if I could keep my travel trailer on the property so I wouldn't have to waste time commuting back and forth to San Angelo."

Amanda fought her racing pulse and tried to stay calm. "But if that's not going to work, I guess I could park my Silversteam at the campground. Assuming, of course, they have a space available. Since it's the busy summer season, they may not."

He lifted a hand. "You don't have to do that."

Amanda folded her arms in front of her. "Sure about that? Because just now you seemed dead set against me camping here."

He flashed a slow, disarming smile. "That's because I thought you were a tourist, not an apprentice."

Apprentice? Strike two for the handsome Texan! "I'm not the apprentice," Amanda said tightly, her temper rising. "I'm the master carpenter."

He pulled the paper out of his pocket and squinted at it as if he couldn't believe the words in front of him.

Then his head lifted and he speared her with an incredulous gaze. *"You're A. B. Johnson Jr.?"*

Amanda wondered if it took him this long to process everything. "Amanda Bliss Johnson. Junior's the nickname I got at work."

"You want me to call you Junior?" he asked, with a hint of humor in his low baritone.

"Or Amanda." She waved a hand. "Whatever. It doesn't matter to me." What did was getting this gig. It would allow her to settle in this ruggedly beautiful place for an entire month before moving on to her next rural job.

Justin McCabe continued to contemplate her as if he either didn't believe she could really be an ace carpenter or wasn't going to be comfortable having a woman undertake such a large job.

Amanda sighed.

Great, just great. She'd gotten up at the crack of dawn to put the finishing touches on a built-in bookcase for a very fussy client, then spent hours getting all her stuff packed up and driving all the way out here. Now, the deceptively laid-back McCabe was acting like he wanted to fire her on the spot.

Deciding it was his turn to be put in the hot seat, Amanda stepped closer. "Do you have a problem with the fact I'm a woman?"

"No." He was clearly fibbing. "Not at all."

Then why couldn't he stop looking at her like he was going to need a protective force field just to be anywhere near her? "I come highly recommended." The defensive words were out before she could stop them.

"I know." He exhaled, beginning to look as off-kilter as she felt. "I just expected a guy. That's all."

A common mistake, given that most of her competitors were male. Still, Amanda refused to let Justin McCabe off the hook. Sensing there was more to whatever it was going on with him, she arched a brow.

There was a beat of complete and utter silence.

He scrubbed a hand across his face. "I did a Google search on your company after Libby told me she had arranged for A. B. Johnson Carpentry to come out and finish the work on an emergency basis. The website said the company was founded in San Angelo, Texas, by Angus 'Buddy' Johnson thirty-eight years ago."

Proudly, Amanda relayed, "That's my grandfather. He still runs the business—although he's supposed to be phasing out of that, too—but he stopped doing the rural gigs a year ago." After much persuading on her part.

Amanda touched her thumb to the center of her chest. "I do them now."

It was McCabe's turn to appear irritated. "So why didn't you make that clear in the communication with Libby? Unless—" he paused, still scrutinizing her closely "—you're trying to purposely mislead people?"

Amanda really did not want to get into this. However, he'd left her no choice. "When I first started doing jobs on my own the company was getting a lot of requests for me that had nothing whatsoever to do with my talent as a carpenter."

Understanding dawned on his handsome face. Along with a hint of anger. Amanda warmed beneath the intensity in his eyes. "So we took all the employee photos off the website and just listed the carpenters by name, or in my case, just my initials and last name. To differentiate me from my granddad we added the Junior to my name. That successfully eliminated all the customers just interested in making up jobs to hit on me."

"Makes sense."

She straightened. "Luckily, that's not going to be the case here."

"No," he concurred, meeting her stern gaze. "It's not."

"Good to hear." Amanda relaxed in relief. The last thing she wanted to deal with was the amorous attention of the tall, sexy Texan. Given how physically attractive she found him, the situation might be just too tempting.

Thinking he was possibly the most easygoing man she had ever met, Amanda drew a deep breath. "Anyway, back to the way the company operates. My grandfather takes the service requests. He makes up the schedule and does all the accounting work required to run the business. The other four employees are all master carpenters, and they work in San Angelo. They all have families, and don't want to be away for days at a time, so I take the gigs on all the remote locations."

When he opened his mouth she lifted a staying hand. "Unless you're not comfortable with that? If that's the case, I'll see if one of the guys wants to do it." She paused again, frowning. "They'd have to commute back and forth, and the two hours' travel time daily would add significantly to the overall cost and time it will take to complete the job."

McCabe shook his head, swiftly vetoing that suggestion. "That won't be necessary," he reassured her. "You're here. You should do it."

Happy that much was settled, Amanda was ready to move on, too. She returned his easy smile. "Then how about you show me everything you want done so I can get started."

* * *

Justin spent the next half hour showing Amanda the bunkhouse they were converting for the opening of the Laramie Boys Ranch. It would house the first group of eight boys and two house parents. There were cabinets to install in the bathrooms. Trim and doors to put on. Bookshelves and built-in locker-style armoires to be constructed in each of the five bedrooms.

Amanda paused next to the mangled drywall and damaged utility cabinet in the mudroom. She brushed splinters of wood from the plumbing hookup for the washer. "What happened here?"

Motioning for the dogs to stay back, well out of harm's way, Justin grabbed a trash bag. "I tried to put the cabinet up myself and it fell off the wall, taking the drywall with it."

Amanda dropped the shards of splintered wood and ripped-up drywall into the bag. Justin knelt to help her gather debris.

"Can you fix it?" He wasn't used to screwing up. Failing in front of a highly competent woman made it even worse.

"Yes." Amanda dusted off her hands and took out her measuring tape.

Justin watched as she set down her notebook and measured the damaged back of the cupboard. "No need to order a new cabinet?"

Nodding, she jotted down a set of numbers.

When she had finished looking around, Justin asked, "What's your best estimate?"

Amanda raked her teeth across her lush lower lip as she consulted the list she had made. "You said you wanted hardwood flooring installed throughout?"

"Except for the bathrooms. Those are going to have ceramic tile."

"The target date?"

"August first."

"Which gives us a little under four weeks." She tilted her head slightly to one side, her hair brushing the curve of her shoulder. "That's an ambitious schedule."

"Is it doable?"

"That all depends. Are you willing to have me work weekends and some evenings, too?"

Until more donations or grants came in, things were really tight. "We don't have the budget for overtime pay," he admitted.

Understanding lit her eyes. "I'll just charge you the regular rate, then."

He paused, tempted to accept yet not wanting to take advantage. "Sure?"

She tucked her notebook under her arm and headed for the open front door. She stepped outside, the sunshine illuminating her shapely legs. "Consider it my donation for your cause. Which, by the way, is a good one."

Justin fell into step beside her as they continued toward her truck. "You think so?"

She tossed him an admiring glance. "Troubled kids need a place to go." A hint of a smile curved her lips. "If that can happen in a beautiful setting like this, more power to you."

"Thanks." Not everyone was on board with his idea for the ranch. It helped to know she was.

The dogs raced forward, suddenly on full alert. A split second later, a car motor purred in the distance.

Two vehicles appeared, the second one a black-and-white Laramie County sheriff's car.

"Another lost tourist?" Amanda joked, her glance roving over him once again. "This one with a police escort?"

Justin shook his head, hoping it wasn't more bad news. "Mitzy Martin. She's the social worker tapped to work with the ranch. She's also on the board of directors. The sheriff's deputy is my brother Colt McCabe. He's in charge of community outreach for the department. I have no idea who the teenage boy with her is...."

Amanda backed up. "Well, obviously you don't need me for whatever this is." Giving the other visitors a cursory wave, she walked to the truck, his dogs trailing behind her, and began unloading her tools.

The teenage boy stayed put as Mitzy and Colt got out of their cars. Both radiated concern as they approached. "We have a favor to ask," Mitzy told him.

Justin looked at the sullen teen slouched in the passenger seat of Mitzy's car, arms crossed militantly in front of him. Pale and thin, he wore a black T-shirt with a skull on the front. His dark ash-blond hair was on the long side. "What's up?"

Mitzy shot him an imploring look. "We need a place for Lamar Atkins to stay during the day for the rest of the summer."

Understandable, but... "The ranch isn't open yet."

Colt inclined his head toward the unfinished bunkhouse. "It looks like you could use a lot of help getting it ready."

That much was certainly true, particularly in the bunkhouse. Justin paused, wanting to make sure he knew what they were expecting him to provide. "You want me to pay him?"

Mitzy shook her head. "Help him work off his community service hours."

"For…?" Justin prompted.

His brother frowned. "Repeated truancy. He's supposed to be in summer school now, but he keeps skipping, and the judge gave him one hour of community service for every hour of class he's skipped. Which amounts to two hundred and thirty-six hours."

Justin muttered a compassionate oath. That was going to take a while to work off.

"If you take Lamar on, and he sticks with the program, he'll be finished with his community service commitment before school starts in the fall," Mitzy urged. "And hopefully will learn something in the process."

Justin looked at the kid. He had his earphones in, his eyes closed. Justin turned back to Mitzy and Colt. Both had also felt the call to help others. Although his brother was now happily married and father to a little boy, Mitzy was as single as Justin was, with as little time for her social life as he. All three of them took to heart the fate of those in need. "Where are the boy's parents?"

Mitzy's expression tightened. "Long gone. Fed up with trying to deal with his defiance, they severed their parental rights and turned him over to the state last March. The court placed him with a foster family in Laramie, but both foster parents work during the day, and they can't be around to constantly monitor Lamar." She paused. "He seems to like them, and they feel the same way about him, but they just can't keep him in summer school."

Justin squinted. "What happens if this doesn't work out?"

"Given that Lamar was already on his last chance when I picked him up?" Colt exhaled slowly. "He'll be labeled incorrigible and put in a juvenile detention center."

Which meant an awful lot was at stake. Justin had seen enough kids spiral downward. He didn't want to be personally responsible for the ill-fated future of another. "I want to help." Wanted to give the kid a safe place to be during the day.

Mitzy regarded him with confidence. "We figured you would."

"But…" Justin cast a glance over at Amanda, who was lifting toolboxes and a power saw out of the bed of her truck. "I'd feel a lot better about it if the place was finished and the live-in counselors were here."

"You still want to be named ranch director by the board?" Colt asked. "Instead of just chief financial officer?"

Justin sighed, frustration growing. "You both know I do."

Mitzy pushed, sage as ever. "This is your chance to prove yourself worthy of the job."

Justin knew Mitzy and Colt were right. This was a prime opportunity to advance his career in the direction he wanted it to go, as well as a chance to help a kid in need. So the situation wasn't perfect. They'd manage. "When do you want to start?"

The duo smiled their thanks. "First thing tomorrow morning," Mitzy said.

"So you're going to personally supervise Lamar?" Amanda asked in shock after Justin filled her in an hour later.

To his aggravation, she seemed to think he couldn't—shouldn't—do it. "Why does that surprise you?" Justin was more than a little irked to find her among the naysayers who were constantly doubting him.

Amanda surveyed the area surrounding her temporary home site. "From the way you were talking earlier as you showed me around, I had the impression you were more of a numbers guy."

Being good at something didn't mean it was the right fit, career-wise. Justin wished he could make people understand that. He followed her back to the trailer. "I studied business and accounting in college."

Amanda chocked the tires so the trailer wouldn't roll. Finished, she stood. "What practical experience have you had working with troubled kids?"

Not enough; he'd found out the hard way. But that, too, was about to change.

"I worked at a nonprofit that helped at-risk teens." He helped her unhitch the trailer.

Amanda undid the safety chains. "And did what exactly?"

"Initially, I was the CFO." Justin pitched in and took care of the sway bars. "Eventually, I coordinated services for the kids, too."

"But someone else did the actual counseling and evaluating," Amanda guessed.

Justin nodded. "Which was quite extensive, given how complicated some of their situations were."

Her expression pensive, Amanda unlocked the hitch. "I'm sure it was."

"But?"

Amanda got into her truck to drive it out from under the hitch. "Facilitating services for an at-risk kid is not the same as actually getting through to him or her." She stepped back out of the cab and headed toward him, her long legs eating up the expanse of yard.

Unfortunately, this wasn't the first time Justin had heard that particular argument. "I can do this." He knew it in his gut. All he needed was a chance.

She gave him a skeptical look, then took out a carpenter's level to check the floor of the trailer. As she moved, the hem of her denim skirt slid up her thighs. "From what you've just told me, Lamar sounds like a tough case." Finding it okay, she stood with a smile. "Forgive me for saying so, but you don't seem like someone who knows much about defying the system."

Justin couldn't deny that was true. He'd gone through life without getting into trouble with authority once. That didn't mean he couldn't help those who had.

He was beginning to feel a little irked. "So?"

"Where's the common ground that will allow you and Lamar to establish any kind of rapport?"

"He'll respond to time and attention."

Amanda shook her head. "You think his foster parents haven't been giving him that?"

"Obviously, Lamar needs even more than what he's been getting," Justin countered. "Which is where I come in."

Amanda activated the trailer's solar panels. "Want my advice?"

"No, but I expect you're going to give it anyway."

Their eyes met. "Leave the life lessons to the social workers. They've had lots of practice and they're good at it."

She went inside the trailer and returned with a rolled-up awning, which he helped her set up.

"Work on getting this ranch finished and ready for the first eight boys. If Lamar can help you do that, fine, it'll be a good deal for both of you." With the awning finally attached, she brushed dust off her hands. "But accept the possibility that the kid might not want to be here tomorrow any more than he apparently wanted to be here today."

"And if that happens?" he prompted, intrigued despite himself by her perspective on the situation.

Her voice dropped a companionable notch. "If he doesn't want to help out, don't force it, because the only way it will ever work is if this is his choice. Not someone else's."

Justin studied her closely. "What makes you such an expert on all this?" *As compared to, say—me?*

A hint of sadness haunted her eyes. "Because I lived it. For a good part of my teenage years I hated everyone and everything."

Now, that was hard to imagine. She seemed so content and comfortable with herself. Sensing he could learn something from her, Justin asked, "What changed?"

For a moment, Amanda went very still, seeming a million miles away. "Me. I finally realized I had a choice to either continue on as I was, which was a pretty miserable existence, or approach life differently. The point is, Justin, you can't help someone who doesn't want to help himself." She sighed. "From what I saw, it didn't look to me like Lamar is there yet."

He grimaced at the truth of her words. "I know he's not."

Another beat of silence. "Then?" she pressed.

I'm not risking another tragedy. It's as simple and complicated as that.

Justin stepped closer, vowing, "I'm going to help Lamar whether he wants me to or not." He paused to take her in, appreciating both her beauty and her strength. "I'd like it if you were on board with that. If you're not," he paused and shot her a laser-sharp look, "I'd appreciate it if you would keep your feelings to yourself."

Chapter 2

"I'd rather work with her." Lamar pointed at Amanda, soon after arriving the following day.

Justin motioned Lamar back to the stacks of paper he had been trying to organize. Some were for state licensing and registration, others were for federal, state and private grants. The biggest—a quarter-million-dollar endowment from the Lone Star United Foundation—was due by the end of July. In addition to that, there were more fund-raising solicitations to send, thank-you letters to write, a tight budget to manage and local building regulations to comply with.

Justin had figured the teen would show up with an attitude, but he wasn't going to let him dictate how things were done. "Not an option."

Lamar slouched in his chair, a scowl on his young face. "How come?"

"Because Amanda's not in charge of you," he reminded the boy mildly. "I am."

The teen returned his glance to the window. "That wood she's carrying looks heavy."

Heavy enough to require the sleek muscles of her gorgeous shoulders and upper arms, Justin noticed appreciatively. What it did for her legs wasn't bad, either.

Justin dragged his glance away from the statuesque beauty in the sleeveless red T-shirt, denim coverall shorts and sturdy work boots. "If Amanda needed our help, she would've asked for it."

"Sure about that? I mean, isn't this place supposed to be about turning kids into well-mannered guys? What kind of Texas gentleman lets a lady hoist all that stuff by herself—even if she is a carpenter by trade?"

Good question. And one meant to make Justin bend to Lamar's strategy. "Nice try."

The kid held his palms aloft. "Hey! I'm just saying…"

Justin eyed the paperwork still needing attention. "Did you get how to use the scanner? Or do I need to explain it again?"

Lamar turned back to the desk with a huff. "I'm not good at this computer stuff."

Which was an understatement and a half, Justin soon found out. In the next thirty minutes, Lamar managed to accidentally shut down the operating system, re-enter a single document three times and delete two files Justin had initially scanned as examples. The only thing worse than his own mounting frustration was the fact that his young charge seemed equally annoyed at his own ineptitude.

"So maybe office work isn't your thing," Justin said

finally, ready to admit that all this assignment had done so far was cost both of them precious time and patience.

Lamar looked wistfully out the window at the vast blue horizon and dazzling sunshine. "Sure you don't want me to go out and at least offer to give Miss Amanda a hand? She still has quite a bit to unload."

The goal was to get Lamar doing something constructive on his very first day, so Mitzy could report back to her superiors that things were going well.

Figuring it would be okay if they both assisted Amanda, Justin stood. "All right. Let's go ask."

Justin and Lamar walked out of the lodge. By the time they reached the pickup truck that Amanda had parked just in front of the door, she had re-emerged from the bunkhouse. She looked from one to the other. Sweat beaded her face, neck and chest. "What's up?" she asked, blotting the moisture on her forehead with one gloved hand.

Justin turned his attention away from the pretty color in her cheeks and the radiant depths of her eyes. "We thought we'd give you a hand with the unloading," he explained.

Amanda stiffened. "That's okay. I've got it."

Lamar gave the pretty carpenter a pleading look. "If you don't let me help, he's going to make me go back to the computer—and I've already messed things up in there pretty bad."

Amanda had no problem turning Justin down.

Lamar, it seemed, was another matter entirely.

She sized up the teenager. "The bunkhouse air-conditioning isn't installed yet. My guess is, even with all the doors and windows open for maximum airflow, it's about a hundred degrees inside. Add physical exertion to that, and it's going to be a workout and a half," she warned.

The tall, lanky teen was evidently unconcerned with the hard physical labor ahead of him, so long as he got out of any more office work. "Okay with me," Lamar said cheerfully.

Justin smiled and offered, "I can help, too."

Amanda frowned. "That's okay…you don't have to. Lamar and I can handle it."

Justin didn't like feeling expendable.

But if this was what it took to get Lamar to realize he could actually enjoy being out here on the ranch, Justin figured he could spare him for one day. "Let me know when Lamar's work for you is finished," he told Amanda briskly. "I'll take it from there."

Amanda knew she had hurt Justin's feelings. There was no helping it. She could not have him underfoot. He was too handsome, too distracting, and she couldn't afford to lose her focus for even a moment.

"You know, if you don't want me around, either, I could go off somewhere and just get lost for a while," Lamar suggested casually as soon as Justin had gone back into the lodge.

Chuckling, Amanda clapped a gloved hand on his shoulder. "Nice try, kid. But you told Justin you'd help carry all this wood into the bunkhouse, so that is exactly what you're going to do." She rummaged around in her truck and returned with a pair of leather work gloves for him.

Awkwardly, Lamar inched them on. "You don't mind taking orders from him?"

Did she? Normally, Amanda liked to maintain her

independence and set her own work agenda. That was what made these rural gigs so appealing. The clients were so busy with their own work, they were less inclined to micromanage her. Best of all, at the end of the day, she could really get away from it all in her home-away-from-home travel trailer.

"Justin McCabe runs this ranch. It's my job to make sure he is happy with the work I do. Yours, too, for that matter, since he's overseeing your community service."

Silence fell.

Lamar stacked more trim wood in the corner, next to a pile of interior doors that needed to be installed. "Don't you want to know what I did to get sent out here?"

Amanda brought in a stack of doorknobs and latch kits. "Truancy, right?"

Lamar scowled. "Justin told you."

They walked back outside for another load. "Yep."

Lamar peered at her from beneath his blond bangs. "Aren't you going to use this opportunity to lecture me on how I'm ruining my life and all that?"

Amanda took in the front of his Pirates of the Caribbean T-shirt. It depicted a rollicking fight scene. "Would you listen?"

"No."

She handed him a bundle of trim wood. "That's what I figured."

Lamar cradled it against his chest. "Which is why you're not lecturing me."

Amanda grabbed a bundle for herself and walked with him toward the door. "I figure there has to be a reason you keep cutting class."

Lamar put down his bundle of wood with more than necessary force. "I hate it. It's boring."

Regular school had been a pain for Amanda, too. Figuring they could both use a rest, she went to the cooler in the corner and brought out two icy grape-flavored electrolyte drinks. She tossed one to him. "What does interest you?" she asked.

Lamar wiped the moisture away with the hem of his shirt. "I like watching TV. Listening to music."

Amanda took a long drink. There had to be something that would help him connect with others. "Do you play any sports?" Even if Lamar didn't qualify for school teams, there were always private athletic leagues to provide a little fun and make him feel involved.

"Nah." Lamar finished half his bottle in a single gulp. "I'm no good at sports, either."

So Lamar had suffered multiple failures, socially and otherwise. Catching sight of his dejected expression, Amanda's heart went out to him. She knew was it was like to be a teenager who didn't seem to fit in anywhere. "What *are* you good at?"

Abruptly, mischief crept into his expression. "Getting out of stuff I don't want to do."

Amanda could see that. "You can't really make a living as a no-show."

"So maybe I'll be a security guard," Lamar boasted, "and sit around and watch those TV monitors."

Amanda couldn't think of anything less interesting, but leery of discouraging him, she smiled. "Could work."

He paced to the window and back. "You're not going to try to talk me out of it? Tell me I have to finish high school and go on to college?"

Amanda held his gaze. "College isn't for everyone."

"Did you go to college?"

Amanda shook her head. "I didn't like high school, either, so I got a GED instead and learned carpentry from my grandfather."

His face grew pinched. "I don't know about the GED," he grumbled, as if it were the worst idea in the world. "All that studying and having to take those tests…"

Amanda could see where even the idea of that would be overwhelming for Lamar, given he'd skipped so much he had to be way behind on his studies. They walked back out to the truck to finish unloading supplies.

"Do you like being a carpenter?" Lamar asked eventually.

"Very much."

He slanted her a wary glance. "How come?"

Trying not to think about the failures in her own life, Amanda offered him a faint smile. "Because I like building things that will last."

It was nearly noon when Justin looked up from behind his desk to see his dad striding into the lodge. As he walked across the spacious living area, Wade McCabe held a large high-velocity floor fan in each hand.

Justin strolled out of the administrator's office to greet him. "Hey, Dad. Thanks for bringing those out." Wade set them down next to the overstuffed sofas and chairs that had been donated by a local furniture store. "Some reason you couldn't run into town and pick them up yourself?"

A very good one, as a matter of fact. "I'm supervising a teenager's community service right now."

His dad looked around, perplexed, noting they were quite alone.

"Lamar's in the bunkhouse, assisting the carpenter. He'll be back in here as soon as they're finished carrying in all the wood from the pickup truck."

His dad paused. "So this is a one-day thing?"

"All summer."

Wade blinked in surprise. "You're not really equipped for that, are you son?"

Justin tensed. *Here we go again.* He turned and walked into his office. "Dad, if this is where you tell me if I'm serious about all this, I need to go back to school and get a degree in psychology…"

Wade looked around the sparsely decorated administrator's office, which at the moment was littered with the paperwork Justin was still trying to get through. "Your mother and I raised you to find what you're good at and do it to the best of your ability." He sank into a chair in front of Justin's desk and gave him a long, level look. "What you are good at, Justin, is finance and accounting."

Justin slid a stack of papers into a mailing envelope, sealed it shut and ran it through the postage meter. "I'm doing that here."

Wade steepled his hands in front of him. "To a much lesser degree than what you were doing five years ago."

Which, for his ambitious father and mother, was unacceptable, Justin knew. They wanted all five of their sons to have the same kind of financial security and success they'd built for themselves, while still holding on to their core values. "It's important work, Dad."

Wade's expression softened. "I'm not discounting that. It's why I made a sizable donation to help get the

Laramie Boys Ranch up and running and accepted a position on the board of directors."

Something Justin was beginning to regret. In hindsight, he saw answering to his father, even among a group of other involved adults, might not be such a good thing. "Then...?"

"Your mother and I are worried about you."

Justin grimaced. "Why?"

"Clearly, you've yet to get over everything that happened in Fort Worth—first your broken engagement to Pilar, and then..."

Justin heard a feminine throat clear, followed by a knock. He and his father turned to see Amanda standing in the open door.

"I'm sorry to interrupt," she said, looking gorgeous as ever, despite her hot and sweaty state. "But have either of you seen Lamar?"

Actually, given the conversation she'd overhead inside the ranch's office, Amanda wasn't at all sorry to interrupt. It sounded as though Justin McCabe needed a break. Having been the target of a great deal of parental lecturing growing up, she knew just how demoralizing such sessions could be. Not to mention the damage they inevitably did to the relationship. Although, unlike her mom and dad—who had seen her mostly as a stumbling block to their happiness—Justin's parent seemed to genuinely care about him.

She continued, "I just got back with more wood and..."

Justin shot out of his chair, his expression filled with concern. "What do you mean you *just got back?*"

Why was he making a big deal out of this? "I had to

run to the lumberyard to pick up the rest of the base-board." She paused. "He didn't tell you?"

Justin shoved a hand through his hair. "I haven't seen him. I thought he was with you."

Justin's father looked on with a mixture of resigna-tion and disapproval.

Amanda felt for Justin. Whether or not the two of them should have seen this coming was a moot point. She swallowed uncomfortably. "He should have re-ported back to you about an hour and a half ago...."

Justin stalked around the desk to her side. "Where could he be?"

Amanda turned to let Justin through. She caught a whiff of soap and man as he passed by. "I don't know." She was, however, willing to help search.

Together, the three of them looked through the lodge. Eventually, they found Lamar sound asleep in the lounge on the second floor. The TV was on, the sound turned all the way down.

Relieved yet still disapproving, Wade McCabe told his son curtly, "I'll leave you to handle this."

Tense with embarrassment, Justin nodded at his dad. "Thanks again for bringing the fans."

Wade nodded and left.

Lamar opened his eyes, stretching lazily. He smelled of sweat and bubblegum. "Hey," he said to Amanda. "You're back."

"Yes." She tried not to think about how much trouble Lamar was already in, and he'd only been at the ranch for half a day. "I am."

Justin clenched his jaw with frustration. "Is this where you've been the entire time she was gone?" he demanded.

"Yeah. So?"

"You were supposed to find me when Amanda no longer needed your help."

Lamar rubbed the sleep from his eyes. "Yeah, well, all you were doing was office work. I'm no good at that."

Justin gave Lamar a reproving frown. "That's not for you to decide. This is community service, remember? To get credit for your time, you have to do what you're told."

Lamar sat up and dropped his feet to the floor. Belligerence radiated from him in waves. "Is it time for lunch yet?" he asked, completely ignoring Justin's reprimand. "I'm really hungry."

Amanda's stomach had been growling for the past half hour, too. "I've got some sandwiches made if anyone wants to join me."

"Sounds good to me," the teen said.

Amanda looked at Justin. Temper again under control, he nodded. Then he cautioned Lamar, "Just don't do that again, okay? For both our sakes, I need to know where you are at all times."

"Okay," Lamar muttered.

Relieved to have that settled, Amanda led the way to her trailer. She invited the guys inside, figuring there was safety in numbers. Wrong. The moment they stepped inside, her refuge felt filled to the brim with testosterone. And much smaller. Especially with Justin standing right beside her. Of course, that was probably because at six foot five his head almost reached the ceiling.

"Wow!" Lamar whistled appreciatively as he surveyed the comfortable space she had worked so hard to create. More a mini-apartment than camper, the back half was all bedroom and bath. The front half of the Airrstream housed the kitchen—with a full-size fridge, microwave, stove, sink and even a tiny dishwasher. The butcher-block tabletop between the roomy banquettes doubled as a work space, and there were plenty of built-in racks for her pantry items and cookware.

"You must really like to cook." Lamar checked out the bins of fresh fruits and veggies, her complex variety of dried chili peppers and some freshly made tortillas.

Amanda nodded proudly. "It's a hobby of mine."

"Where did you learn?" the teen asked.

She opened up the fridge and brought out the three large grilled-chicken wraps with lettuce, cheese and Caesar dressing that she'd made from the leftovers of the previous evening's dinner. "My grandmother and grandfather. Cooking was something they liked to do together, so when I moved in with them I started cooking, too."

"Sounds fun," Justin said.

"It was." It was the first time she'd known what it was like to be part of a happy family.

The handsome Texan's fingers brushed hers as she handed him a flavored sports drink. "Was? You don't do it anymore?"

Trying not to react to the husky caress of his voice, the warm feel of his fingers or the tenderness in Justin's brilliant blue eyes, Amanda shook her head. "Occasionally, but not as much since my grandmother died of congestive heart failure a couple of years ago."

"Sorry to hear that," Justin and Lamar said in unison.

Amanda accepted their condolences with a nod, aware of a growing sense of intimacy she didn't expect. Wasn't supposed to want. And knew would be unwise to encourage. "So," she said, pushing her lingering grief away. "Why don't the two of you tell me a little more about the area. What should I know about Laramie County?"

"There are a number of good restaurants in town," Justin began.

Lamar nodded. "The Lone Star's food is good, and they have live music and dancing, too. Since chicks seem to like that stuff," the teen added helpfully.

Amanda wondered if that was where Justin had intended to take her the first night, when he'd asked her out.

"I do like dancing," she admitted with a smile.

Justin's eyes gleamed. "Then you should make it a point to go while you're here," he said. "With or without a date."

Amanda's middle fluttered with sensation. Adopting her best poker face, she nodded. "I'll keep that in mind."

Wary of letting her thoughts wander where Justin's were obviously headed—into forbidden romantic territory—Amanda guided the conversation to mundane subjects, like the new wind farm and a famous sculptor she'd heard about who worked in bronze.

As soon as the meal was over, she rose. Eager to get back to work, she looked at Justin. "Your dad said he brought two fans that would help cool off the bunkhouse till the air-conditioning is installed?"

Justin nodded. "Lamar and I will carry them over for you."

Amanda smiled. "Great. I'll meet you guys there."

A few minutes later they walked in, and Amanda showed them where she wanted the fans set up. Concerned that there was still a lot of friction between Justin and Lamar, she figured it wouldn't hurt to act as buffer a little while longer.

"I don't know what you had planned for Lamar this afternoon," she told Justin, "but my work will go a lot faster if I have assistance mounting the top kitchen cabinets."

"I'll do it!" Lamar quickly volunteered.

Justin looked at the cabinet lift Amanda had set up, and the bulky stock cabinets. She knew he could see it was not an unreasonable request, even if she could easily have done the job all on her own. "Can you keep him busy the rest of the afternoon?"

"I won't let him out of my sight," Amanda promised.

Justin exhaled, his expression grim. After a long pause, he gazed at Lamar. "No more disappearing acts. Okay?"

The teen nodded, clearly aware he was on very shaky ground with the man supervising his community service.

Justin turned back to Amanda, his eyes devoid of the gratitude she had expected. "I'll be in the office, working on grant applications, if you need me." Justin turned on his heel and stalked off.

Watching him go, Amanda knew she had just made another mistake. She should never have stepped between Justin and his charge. In the end, all she had done was make things worse.

As soon as Justin disappeared from view, she did her best to undo the damage. "You need to give Justin a chance."

His expression stony, Lamar helped her cut a base cabinet out of its cardboard cover. "McCabe doesn't get me the way you do."

Amanda bit her lip. "I'm not so sure about that." While it was true that she could talk to Lamar with ease, Justin seemed to have Lamar's number in a lot of ways.

The boy's jaw tightened. "I see the judgment in his eyes when I screw up, Amanda. I don't need any more of that."

She had seen the disappointment, too. However, it didn't mean Lamar had to return it in kind. "You're going to have to work with Justin while I'm around, and after I leave. So the sooner you try to find common ground with him, the better."

Lamar picked up the utility scissors. "Maybe I could continue my community service with you, wherever you go after this," he suggested hopefully.

Amanda was flattered. She also knew it wasn't the best idea. She cut open the next box. "I don't think the court is going to go for that. They're going to want to see that you can follow the rules and act in a positive manner, no matter where you are or who you're with."

Lamar sulked but said nothing more.

Her point made, Amanda focused on the cabinet installation. She kept Lamar busy until his foster father showed up to collect him at the end of the day.

Only when she'd had a chance to get a shower and clean up a little did she go in search of Justin again.

She found him on the back deck of the lodge with his dogs.

"Got a minute?" she asked, aware she owed him an apology, but unsure if he'd accept it.

Justin measured kibble into five stainless-steel bowls. He had the same brooding look he'd worn when he'd been talking with his father. "It's probably not the best time for us to talk, Amanda."

Not an encouraging start. "We need to clear the air."

After each dog had a bowl of food he turned to her. "Go ahead."

She swallowed. "I'm sorry if I got in the way of whatever you were trying to accomplish with Lamar this afternoon. But I thought a time-out between the two of you might help. And I used the opportunity to tell him he should give you a chance."

His gaze drifted over her before returning ever so deliberately to her eyes. "Bet that went over well."

Like a lead balloon. "He'll come around." Amanda punctuated her words with a hopeful look.

He stood, legs braced apart, arms crossed in front of him. "Is that all?"

She wished. "I have a feeling you blame me for Lamar skipping out on us this morning."

"I'm sure he would have done the same thing whether you were here or not."

She lifted her chin. "Then why are you ticked off at me?"

Leaving the dogs on the patio, he turned and strode back into the lodge. "I'm not."

"And if I believe that, you've got a lake in Odessa you'd like to sell me."

Justin walked down the hall to his office where stacks of paper and letters littered every available surface. Frustration emanated from him in waves as he took a seat behind his desk. "Let's just say it wasn't the best day for me, okay?"

Amanda refused to give him sympathy. He was throwing enough of a pity party all on his own.

"I don't deny there were issues," she countered. "But to be honest, the problems were also of your own making. I mean, really," she continued, goading him with thinly veiled exasperation, "could you have given Lamar a worse task on his first day here?"

Justin's glance narrowed. "What do you mean?"

Not about to let him pull rank on her—because in this instance they were equals—she moved around the front of the desk and leaned against it, facing him. "Lamar was sent here because he can't stand school. So the first thing you do is give him *paperwork?*"

His full attention on her, Justin rocked back in his swivel chair and waited for her to go on.

Her frustration with the situation boiling over, Amanda continued, "Does anyone know why he is skipping so much? Has anyone even asked him?"

Justin's handsome features sharpened with chagrin. "I don't know what he's told others, but I can tell you that I haven't discussed it with him."

Hands cupping the edge of the desk, her arms braced on either side of her, Amanda leaned close enough to search his eyes. "Don't you think you should?" she persisted.

Justin's brooding expression returned. "I'm not his counselor."

Amanda exhaled and sat back. She knew this wasn't her problem, and yet it was. "Then try being his friend."

His jaw hardened. "He's got to respect me first."

Amanda knew better than anyone that a solely disciplinarian approach never worked with a kid like Lamar, just as it had never worked with her when she was ticked off at the entire world. "Set a good example. Inundate him with kindness and patience. The respect will come."

Silence fell between them. She couldn't tell what Justin was feeling. Wasn't sure she wanted to know.

Restless, Amanda stood and began to pace around the room. She paused to look at some of the awards hanging on the wall. There were several for community service and fund-raising, as well as his bachelor's degree diploma from the University of Texas. Also on display were a model and numerous sketches of the Laramie Boys Ranch as it would look when it was completed with a dozen residential bunkhouses, barns and corrals, basketball and tennis courts, and a swimming pool. But the walls were devoid of the kind of pictures that one would expect to see—portraits of family and friends, and kids he had helped in the past. Truth be told, there was nothing uniquely personal here.

Wondering if his quarters at the ranch were any different, she swiveled back around. "I know your heart is in the right place," she said softly, determined to help him succeed with Lamar.

He raked his hands through his shaggy hair and stood. "You just don't think I'm cut out for this."

Amanda paused, her hands curving over the back of an armchair. It was difficult telling someone what they didn't want to hear. For whatever reason, with Justin, it was ever harder. She met his eyes. "Kids like Lamar are complicated. They're tough to reach because they play everything so close to the vest."

His broad shoulders relaxing slightly, Justin roamed closer. She inhaled the brisk masculine scent of his skin and hair, her pulse picking up another notch.

"So how did you get through to him?"

Feeling as if the room was a little too warm and small for comfort, Amanda turned and walked into the spacious living area with its abundant couches. She sank into a big armchair, wishing she could find the right words to reassure him. "I didn't. Not really." Pretending she wasn't oh-so-aware of every masculine inch of him, she looked Justin in the eye, then lamented, "All I can tell you for certain is that Lamar's self-esteem is incredibly low."

Justin rubbed the underside of his handsome jaw. "Which is why he's acting out."

Trying not to notice how good it felt to be with Justin in such an intimate setting, Amanda fought back a flush. "Right."

Justin sat on the sofa opposite her. "Still." Justin paused to look her over lazily, head to toe. "You connected with him a lot more than I did. He followed you around like a lost puppy."

Tingling everywhere Justin's gaze had touched, and everywhere it hadn't, Amanda shrugged. She knew that what she and Lamar had shared had, for the most part, been superficial, that there was much more going on with the teenager than he was divulging. There had to be, given the fact Lamar had been abandoned by his parents before becoming a ward of the state.

Aware Justin was still studying her intently, Amanda slanted Justin a haphazard glance. "Lamar had never actually seen any carpentry work being done, so he was interested in what I was doing."

"Plus," Justin guessed ruefully, "Lamar was trying to get out of more desk work, assigned by yours truly."

"Good point." A more companionable silence fell, and they exchanged smiles. "I want this to work out for you both," she said.

Really listening now, Justin leaned forward a bit. "Then where would you suggest I start?"

Amanda tried to keep her eyes off the sinewy lines of his shoulders and chest. She did not need to be wondering how it would feel to be held against him. And she certainly didn't need to be wondering what it would be like to kiss him!

Amanda smiled and advised, "By doing something with Lamar tomorrow that would get you both out from behind a desk. Something that needs doing that he can feel good about at the end of the day."

Justin took her advice to heart. "I'll work on it," he promised, leaning toward her. "In the meantime, I have a favor to ask."

Chapter 3

"A favor," Amanda repeated, wondering why she was so drawn to him. And even more important, why she was so curious. He was just a client. She shouldn't need to understand Justin McCabe on a personal level, never mind try to figure out why he had taken on a challenge of this nature. And yet, she sensed there was *something* motivating him. Something he didn't like to talk about.

"Don't worry." Justin rose and headed for the lodge kitchen. "It's nothing all that drastic."

Intrigued, Amanda followed him. "I can't wait to hear it, then."

Justin wandered over to the fridge and peered inside. He took out a package of New Braunfels smoked sausage links and set them on the counter. "I volunteered to host a fund-raising dinner and I've got no clue what I need to do to get ready for it…or even what kind of food I should serve."

Amanda couldn't have been more shocked had he proposed marriage. "And you're asking *me?* The carpenter?"

Justin set a skillet on the stove. He opened a bottle of Shiner Boch beer and poured it into the skillet, then added the links and turned the burner on to simmer. "You're still a woman. And you like to cook." He went back to the fridge and brought out containers of premade German potato salad and green beans with almonds. "I figured you would know this stuff."

Amanda did. Unfortunately, she had gone down this particular path before, and it wasn't a mistake she intended to repeat. "Isn't this the kind of thing you should be discussing with your girlfriend?" she asked.

Justin went to the fridge again and brought out two more bottles of beer and a jar of jalapeño barbecue sauce. "Don't have one." He opened both beers and handed her one.

Their fingers brushed, sending a thrill spiraling through her. Amanda took a small sip of the delicious golden brew and studied him over the rim. "Don't have one as in you recently broke up with someone, or don't have one as in you don't want to be in a relationship?" she asked before she could stop herself.

The corner of his mouth quirked up and he took a drink. "You really want to know?"

"I do," she murmured. *Though maybe she shouldn't…*

He let out a long breath, then turned and dumped the green beans into a saucepan to heat. "A couple of years out of college, I got engaged to a woman I worked with." The words seemed to come with difficulty. "Pilar and I were both vying for promotion. But there was only one slot available at the company where we worked, and the competition for it was intense. I'd been there longer, had an edge. So Pilar picked my brain at length about what I thought it would take to land the top job, then passed my ideas off as her own before I could present them to my boss." He took another sip of beer. "Suffice it to say, she got the promotion."

"That's terrible!" Amanda blurted out, stunned by the depth of his ex's betrayal.

"The worst of it was that Pilar didn't think she had done anything wrong." There was a long pause as Justin lounged against the counter. "She said that the corporate world was brutally competitive and to succeed one had to be ruthless. She was only surprised I hadn't done the same to her, or at least tried. But—" cynicism crept into his low tone "—she felt we could still go on, forewarned and forearmed."

Amanda couldn't believe her ears. "Obviously, you felt otherwise."

"I realized I didn't want to be in a relationship where competitiveness was a factor. So I ended it."

"Over her objections," Amanda guessed.

"Yes."

Amanda couldn't blame him for brooding. Setting the bottle aside, she closed the distance between them and squeezed his hand compassionately. "I would have done the same thing in your place," she admitted.

"What about you?" He drained the remainder of his beer. "Is there a reason you don't want to help me out? A boyfriend waiting in the wings who might not approve?"

Hoping Justin hadn't picked up on how attracted she was to him, because an awareness like that could propel them right into the bedroom, Amanda flushed. She moved a slight distance away and worked to contain the emotion in her voice. "I'm not attached, either. Although, like you, I was engaged once, several years ago."

His gaze scanned her face and body, lingering thoughtfully, before returning to her eyes. "What happened?"

"Rob's parents got wind of the fact that I had a less-than-admirable record before I went to live with my grandparents."

His gentle expression encouraged her to go on. Amanda drew a bolstering breath. "They heard from one of their friends, who managed a department store, that I had been caught shoplifting there. As you can imagine, my potential in-laws were not pleased. They had in mind a very different type of woman as the mother of their grandchildren."

He caught her hand when she would have turned away. "So your fiancé broke up with you?"

Amanda leaned into his touch despite herself. "I broke up with him. I didn't want to come between Rob and his family, and I certainly didn't want to have kids with a man whose own parents detested me."

Justin turned around and brought out two plates. "And Rob didn't try to persuade you otherwise?"

Noting that Justin had simply assumed she'd dine with him, Amanda shook her head. "In the end, he agreed a long-standing family quarrel wasn't what he wanted, either."

"And since then…?" Justin asked, seeming to understand implicitly how devastated the whole debacle had left her.

She decided she might as well eat with him—she was starving and he had enough food to feed four people.

"I've had dates here and there, but nothing with the potential to be lasting."

It seemed the kind of guys she wanted to date all had stellar childhoods and stable, loving families. In the end, none wanted to be dating a former delinquent.

The most vulnerable part of her did not want to find out that Justin felt the same way.

Justin loaded their plates with food and motioned for her to sit down at the stainless-steel work island that ran down the center of the room. He took a seat and his smile turned seductive. "So there's really no reason you shouldn't help me, then."

Except that it would bring them closer, and she wasn't sure she wanted to be closer to someone who made her feel this wildly excited and yearning for more.

She liked the way she had been before. Content with what she had, and who she was. Not longing for the Cinderella fantasy of a spellbinding romance.

Aware Justin was still waiting for her answer, Amanda settled onto a high-backed stool opposite him. "Don't you have a mother or a sister or someone else you could ask?" Her mouth and throat had suddenly gone bone-dry.

He added a healthy splash of barbecue sauce to his plate and cut into his sausages with gusto. "I don't have any sisters. My four brothers know as little about party planning as I do."

"There's still your mother," Amanda persisted.

Justin set the barbecue sauce in front of her. "She's a wildcatter, with her own company to run. Not only is she completely inept in the kitchen—to the point that it's a running family joke—she's pretty busy scoping out a new drilling site in the Trans-Pecos area of southwest Texas."

"So," Amanda said, picking up her knife and fork, "it's back to me."

Laugh lines crinkled at the corners of his eyes. "That lunch you served us proves you're an amazing cook."

She kept her eyes locked with his, even as her heart raced in her chest. She took a bite of the meal he had prepared. The sausage was delicious—crispy on the outside, meaty and flavorful on the inside. "This is really tasty, too."

"The supermarket deli made half of it."

Amanda felt her face flush even as she savored the tang of the German-style potato salad. "One excellent home-cooked meal is not going to get you what you want."

"Sure?" His eyes danced with merriment. "Because there are more meals where this came from."

Amanda raked her teeth across her lower lip. She knew he was attracted to her, too. Sparks arced between them every time they were near. "Is this just an excuse to spend time with me?" she asked warily.

He dabbed at the corners of his mouth with his napkin, poker-faced once again. "I said I wouldn't hit on you while you were working here."

And he hadn't. The problem was, she was beginning to want to proposition *him*. At least in fantasy…

Heat climbed from her chest to her neck and face. "I believe that you really do need help for this worthwhile cause, but why does it have to come from me? Surely you could hire a party planner or caterer."

Finished eating, Justin leaned toward her, forearms on the table. "We don't have the budget for that. Plus, word would get out. And since entertaining is going to be part of the ranch director's job…" He let the thought trail off.

Unbidden, another wall came tumbling down. One

that, perhaps, should have stayed intact. "So to help them take you seriously, this has to be well-done," Amanda guessed.

His mesmerizing blue eyes found hers. "You got it."

She bit her lip, intrigued despite herself. "How many guests are you going to have?" She did like cooking for a crowd.

"Twelve," he replied, setting his glass down. "Thirteen, if you'll come and speak to the rest of the guests about your own experiences turning your life around and how it led to you becoming the upstanding adult you are today." He glanced at her admiringly. "Because clearly whatever it is—whatever it takes to connect with an at-risk kid—you have in spades. I can see it in your dealings with Lamar and the way he instinctively relates to you."

Amanda didn't know what was worse. The thought of wanting to hit on Justin—when he was so obviously off-limits and out of her league. Or being simultaneously recruited to plan and cook for his party *and* be the star of his dog-and-pony show on dysfunctional childhoods.

Thoroughly insulted, Amanda set down her napkin and stood. "I have to hand it to you, McCabe. You really know how to make a gal feel good."

He seemed taken aback by her sarcastic tone.

"The answer is no," she snapped. "To all of the above."

And no to the idea of ever making a play for him, as well. Heaven help her, she thought wearily as she strode from the kitchen. *When would she ever learn?*

The next morning, it didn't take Lamar long to notice the atmosphere. "Is Amanda mad at you?"

She'd certainly taken his compliments—and request for help—the wrong way, Justin admitted ruefully.

Wishing he had even a small part of Amanda's natural ability to communicate with troubled kids, Justin asked his teenage charge, "Why would you think that?"

"I don't know. I saw her shoot you this look when she was heading over to the bunkhouse. She was definitely angry."

Justin sighed and ushered Lamar through the lodge onto the back deck, where the sun was already beating down. The heat had risen past an uncomfortable ninety-five degrees, and it was barely past nine o'clock. "I may have ticked her off last night when I asked her to do me a favor that would help out the ranch." Justin whistled and all five dogs came running.

Lamar hunkered down to pet them and was soon covered with doggie licks and kisses. Reveling in the unchecked affection, Lamar looked up at Justin. "That doesn't sound like Amanda. Seems like usually she's happy to help out with stuff. She even volunteers. Like with lunch yesterday. I mean, she didn't have to feed us, but she did."

"Yeah." Justin had also been surprised by this morning's standoffish attitude. "Maybe I just caught her at a bad time."

The only thing he knew for sure was that Amanda had felt used or manipulated. Which rankled. All he had really wanted was to find a way to bring down the barriers she had erected around herself and get to know her better. So something else a heck of a lot more satisfying than just friendship might be possible. But that hadn't happened. Worse, he had undermined whatever small gains he had made in his pursuit of her.

And he was, Justin admitted reluctantly to himself, pursuing her. Despite the fact he had promised not to make a pass at her. While she was working on the ranch, anyway. Once that was done, all bets were off....

"Am I going to be helping her today?" Lamar asked hopefully as he gave the dogs a final pat and rose to his feet.

Justin pushed aside the disappointment that he was still a less than acceptable choice from the teen's point of view. But, like Amanda said, he had to remedy that by giving the kid something he could accomplish and feel good about. "No, you're going to be assisting me," Justin said, ignoring Lamar's immediate scowl of displeasure. "First off, we need to give the dogs a bath."

Dismay quickly turned to trepidation. "All five of them?"

Justin nodded, figuring the task would take a good part of the morning to accomplish. "They need to be bathed before we put on their monthly flea and tick medicine."

Lamar shoved a hand through his hair. "I don't know if I'm going to be any good at that, either."

Justin refused to let fear of failure get in the way, for either of them. "Do you know how to pet a dog?"

"Sure..."

Justin smiled and pressed on, "Do you know how to take a bath yourself?"

The boy scoffed. "Well, duh."

"Then you've got all the skills you need." Justin went into the mudroom off the kitchen and pointed to the shelves. "Grab the leashes, that stack of towels and the box of treats." Justin picked up the rest of the supplies and stepped out onto the long deck that ran along the back of the lodge where the dogs were still waiting curiously.

One by one, Justin roped the leashes to the railing and then snapped the secured leashes to their collars. He asked Lamar to turn the water on and bring the hose up on the deck. Already sweating himself, Justin adjusted the handheld sprayer to the shower setting and handed it over to Lamar. "Let's wet them all down first."

While he did that, which also cooled the dogs off, Justin made sure the towels were well out of the way and opened up the shampoo and conditioner bottles. He handed one of each to Lamar, instructing, "Soap, rinse, condition and rinse again."

The teen nodded, looking both serious and nervous, but Justin knew the kid would do fine once he actually got started. "Why don't you start with Sleepy, since she's the most patient?"

Lamar knelt down next to the dachshund–bassett hound mix. Sleepy lay on her side, lazy as ever and ready for a nap. Already starting to panic, Lamar looked at Justin. "How am I going to wash her?"

"Start with what you can reach." Justin drizzled a line of shampoo down Roamer's spine and began working it into his soaked coat. "She'll get up."

Lamar looked over at Justin and mimicked his actions. The teenager frowned at the dog's fur. "It's not lathering."

"Did you use shampoo? Or conditioner?" Justin asked, belatedly figuring out what had happened. It was an easy mistake to make—the white plastic bottles all looked the same. Only the labels were different.

"Oh. Conditioner, I guess."

"It's okay. Just rinse it out and pour on some shampoo."

Lamar seemed frazzled. It didn't help matters when Woof, who was still waiting his turn, began to bark hysterically.

"It's okay, Woof," Justin said firmly. "Calm down."

Reacting to the excited hound, Fetcher strained at her leash then took it between her teeth. Justin knew it wouldn't take much to chew through it and reprimanded the Labrador–golden retriever mix. "Fetcher, drop!"

Assuming they were involved in a tug-of-war, Fetcher pulled all the harder on the woven fabric lead. Anxiously, Woof intensified his barking and howling. Professor—the poodle–black Lab mix who hated chaos of any kind—began to look for a way out. Any way out.

"Fetcher! Stop!" Justin warned, reaching past Roamer to comfort Professor.

Meanwhile, apparently hating the feel of the shampoo on his back, Roamer rolled around on the deck, trying unsuccessfully to rub the soap out of his coat.

Realizing it would have been better to hook up two hoses, Justin waited while Lamar rinsed the foam off Sleepy.

Justin handed the teenager the appropriate bottle with one hand; with the other he worked to pry the leash out of Fetcher's teeth. "Condition next," he instructed.

Lamar frowned, perplexed. "I already did. Before I shampooed, remember?"

Justin grimaced as Fetcher clamped down harder on the leash and tugged with all her might. Meanwhile, Woof continued making a racket.

Justin had to shout to be heard over the growing commotion. "Condition *after* you shampoo!"

Professor, deciding he'd had enough of the ruckus, began yanking against his leash, using all his weight to pull free. Justin leaped to put a stop to that. Which was, as it turned out, all the opportunity Roamer needed. One jerk of the German shepherd–border collie's long elegant neck and he was out of his collar. Still covered with swirls of shampoo, Roamer left the dangling leash and collar behind, bounded over the backs of Woof and Sleepy and raced across the long veranda just as an unsuspecting Amanda rounded the corner.

One moment, Amanda was on her way to see what all the hubbub was about. The next, eighty-five pounds of wet black dog rammed her legs. The impact knocked her off her feet and sent her sprawling so hard onto the wooden floor of the deck that the wind was knocked from her lungs. Roamer splayed awkwardly over her, equally stunned by the collision. He whimpered and licked her face as if to make sure she was all right. Dimly, Amanda was aware the barking and howling had stopped. She blinked again and saw Justin hovering over her, his handsome face taut with concern. Then she noticed Lamar, who was apparently just as worried.

"Amanda!" Justin physically removed his still-confused dog who sat, suddenly compliant. "Are you okay?" he asked, kneeling down beside her.

Feeling a little better, but never comfortable as a damsel in distress, Amanda started to rise. Justin slid an arm around her waist and helped her into a sitting position. "I'm fine." She looked over at the half-bathed dogs, realizing why there had been so much commotion. She made a face. "You were bathing the dogs all at once?"

"It's what I usually do," Justin admitted defensively.

Lamar edged away, shoulders slumped, mouth tight. "Except this time I screwed it up."

Knowing the last thing the youth needed was another setback, Amanda shook her head and answered in the same tone her grandfather used when she needed bolstering, "No, you didn't. No one did." She paused to give the skeptical teen a long, level look. Then she smiled, letting both guys know she really was okay. "Dogs just get excited sometimes."

His hands still cupping her shoulders, Justin shot her an appreciative look that warmed her almost as much as his tender, protective touch.

"Do you have a dog?" Lamar asked, coming closer.

Amanda let Justin help her all the way to her feet. Realizing belatedly how soggy her T-shirt was, she plucked it away from her chest. She smelled like wet dog—as did the guys. "No. I always wanted one, though."

Lamar leaned down to pet the now-quiet circle of animals. He regarded her curiously, and the sense of near-familial intimacy between the three of them deepened. "Why didn't you get one, then?"

Amanda was aware that Justin was listening intently. "None of the adults in my life wanted to take responsibility, so I knew if I got a pet, I'd be completely on my own. I guess I was worried I'd let him or her down."

"You wouldn't do that," Lamar protested.

It was good to know someone thought so. Unfortunately, Amanda knew better than anyone that she was better at short-term relationships, in general, than anything requiring a lifetime commitment. Only with her grandparents had she been able to forge something lasting. And that hadn't happened until they had taken her in and put her on solid footing.

Lamar turned to Justin, not above pleading, "Maybe Amanda should help us finish giving the dogs a bath.

Then we could do her a favor by helping her with the carpentry."

Amanda didn't want to cut into Justin's time with Lamar. However, she *did* want to boost the teen's confidence. And, given the mess the two guys had made of the doggie baths, it was clear they needed help getting back on track. "Okay."

Justin blinked in shock at her quick acquiescence, which probably surprised him given the irate way she had walked out on him the evening before.

A little embarrassed that she had been so emotional last night—she could have just said no and left it at that—Amanda continued matter-of-factly, "I've got some heavy lifting that needs to be done, and I was headed over here anyway to see if I could borrow you both for an hour or so. Now I won't have to feel bad about asking since I'll be helping you fellas out first."

"We would have helped you anyway," Justin countered, in a way that let her know he was thinking about her curt refusal to *his* request for aid the night before.

Amanda refused to feel guilty about that. It had been a bad idea. It was still a bad idea.

She squared her shoulders and lifted her chin. "Yes, but this way we'll be even."

Lamar squinted at them. "Am I missing something?"

"No," Justin and Amanda said in unison, despite the chemistry sizzling between them.

Again, Lamar took note.

Wanting to move on, Amanda took a deep breath and asked Justin, "So which dog do you want me to bathe?"

Justin paused. "Probably better take Woof. Fetcher's still pretty rowdy."

No kidding, Amanda thought, watching her recommence rolling around on the deck as if wrestling an invisible opponent, her leash once again clamped in her teeth.

"I'll finish Roamer and then start on Fetcher," Justin continued, getting back down to work. "Whoever finishes first can handle Professor."

"So how long have you had your dogs?" Amanda inquired, picking up a bottle of shampoo.

"I adopted Sleepy and Woof when I was still living in Fort Worth and working at a nonprofit there. They came from a shelter. Professor and Fetcher came from families here in Laramie who thought they could handle having a pet and then discovered they couldn't." His voice thickened with emotion. "I found Roamer on the side of the road. He was painfully thin and infested with fleas and ticks. It looked like he had been driven out to the middle of nowhere, abandoned and forced to survive on his own."

Amanda's eyes filled just thinking about it. "That's awful."

Lamar's jaw clenched in youthful indignation. "How can people do that?" he asked fiercely. "When you adopt a dog—"

Or have a kid like Lamar, Amanda thought.

"—it's supposed to be a lifelong commitment!"

Only sometimes it wasn't, Amanda thought sadly. "I guess some people aren't cut out for that kind of responsibility." She waited for her turn with the hose, then wet Woof down and lathered shampoo into his fur.

Lamar became even more irate. "Well, you can count my parents in that tally," he muttered.

Deciding the only thing that would comfort Lamar was total honesty, Amanda confided, "And mine."

Lamar's jaw dropped. "You got ditched by your folks, too?"

Beside Amanda, Justin went very still. She realized these were the kinds of intimate details that Justin had wanted her to share with his dinner guests—to help them understand the plight of an abandoned child, from the child's perspective—and she had declined.

Having shared it once with a man she trusted, and suffered the fallout, she wanted to keep the miserable story to herself.

Yet, realizing it might make Lamar feel less alone to hear her story, Amanda forced herself to continue. "My parents divorced when I was two. I spent the next twelve years bouncing back and forth between their houses." She sighed heavily. "Both remarried and divorced, more than once, so to say it was chaotic is an understatement. I wasn't happy about it, and I showed my displeasure by acting out."

Lamar finished bathing Sleepy before turning his attention to the patiently waiting Professor. "How?"

Amanda shook her head in regret. "I skipped school. Shoplifted. Raided the liquor cabinet of a friend's parents'. Threw parties. Secretly sneaked out to movies I wasn't old enough to see." Out of the corner of her eye, she could see Justin listening intently.

"Wow." Lamar sounded impressed.

Amanda held up a cautioning hand. "It's not as glamorous as it sounds, Lamar. I came really close to ending up in juvie. Luckily, before that happened, I tried to run away. The local police found me and took me to the station, where I officially entered the system, and a sympathetic social worker decided I needed more stability than either of my parents were able or willing to give. She talked my grandparents into taking me in."

Amanda paused, remembering. "They had rules. Lots of them. I had to study for my GED and be respectful, help my grandmother around the house and work as Granddad's apprentice when I had any spare time."

Lamar reached for a bottle, paused, as if unable to decipher the labels. "And that was a good thing."

Noticing he needed the conditioner, Amanda handed it over, and was rewarded with a grateful smile. "Yep. For the first time in my life, I really felt safe. And loved. And cared for." She paused to towel off Woof, taking care to dry his face and ears before his body, just as she had seen Justin do.

That accomplished, she continued her story. "The point is, even though my parents couldn't handle me or my problems, I eventually ended up in a better place. I was happy." She paused to let her words sink in and saw Justin was a captive audience, too.

She turned away from Justin's tender expression. Swallowing, she pushed on. "Even more important, for the first time I saw what a good marriage looked like. It made me realize how important it is to marry the right person from the get-go."

Lamar turned to Justin, a question in his eyes. "Do you think that, too?"

Justin nodded as he toweled off Roamer. "Yes. My parents have a very strong and happy relationship." He smiled at Lamar then turned and caught Amanda's gaze. "Having that kind of love and commitment as a foundation makes for a very good marriage."

"And happy marriages," Amanda concluded softly, pleasantly surprised to find them all on the same page, "make happy families."

* * *

That evening, Justin offered to let Amanda do her wash in the laundry room at the lodge. Given that the alternative was driving into town to use the coin laundry, Amanda took him up on it. As she expected, he wandered in eventually to talk to her.

"Thanks for talking so frankly with Lamar today."

"No problem." Trying not to notice how handsome he looked with his skin bronzed from the summer sun, Amanda smiled.

Justin came closer, inundating her with the intoxicating scent of his cologne. "I had no idea you had such a rough childhood."

Amanda turned her eyes from the hard contours of his chest beneath his short-sleeved white polo shirt. Lower still, beneath the hem of his cargo shorts, were tanned, muscular legs. Covered with a light sprinkling of hair, one shade darker than the chestnut hair on his head, they hinted at just what fine shape he was in.

Mouth dry, Amanda forced a smile. When she leaned over to stuff another handful of lingerie into the washing machine, she ignored the way his eyes trailed over the lace. "It happens. People survive the bad stuff. They move on." She swallowed, giving in to the ever-present urge to take a good, long look at him.

He lounged against the dryer, arms folded in front of him. His lips took on a downward tilt. "Which, in my case, wasn't so hard. Since I had a great childhood."

She knew he was from one of the most powerful clans in Texas—the McCabe family—but that was all she'd been told. "Born with a silver spoon in your mouth?"

she quipped as she added a detergent suitable for delicate fabrics.

He watched her recap the bottle and set it aside. "Yes and no."

Amanda set the dials and started the machine. Enjoying the cool air of the lodge, she folded her arms across her middle. "You're either rich and pampered, bud, or you're not."

Justin grinned, the man in him responding to the womanly challenge in her. "I was well cared for, but I didn't have access to a lot of money. I had chores, the normal allowance for around here. Which made for plenty of incentive to go after a part-time job."

She wrapped her mind around that. "You worked when you were a student?"

His brilliant blue eyes continued to mesh with hers. "From the time I was fourteen."

"What did you do?"

He studied her for a long beat. "A lot of stuff, actually. I bussed tables at Sonny's Barbecue, took tickets at the movie theater, worked in a warehouse, loading boxes onto trucks." He exhaled. "My last two years of college, I got a part-time gig working in a CPA's office, which led to my first job after graduation with a big-ten accounting firm."

"Wow." Amanda became aware that this was beginning to feel more like a date than a casual conversation. "You are well-rounded."

The hint of a smile curved his lips, too. "And you…?"

"Never did anything but carpentry."

He inched closer. "As good as you are at that, you're also really great with kids. Especially the ones who haven't had it easy."

She stepped back. "It takes one to know one."

He stubbornly held his ground, gazing down at her. "It's more than that," he observed. "You have a natural ability to communicate. Just being near you seems to calm Lamar down."

Amanda shrugged. "You're good with him, too."

"Not as good as you."

She leaned against the washer and felt the vibration of the cycle against her spine. "It's not a competition, Justin."

"Good thing." He sighed in something akin to defeat. "Because if it were, no question, you'd win."

And that bothered him, Amanda noted. Probably because he wanted to excel at everything he did. Silence, and an aching awareness, stretched between them. Amanda felt compelled to remind him, "You know there are no perks that come with my presence here tonight or at any other time."

He nodded, accepting her boundary. For now, anyway. "How about we just be friends then?"

Amanda scoffed. Now who was kidding himself? She moved away from the vibrating machine. Looked him up and down. "You and I can't be just friends."

He lifted a dark brow. "Why not?"

Amanda was sure he knew, but she decided to demonstrate the pitfalls anyway. She smiled, gliding closer. Keeping her gaze locked with his, she said brazenly, "I'll show you why not."

Chapter 4

Amanda told herself she was just going to prove her point—that there was nothing real between them—when, truthfully, she wanted to satisfy the desire that had been building from the first moment she had set eyes on Justin McCabe.

It wasn't just that he was tall and strong, and rugged enough to make her feel all woman to his man. Or that he had a heart big as all Texas, a heart that would take in homeless dogs and kids who had lost their way.

It was the way Justin McCabe looked at her, as if she was all that he had ever wanted or dreamed he could have. It was the way he smiled at her, the protectiveness of his touch, the way he seemed to know exactly what she was thinking and feeling, that gave her the courage to rise up on tiptoe, wreathe her arms about his neck and press her lips to his.

It was, she thought wistfully, enough to make her close her eyes and revel in that first electric contact. To savor the intoxicating male taste of his lips, the heat and pressure of his kiss, and the feel of his body pressed intimately against hers.

He wanted her, too. She knew it. Felt it. Relished it. And that was why, more than anything, she had to break off the reckless embrace and pull away.

"Not so fast," Justin rasped, before she could even take a breath. Pulling her right back into his arms, he threaded his hand through her hair and lowered his lips to hers.

Justin had wanted to kiss Amanda for what seemed like an eternity; he just hadn't figured it would happen until the work on the ranch was complete.

However, her sexy move on him had changed all that, made it okay for *him* to kiss *her*. And kiss her he did, savoring the softness of her lips, the heat of her body, the womanly fragrance of her hair and skin. She was strong and lithe, beautiful and seductive, tender and kind. And he wanted her more than the rational part of him knew he should.

Which was why, when she broke off the kiss a second time he had to respect it. Had to lift his head and let her go. She was breathing hard—as was he. Her cheeks were pink, her lips damp. The sweet feminine scent of her dominated his senses.

"That," Amanda said, trembling with desire, "is why we can't be just friends. Because the physical attraction will get in the way."

He was willing to take it to the next level if she was. "So, maybe we should renegotiate our initial agreement…and be friends *and* lovers."

Amanda appeared amused but not really surprised by what he was proposing. "Lovers," she repeated in a whisper-soft voice. "You don't pull any punches, do you?"

Justin tucked a strand of silky blond hair behind her ear. "I'm honest about what I want, what I need."

Amanda released a quavering breath. "Then I will be, too." Her eyes narrowed. "And that won't work, either."

"Why not?"

She picked up her laundry basket and walked over to the dryer. "First, men with families like yours don't get involved with women from backgrounds like mine."

He watched her bend over and pull her clothes from the machine. "You underestimate me and my family."

"Second," she pushed on, "I'm not the kind of gal who can love someone, and leave him and *not* feel bad about breaking his heart."

He grinned at her joking manner and responded in kind. "What if I tell you my heart won't be broken?" he quipped, having an idea what it would feel like to be invited into her bed, and then, just a short time later, summarily kicked out. It would be disappointing as hell to be that close to heaven and then lose it all.

Amanda arranged the clothes in her basket so the frilly undies were beneath her plain T-shirts. "What if I tell you that mine will?"

Silence fell between them. She could tell by the expression flitting across his handsome face that he was weighing the truth behind her teasing words. "You have a lot going on here, Justin. A lot to accomplish in just a few weeks."

As if he didn't know that. He folded his arms across his chest. "It'll get done a lot faster with you here helping me."

"And then I'll be helping my granddad—and his company—by moving on to the next rural gig. I don't want to miss you when I'm gone. I don't want to miss—" she rose up on tiptoe and lightly kissed his lips "—this." Backing away again, she finished with an earnest look, "So it's better we just not start."

"How is the job going?" Granddad asked later that evening over the phone.

"Good." Amanda paced the length of her travel trailer. Usually she loved her cozy little space. Tonight, since she'd finished her laundry and brought it back to put away in her limited storage space, she felt trapped and hemmed in.

"You sound...stressed."

How well her grandfather knew her. "I'm just tired," she fibbed.

"McCabe treating you well?"

Amanda stepped outside into the muggy heat of the night and gazed up at the star-filled Texas sky. She looked over at the lodge. The lights in Justin's office were on. He was probably still working on all the paperwork for those grants.

She rubbed her temples and continued pacing, thinking about the sweet sensuality of his embrace and her passionate reaction to it. "He's a reasonable client." Never pushing her to work too hard. Always wanting her to spend more time with him—as friends. When what she wanted was...

"And?" Her grandfather prodded, sensing there was more.

Amanda struggled to describe Justin without betraying her growing feelings. "He's the kind of man who takes on impossible challenges and sees them through. The kind who never got sent to the principal's office when he was growing up."

"A real role model, hmm?"

She heard the caution in her granddad's tone and felt it, too. "It appears that way," she admitted, telling herself that Justin was not like Rob in any way. Judging by his work on the ranch, when Justin committed to something or someone, he would not back away simply to make his life easier.

"From what I can gather, he's held in high esteem throughout the community, too. Generous. Kind…"

Granddad chuckled. "The same could be said about you, honey."

Amanda felt her halo begin to slip. Her granddad might think she had grown up to be perfect, despite her teenage troubles. She knew otherwise.

"I'm sure Justin thinks you're amazing, too."

"At the moment, maybe," Amanda allowed with a sigh.

She couldn't help but think if she stayed around too long, she would do something that would demonstrate just how wrong she was for a guy like Justin.

She didn't want to see that look in his eyes, the one that said she'd let him down or somehow embarrassed him in front of his family. She didn't want to go back to feeling less than admirable. And the way to prevent that, she knew, was to stick to the tried and true. Her carpentry, life on the road, her devotion to her grandfather, and little more…

"But back to business," Amanda said, pushing her conflicted feelings aside. "How are things on your end, Granddad?"

"Busier than usual, that's for sure. I'll have to fill you in when you come home."

Amanda ducked back into the air-conditioned comfort of her trailer. "That sounds good." She let out a wistful sigh

Granddad paused; as always he read more of her thoughts than she would have liked. "You know, if you're tired of traveling, you could work here in San Angelo exclusively again."

She chuckled. "And miss out on all those high-paying gigs?" The ones that brought an extra cushion of solvency to the family business and made up for the overall loss of revenue as her grandfather made the transition into retirement.

"I understand why you took over for me after you ended your engagement to Rob, that you needed a change of scene," Granddad continued soberly. "But you don't have to keep running away."

Amanda harrumphed. This was an old argument, one neither of them was likely to win. "I'm not running away, Granddad."

"Mmm-hmm. When I was sixty-eight, I would have believed you. Now that I'm seventy, I know better."

She laughed out loud. Leave it to her granddad to make a joke to break the tension. "I do miss you, Granddad," she said fondly.

"Then how about you come home this weekend? Spend a day or two in San Angelo so we can really talk."

Knowing that "conversation" would end up being a full inquisition into her current situation, Amanda hedged, "I'll have to see how things go work-wise, but maybe I will." Leaving the ranch and Justin—if just for a night—could put everything into perspective.

On the other hand, maybe rushing through to the end of this job was the best way to go. The sooner she stopped seeing Justin every day, the sooner she would stop risking another kiss. The sooner she would stop fantasizing about him.

Aware that her grandfather was waiting for an answer, Amanda said, "I'll just have to see."

She heaved a sigh of relief when he agreed to leave it at that.

"I smell the bacon cooking, too, fellas," Justin told his canine companions at eight-thirty the next morning. "But you're out of luck because I don't have any to give you. And Amanda has not invited us to share."

All five dogs remained at the back door of the lodge, eyes looking up at him hopefully, tails wagging.

"We can't just barge in on her," Justin continued. "Especially since she started working before the sun was even up this morning and is now on a well-deserved meal break."

Professor whimpered with excitement. Roamer let out a short, demanding bark. Then Sleepy, overwhelmed with excitement, began to sniff and circle. "Oh, no," Justin said. That was all he needed—a hot mess on the mudroom floor.

Swiftly grabbing Sleepy's collar before the dog could squat, Justin ordered sternly, "All right, fellas, I'm letting you out, but you stay with me." He gave the dogs the hand signal to heel and opened the back door.

To his relief, they stayed by his side.

He led the way down the steps to the grassy area favored by the dogs. Sleepy immediately got down to business. Woof followed suit. Professor sniffed the air and sprinted off.

His four friends darted in pursuit.

Muttering under his breath, Justin raced after them.

He caught up just as they reached the door to Amanda's trailer, where the tantalizing smells of freshly cooked bacon, waffles and strong coffee abounded.

Woof let out a loud bark. Then another. The rest joined in, and suddenly it was like the inside of a kennel. Justin put two fingers between his teeth and let out a long, sharp whistle. "Sit!" he commanded.

The trailer door opened and Amanda stepped out. Damned if she wasn't a sight for sore eyes, with her butterscotch-blond hair swept into a clip on the back of her head, cheeks flushed pink and her eyes glinting with humor. She wore a hot pink T-shirt and cream-colored overall shorts that showcased her long, tanned legs. On her feet were the steel-toed construction boots she wore when she worked.

She smelled like breakfast and warm maple syrup. It was clear, from the empty plate in her hand, that she had just finished eating. She mugged affectionately at the dogs, who were now sitting patiently in a semicircle, begging for scraps. She smiled at them, then turned to Justin. "Everything under control as usual, I see."

Her teasing hit the mark. "No kidding," Justin retorted drily.

His lovable mutts couldn't seem to stay away from her any more than he could. Chuckling, Amanda went inside and came back with crisp slices of bacon. She broke them into pieces and tossed a section to each dog.

They downed it quickly, licked their chops and stared at her as if in love. Justin knew how they felt. There was something captivating about her. Something that made him want to stand here and talk with her all day.

"I called the heating and air-conditioning company," he said. "The unit they were waiting on finally came in. They'll be out to hook up the bunkhouse HVAC today, so starting tomorrow you'll be able to work in air-conditioned comfort."

"That's nice."

"I feel bad you've had to work in such blistering conditions."

"That's okay, I'm used to the heat…it's nothing I can't handle. But thanks for thinking of me. I'm sure Lamar will appreciate it, too. Though he hasn't complained, I know he's not as used to working in the sweltering temperatures as I am."

Curious, he moved closer. "Are you going to need his help today?"

She met his gaze. "If you can spare him, I'd love it."

Justin nodded. Beside him, the dogs continued to pant and look at Amanda adoringly. "I'll send him over to help you as soon as he arrives." Could this conversation get any more inane?

"Thank you." She paused as her next thought hit. "Have you had breakfast yet?"

He grinned. Now they were getting somewhere. "Does a bowl of cereal at dawn count?"

Her smile broadened. "Hang on." She slipped inside the trailer. Half a minute later she returned with a foil-covered plate and quarter-full bottle of maple syrup. Breakfast to go. Not exactly what he'd had in mind…

Amanda handed the food over, being careful not to touch him during the transfer. "This will make us even," she said cheerfully, "since you cooked me dinner the other night."

Justin would have preferred to be invited in, even for a few minutes. But it was clear that wasn't going to happen. Amanda had set the boundaries the night before. She was going to maintain them whether he wanted her to or not.

An hour later, Lamar had arrived and was hard at work helping Amanda. Justin was in his office compiling more data for the grant applications when he received a phone call from Libby Lowell-McCabe. She asked him to drive into town for a meeting at the Lowell Foundation offices, to discuss the particulars of the fund-raising dinner he was going to be hosting.

When Justin arrived, he was not surprised to see three of the Laramie Boys Ranch board members. They were a hands-on group. He greeted Miss Mim, the retired librarian and long-time community leader first, then social worker Mitzy Martin and finally Libby, the board's chairwoman.

Libby motioned for everyone to sit down then turned to Justin. "Do you want the good news first, or the bad?"

That was easy. "The good."

Libby smiled. "The guest list for the fund-raising dinner at the ranch is coming along nicely. We've got firm commitments from all the board members, plus reporters from the *Dallas Morning News* and the *Houston Chronicle,* and two TV news folks who are considering doing features on the ranch for their respective stations, as well as representatives from several major charitable foundations in Fort Worth and Corpus Christi."

Suddenly feeling the pressure mounting to make the event a success, Justin said, "So what's the bad news?"

"The only time we can get everyone together is Saturday evening."

Saturday. "As in tomorrow night?" Justin needed to make sure he understood.

Miss Mim lifted a hand. "We know it's short notice," she said quietly.

It wouldn't have been for any of them, Justin thought. The three women in the room could throw together a party on a moment's notice, and had done so plenty of times in the past year and a half as they toiled to turn the boys ranch from dream to reality.

"And probably very overwhelming for a guy," Mitzy Martin added kindly. "Which is why we're offering to do all the cooking and meal prep for you."

Irked to be thought of as incapable in any regard, Justin said, "That's not necessary. I can handle it."

Libby studied him. "You're sure? Because we really need the funds that publicity like this could bring in if we're going to expand the ranch anytime soon."

"I'll make sure all goes smoothly," Justin promised.

He and the three women talked some more about the event. They all approved his proposed menu. After Mitzy left to drive Miss Mim home, Justin stayed behind to talk to Libby. "How is the search going for counselors?"

Libby beamed. "We've located three husband-and-wife teams who would be perfect. I only wish we could build two more bunkhouses and hire them all."

So did Justin, but that would mean raising another million dollars, no easy feat. Especially since he had already donated the majority of his own inheritance to purchase the land and build the lodge. "What about the director position?"

Libby's expression grew conflicted, but she looked him in the eye. "We have a lot of qualified candidates with varied backgrounds. And we're looking at all of our options."

Which meant it probably wasn't going to be him. Disappointment knotted his gut. He leaned forward in his chair. "Am I still in the running?"

"Yes. Of course. You're the founder of the boys ranch, after all. If it weren't for you and your unwavering commitment—and the considerable funds you've put in—it wouldn't exist."

"And yet…?" Justin prodded, sensing there was something holding him back in their view.

Libby clasped her elegant hands together. "The board wants to make sure whoever holds the position can really relate to the kids and put him or herself in their shoes."

"Or in other words, you all think I won't be able to empathize enough with the kids to be effective."

Libby nodded reluctantly. "That pretty much sums it up, yes. I'm sorry, Justin."

First, Amanda basically—and erroneously—had told him he was out of her league, and now this. Justin wasn't sure he wanted to know what was next.

Amanda wasn't sure what had happened with Justin at the board meeting in town. All she knew for certain was that his expression was unusually pensive when he walked into the bunkhouse kitchen to resume supervision of Lamar.

"So what do you think?" Lamar asked Justin proudly.

Justin surveyed the unfinished store-bought cabinets, butcher-block countertops and newly laid wood floor. All had been perfectly leveled and installed with Lamar's help.

Eagerly, the teen stepped back to point out, "Adding the crown molding really makes the cabinets look a lot fancier, don't you think?"

Justin studied the clean, elegant edges and turned back to Lamar with approval. "You guys did a really nice job. The whole thing looks custom-built."

"Or at least it will when we get everything stained and varnished," Amanda said with a smile.

Justin smiled back at her. "So what's next?" he asked, coming nearer.

"We'll build the bookcases and wall lockers in each of the bedrooms. And of course we'll make sure those are nicely trimmed, too. Then we'll add the cabinets to all the bathrooms."

Justin's eyes locked on hers. "Can you have at least one bedroom and bath done by Saturday evening?"

It would be pushing it, but since it seemed so important, Amanda nodded. "Sure," she said. "Although nothing will be varnished yet."

"That's okay." One corner of his mouth quirked as he turned back to Lamar. "I'm going to need some extra help tomorrow for a fund-raising dinner, here at the ranch. I know it's Saturday, typically you get that time off, but I would appreciate it if you could help out with the preparations, serving and cleanup. Of course, any hours you put in will count toward your community service."

Justin's tone was amenable, yet Lamar was wary. Probably, Amanda thought, because he worried he would be out of his element and end up falling flat on his face.

"What exactly would I have to do?" Lamar asked nervously.

Justin either missed or chose to ignore the teen's unease. "A little of everything, probably." He brushed off further questions, assuring, "We'll figure it out as we go."

Famous last words, Amanda thought.

"In the meantime—" Justin paused to check his phone and punch in something on his keyboard "—I've got to get a list together and go back into town to buy groceries. I need your help for that, too." He slid his phone back into his pocket.

Lamar dug in his heels. "I'm helping Amanda," he protested.

Realizing that tempers were about to flare once again, Amanda put a soothing hand on the teen's shoulder. "It's okay, Lamar. I'm just going to be measuring and cutting wood this afternoon. There's still plenty for you to help me with the next few weeks, when Justin doesn't need you to assist him."

Lamar relaxed beneath her maternal touch and reluctantly acquiesced. Justin smiled with relief and the two guys strode off. Fifteen minutes later, they got into Justin's truck and drove away.

Amanda went back to work.

While they were gone, she wondered how it was going.

She found out when they returned.

The moment Justin cut the motor, Lamar stormed out of the pickup and started for Amanda.

Justin followed. "Lamar. Come back here."

As out of control as Justin was in control, Lamar spun around to shout, "Why should I? You don't want me around. Admit it! You're just doing this 'cause you have to, same as me!"

"You're wrong about that, Lamar," Justin replied.

But, Amanda could see, Lamar didn't believe him. In fact, wouldn't have believed anyone at that point.

All five dogs, who had been hanging out on the porch of the lodge, stood and came forward, tails at half-mast. They seemed to be as concerned about Lamar's upset state as Amanda. She took off her goggles and gloves, set them on the table and walked toward the guys. "How about I give you fellas a hand? I imagine there's a lot of stuff to unload."

When Lamar looked over at her, the fight seemed to seep out of him. He ducked his head and moved for the truck's rear doors.

There were a lot of groceries, Amanda noted. Cases of sparkling water, soda and tea. Butcher-paper-wrapped meat. Four gourmet pies from the Sugar Love bakery. Fresh vegetables, fruits and herbs. Together, the three of them carried everything in and set it on the counter.

Lamar still wouldn't look Justin in the eye. "Now can I take a break?" he bit out before Justin could say anything more. "I didn't even have lunch, you know!"

At that, Justin looked completely taken aback.

Once again, Amanda felt compelled to intervene. She placed a comforting arm around Lamar's thin shoulders, not sure why, just knowing the kid brought out the mother in her. "I've got some sandwiches already made in the fridge in my trailer," she told the teen lightly, noticing he was near tears and struggling to hide it. "Why don't you go cool off and help yourself to a few of those? There are chips and apples, too."

Lamar's grateful expression reminded her just how

downtrodden he was. "Thanks, Amanda." He pivoted and left the lodge, pausing only long enough to pat the dogs on the porch before crossing the lawn.

Amanda turned back to Justin, sensing he needed comforting, too. "I'm assuming you didn't have lunch, either," she remarked drily.

Broad shoulders slumping, he scrubbed a hand over his eyes. "You're right. I didn't."

"We could take care of the stuff here, wait a minute and then both go over and join Lamar."

He exhaled and shot her a gruff look. "I appreciate the way you're able to calm Lamar down, but you don't have to take care of us."

It was the first time he'd rebuffed her help. She found it—and him—oddly fascinating. Unable to help herself, she stepped closer. "I do if I want to coexist in peace." She emptied produce from a bag. "What happened at the store, anyway?"

Justin grimaced. "I wrote out a list for Lamar of stuff I figured would be easy to find." Justin reached into the pocket of his jeans and brought out a crumpled-up piece of paper. "Another for me, with the harder stuff, like fresh basil."

That sounded fine. "And then?"

"We each took a cart and then...nothing." Justin opened the fridge and set the meat on a shelf, the vegetables in the crisper. "I'm done with my list, and I look around...and where is he?" Justin continued, clearly exasperated. "The magazine rack, looking at motorcycles!"

Amanda stepped in to hand Justin the rest of the refrigerator items. "He didn't get anything on the list?" she asked in dismay.

"Nope." Justin shook his head. "Not a single item. He didn't even have his basket with him anymore."

Unable to understand this—Lamar was always so helpful when he was with her—Amanda scrunched up the plastic bags and put them in the recycling container. "What did he say when you asked him about it?"

Justin lounged against the counter, arms folded in front of him, his big body simmering with pent-up frustration. "That he's no good at grocery shopping and shouldn't be required to do it."

That sounded like the contemptuous, passive-aggressive kid who had been sentenced to community service. Eager to hear the entire story, Amanda settled next to Justin. "And you said?"

"I'll help you. We'll start with the olive oil and the butter." Justin shook his head. "But he wouldn't cooperate there, either. Wouldn't even give a half effort. All he would do is stand in front of whatever shelf I directed him to, and look at the packages, and sometimes pick something. Never, of course, what we were looking for."

Amanda wished she could reach out and comfort Justin without it being misconstrued. "He was probably just angry because you reprimanded him in public."

Glance narrowing, Justin met her gaze. "I wasn't reprimanding him. I was just trying to get him back on task."

Amanda chided, "Trust me. People know when you're not happy." He had a very expressive face, very expressive eyes, a very willful nature. Only right now, that strong will wasn't helping.

Justin winced and scoured a hand over his jaw. He hadn't shaved yet today. The resulting stubble gave him a very rugged, masculine look she itched to explore.

Mistaking the reason for her silence, he finally muttered, "I suppose you could have done a better job?"

She wasn't about to lie, but didn't want to rub it in, either. "That's really not the point, is it?" She gave him a long, level look. "You're the one running this ranch."

"For now." Frown lines bracketed his sensual lips. He came another step closer. "It may not be for much longer, if I can't even get through to one kid in need."

"Give it time," Amanda advised. "In the meantime, try an apology. Trust me on this, Justin. A few kind words of compassion can work wonders."

Justin gathered her close. He wrapped both his arms around her middle. "For me, too," he admitted in a low voice.

His mouth was so close she could feel the heat of his breath on her forehead. "What do you mean?"

He rubbed his thumb across her lower lip, tracing its shape. His eyes took on a sexy shimmer. "It helps having you here with me. More than you know."

The tenderness of his voice obliterated her defenses even more. "Justin—"

He tunneled his hands through her hair and lifted her face to his. The sound of his husky laughter warmed her heart. "Just one kiss, Amanda. That's all I'm asking." He gave her no chance to refuse.

At the first touch of his lips to hers, Amanda splayed her hands across his chest. She swore to herself she wasn't going to yield to temptation, but before even a second had gone by, her lips had parted under the seductive pressure of his. Her knees weakened and her heartbeat sped up. Wild longing swept through her. And suddenly she was kissing him back with all the wonder and affection in her heart. By the time the possessive caress ended, she was tingling from head to toe. And worse, on the verge of falling harder and faster for Justin than she ever dreamed possible.

Scared by what that could mean, she pushed away from the unyielding hardness of his body. "Justin. We can't do this."

He frowned, perplexed, then reluctantly stepped back.

"You have to concentrate on helping Lamar now," Amanda reiterated firmly. "And nothing else."

As much as he hated to admit it, Justin knew that Amanda was right. The main goal was to make Lamar feel good about himself, to put him in situations where he would thrive, not struggle. Ashamed he had lost sight of that, even for a short while, Justin went in search of the boy.

In not acting swiftly enough, he had failed Billy. He would not do the same to Lamar.

Luckily, it didn't take Justin too long to find the missing teen. He was sitting in Amanda's trailer, all five canines sprawled on the floor at his side. A half-eaten sandwich and a nearly full bag of chips was spread out on the table. For someone who had professed to be starving, he didn't appear to have much of an appetite. "Got room for one more?" Justin asked.

Lamar just looked at him and sulked.

Justin slid into the banquette across from him, ready to do what he hadn't done before. "I'm sorry if I was a little short with you back at the store," he said sincerely.

"Yeah, well," Lamar admitted reluctantly, "I probably should have tried a little harder to find some of that stuff, even if I didn't know what half of it was."

Justin took the admission for the peace offering it was. He helped himself to a chip. "That's good to hear. But you need to know that my grouchiness had nothing to do with you. I was ticked off because the ladies on the board of directors don't think I can pull off this party because I'm a man, and I realized when I was in there, trying to buy all this stuff, that they're probably right."

He retrieved a sandwich from Amanda's fridge and sat down to unwrap it. "The truth is, I don't know what I'm doing. I mean, I can cook guy food till the sun comes up. But a dinner party?" Justin forced himself to take a bite. He swallowed and squinted at Lamar. "As much as I hate to admit it, they're right. I am out of my league. Way out of my league."

Lamar picked up his sandwich and began to eat. "Then why do it?"

"Because if I don't, I won't get the job I want, and I really want to be the director of the Laramie Boys Ranch."

"Why?"

"Because I know I have what it takes to run the place and help kids just like you. And I want to be given the chance to try."

Lamar munched on his sandwich and thought about that for a long moment. "They really said you couldn't do this because you were *a guy?*"

"Yep."

Lamar slammed a palm on the table. "Well, that's just *wrong.*"

Justin chuckled, aware this was the first time in his life he'd been subject to gender discrimination. On the job, anyway. "My opinion exactly."

Lamar went to the fridge. He took out two apples

and tossed one to Justin. "I don't know a lot about that stuff, either, but I can probably learn." He sat down opposite Justin. "I mean, heck, I'm learning carpentry pretty quick."

Justin polished off his sandwich and started on his apple. "You sure are."

Lamar leaned forward enthusiastically. "Just tell me what you need, and I'll do my best to deliver. And Justin? Thanks for apologizing." Lamar swallowed, seeming suddenly emotional. "It means a lot to hear someone besides me say 'I'm sorry.'"

Amanda was back at work when she saw Lamar and Justin come out of the trailer a short time later. One look at their body language told her they were no longer at odds. Consequently, Lamar assisted Justin at the lodge for the rest of the day. Relieved that things seemed to be going better, Amanda kept to herself, working late into the evening. Given how long the lodge lights were on Friday night, Justin was burning the midnight oil, too, getting ready for the fund-raiser.

She was tempted to pop in and see how things were going, but mindful of her refusal to be drafted into catering and cohosting duties by a man she found extraordinarily attractive, she stayed away.

Justin, she was sure, would do fine without her. And if he didn't, it really wasn't her problem. Even if it inexplicably *felt* like her problem...

Eventually, she went to sleep, only to dream of Justin, and the kiss they had shared, all night long. Frustrated, and knowing she couldn't allow it to happen again or she really would fall hard for him, she got out of bed and started her day early.

Lamar was back bright and early Saturday morning.

On track to finish building one bookcase and wall-mounted wooden locker as promised, Amanda labored in the bunkhouse all morning. Lamar hosed down the porch, cut and edged the grass, and could be seen going in and out of the lodge all day long. Justin did not appear.

At five, she had completed the installation of the bathroom cabinets, and was finished for the day. Not sure what she was going to do during the fund-raising party—maybe go into town, see a movie or drive to San Angelo and see her grandfather—she headed for her trailer and a quick shower.

She had just put on clean clothes and run a comb through her hair, when she heard footsteps outside her trailer. "Amanda!" Lamar pounded on her door, his voice frantic. "It's an emergency! You've got to come quick!"

Chapter 5

Amanda raced after Lamar, her heart pounding. The dogs were running back and forth across the deck at the rear of the lodge. The unpleasant smell of something burning scented the air. "What happened?"

"You'll see." Lamar darted up the steps. Amanda followed him through the lodge and into the kitchen.

A grim-faced Justin stood next to the stove. In front of him were two big charred pieces of still-smoking meat. Aghast, Amanda could only stare.

His expression hardened. "I didn't hear the timer go off."

"Now what are we going to do?" Lamar cried, acting as if this were a disaster of the first magnitude.

"What we're *not* going to do is panic." Amanda turned back to Justin, who was still standing there looking like he wanted to punch something. Preferably himself.

"How long before guests arrive?"

His dark gaze got even darker. "Less than an hour."

Still shoving his hands through his hair and racing back and forth, Lamar reported, "And the main part of dinner is all burned!"

Amanda knew how much was riding on this—for the ranch, the prospective kids and Justin personally. Not to mention the fact that Lamar needed a "win."

"Now, now, let's stay calm," she soothed, moving closer to inspect the charred beef. Her many years in the kitchen had given her lots of experience in fixing unexpected culinary mishaps. Ignoring Justin's bleak expression, she switched on the exhaust over the stove. "Lamar, can you open a few windows and go to the bunkhouse and bring in one of the big floor fans? We've got to get the smoky smell out of here."

"Sure." Glad to be part of the solution, Lamar dashed off, opening windows in the dining area as he went.

His body tense with disappointment, Justin opened the heavy window above the kitchen sink and then turned to her. "Look, I appreciate you coming over," he told her, with a shake of his head. "But there's nothing you can do to rescue this. It's my screwup. I'll be accountable."

A wave of unexpected empathy wafted through Amanda. This was one time when her history of cleaning up after her own failures, of which there were many, would come in handy. One time when she could show Justin a thing or two...

Refusing to be dragged down by his sour mood, she mugged at him playfully. "Oh, ye of little faith!" She cut a deep slit in the center of the scorched beef tenderloin and checked out what was left. "See?" She elbowed him, prompting him to look. "Inside, the meat is still quite edible. All we have to do is cut off the burned part and see what we have to work with."

Justin reluctantly stripped down one hunk of charred beef, while she did the other. By the time they had finished cutting off the barklike crust, they had a good two pounds of nice, tender high-quality beef that smelled as if it had done time in a smoker, not such a bad thing when it came to Southwestern-style cuisine.

Justin studied the remains and rubbed a hand across the tense muscles at the back of his neck. He saw the value in salvaging the edible meat. "Unfortunately, that's not enough to feed fourteen people."

Amanda set the burnt pieces aside for later disposal. "It is if we turn it into something else, like beef barbacoa enchiladas."

Justin gave her a steady look that sent heat spiraling through her. She had the feeling that if the situation hadn't been so dire he would have swept her off her feet and kissed her. Suddenly, hope glimmered in his eyes. "Do you know how to make that?"

Amanda pushed aside her earlier decision not to get involved with this dinner. The future of the ranch—which could help a lot of boys like Lamar—was at stake. She thought about all the times she and her gran had cooked for her granddad and his buddies when they gathered to play poker or watch sports on TV. "I do. Plus, I have all the ingredients we need in my kitchen."

While Justin worked on shredding the beef into bite-size pieces, Amanda and Lamar strode back to her trailer. They returned with their arms full of groceries and two large glass baking pans. Using dried chiles and chicken stock, she quickly whipped up a red sauce.

While Lamar stirred the bubbling sauce, she softened the tortillas and diced two onions. She showed both guys how to put a spoonful of meat into the center of the softened tortilla, and add a teaspoon of onion, before rolling them and putting them seam-side down in the baking pan. She covered the rolled enchiladas with the red sauce and a sprinkling of crumbled *queso fresco*.

"What are we going to serve with it, though?" Justin asked.

Good question. "What were you going to have?"

"Roasted vegetables." Justin pulled baking sheets out of the fridge, and showed her the sliced squash, zucchini, onions and baby carrots, all ready to cook. "And field greens with buttermilk dressing."

"That's all good. It'll work nicely with the enchiladas."

Justin breathed a sigh of relief, as did Lamar. Amanda smiled. Whether the two guys knew it or not, they really were becoming a team.

"Any appetizers?" she asked.

Justin opened up the fridge again. He brought out several nicely prepared serving platters. On them were water crackers with blue cheese and walnut spread, stuffed mushrooms—which had yet to be baked—and chilled shrimp with cocktail sauce.

"All would have been perfect as a prelude to beef tenderloin," Amanda observed thoughtfully.

"That's what the book on entertaining said." Justin paused. "But none of that goes with enchiladas, does it?"

"Let me think." Amanda studied the repast. "The shrimp will be okay if we add a little lime juice and cilantro to the cocktail sauce. We can quickly make fresh guacamole and *pico de gallo* to top the water crackers, or substitute chips for the crackers, if you prefer. What's in the stuffed mushrooms?"

"Cream cheese, breadcrumbs." Justin looked at Lamar, who dutifully supplied, "Other stuff…"

Amanda laughed. When Justin produced the recipe, she glanced at it. "I think this will probably be okay." It wasn't Southwestern, but it was neutral enough in flavor to accompany the spicier dishes.

"So we're good?" Justin asked.

Amanda nodded. "I think so."

With less than twenty minutes to go before the guests arrived, Lamar chopped up the burned meat and carried it out to the dogs, who were delighted with their savory treat. Justin worked on cleaning up the lodge kitchen, and Amanda returned to her trailer to prepare the *pico de gallo* and guacamole.

By the time Justin came over to assist, she was done. Noting once again how small and intimate her space seemed with the big, handsome Texan in it, she handed him large bowls of both dips, along with a fresh bag of tortilla chips. With a tingle of awareness sifting through her, Amanda gulped in a bolstering breath and kept her mind on his goal—which was to entertain successfully that evening.

She flashed a brisk smile, meant to demonstrate just how emotionally uninvolved she was. "Here you go. You should be all set. Oh! And I wrote down the temperature and time for the enchilada bake. You'll want it to finish about ten minutes before you plan to serve the main course, so it will have time to set."

A mixture of tenderness and gratitude dominated his handsome features. "I don't know how to thank you."

Aware she had to find the strength to keep her guard up now that the crisis was averted, she swallowed and moved away. "I realize this was a singular occurrence."

He tracked her with his eyes. "It doesn't have to be."

Oh, how she wished that were the case.

The sound of a car motor—make that multiple motors—could be heard coming up the driveway.

"I hope it goes well."

Justin caught her wrist. "Come to dinner."

A jolt of electricity coursed through her as his warm fingers grazed her skin. But, out of an increasing need for self-preservation, she slipped from his light, beseeching grasp and stepped away. She held the door open for him to exit her trailer. "I couldn't."

Reluctantly, he moved to leave, strong arms full. "Even as my guest?"

Amanda knew he wanted her there. Obviously, as culinary backup, to help with the dinner. To make sure all went smoothly with the rest of the cooking and serving. And yes, he was grateful for her assistance and happy with her now. But one day, he might not be. Especially if his family—who were pillars of the community— did not approve of him getting involved with a woman from the wrong side of the tracks.

"You have to go," she said urgently, telling herself that if they were lucky they could one day be casual friends. And only casual friends.

Justin gave her another look that indicated there would have been a lot more persuading on his part were the guests not already parking their cars and trucks. Then they heard the sounds of doors slamming, voices filling the air.

"And good luck tonight." Amanda would be thinking of him—and Lamar—whether she wanted to or not.

Amanda was trying to figure out how to make her getaway—not an easy feat since the driveway was filled with a dozen vehicles—when her cell phone rang. She picked up, happy for the distraction. The last thing she needed to be doing was standing here thinking about how it would have felt to be Justin's cohost—or date—on an evening such as this. "Hey, Granddad." Amanda smiled.

"Hey there yourself, sweetheart," A.B.'s voice rumbled over the phone. "I haven't heard a lot from you the past few days, so I thought I'd check in, see how the job is going."

"Oh. Great," Amanda was able to say truthfully.

"You need any more help? I can always come out to assist."

Amanda knew that bored tone. Her grandfather was feeling hemmed in. Unfortunately, there'd been a role reversal in their relationship. Now, she was the one looking out for him. "Doc Parsons said no more traveling jobs, remember? You're supposed to be phasing into retirement. Which means you can continue to *run* your business as long as you don't do the carpentry work, too!"

"Yeah, yeah, yeah…" Granddad harrumphed. Moving on, as always, when the talk got too uncomfortable, he said, "So, you're good?"

Was she? Talk about a loaded question! How all right could a woman be when she spent all her private time yearning for a man who was off-limits to her? But leery of letting her granddad know that, Amanda adapted her usual cocky attitude. "I'm fine. That foster kid I told you about is helping me part of the time."

"How is he working out?"

"Nicely," she reflected fondly. "Lamar seems to have a natural talent for carpentry."

"Maybe you can recruit him to apprentice with you, once he graduates from high school."

If Lamar graduated from high school, Amanda thought. To her grandfather, she admitted, "I've been thinking the same thing."

"Then?"

"I'll talk to him about it when the time is right."

"Everything else okay?"

She felt herself getting defensive. "Why wouldn't it be?"

"You tell me. I have a feeling you've got something on your mind."

Make that some*one,* Amanda thought, looking out her trailer window and watching the guests move from the lodge over to the bunkhouse, en masse, the dogs bringing up the rear. Finally, she said in the most off-hand manner she could manage, "There's a fund-raising thing going on at the ranch tonight."

"Ah." A.B. knew how uncomfortable things like that made her, especially when they involved the movers and shakers of Texas society.

"If you need a break, why not do what I suggested earlier and come on home tonight? I've already made plans to go out and play poker this evening, but we could have breakfast tomorrow. Maybe see a movie in the afternoon."

That sounded good. Anything to get her mind off Justin. And Lamar. And whether or not this dinner would help raise the funds the ranch so desperately needed to continue expanding.

The truth was, she missed her grandfather. Missed his steady, reassuring presence. Amanda smiled, already feeling better. "Okay, Granddad, I will. I'll see you later, okay?"

"Travel safe." A.B. ended the call.

She slid her cell phone into her purse. She'd just found her keys when a rap sounded on her door. It was Lamar. He was grinning from ear to ear this time, clearly in the flush of victory. "Amanda! You've got to come over to the bunkhouse and tell them all about the stuff you've been teaching me. The reporters especially are really impressed."

Amanda could have passed on the opportunity to sing her own praises, but she wasn't about to let Lamar lose the chance to feel good about himself and what he had accomplished. She looked down at her sleeveless navy blouse, knee-length khaki walking shorts and flats. Thought about changing into something more on par with the dresses and sport coats the guests were all wearing, and decided what the heck. She was who she was. And she wasn't a guest. There was no sense in pretending she was one of them.

She set her purse, phone and keys aside, and walked out with Lamar.

"And Lamar helped you with all of this?" Wade McCabe asked, clearly impressed, as he and the other guests examined the quality of the kitchen cabinet installation.

Glad Wade seemed to be coming around to what his son was trying to accomplish here, Amanda nodded.

She had seen how much it meant to Justin to have his father's approval. "Lamar also helped cut and add the trim that gives the cupboards a more custom look. And, of course, all the woodwork in the bunkhouse will be finished with stain and a finish that will feel silky to the touch."

"I'm going to help with that, too," Lamar proclaimed. Catching himself, he said, "That is, if Amanda agrees."

Catching Mitzy's knowing glance, Amanda smiled and added hastily, "I'd welcome the help if it's okay with the boss."

She didn't want anyone—especially the social worker in charge of Lamar's case—thinking she was undercutting Justin's supervision of the teenager.

Justin nodded his approval. "As far as I'm concerned, the more Lamar learns, the better." His customary confidence back, he winked at Amanda. "Especially since he has such a great teacher."

"I have a great student," she replied. Lamar beamed. The group was all smiles as they headed back toward the ranch house.

Libby fell into step beside Amanda. "Have dinner with us," she urged.

Amanda looked at the chairwoman of the board. "Thank you." She appreciated the sincere invitation. "But I'm really not dressed."

Libby glanced at her own cotton sheath, then back at Amanda's knee-length shorts and blouse. "Nonsense! You look great. And if we're to make this ranch all it can be, we really need your input, as well as Lamar's."

Justin wasn't surprised that Amanda had been asked to dine with them. He'd issued the same invitation for all the same reasons. He was surprised she agreed, but once she did Lamar felt comfortable enough to join them, as well.

Both fielded a lot of questions throughout the meal. Amanda talked about learning the art of carpentry. Lamar discussed how much he liked being at the ranch and learning a trade that might someday turn into a job. The ranch was *much* different than school.

There, it was all about grades, the future and the pressure to get stuff done. At the ranch, when he was with Amanda, it was all about being in the moment. He admitted he was hoping Justin would let him keep on working there, even after his community service was finished.

Justin spoke about their plans to expand the facility one bunkhouse at a time. Costs were discussed next. Justin detailed the various ways they had been able to limit building and construction expenses, without sacrificing comfort or quality.

By the time the reporters and most of the board members, including his father, had left, Justin was certain the project would be getting positive press, as well as donations from the charitable foundations present that evening. Best of all, he'd begun to feel like he could finally put what had happened with Billy completely behind him.

The board members were pleased, too.

"I can't tell you how happy I am to see you doing so well here," Mitzy remarked to Lamar as she helped to clear away the dessert dishes.

Libby nodded agreement. "I never saw the 'before' attitude, but you are obviously thriving in your community service here."

"It's pretty easy with Amanda—and Justin—around," Lamar said shyly.

"That's good to hear." Mitzy put the plates in the dishwasher and smiled again. "Dinner was great, by the way. Although I am curious." She turned to Justin. "Why did you change your mind about the menu? We thought you were cooking whole beef tenderloins."

"He was until he screwed up and burned the meat," Lamar blurted out. "But then Amanda saved the day and showed us how to make enchiladas and change around the other stuff so it would go with it, and... Uh-oh." Lamar turned pale. "Was I not supposed to say that?"

Justin held up a hand, not the least bit upset. "Lamar's right," he said. "Amanda did save the day."

Flushing self-consciously, Amanda shook off the praise. "It wasn't that big a deal."

Justin was determined to give her the accolades she deserved. "Nonsense." He turned to their two remaining guests. "Dinner would have been a disaster had Amanda not stepped in at the last minute to help us."

Libby and Mitzy exchanged approving smiles. "Well, then, thank you again for being so charitable," Libby told Amanda.

She wished more credit was going to Justin—after all, he was the one who had founded the ranch and worked so hard to make it happen. "I'm all for good causes. And the boys ranch is definitely one of them."

The cleanup and conversation continued until almost midnight.

Still chattering about how much he loved the ranch, Lamar hitched a ride back to town with Mitzy and Libby.

Justin and Amanda were alone once again.

Which, considering how attracted she was to the evening's host, was perhaps not such a good thing.

Taking a deep breath, she stepped away from the driveway and onto the grass.

A full moon and stars shone in the velvety-dark Texas sky, and a warm summer breeze blew across their bodies. It couldn't have been a more romantic setting, which was why, Amanda knew, she had to bid the handsome man beside her adieu.

She slid her hands into the pockets of her shorts, broke away from the quiet intensity of his gaze and took off in the direction she needed to go. "I better head back to my trailer."

Justin caught up with her in three quick strides. He slid a protective hand beneath her elbow. "Let me walk you."

She tingled at the protectiveness of his touch. For both their sakes, she eased away. "Really," she reiterated firmly, working hard to keep their mutual attraction at bay. "It isn't necessary."

This time he kept his distance, even as he walked companionably beside her. "I know that." He sent her a gallant look. "I want to do it."

They continued across the grass. It felt like the end of a date. It wasn't a date. She had to remember that. Struggling to maintain her composure, Amanda looked up at him as they reached her trailer. "I know you're grateful for my help this evening…" she began.

He tilted his head to one side. "Very grateful." His voice slid over her like a caress.

"But it doesn't mean anything other than I was being neighborly," Amanda insisted.

His gaze swept over her before returning with patient deliberation to her eyes. "Good to know."

It astounded her, realizing how much she yearned to kiss—and make love—with him. "So…?"

Tenderness glimmered in his expression. "It still means a lot to me. You were a huge help tonight with the fund-raising."

"I didn't do anything other than tell the truth."

His lips took on a seductive curve. "Then how about telling it now?"

Amanda lifted her chin, her heart thudding in her chest. She ignored the tingling sensation in her middle. "I don't know what you mean."

"Yes, Amanda, you do."

Amanda glanced at him, trying to figure out how to persuade him otherwise. Inside the trailer, her phone rang. She frowned and looked at her watch. At this hour, there was only one person it would be. "Hang on. I've got to get that."

She stepped inside her trailer and picked up her cell phone. "Hi, Granddad. Um, no." She paused, listening. "It's a long story. Suffice it to say, I got distracted working on something here, and before I knew it time got away from me." She paused again, aware Justin could probably hear every word she was saying. "Um, I don't think so. How about I call you tomorrow? Yes."

She said goodbye to her grandfather and walked back outside. Justin was standing, legs apart, hands braced on his waist, surveying the ranch. The quintessential cowboy. Only he wasn't a cowboy. And he didn't have a hat.

He pivoted to her, concern etched on the rugged planes of his face. "Everything okay?"

Wondering what it would be like to come home to a

man like him every night for the rest of her life, Amanda said, "That was my grandfather. I had told him I was going to drive to San Angelo this evening and spend the rest of the weekend with him. Only…"

"You got caught up helping me."

Amanda breathed in, wishing Justin didn't smell and look so damn good. "Right."

"Are you going to see him tomorrow?"

"I'm not sure."

"You've got the day off."

It wasn't that. It was that the moment Granddad saw her, and asked her even a few questions, he would know she had feelings for Justin. And since her grandfather had no qualms about inserting himself into her love life, particularly if he thought she needed protecting…

Emotion roiled through her. She did not want the situation getting any more uncomfortable than it already was. "I'll think about it, okay?"

Justin watched her, as if knowing she was still keeping a lot more to herself than she was telling him.

"Anyway, back to what we were talking about…" Amanda started.

His irises darkened to the color of midnight as he listened intently to what she had to say.

"Just because we worked well as a team tonight, and have done a pretty good job getting Lamar back on track, doesn't mean we should read anything else into it."

The air was suddenly still enough to hear a pin drop. "Like attraction," he said.

Their gazes collided. "Right."

He moved subtly closer and flashed her a grin,

all confident male. "Except I am attracted to you, Amanda."

And not afraid to face it.

She held up a staying hand. "And I'm attracted to you, too, Justin, but…"

Slowly, purposefully, his eyes locked on hers, he invaded her personal space. "But what?" he asked huskily.

She shivered when his hands lightly cupped her shoulders. "But there's a lot more than the physical component to a relationship, and I want a relationship, Justin." She lifted her chin. "The kind that lasts."

He lifted his broad shoulders. "So do I." His voice was silky-soft, contemplative. And somehow dangerous in a deeply sensual way.

Panic welled, along with desire. Ignoring the fluttering of her pulse, she advised coolly, "Then you should pick more wisely."

Justin used his leverage on her to bring her closer still. Smiling, he said, "I am."

Chapter 6

Amanda knew it was a mistake to get so involved with Justin and this ranch when she was only going to be here a short time. It was an even bigger folly to let herself get emotionally attached to him. But she couldn't seem to help it. Whenever he looked at her that way, touched her, took her face into his hands and bent down and kissed her, all her resistance fled.

Her heart was wide-open. And what her heart wanted, she reluctantly admitted to herself, was him.

Amanda followed his lead and opened her mouth to the insistent, warm pressure of his. He kissed her again, harder, deeper. She moaned as his tongue swept the inside of her mouth. Another ribbon of desire unfurled inside her. Eager for more, she wrapped her arms around his shoulders and clasped him to her.

He pinned her against the side of the trailer, his body

hard and muscular and hot. So hot. Something unexpectedly wanton was unleashed inside her. She moaned again and he continued kissing her with that mixture of confidence and tenderness that completely undid her. Trembling and aching to be filled, she arched against him. She could feel his heart pounding against her chest. And still it wasn't enough.

All restraint fled. His hands slid lower to cup her bottom, ardently holding her against the proof of his own mounting desire. She melted against him, surrendering to the erotic thrill of being held in his arms—to him. And damned if he didn't take her up on her offer.

"Amanda," he whispered against her mouth. He lifted his head, his eyes dark and hungry. "Stop me if you're going to," he said, his voice raspy and low. "Because if you don't…"

She didn't care what they had promised each other before. All that mattered was what she felt now.

"I don't want to stop you," she whispered back. She didn't want to stop any of this.

Taking him by the hand, she led him inside her trailer.

Their eyes met again. They kissed their way through her kitchen, past the bath and to the queen-size bed. Arms around each other, they tumbled, laughing, onto the mattress.

Justin rolled onto his back, tugging her over him, and kissed her again. And again. As if kissing were an art in and of itself. And heavens, Amanda noted blissfully, did the man know how to kiss! He stroked and invaded, tempted and caressed, adored and seduced, until nothing mattered but this moment, this night, and the two of them.

* * *

Justin had wanted Amanda since the first second he'd set eyes on her. That wanting had grown exponentially with every moment since. She'd wanted him, too, even though she'd tried to hide it beneath her confident, independent demeanor. But with her lithe, hot body sprawled on top of him, their legs intimately entangled, there was no more pretending.

Her nipples were taut. Her breath, erratic.

Rock-hard, he rolled her onto her back and turned his attention to unbuttoning her blouse, gently removing it and then her bra. She watched, with a look as sweet as heaven, as he bent to her breasts and kissed the pale orbs and rosy tips. "Damn, but you're gorgeous," he breathed, disrobing her the rest of the way.

She was soft all over, feminine. Just as he'd known she would be. A perfect breast in each hand, he kissed her languidly. She wrapped her legs around his waist, and kissed him back.

With her help, and a little more laughter from both of them, they were undressed in a minute flat. Then all amusement faded as she fisted both hands in his hair, sighed his name, and kissed him once again. Deeply. Passionately. Irrevocably.

The knowledge that she wanted him just as much as he wanted her sent another surge of heat soaring through him. Justin slid down her body, stroking her beautiful breasts, the deliciously flat plane of her stomach, the sensitive sweep of her lower abdomen, her smooth thighs. Homing in on the most womanly part of her, he sought out every sweet sensitive spot, until at last she gasped, lifted herself to him, and came apart with an exultant cry.

The depth of her satisfaction lit a fire beneath his own need.

He found the condom that had been in his wallet since he didn't know when. Their gazes caught for a long moment and the air between them hummed with anticipation and the yearning for more. Her hands trembling slightly, she helped him put it on, and then they were entwined in each other's arms again.

When she kissed him, it felt as though he'd been welcomed home. He had his mouth on hers and his hands beneath her hips, first lifting her to take him, then pressing her down against the sheets. She felt so good, so right, undulating beneath him. He possessed her with everything he had. When they came, it was together, hard and fast, and he surged into her, taut and deep.

She buried her face in his neck as the tremors subsided. Reveling in their closeness, he breathed in the sweet, womanly scent of her. And he knew. This... Amanda...was what had been missing in his life.

Amanda clung to Justin, willing her heart to slow, her feelings to come back under control. The first she eventually managed. The second...well, she didn't think she would ever get past what had just happened. At least, not to the point where she could erase it from her memory. Which was why she had to put some distance between them. Now.

With a soft exhalation of regret, she untangled her body from the hard length of his and sat up. He lay on his side, watching with lazy satisfaction as she pulled on a robe. Amanda swallowed, not sure why she had fallen so hard and fast for Justin McCabe, just knowing that she had. And that her feelings, as intense as they were, might not be returned. That in his view, she might never be more than a conquest, or a woman he would like to bed and just be friends with. A notion, she knew, that could break her heart.

Finding her way back to sanity, she cleared her throat and regarded him with every ounce of common sense she possessed. "Well. As wonderful as this was…"

"You're kicking me out," he guessed, his voice rough.

She didn't want to. She also knew how easy it would be to forget all the reasons they'd never work out, and surrender her heart and soul to him. She couldn't let that happen. Couldn't stand to have her self-esteem crushed again. Because even if Justin didn't mean to hurt her, in the end, he would.

And if she'd barely recovered once—with a man she had come to realize she'd never truly loved—she would not survive this.

Amanda shoved the hair from her face and twisted it into a loose knot at the nape of her neck as she paced. "It's no surprise that we made love tonight, or why."

He did a double take, but she forced the words out. "However, you have to know that we can't continue this."

He caught her wrist as she passed and drew her down to sit beside him on the bed. He looked like a male Adonis with the sheet drawn loosely to his waist. A slight smile curved his lips. "You're going to have to clue me in," he said with a bewildered shake of his head. "Because I thought we made love because we are incredibly attracted to each other."

Amanda averted her gaze from the muscular splendor of his bare chest. She resisted the urge to bury her fingers in the swirls of hair around his flat male nipples. "That was part of it."

His eyes lingering everywhere he had previously caressed, he took her hand and turned it palm-up. "What was the rest of it?"

Pushing aside the memory of the way he had just made love to her, not to mention the tingles still rippling through her body, she forged on, "You had a culinary emergency. I helped you out."

He held her open palm in his and traced her lifeline with the tip of his index finger. "It was lot more than just cooking together that propelled us into your bed."

Ignoring the need to join him there again, she met his gaze and didn't look away. "Listen to me, Justin." Deliberately, she tried again to talk sense into him. "When a man and a woman successfully entertain together, the way we did tonight, they can end up feeling like a couple even without an intense physical attraction for each other."

Tenderness filled his eyes. "And you know this because…?"

Sadly, Amanda admitted, "Because it's happened to me before."

He let her hand go. Continued watching. "With your ex-fiancé?"

Her throat dry, Amanda nodded. "His family owns a custom home-building business. They take on high-end clients, people who require wooing and entertaining."

Amanda sighed. "When Rob joined the business, he was expected to do that, too." She frowned, recalling, "He had one couple in particular he was trying to sign. The man and his wife were both incredible cooks, and they wanted a builder who shared their passion.

"I was putting in some custom carpentry on another home his family's company was building, and Rob knew I liked to cook so he came to me for advice." Amanda threw up her hands in dismay and shook her head. "One thing led to another, and the next thing I know I'm not just giving Rob advice on what to cook, but I'm in the kitchen with him…"

Aware Justin was listening intently, Amanda continued relaying her story. "Suffice it to say, the clients signed, and Rob was delighted. He took me out to dinner to celebrate his successful deal. We did a few more dinners." Her face flushed as she forced herself to go on so Justin would understand. "We ended up in bed. And we felt like such a great couple we became engaged."

Justin studied her, all empathetic male. "Which lasted until Rob found out about your background."

Amanda nodded, a mixture of pain and regret flowing through her once again. "Which is when it all fell apart." She drew a deep breath and stood. "The thing is, if I hadn't stepped into the role of Rob's helpmate, or partner or whatever you want to call it, we never would have ended up in bed together, just like you and I would never have ended up in bed together tonight."

Rising to his feet, Justin put his hands on her shoulders and waited until she looked him in the eye. "You're selling us short," he said with a look of sheer male annoyance.

Amanda tried not to think about how magnificent he was, with clothes and without. How incredibly, sexily masculine. "Don't you see? I can't romanticize what happened tonight the same way I did before."

"I don't think you're doing that. I think you're running from what just happened because you're scared that what we've got might have the potential to be something real. Or lasting," he said, taking her into his arms.

The hardness of his body pressed against hers, he dropped a kiss on her temple, another on her cheek, the corner of her mouth. He paused to give her a long, hot, openmouthed kiss that she couldn't help but return.

"And the way you're responding to me now proves it." He kissed her thoroughly.

Amanda knew she shouldn't give in to Justin again, shouldn't give in to this. But the moment he touched her, self-control vanished.

She let out a tremulous sigh. "Maybe just once more, to satisfy our curiosity about each other," she conceded.

"I'm all for making love again." He tumbled her back onto the sheets as if they had all the time in the world. Only, as it turned out, it wasn't once more. It was two more times. After which, Amanda was so replete and content she didn't have the will to toss him out. Instead, she spent the night clasped in his arms.

The next thing she knew, it was morning. Sunlight was slipping past the edges of the window blinds. She was alone in her bed. Sighing groggily, Amanda sat up and looked at the clock. To her amazement, the morning was half gone.

Not surprised that Justin had taken off, but happy he had been kind enough to let her sleep in, she stretched, got up and headed for the shower. She came out and had just gotten dressed when there was a rap on her door. Justin was standing there, compelling as ever. In deference to the intense heat of the July day, he was dressed in cargo shorts and a V-necked T-shirt.

"Hey there, sleepyhead."

His endearment sent a thrill coursing over her skin.

"Ready for some breakfast?"

Was she? And if they did eat together, would it lead to more lovemaking on the one day both of them could afford to take off?

"'Cause if you are…" Justin's voice was a sexy drawl.

Before Amanda could answer, she heard a vehicle coming up the lane toward the lodge.

They turned toward the sound. "Expecting someone?" Justin asked.

Amanda was about to say "no" when the white pickup truck came closer and she caught sight of the familiar green letters emblazoned on the side. "Actually," she bit her lip, "it's my grandfather."

A. B. Johnson was everything you'd expect a self-made man to be, and more. Justin figured the carpenter was in his late sixties. He was fit, strong, robust and nearly as tall as Justin.

A.B. got out of the truck bearing his name and company logo. He strode straight to Amanda, wrapping her in a bear hug. Blushing fiercely, she hugged him back. "Granddad! What are you doing here?"

"I came to see how you were holding up." The white-haired man released her and turned to Justin. "A. B. Johnson, here. Or Angus, if you prefer. And you must be…?"

Happy to meet the man who had played such an important part in Amanda's life, Justin extended a hand. "Justin McCabe."

Angus looked from one to the other. "Am I interrupting something?"

"Not at all," Justin replied cordially. "I just stopped

by to invite Amanda to have breakfast with me at the lodge. I'd be honored if you could join us, too, sir."

Amanda gave Justin a look that reminded him that *she* hadn't said yes. Not that he figured there was ever any doubt, any more than there was really any doubt that she would make love with him again when the time was right.

A.B. smiled. "That'd be nice, thanks."

Justin ignored Amanda's obvious wish that he hadn't extended the invitation as the three of them walked toward the lodge. A.B. paused to greet all five of the dogs, who had been standing sentry on the porch. Tails wagging, each got petted in turn.

Inside the lodge, two places had been set, complete with floral centerpiece, on the long plank table.

Justin added another place setting and headed for the stove. "Hope you like pancakes," he said over his shoulder.

Her grandfather grinned. "I sure do."

Gesturing for them to have a seat, Justin poured three mugs of coffee, then set cream and sugar on the table.

Conversation quickly turned to carpentry. "How much do you have left to go?" A.B. asked.

Amanda slipped easily into business mode. "We're halfway done with all the carpentry. Then we'll have to stain and finish everything."

Justin didn't want to think about the time when Amanda would leave. He liked having her at the ranch.

A.B. turned to Justin. "My granddaughter making the grade?" he drawled, his faded eyes twinkling.

Realizing he and A.B. had something very important in common—a deep and abiding affection for

Amanda—Justin smiled back. "By leaps and bounds, actually."

A.B.'s glance narrowed, considering. "You cook for all your help?"

Amanda cringed at the protective tone. "Granddad…"

Justin winked. "Just the special ones." He brought a platter of sausage patties out of the oven, and set that and a plate brimming with golden flapjacks on the table. He added butter and two kinds of syrup then went back to make some more.

"Although," Justin continued, pausing to bring out a pitcher of juice, "I did have an ulterior motive in asking Amanda to eat with me this morning."

Could it get any worse? Amanda wondered, barely resisting the urge to duck for cover. First Granddad, arriving unexpectedly, obviously because he suspected that something was up with her. And now he was watching her every move, and Justin's, too!

"Really." Granddad sat back in his chair.

"I'm sure Justin just wanted to thank me for giving him a hand with the fund-raising dinner last night."

"What I really wanted to do," Justin clarified, with the gallantry for which the McCabe family was known throughout Texas, "was talk to you about the future."

Oh, no, Amanda thought with a sinking heart. *Please tell me he's not going to ask Granddad for permission to date me.* "Not necessary," she declared with an airy wave of her hand.

Justin just smiled and continued talking to her grandfather as if she hadn't objected. "Did Amanda tell you she'd been teaching carpentry to a teenage boy named Lamar Atkins?"

Granddad folded his arms across his chest. "She did."

Justin stacked the second batch of golden hotcakes on the plate and carried them to the table. "Good, 'cause I have to tell you that what's been going on here is nothing short of amazing."

Joining them at the table, Justin explained the circumstances that brought Lamar to the ranch and the attitude the delinquent teenager had when he arrived. "Everyone's impressed at the impact Amanda's been able to have on Lamar."

"Doesn't surprise me," her granddad declared, slicing into a crisp sausage patty. "My granddaughter has always had an enormous heart. Plus, a real talent for carpentry."

"To the point," Justin agreed, adding food to his plate, "that I'm hoping I can convince her to stay on, once she's done with the contracted work."

Amanda blinked. No way had she seen this coming! "In what capacity?" she asked.

Justin reached for the maple syrup. "Carpentry instructor."

"Hmm." Her grandfather scratched his ear thoughtfully.

Amanda didn't know what to think. She had not expected the two men to join forces. The only thing she did know was that, after having made love with him, it would be torture to work with Justin if they weren't going to become romantically involved.

And common sense told her that, over the long-term, they would not be.

"Thanks, but I already have a job," she said tersely.

Justin studied her as if looking for a way to bypass her opposition and change her mind.

Finished eating, Granddad pushed his plate away. "Despite the fact that helping people in need is always a good thing, my granddaughter's right not to rush into anything. There's a lot to consider. The overall stability of this situation, for instance."

Amanda relaxed in relief.

Justin rose, more determined than ever. "Want to have a look around?" he asked A.B. "See what I've been able to accomplish so far?"

The next thing Amanda knew, the three of them had piled into Justin's pickup. They drove the entire two-hundred-acre property. Went to see the neighboring ranch where the boys would learn to ride and care for horses under the tutelage of Dylan Reeves. Then they visited the park ranger station at Lake Laramie, where the boys would go once a week to assist in whatever way necessary. And finally they were back to the boys ranch, where they toured the bunkhouse, and then the lodge, and finally settled in Justin's office.

There, the talk turned to the problems and pitfalls of starting any new business from the ground up, whether it be for-profit or nonprofit. Before long, Justin was getting out his books. Her grandfather eagerly took a look, curious to see exactly how and where the boys ranch money was being spent.

Then, satisfied that Justin was an accomplished financial manager, A.B. offered to help Justin put together a financial prospectus on just what it would cost to set up an on-site workshop and offer carpentry instruction at the ranch for all the boys.

The talk grew even more detailed and intense as the two men bonded.

Confused and a little annoyed, although she couldn't exactly pinpoint why, Amanda eased out of the room. Given how pleasurably her morning with Justin had started, this was not the way she had expected her day to go.

"I have the feeling you're ticked off at me," Justin said that evening after her grandfather had headed back to San Angelo.

Well, he wasn't completely clueless. That was good to know.

"Why would I be ticked off at you?" she challenged sweetly.

His brow furrowed. "You tell me."

Her heart kicked up a notch. "Mmm, no." Amanda inched off her gloves and tucked them into the pockets on her knee-length overalls. "You go first."

Justin narrowed his eyes. "I think you're jealous that I spent most of the day with your granddad instead of you."

Amanda moved her safety goggles to the top of her head and swallowed against the sudden dryness in her throat. "You're partially right." She turned off the miter saw, unplugged it and walked out of the bunkhouse.

At seven o'clock the sun was inching toward the horizon. This time of summer, sunset was still an hour and a half away. Peace of mind seemed even more distant.

Justin shut the door behind them and came close enough for her to see the hint of evening beard lining his stubborn jaw. "Then suppose you tell me the rest of it."

Amanda struggled to maintain her composure in the

face of all that masculine determination. "My grandfather has never approved of any guy who has shown an interest in me, including my ex-fiancé."

"Seems like A.B. might have had a reason, since your ex was obviously a jerk."

Amanda stiffened, hating it when he was right. "That's not the point."

He cocked a brow. "Then what is?"

She refused to be seduced by the satisfaction in his low voice. "Granddad likes you, Justin. A lot."

He didn't back off in the slightest. "I would think that would be a good thing."

"Well, it's not!" she scoffed. "I don't want the two of you being all buddy-buddy." *Especially under the circumstances.*

He stepped even closer, inundating her with his intoxicating scent. "Why not?"

Amanda put up a staying palm. "Because it makes things too complicated."

"In what way?" He caught her wrist and lifted it to his lips.

Skin tingling, she pulled away from him and walked to the edge of the bunkhouse porch. "In a way that leaves too many people getting hurt."

He went very still, his expression inscrutable as he waited for her to go on.

Knowing it had to be said, even if she didn't want to have to say it, Amanda continued, "Because, like I said last night, if I keep seeing you, this—whatever this is—will end badly."

He came several steps closer, his gaze roving her upturned face. "It doesn't have to."

"Doesn't it?"

He shook his head, his expression sober, intent. "I'd never hurt you, Amanda."

Amanda only wished she were that naive. "I'm sure it eases your conscience to think so right now," she said. He was a McCabe, after all. And McCabe men did not hurt women.

But that didn't mean they would have a happily-ever-after ending, either. Especially with any real, long-term commitment between them out of the question.

Justin threaded his fingers through her hair, cupping her head with his hand. "Listen to me, Amanda. My conscience doesn't need easing where you're concerned, because I haven't done anything wrong. And for the record, I like your grandfather. He's a great guy. Very down-to-earth."

Aware they were veering into dangerous territory, Amanda said, "A.B. also knows something is going on between the two of us."

"I know that. I could tell that right away." He leaned closer still. "But even if I hadn't intuited that, I would have found out. Because after you left the office this afternoon, he asked me what my intentions are toward you."

Dismayed, but not really surprised, Amanda eased into a sitting position on the porch railing. "What did you say?"

Justin chuckled. "I said that I didn't know yet. That you were really kind of ornery and independent, and you liked to cook." He shook his head as if that were the worst complaint yet. "And what man could possibly want a woman in his life who knows how to turn burned filet of beef into the most delicious barbacoa enchiladas anyone has ever tasted?"

Amanda rolled her eyes. "Will you be serious?"

Justin gripped her wrist and tugged her to her feet. "I *am* being serious." He wrapped his arms around her waist and brought her snug against him.

"When A.B. mentioned that you didn't have an ideal background, I told him I already knew that, and it didn't matter to me...and it wouldn't matter to my family, either." He paused to make sure his words were sinking in. "Because McCabes know it's not the name that makes a person worth having. It's what's in a person's heart. And your heart, Amanda, is pure gold."

Chapter 7

"Have you given any more thought to my proposal?" Justin asked Amanda on Monday, after Lamar had left for the day.

The truth was, she hadn't been able to think about anything else. The idea of staying on and helping create a program to teach kids like Lamar was incredibly enticing—even without the added bonus of working by Justin's side.

Amanda attached the slide for a cabinet drawer. "I'd be happy to help you design the program, but I can't sign on as a full-time instructor." *No matter how much a part of me would like to do so.*

He favored her with a sexy half smile. "Not even if your granddad thought it was a good idea for you?"

Amanda picked up the other slide and fastened it, too. "He wouldn't."

Justin didn't say anything for a moment. Then he took his cell phone out of his pocket, punched in a number and handed her the phone.

"Hi, honey."

Familial warmth spiraled through her as she set down her drill. "Granddad?"

"Justin thought it would help if I told you I want you to do this."

She glared at Justin, only to have him grin back at her in a way that made her hormones surge. Pacing a short distance away, she continued talking to her grandfather. "I can't teach classes here. I have two jobs after this one, remember?"

"Not to worry," A.B. assured her. "I took care of it."

Amanda tensed. "What do you mean 'you took care of it'?"

"We'll discuss it next time I see you."

Amanda willed herself to hold her own with these two determined men. Shielding her face with her hand, Amanda avoided Justin's eyes. "Granddad, I know this is a good cause, but I have a responsibility to your business." One she took very seriously.

"Nothing trumps kids in need. Let me know if you and Justin require anything else from me." And just like that he ended the call.

Astounded, Amanda turned to Justin. "The two of you are ganging up on me!" Her heart took another little leap of anticipation as he neared.

A seductive tilt to his lips, he held her gaze in an increasingly intimate way. "I'm going to do what I have to do to make this situation work. So," he said finally, assuming—and rightly so—that she would help him in the end. "Do you have time to get started designing an apprenticeship program tonight?"

* * *

An hour later Amanda had showered and changed into clean clothes. She met Justin in his office at the lodge, and though she'd braced herself for the prospect of spending another evening with him, nothing could have prepared her for the way he looked when she strolled in.

For starters, he had showered, too. Not a bad idea after a day spent running in and out of the Texas summer heat. He'd put on a pair of faded blue jeans, and an olive-green button-up. Shirttail out, sleeves rolled to just beneath the elbow, first couple of buttons undone, he looked relaxed. Sexy. And, to her secret disappointment, completely ready to get down to business.

Already behind his desk, he motioned for her to sit down.

"Your grandfather sent me a list of all the equipment we would need, as well as a list of prices and places where we could buy the brands he recommends."

Glad she had opted for a casual sleeveless turquoise blouse and a pair of ankle-length white denim slacks, she took the pages he handed her. The data was so well organized it didn't take long to glance through it. Amanda smiled. "This looks good. Which is no surprise. Granddad is as good with numbers as you are."

He rocked back in his chair. "I take it that isn't your forte."

Amanda sat back and tried to relax. "You've got that right. Which is why I've been dreading the day that Granddad asks me to take over the running of A.B. Johnson Carpentry."

He eyed her curiously. "Not interested?"

Amanda frowned and tried not to remember how good Justin's lips had felt moving over hers. They weren't going there again, she reminded herself. "It doesn't matter if I'm interested or not in handling the business side of things. Granddad spent his entire adult life building that company. The income the firm generates funds his retirement. I owe it to him to take over when the time is right."

Justin's eyes darkened protectively. "You should tell him how you feel."

Amanda shook her head. "I can't disappoint him like that. He's been too good to me. And who knows? Maybe by the time we actually get to that point, I'll find I *like* making out schedules, meeting payrolls and crunching the numbers."

Justin snickered, clearly not believing her for one second.

"Okay," Amanda conceded. "So maybe I won't love it, but I'll learn to like it."

A muscle worked in his jaw. "Sounds more likely."

Silence fell. Justin went back to looking at the numbers. A little bored, and a lot restless, Amanda glanced around. She saw a stack of folders fanned out on the edge of his desk. All had photos of teenage boys clipped to the front. She inclined her head. "Are these the first kids who have been chosen to live here?"

"No." Justin rose and went to the file cabinet. He brought out several more thick stacks of files and handed them to her. "These are the first two hundred candidates. Somehow, I have to figure out who is the most deserving and pick eight."

Amanda's heart sank as she flipped through the top dozen or so.

"Yeah." His eyes darkened. "I guess I didn't think about this part of running the ranch, either."

Her throat tightened. She looked through more photos. "All these kids need placement?"

Justin raked his hands through his hair and left them clasped on the back of his neck. "The hell of it is, I don't know where to begin, or even what criteria to use." He sat back down in his chair. "Should I take only kids from Laramie County when I know that some of the kids who are living in the inner city need safe haven, too? Should I select the kids who've been bounced in and out of different foster homes more times than they can count? Or someone who's never done anything to get in this situation—*except* have the misfortune to be orphaned? Or someone who has been in the system for practically their entire life and is desperate for a place to call home?"

Put that way, it did sound insurmountable. Amanda resisted the urge to comfort him physically. Instead, she sat primly in her chair, legs crossed at the knee, hands clasped on top of them. She was just a bystander here. "Mitzy can't help you?"

Justin shook his head. "She said it's really up to me, and/or the new director. What 'we' think on a gut level after reading the files. Because, from the social services department's perspective, they are all deserving candidates."

Amanda ruminated on that.

"On top of that," Justin continued in a low, husky voice, "I'm looking at the cost projections your grandfather sent me of what it would take to start up a barebones training program in carpentry, versus what it's going to take to get another bunkhouse or two built so we can bring in another eight to sixteen kids."

For the first time, she felt the weight he carried on

his shoulders, understood the enormity of what he was trying to do. And respected his courage for having taken it on.

She rose, ready to offer much-needed solace. "You want to know what I think?"

He grinned at the hint of mischief in her eyes and stood, too. "Somehow I think you're going to tell me," he drawled.

She handed the stack of files back to him. "If you're going to dream, dream big—and go after it all. Use the vocational program to show what you're planning to do for these kids, and that in turn to convince people to donate and give the ranch the big monetary grants."

They locked eyes for a heart-stealing moment. "That was the plan."

Amanda put up her palm for a high five. "Time's a-wastin', then." After they slapped palms she stepped back. "Let's get started writing up those skill lists and course descriptions." Once again, inexplicably, undeniably, they were a team.

Amanda spent the next few days working hard on the carpentry with Lamar at her side. Her evenings were spent with Justin, putting together a proposal for the board of directors. Included in their pitch was an innovative way to pay for the required equipment, insurance and instructor.

"Let's just hope the board goes for it." Justin monitored the pages coming out of the printer as they burned the midnight oil the evening before the presentation.

Amanda laid the folders side by side. "If the interest they all showed when they were touring the bunkhouse the other night is any indication, they will," she assured him with a smile.

Justin walked the first set over to her. Their fingers brushed as the proposal changed hands. "Thanks for agreeing to be the instructor."

She still wasn't quite sure how she'd gotten talked into it; she just knew she couldn't turn away from those kids in need. Not yet, anyway. Ignoring the sensation the brief contact generated, Amanda shrugged. "Part-time. For the first year or so," she reminded him. After that, they would have to see.

The second copy came out of the printer. "No one is going to be able to fill your shoes."

Amanda accepted it and continued assembling the material, one folder at a time. "Funny. That's what I expected my granddad to be saying right now about leaving his business." She caught her index finger on a sharp edge of paper. Amanda lifted her hand to her mouth. No blood, but it still stung.

"You know why he's not?" Justin continued. "He saw what everyone else did—how great you are with kids."

And you, Amanda thought. But not wanting to clue Justin in to her grandfather's matchmaking, she merely smiled and put her still-stinging fingertip to her mouth. "What time is the presentation to the board?"

"Seven tomorrow evening. Want to go together?"

As long as it wasn't a date. And it apparently wasn't. "Sure." Amanda paused. "What should I wear?"

He brought over the third and fourth sets of documents. "Whatever you're comfortable in."

She checked her throbbing fingertip. Actually, it was bleeding, just a little. "What are *you* going to wear?"

He set down the papers, left the office and came back with a first-aid kit. "Shirt and tie."

He opened the kit and took out a tube of ointment. Amanda's heart leaped as he came toward her. "Jacket?"

He took her finger, inspected it and dabbed some of the salve on her fingertip. To her relief, her finger stopped stinging right away.

"Probably not, given how hot it is."

She was thrumming with something akin to desire as he tended to her wound. She forced a laugh. "No kidding. Will July ever end?"

"I hope not." He put on a Band-Aid, followed by a kiss that seemed to say oh-what-I-could-do-to-you-if-I-had-a-chance. A thrill swept through her.

Aware just how little it would take to persuade her to make love with him on the office floor, Amanda recoiled breathlessly. "What was that for?"

"All the work you've put in." He bent his head and kissed her again, more deeply and erotically. "Because I couldn't have done this without you."

Amanda wanted to believe that. Just as she wanted to believe they could make love one day, be friends the next and even work together for the next year without any repercussions.

But the womanly part of her, the part that had been devastated by her last breakup, knew otherwise. There was no doubt in her mind that a romantic liaison between them would be fraught with emotional peril.

Finger taken care of, she forced herself to go back to the task at hand. "Yes," she said over her shoulder, pretending his kisses hadn't affected her at all, when she was nothing but a puddle of need inside. Hot, melting, lusting need. Her back still to him, she drew in a bracing breath. "You would have done fine. Nothing gets in the way of a McCabe and his goal."

Lazily, Justin strolled back to the printer, which had stopped spitting out pages while he kissed her. "You see me as that determined?" His expression was inscrutable.

His easy calm was as maddening as her own welling desire. Amanda smiled. "And then some."

And not just when it came to the boys ranch, but to her, as well.

The question was, could she—would she—keep him a heart's length away?

The next evening Justin and Amanda drove into town together and went to the Lowell Foundation building. In a conference room next to Libby's office, the six board members listened intently while Justin and Amanda made their presentation.

When they had finished, they opened up the floor to questions. Mitzy went first. "So the cabinets and bookshelves you and the students make in the shop will be sold for profit?"

Justin expanded on that idea. "The money from that will pay for the necessary materials, insurance and Amanda's time as instructor."

"Sounds great," Miss Mim said.

"I'm curious, though." Libby turned to Amanda. "You have no background in either teaching or philanthropy. So how did you become interested in tackling something like this?"

Amanda found the spotlight on her. "To be honest, I never even thought about it until I met Lamar Atkins. Looking at him was like looking at myself at that age. It really took me back."

"How so?" Wade McCabe probed.

Amanda gave Justin's father's question the consideration it deserved. "I know what it's like to grow up failing in every aspect of your life. If it hadn't been for my grandfather, if he hadn't helped me see that I could succeed at something, I don't know what would have happened to me. But the skills I learned from him gave me a way to feel good about myself as well as a way to support myself and provide a valuable service to others."

She paused to look all six board members in the eye. "I want to be able to do that for others. I want to help get the program up and running and make sure that you find someone able to step in when I leave to go back to my family's business, full-time, one year from now."

Mitzy jumped in, "Would you be amenable to staying on if we offered you a more substantial role in the boys ranch from the get-go?"

Amanda shot a look at Justin. He seemed just as caught off guard as she was. "What do you mean?"

Libby smiled. "We've all been talking since the dinner last Saturday. We all concur. We think you're the director we've been looking for."

"Ice cream," Amanda repeated to Justin, still in shock. "You want to take me for ice cream after what just happened in there?"

He grinned as if he hadn't just sustained a major disappointment. "My mom used to say troubles go down better with ice cream." He put a light hand on her spine and guided her toward the Dairy Barn down the street. "Might have been more of a woman thing, but we all liked to eat so we were on board, and darned if she wasn't right."

At the window, Amanda ordered strawberry ice cream with whipped cream and a sprinkling of nuts. Justin ordered the chocolate-toffee-vanilla crunch with extra candy on top.

Because all the tables were full of other couples, they took their sundaes down the street a bit to a bench along a deserted part of Main Street. Amanda had no idea where to start so she began with the basics. "Thanks for the ice cream."

He settled beside her. "Thanks for helping on the proposal and going with me tonight."

There were several inches between them, but she could still feel the warmth emanating from his thigh. She watched the people playing on the mini-putt course across the street. "I still can't believe they offered me your job."

His mouth crooked. "It wasn't my job."

She turned slightly to face him, her knee bumping his slightly in the process. "It's the one you wanted."

He dipped his head in acknowledgment. "Which is different from actually getting it."

This wasn't fair. Amanda faced forward once again. "I'm going to turn it down."

He caught her hand. "Please don't do that."

She looked him in the eye.

"I admit, when Libby first brought it up, I was a little ticked off."

"As well you should be!" Amanda burst out. His eyes darkened. "But the truth of the matter is, they were probably never going to give it to me anyway. I don't have what it takes to relate to kids in trouble the way someone like you—who's actually been there—does."

Amanda had never met anyone so selfless. "Lamar thinks the world of you now."

Justin sighed. "But he probably wouldn't, had you not been there to build a bridge between us." He released his hold on her and went back to eating his ice cream. "I admit, until now, I didn't understand what all the board members were talking about." He frowned. "I didn't see why intuitiveness and instinct were such an essential part of the director's job."

Justin turned back to her in all sincerity. "But having seen the miracle you worked with Lamar in just a few short weeks, I now realize we have to have someone at the top who the kids feel completely comfortable going to with their problems. Someone who is cheerful and energetic and charismatic. Someone who just 'gets it,' and has had the experience of turning her own life around." He entwined his fingers with hers. "That person, Amanda, is you."

Amanda was deeply touched by his faith in her, but she still had her doubts. "That part of the job I could probably handle. It's the rest of it, Justin. The thought of all the paperwork and the grant applications and meetings with big-time donors that overwhelms me."

He nodded in understanding. "First of all, I'm not going anywhere. I'll still be the chief financial officer, as well as the assistant ranch director. I'll handle as much of that as you want me to handle. All you'll have to do is delegate and then give the final signature. And you'll have time to teach the kids carpentry, too, on weekends or evenings when they're not in school."

It was still a big decision. "I'm going to have to think about it."

Again, he understood. "I figured as much. So why

don't you take a couple days off, maybe go to San Angelo and see your granddad and talk to him. And then go from there."

Amanda thought about calling Granddad and letting him know she was coming, but if she did that, he'd want to know why she was showing up in the middle of a work week and she didn't want to hash it all out over the phone. She wanted to see the look in his eyes when she laid it all out for him. She wanted to see his gut reaction. So she went back to the ranch, said goodbye to Justin and hit the road. Traffic was light that late in the evening, and she made it to her grandfather's home in San Angelo in a little over an hour.

As she expected, he was still up, watching a late-night comedy show. What she hadn't expected were the stacks of what appeared to be legal papers spread all over the dining room table.

Business evaluations. Several different purchase offers. A proposal for breaking down the business, and dissolving it. "Granddad, what's going on?"

"I'm thinking of selling the business."

"Why?"

"Because if I were to sell it now, along with the existing contracts for the local homebuilders and home-improvement stores, I could make enough to pay my expenses the rest of my life—and leave you a little something in the bargain."

Amanda sat down in shock. "I thought you wanted me to take over the business."

"Originally, I thought it *would* be the best way. Then, as time went on, I saw how uninterested you were in the financial side of the business. I realized it wouldn't be so much of a gift as a burden were I to turn it over to you."

No wonder he had been so enthusiastic about her taking a job at the boys ranch. "When were you going to tell me all this?"

"The next time you came home, or when the job you're working on now is done. Which brings me to my next question." Granddad paused. "Why are you home?"

Briefly, Amanda explained.

Granddad shook his head. "Fate works in mysterious ways, doesn't it?"

It certainly did.

Amanda studied him. "You really want me to take this job?"

"I want you to do what will make you happy," Granddad replied.

And strange as it was, when Amanda thought about happiness, Justin McCabe was the first thing that sprang to mind.

Chapter 8

"Your granddad's selling the business?" Justin asked in disbelief when Amanda returned two days later.

Trying not to think how much she had missed him, Amanda said, "He's been fielding offers for a while now. He just didn't know how to tell me."

"How do you feel about that?"

"Honestly? Relieved." And strangely adrift, too. As if the future she had seen for herself—even if she hadn't really wanted it—was gone. But there was a lot that was positive in the situation. She had to remember that.

Aware that Justin was watching her closely, Amanda forced herself to continue bringing him up to speed. "With the deal Granddad decided to accept, he'll be all set, in terms of his retirement. His employees will be taken care of, too. The only things that will change will be the name of the company and they'll bring in a day-to-day manager. Plus, the new owner has agreed to place orders with the boys ranch carpentry shop once we get that up and running. So, in the end, it's all good."

Justin poured her a cup of coffee and watched as she stirred in generous amounts of cream and sugar. "I take it that 'we' means you've decided to accept the job?"

Amanda returned his smile. It would be so easy to get lost in his easygoing charm. In him. "With trepidation—" *and the fear I'll end up letting everyone down* "—yes, I have."

"As I said before, I'll help you handle the paperwork end of things. I know initially it can be overwhelming."

Amanda widened her eyes. "Even for you?"

He sat down beside her. "When I came up with the idea to start the ranch, I thought it would be simple. I'd buy the land, and build a lodge, and start taking kids in. It turned out to be a lot more complicated than that."

She took a sip of the hot, delicious coffee. "How so?"

Ruefully, Justin admitted, "Well, even with the money I threw into the project, I was far short of what was needed." He went on to explain about fire codes, zoning regulations, building permits and other bits of red tape he'd had to cut along the way.

Amanda blinked. "Wow. I had no idea."

"Not to worry." He patted the back of her hand. "Most of this has already been done. I'll walk you through anything that's left, like the final series of inspections."

Warmth flowed through her as she studied the loving way his palm covered her hand. "I don't know how you manage to do all this."

Justin got up and went to the fridge. He came back with a chocolate bar. "Hey, the Alamo wasn't built in a

day and neither was this. And we're further along than
you think. Although, there are a few things that have
to be done right away."

Amanda accepted the half he gave her. "Like what?"

"Tomorrow morning you have to go into town to
go over your employment contract with the ranch attorney, Liz Cartwright-Anderson. The appointment is
at nine o'clock."

Glad for the sugary pick-me-up, Amanda savored her
share of the dark chocolate. "Will you be there, too?"

He smiled. "What would you prefer?"

"For you to accompany me." The words were out before she could prevent them. She had the feeling that
with Justin by her side she would feel less overwhelmed.
"That way, if there are any issues," Amanda continued,
a little lamely, "although I'm not sure what those might
be…then…"

"I'll be there, to help expedite the signing," Justin
promised.

Nodding in relief, Amanda crumpled the wrapper
in her hand.

"It's not a problem. I'll just call Lamar's foster parents and let them know we'll pick him up in town. He
was supposed to spend the morning at the high school
signing up for fall semester classes, anyway." Justin
stood and took his empty mug over to the dishwasher.
"So, are you ready to pick out your new quarters?"

Amanda followed suit. "What do you mean?" Once
again, she felt three steps behind.

"Well, obviously, as director, you're going to have
to reside in the lodge, same as me, so…why don't we
go upstairs and have a look?"

Amanda had never been in the wing that housed

the staff quarters. The only time she'd been upstairs at all was the day they had gone looking for the missing Lamar, and then only so far as the TV lounge.

A lot was changing, very quickly. She fell into step beside him. "Who else is going to live on the property?"

"Well, for right now, you and me. Eventually, when we get up to full capacity of 20 cabins and 160 kids, we will have other staff. A registered nurse, an academic or vocational advisor, and if we're really lucky, and are able to build a barn and acquire some horses, someone to run the stables."

"You're ambitious. I'll give you that."

"Yeah, well, if you're going to dream, dream big, right?"

When Amanda smiled up at him, a sizzling look of awareness zinged between them. The moment passed when he motioned for her to follow him. Justin led the way up the stairs, past the common rooms and the library to the door marked Staff Only. "There are five suites. I've got the one at the far end of the hall. Which one would you like?"

Amanda walked up and down the hall. The rooms were all the same and held a desk, queen bed, dresser, reading chair and ottoman. "You can add anything you like. Television, computer, stereo, rugs, curtains, whatever."

It was nice, but… "Can I put a kitchen in there?" Amanda joked.

"No, but you can use the one downstairs anytime you want, since we're planning to share the cooking and cleanup chores with the kids and the other staff, rather than hire someone to do just that."

"Makes sense." Amanda walked back to check out the rooms once more.

Justin was at her elbow. "Hard decision, isn't it?"

More than he knew. Should she choose the one next to his, or select one as far away as possible?

"Want to flip a coin?" he quipped.

Amanda shook her head. "I think I'll take the one closest to the main hall." *And farthest from you.*

He looked at her, his expression maddeningly inscrutable. Was he disappointed or relieved, she wondered?

He slid a hand beneath her elbow. "Want me to help you bring your things in?"

Her pulse quickening, Amanda moved on ahead of him. "Actually, I think I'd rather stay in the trailer for a few more days and not waste time on moving my belongings when we have so many other, more pressing tasks."

He gave her a long look. "Sure? I don't mind. It probably wouldn't take long."

Amanda's throat felt suddenly dry. Being so close to him was going to be an adjustment. "No, that's okay." She smiled briskly. "I'll get to it eventually." *Just not today.*

"Okay, we've gone over the duties of the job, and the personal leave and time-off policies," attorney Liz Cartwright-Anderson said the following morning. She went down the list in front of her. "Which leads us to the fraternization among coworkers policy."

Liz's unexpected announcement sent Justin into a coughing fit. Several board members raised their brows. Amanda worked to contain a flush of embarrassment while Liz handed over papers to both Justin and

Amanda. The three members of the board of directors in attendance already had their own copies, it seemed.

Liz continued matter-of-factly, "We had intended to go over this with you and Justin separately, but since you're both here today, we'll go ahead and do it jointly."

Which meant what, exactly? Amanda wondered, feeling even more embarrassed. The look on Justin's face said he was as surprised and uncomfortable with the discussion as she was. Working to maintain her composure, Amanda turned her attention back to Liz, who was still referring to the fine print on the contract in front of her. Liz read, "Dating a coworker is allowed, as long as disclosure is made to the board and a release is signed by both parties stating that both parties accept full responsibility for what does or does not happen within the bounds of said relationship."

"And if I were to choose not to disclose?" Amanda asked.

"Then that would be grounds for dismissal," Liz informed her.

Which would not be the end of the world for her, but it would devastate Justin, who had put his heart and soul into building the boys ranch. Amanda flushed. "Then I disclose that…um… Justin and I… Well, we aren't actually dating or anything…"

"But there is a spark," Miss Mim chimed in.

Amanda looked over at the retired former librarian. She nodded, affirming it to be so. Even though she and Justin had pretty much decided not to act on the chemistry again.

Libby smiled. "We all realized that the night of the party."

"But it didn't keep you from offering me the job," Amanda said in amazement.

Libby exchanged glances with the other two board members. "You're going to fall in love sometime, somewhere. So is Justin. And the fact is, you two do make a good team. You work well together, you treat each other with respect." She smiled amiably. "So, as long as your private life remains private, and doesn't affect your work, then the board has no problem with whatever may or may not be developing there."

"Well, that was interesting," Amanda said half an hour later when all the papers were finally signed, and she and Justin had left the attorney's office.

"No kidding," Justin agreed. "I wish I could have forewarned you, but I didn't know it was coming."

Now that it was over, Amanda could chuckle. "I could tell that by your coughing fit."

He shook his head in comical lament and took her hand in his. "Well, at least we have the approval of the three ladies."

Feeling far too vulnerable for comfort, she pulled away. "The only problem is we're not dating, Justin."

He advanced on her, a sexy glint in his eyes. "Right."

He had a way of getting under her skin, like no other man. She turned to him in indignation. "We're not!"

He took her hand in his and lifted it to his lips. Lightly kissing the back of her knuckles, he teased, "So far."

Tingling from the seductive caress, Amanda disengaged her hand from his. Ignoring the racing of her heart, she stepped back and vowed, "It's not going to be an issue anyway. We have so much to do to get ready to open."

Justin glanced at his watch. "Speaking of which, we better get over to the high school to pick up Lamar so we can take him back to the ranch."

But Lamar was not in the school library, where registration was being held. Things went from bad to worse when his guidance counselor said she hadn't seen him at all. Amanda and Justin looked at each other. "His foster mom said she dropped him off this morning at eight, and that she watched him walk into the building," Amanda said.

The guidance counselor frowned. "Well, he must have walked right back out again, because if Lamar had been in this library I would have corralled him right away and signed him up for fall classes. And when you do see him, remind him that tomorrow is the last day for late registration for existing students."

"We will," Amanda promised. "So now what?" she asked Justin.

He held the lobby door for Amanda. "I'll call my brother Colt."

At the sheriff's department? Amanda faced Justin on the sidewalk under the portico at the front entrance of the high school. Funny, they weren't old enough to have a teenage child, but it sure felt like they were parents of the same wayward teen at the moment. "Won't Colt have to notify the court—which could lead to even more trouble for Lamar?"

Amanda knew the teenager had broken the rules, but she didn't want to see him end up in juvie, especially when he'd been doing so well all summer.

Justin placed a comforting hand on her shoulder. "We

can trust Colt to do what's right for this situation. He may be a sheriff's deputy, but he's also the community liaison who runs the department's outreach program for troubled teens. That gives him some latitude. Not a lot, but enough."

Wondering if he should have seen this coming, Justin searched the rest of the high school grounds. Amanda went over to Lamar's foster home to see if he had turned up there. And Deputy Colt McCabe went up and down Main Street, checking out all the businesses. They also scoped out the movie theater, the putt-putt course, the Dairy Barn and the bowling alley. Unfortunately, there had been no sign of Lamar anywhere when the three of them met up in the park at the center of town.

"He was supposed to work at the ranch this afternoon," Amanda fretted. It was close to noon.

Colt frowned. "He doesn't have a car or a driver's license, so he couldn't have driven there on his own."

Unless he had done so illegally, Justin thought, with a growing sense of unease.

Amanda sighed. "It's too far to walk." Her delicate brows knit together. "Do his foster parents own any bicycles?"

"There's one way to find out," Justin told her.

Fifteen minutes later, they knew what mode of transportation Lamar had selected. A blue ten-speed bike.

"I think we should head back out to the ranch," Amanda said to Justin.

He agreed and they walked back to his pickup truck after promising Colt that they would keep him apprised of the situation.

"You okay?" Justin asked when Amanda hopped

into the cab. He slid behind the steering wheel. She looked pale and upset. As if this might be too much for her to handle.

Her lips tight with worry, Amanda buckled her seat belt. "I'm just beginning to realize what a big responsibility this is."

A memory of a past failure assailed Justin. *This is not like what happened to Billy Scalia. It's just a momentary blip in the effort to save Lamar. She knows it. I know it, too.*

"You're up to it," he told her finally, determined as ever. "We both are."

To Amanda and Justin's mutual relief, the bike was parked next to the steps leading up to the front door of the lodge.

Lamar was out back with the dogs, drinking water from the hose. He looked hot and sweaty and immediately jumped to his feet when he saw them. "Where have you been? I was ready to work half an hour ago!"

"We were looking for you." Amanda put a hand to his face and winced at the heat of his skin. The poor boy was sunburned everywhere.

"I was supposed to be here," Lamar insisted.

Justin shook his head. "You were supposed to be at the high school, signing up for classes."

He unlocked the door to the lodge and the three of them went in. The blissful cool of air-conditioning hit them. With a light hand on Lamar's shoulder, Amanda guided him into the kitchen. She sat him on a stool at the work island and went to the pantry for a big jug of electrolyte drink.

Justin got down three tall glasses and filled them with ice.

Amanda rummaged around and brought out some salty pretzels, too. "So what happened?" she asked.

Lamar was clearly about to prevaricate, but he took another long look at their faces and his shoulders slumped. "I don't want to go back to that school, okay? It just… The thought of it… I can't do it. I can't go there again. That's all."

Which means something is going on. Amanda wrung out a clean dish towel with cool water and draped it over the back of Lamar's neck. "Are you being bullied?"

He made a face. "No. Of course not."

"Is it because you don't have any friends?"

Lamar scowled. "I'm not the rah-rah, join-a-club type. And everybody at Laramie High School does something extracurricular."

"It's a good way to meet people and make friends," Justin pointed out.

Lamar snorted and stuffed pretzels into his mouth. He followed it with a long, thirsty drink of Gatorade.

Figuring it was best to let that go for the moment, Amanda asked, "How long did it take you to get out here on the bike?"

"Three hours."

"It's thirty-two miles."

"I know that *now*."

Alarmed, Amanda continued, "You could have gotten heatstroke."

"Yeah, well…"

Justin went off and returned a moment later with a can of sunburn cream. He handed it to Amanda. Wordlessly, Lamar covered his eyes and mouth and let her apply it. As the medicinal smell filled the kitchen, Amanda continued trying to get through to their young charge. "We were really worried about you, Lamar."

The teenager looked her in the eye, near tears. Whether from sheer physical exhaustion or shame, Amanda couldn't tell. "I'm sorry," Lamar said thickly.

Justin stood, arms crossed. "Sorry's not going to cut it with the judge if it happens again."

Flushing, Lamar complained, "I was just trying to get to my community service work."

"You were running away from something you didn't want to face."

Like high school. Classes. Studying.

Lamar turned to Justin. "Can't I come here, instead of going to LHS during the day? Or keep working with Amanda, wherever she goes next, on more community service or something?"

Justin shook his head. "Amanda is going to be working here. She's been named the ranch director."

Lamar blinked, clearly surprised to find her the boss. "What does that make you?" he asked Justin.

As before, Justin took the demotion well, saying calmly, "Founder, CFO and assistant ranch director."

Amanda couldn't help but admire him. In his place, she wasn't sure she would have been so gracious.

"Well, between the two of you it seems like you're calling all the shots," Lamar pointed out. "Can't you *please* talk to Mitzy Martin? And get her to let me stay, even after my community service is up?"

Hours later, Justin stood in the doorway of the administrator's office and asked, "Not quite the way you would have expected your first day as director to go, was it?"

Amanda looked up from the stacks of papers on her desk. Just reading through the summaries Justin had prepared for her had taken the better part of an hour.

She dropped her pen, aware she'd never thought she would be a desk jockey, either. "At least Mitzy agreed with us that Lamar should be placed here as a student as soon as the ranch opens."

Justin took a seat in front of her desk. "We have our first kid selected, anyway."

Amanda smiled ruefully. "Only seven more to go."

His gaze trailed over her face and hair as sensually as a caress. "How about you take a break?"

Amanda threw down her pen. "You're right." She rose, massaging her aching lower back. "I should head over to the bunkhouse and get at least a *little* of the carpentry done today."

Justin stood, too. "That's not what I meant." He strode toward her, not stopping until he towered over her. "The carpentry can wait till tomorrow."

Amanda pushed aside the temptation to fall into his arms. She batted her lashes at him. "Says the person who isn't responsible for getting it done."

He stepped aside to let her by. "As your assistant, I'm responsible for everything you're tasked with and don't get done."

Amanda paused, wondering where she'd left her purse. "I'm beginning to like the way you think."

"Seriously, we should take the night off and do something fun."

Was he talking about a date? "Such as…?" Amanda asked, the search for her handbag temporarily forgotten.

Justin continued, "You've met Colt and my dad. I'd like you to meet the rest of my family. Three of my brothers who aren't normally in Laramie are here for my mom's birthday celebration. I'd like you to get to know them."

Amanda tensed. She'd been unwelcome before at family gatherings. She had no desire to be so again. "I don't want to intrude."

He reassured her with an easy glance. "Other people, friends of the family, will be there, too."

When that didn't help, Justin paused, took her hand in his. "It would mean a lot to me if you would go with me," he said quietly.

Put that way, how could she refuse?

Chapter 9

Maybe she should have refused, Amanda thought an hour later as Justin drove toward his family's ranch in southeast Laramie County.

He sent her a teasing sidelong glance. "You can't be nervous."

Amanda reminded herself she had already met Justin's dad, and Wade McCabe had been very nice to her. "Should I be?"

He considered this as if it were a matter of great complexity. "Hmm."

"You're not helping!"

Justin chuckled. He drove past the gates of the ranch between the vehicles parked on the sides of the long, winding drive. He cut the ignition and turned to her, a devilish smile on his face. "Let's put it this way. McCabes stick together. So meeting them for the first time as a potential…ah…*significant new person*…can be a little like running the gauntlet."

Amanda rolled her eyes. "Now you're making me feel relaxed." And what was a significant new person by the way? Was that like a girlfriend? A special friend? Also known as a friend with benefits?

Mistaking the reason behind her unease, Justin reminded her, "Your granddad put *me* through the third degree."

Amanda pinched the bridge of her nose and briefly closed her eyes. She couldn't help but think everyone was jumping to conclusions a bit. It wasn't as if she and Justin had done anything more than spend one night together. They hadn't actually started dating. They hadn't made love again, although he had kissed her again. And now that they were working together, she wasn't sure they ever would take it any further. Especially since his relationship with the woman he had previously worked with hadn't ended all that well.

Aware he was waiting for her reaction, Amanda sighed. "Sorry about that."

"I'm not." Justin unlatched his safety belt, grabbed the present he had tucked behind the seat and came around to help her out of her side, as if it were a date. Or maybe he was just being polite, since he had obviously been raised as a true Texas gentleman. "It just means your granddad cares."

As they approached the big, beautiful ranch house, her heart was pounding. She swallowed and struggled against her nerves. Justin had told her not to bring a present; he'd said the one he'd gotten would be from them both, but was that the correct thing to do?

On the other hand, how could she have brought an

appropriate present for a woman she had never met? A lady wildcatter, no less?

Amanda forced herself to relax. "So you're saying your family will be every bit as 'curious' about me as my granddad was about you," she said finally.

Justin slid a hand beneath her elbow. "In their own way, yeah."

She leaned into his comforting touch, inhaling the brisk masculine scent of him. "What is their own way?" she asked, savoring the leather and sandalwood fragrance of his cologne.

Justin paused, then backed her over to the shade of a nearby tree. From the rear of the house, they could hear the sounds of voices, laughter and live music. "My mom and dad are both very outspoken when it comes to their opinions. But they are also very kind and respectful of others."

"That's good to know."

He gave her arm a comforting squeeze. "It's going to be okay. You'll see."

Moments later they were moving through the elegant, comfortable interior of the home, depositing the gift on the table with dozens of others and moving back through the kitchen, where a catering staff was busy. There, in the center of activity, was the "birthday gal" who looked about as far from the 60 sparkling on her jaunty crown as could be. Justin's mother was several inches shorter than the six-foot-tall Amanda. She was also lithe, dark-haired, bursting with energy and every bit as attractive as her husband and sons.

Justin encompassed her in a hug. "Happy birthday, Mom."

"Thank you. It's so wonderful to have you all here

today." She embraced him again before stepping back. Extending her delicate hands to Amanda, she said, "I'm Josie."

"Amanda Johnson."

"The lovely carpenter everyone's been talking about." Looking absolutely delighted to have her there, Josie squeezed Amanda's hands warmly. "So, are you here as Justin's date?"

"No," she said, at the same time Justin said, "Yes." Josie laughed. "Well, that answers my question!"

"We're friends," Amanda insisted, her face as hot as a prairie fire.

Josie's smile broadened. "Always a good start to any relationship." She plucked champagne flutes off a passing tray, handed one to each of them and clinked glass with theirs. "And exactly what I want for my birthday, too!"

Obviously knowing where *this* was going, Justin attempted to head Josie off. "I—we—brought a present, Mom."

"Yes, but you know what I want. What I *always* want," Josie teased.

Amanda waited to be illuminated.

Justin merely chuckled and shook his head.

"More grandkids, more weddings and more happily-ever-afters," Justin's dad cut in, as he came up to join them.

Amanda's face grew even hotter, but she kept her smile pasted in place.

"So you think about that tonight," Josie said, going on tiptoe to kiss her son's cheek. "Because I want all my sons to be as happy as their dad and I are."

"And speaking of our other sons…" Wade said with

a broad smile, appearing to want the same thing as his wife. "The rest of your brothers are out back, waiting to say hello to you and Amanda."

Justin took Amanda's hand. "Then we won't disappoint. See you later, Mom and Dad."

Amanda and Justin moved off. It was all Amanda could do not to moan in dismay. "Your mom doesn't mince words, does she?"

Justin heaved a sigh. "Her heart wants what it wants. Which is all of her sons happily married with families of their own."

"How many have done that so far?"

"Two."

The back lawn was filled with people. White-coated chefs stood over commercial-sized grills. The air was scented with fragrant mesquite wood and barbecued beef and chicken.

His hand on her spine, Justin led her through the crowd, introducing her to guests and extended family. Finally, they found Justin's brother Colt. The sheriff's deputy had a lovely wife and a three-year-old son. An ancient Bernese mountain dog was by the child's side. The sight filled Amanda with an unexpected wish for a child of her own. *Justin's child...*

Next up was Justin's brother Rand—a big, strapping, macho-looking guy. Justin hugged his brother, who appeared to be there without a date. "Heard Mom's ticked off at you again."

"Yeah, well." Rand waved a hand. "What can you expect when you put a devoted environmentalist and a lady wildcatter in the same space?"

Derek, a venture capitalist based in Dallas, was as

well-dressed as you might expect. He had an infant daughter cradled in his arms.

Justin's oldest brother Grady, a Fort Worth real estate developer, and his wife, Alexis, were supervising their little girl and several other small children on the backyard play set. Grady smiled at Amanda. "Colt said you're going to be starting a carpentry program at the boys ranch."

Amanda nodded. *Here's where it could get tricky.* "I am," she said, content to leave it at that.

Justin slid his arm around her waist, the proprietary nature of the gesture unmistakable. "She's also been named ranch director," he announced casually.

Grady turned back to Justin with a quizzical frown, clearly shocked. "Isn't that the job *you* were angling for?"

Word of Amanda's appointment spread like wildfire, and though Justin's parents offered their congratulations, Amanda could see that Josie had reservations about the unexpected turn of events. She wasn't surprised to see Justin and his mother take a moment alone a little later in the evening. He returned to her side ten minutes later, his expression tense. "Everything okay?" Amanda asked.

Justin merely looked at her. "Want to get out of here?"

"Won't your mom object?"

His lips tightened. "She'll know why we left."

They walked down the driveway. "Why do I have the feeling this has something to do with me?" Amanda asked uneasily.

Justin fished his keys from his pocket. "It doesn't."

"The director's job, then," Amanda persisted.

Hurt simmered just beneath the surface of Justin's expression. He opened the passenger door for her then propped one arm along the edge and rested his head against his taut biceps. His eyes searched hers. "Our family has a cabin cruiser out at the lake, if you want to go...."

Sensing he *really* needed to get away, Amanda replied, "Lake Laramie it is."

After ten o'clock, the area around the boat slips was peaceful, with only the occasional pocket of activity. Out on the lake, however, you could see boats here and there, their safety lights blinking.

Justin helped her onto the deck, undid the ropes and climbed aboard. Minutes later, they were cruising across the lake, the stars and half-moon nestled in the black-velvet sky, the warmth of a Texas summer night surrounding them. Justin drove the cabin cruiser until he found a deserted cove, well away from other boats. He cut the engine and dropped anchor, but left a few lights on deck, for safety, as well as the soft lights in the cabin below. For a while, they sat there in the semi-darkness, accompanied only by the soft lapping of the water against the boat, the hum of cicadas on shore. The quiet was a blessing after the hubbub of the party.

Eventually, Justin went below and came back with a couple of long-necked beers. "You know, you don't have to talk about whatever-this-is if you don't want to," Amanda said.

He twisted off both caps. "I want you to hear it from me, not someone else."

This did not sound good.

He sighed, settling beside her on the bench seat next

to the rail. "And if I don't tell you, you will hear it elsewhere."

Amanda took a sip of the cold, delicious beer. "Okay."

He opened up his wallet, removed a worn photo and handed it to her. It was a young kid with dark hair, olive skin and hauntingly-old-for-his-age eyes. The eyes of a person who had seen and experienced too much. "Who is this?"

Justin swallowed. "Billy Scalia. A kid I was trying to help back in Fort Worth, when I worked at the nonprofit there."

Their fingers brushed as Amanda returned the photo. "I take it the story did not have a good ending."

He ducked his head. "He died."

The pain and unjustness of that seemed to transfer from Justin to her. "Oh, Justin…" Amanda touched his arm.

Justin caught her hand and pressed it flat against his chest. "His older brother was in a gang and had gone to jail. Billy's mother was desperate to keep the same thing from happening to Billy, so she enrolled him in our after-school program. I was put in charge of coordinating services for him. I got him a grief counselor and a tutor, and signed him up for all sorts of sports and activities, anything to keep him busy and off the streets…out of that gang."

The heat of his body seeped into her palm. "But it didn't work," she guessed.

Frown lines bracketed Justin's sensual lips. "His brother's gang kept coming for Billy, wanting him to join. The peer pressure in that neighborhood is huge. His mother knew Billy wouldn't make it if he stayed, and she couldn't afford to get out on her own. I was working on a solution for both of them. She was even willing to put Billy in foster care for a while, if that kept him safe."

"But Billy didn't want that."

Justin let her go. He picked up his beer again, took another sip. "He didn't want to leave his mom, because then he felt the gang would blame her, and she wouldn't be safe." Justin stared out at the water. "Before I could get things worked out, the peer pressure got too much. Billy joined the gang on behalf of his brother and died during the initiation robbing a liquor store."

"I'm so sorry, Justin…." Amanda's eyes filled with tears.

He turned back to her, mouth grim. "That's why I left the nonprofit and decided to start the ranch, because I knew there were a lot of kids out there, some with parents who cared, some without, all needing a safe, quiet place to go, out of the inner cities. I wanted kids who lack the kind of positive nurturing background I grew up with to have that type of love and support in a residential setting."

Admiring his inherent gallantry more than ever, Amanda vowed, "And the Laramie Boys Ranch will be that."

Justin nodded in determination.

Knowing what he'd just told her was somehow connected to whatever words had been exchanged between Justin and his mother back at the ranch, Amanda guessed, "Your mother liked the idea of the ranch." *How could she not?* "But she thinks you should be director. Not me."

Justin squinted. "It's worse than that."

Amanda traced the condensation on the bottle with her fingertip. "Tell me."

Another grimace. "She thinks, deep down, I'm afraid of failing another kid. That I let the director position go deliberately, and didn't fight for it as hard as I could have, because I'm already getting ready to quit the ranch—the way I quit the nonprofit and the big accounting company before that."

Wow. "Are you?"

Justin drained his beer and set it aside with a decisive thud. "No. The ranch is where I'm meant to be, Amanda." He paused, letting his words sink in, then stood and walked toward her. "I may not have the exact right background for it, but I'm a fast learner, and I'm going to do whatever it takes to make it a success."

"Even if that means ceding the director position to me."

He was only inches away, leaning over her. He met her gaze, his good humor returning. "That's not the sacrifice you may think it to be."

His sexy rumble sent a thrill soaring through her. "Really? How come?"

He smiled when she defiantly angled her chin and gazed into his eyes. "Because having you as my boss means I get to see you every day...and every night."

Amanda sucked in a breath. "And that's a plus?"

He sifted both hands through her hair, came nearer still. "Oh, yeah..."

His kiss spiked her pulse sky-high and weakened her knees. Amanda swayed against him, another thrill soaring through her. "If I thought it was just the sex..." she moaned between kisses.

"It's not." Justin deepened the angle and the sweetness of the caress and kissed her more passionately. "You know it's not...."

Amanda was beginning to see that.

Beginning to want to let herself go. Loving the way he challenged her, the way he wasn't afraid to take passion to the limit, Amanda slid her arms around his neck, pressed her body full against him and locked her mouth on his in a slow, sexy kiss that soon had both their hearts pounding. She felt the sandpapery rub of his beard and savored the exciting masculine taste of his mouth, the tantalizing tangle of his tongue with hers.

He made her feel so wanted. Needed. He was so big and strong, so unbelievably tender and patient in his pursuit of her. So good at getting her to live each moment to its fullest. To know that all that was wonderful was yet to come.

They descended the steps to the cabin and made their way to the double bed against the wall. He clasped her to him and she could feel the hard evidence of his desire. The heat. He kissed her so thoroughly it stole her breath. His hands slid beneath the hem of her blouse to caress her bare midriff. Sensation swept through her. Buttons were dispensed with one by one. On her shirt. Then his. "I want you," he whispered.

"And I want you," she gasped, her nipples budding beneath her bra. Lower still, dampness pooled.

And still he took his time relieving her of her skirt, her shoes. When she was clad only in a bra and bikini panties, he brought her to him. The air between them reverberated with excitement as he took in the swelling curves of her breasts spilling out of the lace, the jutting nipples visible beneath the thin fabric.

She spread her hands across his naked chest, exploring the silken skin and smooth muscle. The hardness and heat of his pecs. The width of his shoulders, his taut biceps. She nipped at his throat. "If we were to have a beauty contest, it's hard to tell who would win." She smiled against his skin.

He kissed the sensitive spot behind her ear. "You think?"

She let her gaze drop lower still, to the fullness hidden beneath faded denim. Her fingers eased beneath the waist of his jeans, finding his hot, hard length. "I do…" she observed playfully as her libido roared. "I've never seen a man with such an amazing physique." She kissed his chin, the underside of his jaw, his cheek. "And that face…" So ruggedly handsome. So male. So perfect in every way from the brilliant blue eyes to his rumpled chestnut hair.

He chuckled softly at the enticing ministrations of her hand, catching her lips with his in a long, sensual kiss. "That," he said as he unclasped her bra and eased it off, "is a compliment that can go both ways, woman of my dreams…"

With a wicked grin, he dropped the lacy garment to the floor and bent her backward over his arm. Tenderly, he kissed the slopes and valleys before settling on the exquisitely sensitized tips. Pleasure filled her with hot, mesmerizing waves. The last of her inhibitions fled. Wanting only to be his, she shuddered and let out a whimper of need.

Together, they shucked off his jeans and briefs. Her panties followed. Still kissing, they stretched out on the bed. At first facing each other. Then with Amanda on top, astride him. Hands on his shoulders, she kept him right where she wanted him, tempting him with kisses and caresses until he was as desperate to have her as she was to have him.

He flipped their positions.

His hands trapping hers, he moved lower, finding the silkiest, sleekest part of her in a slow, hot invitation. Amanda gasped, surging upward, and then there was no more waiting, no more playful foreplay. Eyes heavy-lidded and sensual, he moved over her and possessed her in a way that commemorated what they felt. In a way that promised even more satisfaction in the days and night ahead. In a way that said she was his. And he was hers. And for the moment, Amanda knew, that was more than enough.

Chapter 10

Amanda accepted a cup of coffee from Justin. "You want to have a meeting every morning at eight?" She'd barely stepped out of her trailer when he was on the front porch of the lodge, waving her inside.

He favored her with a sexy smile. "I think it'll help keep us on track if I know what you have on your to-do list and you know what I have on mine. We'll add the rest of the staff as they're hired on, too."

"Okay," Amanda said, slipping off her tool belt and setting it on the floor.

He got out his list. "Do you want to move into this office or would you prefer to take the one next door?"

Amanda blinked, beginning to feel overwhelmed again. "Aren't they both the same size?"

"Yes." Justin nodded affably at his current office.

"But this one is closest to the living area, the one next door is closest to the kitchen."

She grinned back. "Well, then it's settled, I'll take the one closest to the kitchen."

He looked into her eyes as tenderly as he had made love to her the night before. "So you want to move all the files over there?"

Deep breath. "How about we leave them with you for now, since you know what most of them mean?" *And I'm not sure I ever will...*

Nodding, Justin moved on to the next item on his list. "The application for the big Lone Star United Foundation grant has to be signed and postmarked by Friday."

"That's the big one we're hoping to win?"

"Yes. Although there are several others that are due next week, and then another batch to start applying for right after that."

"So this grant application business..."

"Is a continuous process, since the deadlines occur all year long. But like I said, I'll fill them out as long as you want me to do so. All you have to do is read through them and sign them."

How hard could that be? "No problem."

"We have inspectors from the state social services department coming out tomorrow to do a preliminary inspection."

Amanda moved closer. "Why preliminary?"

"They want to have a look around and red-flag anything that will need correcting before the licensing inspection the last week of July."

She inhaled the masculine scent of him, wishing they were back in the bedroom instead of hanging out here discussing business. "Is it going to be a problem that the bunkhouse isn't finished?"

He inclined his head. "I doubt it, but they're going to need a firm date for when it *will* be done. And I would advise that to be at least a week before the final inspection, in case anything comes up on our end."

On more solid ground now, Amanda vowed, "I'll do an assessment when we're through here, and let you know."

His handsome features softened in relief. "Okay."

Without warning, the dogs jumped up and headed en masse for the front door.

Barking heralded a vehicle approaching the lodge. Justin went to the door. "Were you expecting a visitor this morning?"

"Granddad!" Amanda engulfed him in a big hug. "I didn't expect you this morning." How did he always know when she needed bolstering?

A.B. reached into his truck. "I have some papers for you to sign."

Amanda sighed at the sight of the legal documents. "Seems to be a thing lately." Briefly, she explained her visit to the attorney's office the day before.

They walked inside the lodge and settled in the living room area. "Well, if it were just you and me, I wouldn't require you to sign anything. But the new owner wants everyone who isn't moving over to the new company—which is basically just me and you—to sign a severance agreement with a noncompete clause."

Amanda looked over the contract, feeling unexpectedly nostalgic. "It says I can no longer work in San Angelo."

"But," A.B. pointed out cheerfully, "there's nothing preventing either of us from working in Laramie County. My attorney and I made sure of that."

Amanda signed where indicated. "What about the work left on the bunkhouse?"

Granddad pointed out an addendum. "I had everything here excluded from the sale, since it was the one project I had that was still ongoing. But, now that you've signed on as director…"

"It wouldn't be right for me to charge to finish up the bunkhouse, given that as of today I'll be drawing a salary for my work here."

A.B. smiled. "How is the bunkhouse going?"

Amanda leaped to her feet. "Want to come over and take a look?"

Together, they went through all she'd done. "You have what—three bedrooms and baths to go?"

"Plus the wide-plank oak floor," Amanda affirmed.

Granddad contemplated the stacks of flooring in the main living area. "How long do you have?"

Amanda shoved her hands in the pockets of her coveralls. "Less than two weeks to completion."

A.B. whistled. "And it's just you and Lamar?"

"When I have him, yeah."

Granddad understood why she felt overwhelmed. "Looks like you need some help."

Justin walked in to join them. "That we do," he said.

Amanda turned back to her grandfather. "The only problem is, you can't do this kind of heavy lifting anymore."

A.B. harrumphed. "That's not what Doc Parsons said. He said I can't do carpentry all day and then travel to and from a job. I can do one or the other just fine."

This was an old argument. "You promised Gran before she died that you would enjoy your retirement the way she never had a chance to before she became ill."

Granddad sighed. "You want the truth? It can get a little boring."

"I say let him help," Justin urged.

Lamar walked in, his backpack slung over one bony shoulder. He grinned. "The more, the merrier, isn't that what they always say?"

Amanda put the heel of her hand against her forehead. There was way too much testosterone in the room. "Y'all are ganging up on me, and it's not fair."

A.B. hooked an arm around her shoulder. "Relax, honey. It's all going to get done, and in record time. You'll see."

Before Amanda knew it, she'd been escorted to one of the bathrooms to begin installing the premade cabinetry with Lamar's help. Justin was tapped to carry the pieces of wood for the lockers and bookshelves to the cutting station set up in the dining area. He and her grandfather spent the morning measuring, cutting and sanding down the edges of all the required pieces. By noon, the necessary wood was stacked in each remaining bedroom. By evening, they had the storage units installed. The cabinets in the bathrooms were done. All that was left was the flooring.

"If the four of us work on it together, we could knock it out in two, three days max," A.B. said. "Then all that will be left is the staining and finishing."

Justin tilted his head respectfully at her granddad. "Helps to have another pro around."

Granddad smiled and slapped Justin on the back. "Helps to feel needed again."

A little irked to see her grandfather so chummy with a man she wasn't sure would be a permanent fixture in her life, Amanda retorted, "Well, be that as it may, you can't drive all the way back to San Angelo tonight, Granddad."

"Honey, I have to get the papers to the attorneys tomorrow. But I can come back the day after."

She could see how tired he was. "I don't want you driving home alone tonight."

Justin stepped in to help with the persuasion. "Why don't you bunk in one of the guest rooms tonight? Get a good night's sleep and then head home tomorrow morning."

"Please, Granddad," Amanda reiterated.

"All right," he relented. "If it will make you feel better, I will."

"Thanks for talking sense into Granddad," Amanda said several hours later. It was nearly midnight, but Justin was still elbow-deep in paperwork. She had been trying to get caught up, too.

He pushed away from his desk and leaned back in his chair. "No problem. Although I think you worry a little bit too much. A.B. may be seventy but he's in fine physical shape."

Amanda propped her hands on her hips. "Only because he hasn't been overdoing it."

Justin tilted his head, considering. "Is that your only objection?"

Amanda wandered closer. She stood facing him, with her hips propped against the desk, arms folded in front of her. "What other issue could I have?"

"I don't know." Narrowing his gaze, he studied her a long moment. "That's why I'm asking."

Amanda drew up to her full height. "I heard you talking to Granddad earlier today when we were working about the possibility of him working here."

Justin looked up at her, running his palm over the arm of his chair. "That's right. If he wants to work in the carpentry shop, teaching the kids the same way he taught you the trade, we'll put him on the payroll."

Amanda tensed despite herself. She met his level gaze. "I wish you had discussed that with me first."

Justin paused. "Are we talking about his health? Or something else?"

Up to now, the only one who could read her like a book had been Granddad. Trying not to make too much of Justin's ability to read her, too, Amanda said cautiously, "He was really happy to be here helping out."

Justin nodded. "And that's a problem because…?" he probed.

What if I don't work out and the board decides I'm not right for the job after all? What if none of this works out?

Would she and her grandfather both be set adrift, with no family business to fall back on? "It's too much of a commute for him," Amanda said finally. *Too much of a risk for me.*

And the key to her happiness, she had learned long ago, was to keep her life safe and simple.

Justin caught her hand in his, turned it so their fingers entwined. "So we'll set up accommodations for your granddad, whenever he is here, or find a place for him nearby. These are all details that can be worked out, Amanda."

She knew that.

Justin came closer. He touched her chin, angling her face up to his. "So what's the real problem?"

It was time to confide. "I'm feeling overwhelmed."

He released a long torturous breath. "Me, too." Amanda peered at him through lowered lashes. "You don't look overwhelmed," she pointed out.

He winced. "Paperwork, I can handle. A miter saw and nail gun—" he made a comical face "—not so much."

She waved off his anxiety. "Flooring is easy. Particularly if someone else is doing the measuring and cutting. All you have to do is line it up, drop it down and hit it with the hammer so it's nestled in tight."

He grinned confidently at her. "I imagine you'll help me until I get the hang of it."

Amanda grinned back. "I imagine I will."

Silence fell. Their smiles returned. Despite her hefty agenda, Amanda found herself relaxing.

Had her grandfather not been sleeping upstairs… But he was, she reminded herself sternly. So nothing of an amorous nature was happening tonight. Or would be on most nights, since they had to keep their private life out of the work realm.

Figuring this was good practice for the self-restraint that would be required of them in their new positions, she looked at her watch. "Well, it's late…" she said in a wistful tone.

He nodded, looking as if he were feeling, wanting, the same thing. Knowing, at least for that night, it wasn't going to happen.

Amanda cleared her throat, disengaged their fingers and moved away. "We probably should both get some shut-eye. The state inspector is going to be here at nine tomorrow morning." Since they couldn't make love to-night, maybe not tomorrow…or the day after, it would help to stay busy.

She would focus on that.

"We see two problems that need to be addressed right away," the inspector told Amanda and Justin when he had finished the following day. "All the carpentry equipment and materials need to be secured when not in use, preferably in a building of some sort."

"Will a portable building work?" Justin asked.

The inspector nodded. "As long as there is a lock on it. Second, the travel trailer has to be removed from the property right away. The sooner the better." The inspec-tor handed them their copy of his report. "Naturally, when I come back the last week of July, I'll expect to see the bunkhouse completely finished and ready for move-in."

When the inspector had gone, Justin turned to her. Obviously noting this was not good news to her, he pointed out matter-of-factly, "You were going to have to move into the lodge anyway."

Amanda walked back to the office that had been as-signed to her. At the moment it contained a desk, chair and lamp, and little else. "I didn't think I would have to do that until the ranch opened." If then. She'd been hop-ing to wangle a way out of moving in, on some grounds or other. The truth was, she didn't want to be that physi-cally close to Justin. Or get so emotionally entangled with him that she couldn't imagine a life without him.

Justin lounged against the desk, his knit shirt taut across his broad shoulders, looser over his abs. "Where do you usually park the trailer when you aren't living in it?"

"I'm always living in it. At least, I have been since I bought it a few years back."

He looked at her candidly. "You don't have an apartment or a house?"

She placed the report front and center on her desk and sank into her chair. "No. This is the only home I have. With the exception of my old room in my granddad's house. I mean, I can always go there, and I do from time to time. But the trailer is my home."

He studied her with an emotion she couldn't identify in his eyes. "A home you don't want to give up."

"Would you?"

He stepped closer. Reaching down, he drew her to her feet. "I sold my condo to live here."

Amanda flushed. "That was different. You bought the land and oversaw the building of the lodge and the bunkhouse. So this has to feel like your home now."

Justin drew her into his arms and slid a possessive hand down her spine. "It will feel like your home, too," he promised. Cupping her face in his hands, he kissed her with all the pent-up emotion of the day. Tempting her again and again, sweetly and evocatively, not stopping until she felt wanted beyond all reason.

Suddenly aware that things were moving way too fast, that if this continued she would feel even more confused and vulnerable, Amanda wriggled free of his embrace. "And that's another thing." Without her trailer home, without comfort and privacy… "We're not going to be able to do *this* anymore, either."

"Sure we will," Justin countered with a slow, sexy smile. "If we plan for it."

Talk about determination! She smiled as she studied him, suddenly feeling reinvigorated. "You really expect…?"

His eyes crinkled at the corners. "To keep making love to you? Yes, Amanda." He kissed the nape of her neck. "I do."

The irony was not lost on Amanda as she hooked up her trailer to her pickup truck and drove it several miles down the highway to the campground Justin had assumed she wanted the first time they met.

Luckily for her, the Lost Pines Campground had a vacant slot at the far end of the park. There was no view of Lake Laramie where she was situated, but there was enough sunlight coming through the surrounding trees to power her solar panels. There was also an electric hookup in case her batteries ran low.

When she returned to the ranch around noon, she found a note from Justin on her desk saying that he and Lamar had gone to San Angelo to purchase a large shed and would not be back until much later.

"Well, fellas," Amanda told her five canine companions. "It looks like it is just us for the rest of the day."

Twenty minutes later she was proved wrong.

A gleaming yellow truck with license plates that said WILDCAT drove up. Josie McCabe got out, a huge beribboned gift basket in her hands. She smiled as Amanda and the dogs approached. "Is Justin here?"

Amanda explained where he had gone.

"Oh, dear. I had hoped to speak with him, and leave him this peace offering, before I left town again."

"You can wait," Amanda offered.

Josie shook her head. "Actually, I can't. But perhaps it's just as well you and I have a chance to talk privately, Amanda."

Able to see that a number of the items in the basket needed to be refrigerated, Amanda led the way inside the lodge. "It's okay, Mrs. McCabe. I understand why you would have been upset that I got the director job over Justin. It was an unexpected turn of events."

"But, according to both Justin and my husband, as well as the other board members, it's the right solution for what has been an ongoing problem."

That, Amanda thought, remained to be seen. "I've only been on the job a couple of days." And so far all she'd felt was overwhelmed.

"Which is plenty long enough for the situation to throw a monkey wrench into the relationship between you and my son."

Her hiring *had* made things awkward, at least at times. But how had Josie known that? "We don't have a relationship." At least, not an official one.

Josie set the fresh fruit on the counter. "He brought you to the party."

Amanda took the smoked meats and cheese and set them in the fridge. "He thought it was a good opportunity to introduce me to the rest of his family all at once."

Josie unpacked a box of cookies and another of cupcakes from the Sugar Love bakery. "Did he also tell you he hasn't brought a woman home since he ended his engagement to Pilar?"

Trying not to make too much of that, Amanda left the cookies on the counter and put the cupcakes in the fridge. "Maybe he just thought it was time he got back in the saddle again." As soon as the words were out, she clapped a hand over her mouth. "I didn't mean for that to come out the way it sounded."

Josie laughed. "It's time for Justin to get back in the saddle and fall in love. For real, this time. I think you could be the one." A fretful look crossed her face. "I also think working together under such pressure could ruin things for you as a couple, and/or detrimentally affect the boys ranch."

Amanda had much the same fear but pushed it away. "It won't," she reassured Josie.

The older woman studied Amanda. "How can you be so sure?"

"Because," Amanda replied sagely, "I know what this dream means to Justin. I know how hard he's worked for it, how much he is willing to give up—" *including his pride* "—to see it become a reality. I won't get in the way of the success of the ranch. I'll quit before I see that happen."

Justin came back around seven that evening. Amanda was in the bunkhouse staining cabinets a beautiful honey oak. "Need some help?" he asked, admiring her handiwork.

Amanda paused, not sure she wanted to feel any closer to him at the moment. And every time they labored together—at anything—they ended up feeling like more of a team. She gave him the skeptical once-over. "Careful. You could get this on your clothes."

He tugged on some plastic painting gloves and reached for an applicator. "I think it will be okay."

For a few minutes, they worked quietly side by side. "So how did your day go?" Amanda asked eventually.

"Good. It took some doing, but Lamar and I finally

found an aluminum storage shed with a floor that's big enough to hold all your gear plus a fair amount of wood. It's being delivered tomorrow morning."

Their forearms touched as they both reached for the paint tray at the same time. "That's great," Amanda said.

They finished one room and moved into the next. "I saw a gift basket on the kitchen counter with a card from my mom."

Amanda concentrated on the staining. "Yeah. She was here around noon. She wanted to make peace with you." An awkward silence fell. "She's sorry the two of you argued."

Justin snorted. "But probably not sorry for what she thinks."

"She has a right to her opinion."

Hurt glimmered in his eyes. "I wouldn't figure you'd be on her side in this."

Amanda shrugged. "That doesn't mean I agree with her." *Or think this could ruin our...whatever.* "I do think she has a right—as your mother—to worry about you."

"I'm a grown man. I can take care of myself," he bit out.

Amanda shot him a droll look. "I can see that." She waited until he met her eyes, then continued. "My point is, when I was growing up, I would have given anything if I'd had a mother who worried about whether or not I was doing the right thing."

His glance narrowed. "What did your mother worry about?"

Ruefully, Amanda admitted, "Whether or not I would interfere with her happiness."

"And your dad?"

"Worried about whether or not I would interfere with his happiness."

Compassion softened his handsome features. "That sucks."

Amanda refused to pretend otherwise. "Yes, it did. Fortunately, I eventually ended up with Granddad and Gran and they showed me the way families should be. You're lucky enough to have that, so…" *Don't look a gift horse in the mouth!*

He rubbed the back of his wrist beneath his chin. Squinted. "Hmm. Remind me of what my parents think about my life's work?"

Exasperated, Amanda replied, "You have a dad who thinks you're on the wrong path and a mother who thinks you *might* be on the right path but worries that if you stay the course, you could mess up your…" Oops. Damn. She hadn't meant to reveal that part of her talk with Josie.

"Mess up my what?" Justin demanded.

Amanda went back to painting. "Whatever this is with us."

He blinked. "She said that?"

Amanda drew a deep breath, expecting to inhale paint stain and instead getting a whiff of the soap and sunshine scent of his hair and skin. Still working, Amanda eased away. "Actually, I think she said our working together might throw a monkey wrench into our relationship."

Justin finished up the inside of a cabinet, without taking his eyes off her. "My mom called it a relationship?"

"Her word, not mine."

Justin's eyes gleamed mischievously. "I like that word."

With effort, Amanda continued to concentrate on her task. "Even if it's not apt?"

"Who says it's not?"

Amanda moved on to the next room. "You're digressing."

He picked up the paint tray. "I am."

Amanda settled before yet another cabinet. "And you are bringing the personal into the workplace."

Justin set the tray down. "Since the ranch isn't officially open yet and it's only the two of us, I don't think anyone else will mind."

She turned. "Justin…"

He stripped off one glove then the other, dropped them and took her by the shoulders.

"Just one kiss, Amanda." His lips hovered just above hers. "And then we'll get back to painting…"

"Staining," she corrected.

His eyes shuttered. "Whatever."

The next thing she knew, he was kissing her and she was kissing him back.

"So, what's the verdict?" he asked when he had finally lifted his head. "Is working together *helping* our relationship?"

Well, it certainly wasn't hurting it. Amanda lifted her lips to his for one more kiss. His head lowered, slowly, deliberately, and she said, "I think it just might be."

Chapter 11

It was midnight by the time they had finished. As Justin walked Amanda away from the bunkhouse toward the lodge he caught her hand in his. "You can't go back to the trailer tonight."

Amanda swung around toward him. It amazed her how much she wanted him, how much she *always* wanted him. The ferocity of her need put her off balance, and she pulled away from him but couldn't quite make herself disengage her fingers from the warmth and strength of his. "I'm tired."

He let go of her hand long enough to encircle her shoulders and pull her close. His lips brushed the top of her head. "Exactly."

His casual gesture felt profoundly intimate and conjured up an even deeper need for affection. Aware that it would take very little for her to go up in flame, and reveal just how deep her need for him went, she forced herself to create some distance between them. Then she flashed him an officious smile and said, "Seriously. I want a long, hot shower." *Preferably with you in it. But we can't have everything....*

He fought a smile. "We have that here, you know."

"I need clean clothes."

He let out a low laugh, his eyes dark with desire. "You can borrow some of mine."

Amanda quivered, thinking just how sexy it would be to sleep in one of his shirts and nothing else. Aware of just how close she was to surrendering to him, heart and soul, she lengthened her strides. "I also want a bed to sleep in." Reading the seductive direction of his thoughts, even as he fell slightly behind, she said over her shoulder, "My bed, not yours."

He caught up with her easily, and his gaze caressed her face. "Lucky you. We have a bed just for you right upstairs, down the hall from mine. In fact, we have an entire bedroom suite with your name on it. A bedroom, I might add, you are already supposed to be moved into."

Noticing her boot lace flapping, Amanda stopped at the front steps of the lodge, propped her leg on a step and bent to tie it. "I'm getting there," she replied irritably. Not sure why she was resisting the inevitable, just knowing that she was.

He paused beside her, his eyes roving her bare knee and calf with a lover's intent. "Not fast enough."

Another quiver ran through her. Aware her nipples were hard beneath the soft cotton fabric of her T-shirt, Amanda straightened. She ran a hand through her bangs, pushing them off her face. "You," she muttered with a beleaguered sigh, "are incredibly persistent."

His lips curved with a tenderness that she found even more distracting than his ardor. "And hungry," he allowed. He hooked his thumbs in the front belt loops of his jeans and rocked back on his heels. "Let's raid that gift basket my mother brought. She may not know how to cook for her five sons, but she does know how to feed us."

The culinary gifts had looked delectable. And, like it or not, she was too tired to cook, and there were no open restaurants anywhere close.

Amanda gave in—on this. "Okay, I will make a deal with you. I'll shower here and borrow your clothes, but only because mine are so sweaty. And I will sit down to eat with you, but then I'm going to my trailer to sleep." Her look confirmed there would be nothing after that for either of them to regret.

He relented, eventually, shaking his head in admiration. "You drive a hard bargain."

"I do." Together, they walked inside, stopped to pet the dogs then headed up the stairs to his quarters. Not about to go anywhere near his bed, Amanda lingered in the doorway while he plucked a chambray shirt from the closet and a pair of gray cotton jersey workout shorts from the shelf. He stopped at his bureau. "Boxer briefs or commando?"

Amanda smiled, knowing how dangerous it would be to go there. "You will never know," she teased. "And neither, thanks."

His eyes glinted in return. "Soap? Shampoo? Towel?"

That was easy. "All of the above, please."

He produced the necessary items, and left her with the ease of a Texas gentleman, born and bred. "I'm going to shower, too. I'll meet you downstairs in ten."

Amanda called after him, "Make that fifteen."

* * *

Amanda took her time in the shower, hoping the hot, invigorating spray would loosen the tightness of her body and the need throbbing through her. Instead, all it did was give her time to think about what it would be like to make love with Justin again, and to figure out if she could do so without falling hopelessly in love with him.

The answer? She wasn't sure. All she knew, as she got dressed in his shirt and shorts, gathered her dirty clothes and work boots, and walked barefoot down to his kitchen, was that she would never stop wanting him. Never stop relishing what they already had.

As she expected, he was waiting for her in the kitchen. He, too, was barefoot and wearing a pair of dark gray workout shorts that hit at midthigh and left his long, muscular legs open to her perusal. A white V-necked knit shirt nicely delineated his broad shoulders and flat abs. Crisp hair was sprinkled below his collarbone and on his limbs. She inhaled the soap and cologne scent of him and felt her mouth grow dry.

He handed her a tall glass of icy lemonade. He seemed to intuit that her emotions were in turmoil, even though his expression was casual. He brought the platter of hickory-smoked meats and cheeses to the table, and added a loaf of hearty sourdough bread and some spicy mustard from the fridge. "You'll be happy to know I texted my mom."

Amanda watched him open jars of olives, pickles and jalapeño peppers. She thought about the conversation they'd had earlier—one that had seemed to go nowhere at the time. "What did you say?"

Grinning, he brought down two plates. "'Thanks for

the peace offering. Amanda likes you a lot even when you're wrong.'"

Amanda laughed ruefully. She added napkins and silverware then sat beside him at the kitchen island. She propped her chin on her hand and studied him. Although not yet dry, his hair was rumpled and very touchable. "You always have to have the last word, don't you?"

He turned on his stool so he was facing her. He tugged at a lock of her still-damp hair. "Pretty much." His husky voice sent shivers down her spine.

Amanda swallowed. "Did she text you back?"

His gorgeous blue eyes crinkled at the corners. "Yep."

Their eyes met, held. "What did she say?"

"'I love you.'"

The sober words hung between them. "That's it?"

He nodded. Another poignant silence fell. "I'll give her this," Amanda said, feeling a hint of moisture gather behind her eyes. "Your mom knows how to put an end to an argument."

Justin nodded, looking touched, too. "That she does."

Talk turned to the ranch, and all that had yet to be done, as they made sandwiches and savored each bite. They finished off their late-night snack with German chocolate cupcakes from the Sugar Love bakery. Replete, they rose to put the leftovers away and do their dishes. In a corner of the kitchen, the five mutts watched them with sleepy eyes.

Amanda walked over to give them their post-meal tidbits. Finished, she patted each one on the head. "The dogs are tired."

Justin nodded. "They're wondering why *we* aren't asleep."

Amanda realized there was still so much she wanted to know about Justin. She sauntered back to him, acutely aware of what she was wearing and what she was not. If she weren't so worried about having her heart broken again, they would have headed straight to bed. Working to keep it casual, she sat down to put on her boots, without socks this time. "What's your normal bedtime?"

His eyes gleamed wickedly. "Depends on what I'm doing."

Best not go there. She sent him a casual look over her shoulder. "Quit dodging the question." They needed to get back on non-innuendo-laced turf.

"On a normal work night, I am usually in bed by eleven. Weekends can be later." He paused, expression deadpan. "Lately, there have been nights when I've hardly had any sleep at all."

She chuckled despite herself. "Got to watch that. Some habits can be hard to break," she warned with mock solemnity.

He came toward her. Taking her hand as if he were a knight assisting a princess, he drew her to her feet. His hands circled her waist, bringing her closer so her breasts grazed his chest. "There are some habits I don't want to break."

How well she understood that, Amanda thought, as an aura of pent-up longing surrounded them.

Tingling, aware she should have put her bra back on whether it was sweaty or not, she withdrew her hand from his and took a step back. "Well. Thanks for the meal."

He held her eyes, a lot more intimately. "Thanks for keeping me company."

Her yearning multiplied. She struggled, then calling

on every bit of self-control she possessed, found her resolve. "But I better go."

He touched her arm. "I'll escort you."

Amanda slipped away from him, grabbing her bundle of dirty clothing and her purse. She held them in front of her like a shield. "Thanks for the offer, but that's really not necessary."

He leaned down and touched his lips to her temple, clearly aware she was using politeness as a shield. "Exactly why I'm doing it."

Amanda thought about arguing but decided that it would delay the inevitable.

She got in her pickup truck. Justin got in his.

It only took five minutes to reach the campground and drive through the rows and rows of trailers until they reached hers. They both parked their vehicles.

The grounds were quiet and mostly dark.

He followed her to her door. She looked at the handsome contours of his face and felt a tremor go through her. "I really am not inviting you in," she whispered.

He stepped closer and she forgot to breathe.

"A good-night kiss here will do just fine." Her heart racing, Amanda lifted her hands to his shoulders. Their lips met. And once the kiss started it seemed impossible to stop, even more impossible to control. She groaned. "You really are testing my willpower."

He brushed his thumb across her cheek. "And you're testing mine."

"Justin…"

Aching with need, she pressed her face into his shoulder. Her heart and body sent conflicting signals to her brain. Her body won.

She let out a heartfelt sigh, lifted her head and looked

into his mesmerizing blue eyes. She could pretend all she wanted. Deny it all she wanted. But the truth was, she wanted to take it to the next level with him. Wanted…well, she wasn't sure what she wanted, except him. And that wasn't going to change. She splayed her hands across his chest, felt the rapid thud of his heart and slid them lower. She itched to undress him. To…

Amanda caught her breath, then whispered, "I'm thinking you better come in before we give the other campers a show."

His voice caressed her as surely as his eyes. He bent to kiss her temple. "I'm thinking the exact same thing."

Amanda didn't know what it was about Justin, but the minute they were alone together she started to glow from the inside out.

She took his hand and led him to the bed, sliding her fingers beneath the hem of his T-shirt and tugging it up and over his head. She dropped it onto the floor. "Anyone ever tell you that you are so darn irresistible it's mind-boggling?"

He started at the bottom of her shirt and unbuttoned his way up. A second later, it, too, was coming off. Slowly—over her shoulders, down her arms.

His hands skimmed across her ribs and upward. "Did I ever tell you that you have the most beautiful breasts?" His smile was slow and sure, and so hot it could have started a fire.

He bent to kiss a nipple. Her eyes closed as he stroked and suckled. A shiver racked her body and she couldn't catch her breath. She opened her eyes then impatiently reached for the waistband on his shorts. "Everything about you is beautiful, too."

The flatness of his abs, the smoothness of his skin, the sheer masculinity of his hips and lower abs, and... that, too...

Amanda laughed in surprise. "You're..."

"Commando. Mmm-hmm." Clearly aroused, he caught her against him, found the waistband of her borrowed shorts and eased them down. "And what do you know," he chuckled as the shorts hit the floor. "You're commando, too."

"Commando with boots." She glanced at her feet.

He slipped off his moccasin-style leather loafers and bent down to untie her laces.

"Naked is better."

"It certainly is."

The next thing she knew, her boots were off. Still kneeling, he hauled her in tight against him, parting her thighs and giving her a kiss that was long and wet and deep. Her hands were in his hair as he proved he knew her body better than she did. A whimper escaped her throat. Then, suddenly, she was catapulting over the edge, a quivering tangle of sensation. "I want more," she whispered, urging him up.

He joined her on the bed. "We'll have more," he said, his voice husky with promise. He caught her against him, his mouth meeting hers in perfect harmony. The kiss was slow and romantic. Rough and heartfelt. Tender and easy.

He was claiming her completely in the most primal way she had ever allowed, and she reveled in the heat of his body, the proof of his desire. The shocking extent of his need for her, too.

She relished the tenderness, the knowledge that something about this, the way they couldn't help but come together, had opened up her heart. Made her want to want and need him, the way she had never wanted or needed anyone before.

Justin knew, much as Amanda pretended otherwise, that there were still barriers between them. The fact that she didn't think she was good enough for anyone worthwhile. The fact she liked to keep one foot, if not her whole body, out the door. The fact that she didn't want to think about anything more than the moment she was in.

In the past, he'd felt the same way.

Now, things were different.

Now he wanted her with him, pressing her warm curvy body into his until neither of them could think. He wanted her soft, silky hands sliding all over him. Just as they were now. He wanted her on top of him, kissing him madly, and then beneath him, surrendering softly.

He wanted her open and wet and willing, moaning and wrapping her legs around his waist. He wanted to go deep inside her and feel her clench around him. And even when she did that, her hips rocking up against his, he couldn't get enough.

He met her eyes as they began to move in tandem.

Harder, faster…slower, deeper.

Until they were both sighing and panting for more.

And they gave it. One to the other, wildly, passionately, until at last there was no more holding back, no more seeking the best connection yet. They were soaring, pinnacling, the thundering ache in his body replaced by the shimmering satisfaction they gave each other, and the lingering yearning in his heart.

* * *

Justin fell asleep with Amanda wrapped in his arms. He awakened as the first light of dawn was slipping in through the windows. Easing away from her, he rose from the bed and began to dress.

Amanda slept on, looking like an angel. With regret, he went in search of his wallet and keys. They were on the table at the front of the trailer, next to an application for a long-term lease for a space at the Lost Pines Campground.

Amanda's writing was all over it.

He was still staring at it when she came up behind him. Wrapped in a robe, she slid her arms around his waist and laid her head against his shoulder. He turned slightly, so he could put his arms around her.

She looked up at him, frowned as if perplexed. "Is something wrong?" Her voice was soft.

Ask her. "Are you thinking about keeping the trailer here indefinitely?" he asked finally. When she had personal quarters back at the ranch and him just waiting for her to move all the way in? What did this mean?

Her eyes giving nothing away, Amanda lifted her shoulders. "Well, I have to park it somewhere, since I can't keep it at the ranch anymore. It makes sense for it to be nearby."

There was certainly one reason he would not only understand but applaud that decision. Justin scrutinized her closely. "So we'll have a place to be alone besides a hotel room or my family's houseboat?"

Amanda hesitated, running a hand through her tousled blond hair. "Well, sure," she said finally.

Justin tensed. So that wasn't it.

"I just feel better if my home is nearby," Amanda

said finally. "Even if, technically, it's going to be a home away from home, once the ranch opens and the kids start arriving."

Justin guessed he could understand that. Especially since the trailer was the closest thing she had to a home of her own.

He pushed his worries aside. They had time to work all this out. Meanwhile, with everything they had on their agendas, they couldn't afford to get bogged down in minutiae. "I've got to get back to the ranch and take care of the dogs."

Reluctantly, she led him toward the door. "I'll see you later, then."

Later, Justin thought with a twinge of disappointment, as he kissed her again and headed out.

When all he really wanted was the here and now. And the promise that, at the end of the day, she wouldn't decide their love affair was too complicated and slip out of his life as swiftly and unexpectedly as she had come in.

Chapter 12

An hour later, Amanda was in the office. Justin stood beside her desk, multiple stacks of papers in hand. "The first is the application for the state licensing board. The second and third are both small-grant applications. They're all ready to go. They just need to be signed and mailed."

Acutely aware of how good he looked in his beige knit shirt, casual green cargoes and work boots, Amanda accepted the files he handed her. "I can handle that."

His tall frame radiating barely leashed energy, he waited until she had set them aside before continuing. "You're going to need to read through them first, though, so that you're familiar with all the information and to make sure all is as it should be."

Amanda hated paperwork, but she also knew this was part of being ranch director. She was going to have to learn to like it. She put the folders back, front and center on her desk and flashed a smile. "No problem."

Justin reached for another folder. "We've received notice from the state that we're being audited."

Her heart sank as she saw the letter containing the list of all the items the state wanted to review.

Picking up on her panic, Justin curved a reassuring hand over her shoulder. "It's no big deal," he said, giving her a brief, comforting squeeze. "We have to do this periodically to maintain our nonprofit status. As CFO, I'll handle that."

Thank goodness. Amanda would not have known where to begin.

He removed his hand and continued down his list. "You saw the email this morning from Mitzy?"

Amanda had just read it when he walked in. "About Lamar." It was part good news, part bad.

Justin nodded, looking as concerned as she felt. "You want to tell him of social services' decision when he comes in?"

Amanda replied, "I'd like us to do it together, if it's okay with you." She lifted her eyes to his and felt a tiny thrill sweep through her when their gazes meshed.

"Sounds good." Apparently a lot better at keeping his emotions out of the workplace than she was, Justin sorted through his notes with laudable efficiency. "There was also a request for phone interviews from the local paper. They want to get your feelings about being named director of the ranch before they go to press this afternoon."

An interview? Already? Heaven help her. She felt so overwhelmed she could barely breathe. "What do I say?"

"Whatever you want. Although I have to warn you. I know that reporter. She's always looking for the sensational side of every issue, to jazz up her copy. She'll probably ask you how you feel about beating me out of a job everyone knew that I wanted." Justin paused. "She asked me."

"What did you say?"

"That I agree you have that something special the board has been looking for all along, and you'll do a tremendous job here."

Amanda caught her breath. "You really mean that?"

Nodding, he locked eyes with her, his expression every bit as tender and giving as when they made love. "I do," he said softly.

Talk about gallantry. Justin was a bighearted Texan, through and through. The kind of man she had always dreamed about but never believed truly existed, until now.

"And don't forget the TV news producer from KTLZ is coming out to do the advance work on the segment about the ranch later today."

Amanda made note of that on her own incredibly long to-do list.

"I'm still working on the big grant application." He pointed to the stack of at least one hundred pages, if not more, on his desk. "That's due at the end of next week."

Amanda blinked at the enormity of the application. "That's it?"

"What I've compiled so far," Justin allowed. "There's still a ways to go."

Feeling like she would perish if she had to sit, trapped, behind that desk one second longer, Amanda rose and paced toward the window. She looked out at the lawn, saw the bunkhouse, which still needed a lot of work.

Justin put down his folders and came toward her. He stood behind her and massaged her shoulders. "It's okay. I've got it," he reassured.

Amanda trembled. "But should you have to?" she couldn't help but ask.

She pivoted toward him, her arm grazing the hard musculature of his chest. "I'm beginning to feel like I'm all hat and no cattle—not only full of it for even taking this job, but completely incompetent!"

One corner of his mouth quirked up at her self-effacing description. "Stop being so hard on yourself. You'll feel differently about everything once everything is set up and the counselors and kids start arriving. When you have seven other boys to help acclimate and mentor, you'll not only be completely in your element, you'll know why the board wanted you as director."

Amanda didn't doubt she would be able to do a good job mentoring the boys, and looked forward to setting up the carpentry shop and teaching woodworking. But as for the rest of it, the business matters she was inundated with now—or rather simply signing off on—how much of that would she ever actually be capable of doing?

She met his tender, reassuring gaze. "It still seems unfair, Justin. I'm the ranch director. Yet you're still doing all the administrative work."

"You'll transition into a lot of it as time goes on. Although, to be honest, I imagine we'll both continue doing double and triple duty until we get fully staffed. There's simply no other way to get everything accomplished."

"That's true." She leaned her head on his chest, absorbing his warmth and strength.

He stroked a hand down her spine. "The most important thing is getting the kids settled. And speaking of wayward teens…" Justin smiled as a car door slammed outside.

A minute later, Lamar walked in.

Justin and Amanda met Lamar in the living room. Figuring it would be more comfortable than her office, Amanda motioned for the teen to sit on the sofa. She and Justin pulled up chairs on the other side of the coffee table. "Social services has decided you will be our first residential student," Amanda informed him, watching as Lamar beamed with delight. "On one condition." Amanda paused. "You have to agree to attend Laramie High School in the fall. And you have to be serious about it. No more skipping classes."

Resentment surfaced, as expected. "I told you both. I hate it there."

"Doesn't matter." Justin backed Amanda up firmly. "This is nonnegotiable."

Amanda handed Lamar the course catalogue. "To reserve your slot in the first bunkhouse, you have to sign up for classes at LHS today."

Lamar slouched in his chair, all belligerent teen. He thumbed through the catalog listlessly, then shoved it back toward Amanda. "You decide."

Amanda figured that was as far as Lamar was willing to go when it came to cooperation. She picked up a pen, wrote his name and grade across the top of the form, and looked at the instructions the guidance counselor had sent along with the course list. "Okay. Well, first, you have to sign up for Remedial Math and Remedial Language Arts/English, to get you caught up on the requirements. You also have to take World History and Physical Science over again, too, since you flunked both of those last year."

Lamar scowled and started to rise. "Whatever you say."

Amanda shook her head and motioned for him to sit back down. "You're not done yet. You have two more slots left. One can be Physical Education."

Lamar groaned. He put his hands on either side of his head in a demonstration of abject misery. "I hate P.E."

"Everyone does, except the jocks," Justin sympathized. "But it's required. And it doesn't involve studying."

Lamar harrumphed. "Ha! I wish! The coach gives written tests on the rules of each sport."

Justin was briefly taken aback. "Then we'll find a creative way to help you learn the rules, either through practice or watching games on TV, which even you have to admit that you like."

Amanda understood what it was to hate the academic classroom and feel as though you just didn't belong in the traditional school environment. "There is a woodworking class for an elective." She glanced over the description. "Basically, you learn the fundamentals."

Lamar rolled his eyes. "I already know them."

"Which should make it easy for you to excel. And maybe even help some of the other kids who are struggling."

Her attempt to look on the bright side failed. The silence grew even more tense. Finally, Lamar shoved his hands through his hair. "I really have to go to LHS?" he asked miserably. "Again?"

Amanda wished she could tell him there was another option, but social services was not currently offering studying for the GED exam as an alternative path for a habitual truant. With a sigh, she nodded. "If you want to stay here on the ranch, yes, you have to attend the local high school.

"We'll make sure you get the extra help you need to get caught up," Justin reassured the boy. "Even if it means hiring tutors."

Lamar looked even more distraught. For a long moment, he seemed to want to say something. Finally, he stared glumly at Amanda and lifted a shoulder. "Fine. Can I go to work on the bunkhouse now?"

Amanda nodded. "I'll be right with you."

Lamar dashed out of the lodge. The dogs greeted him on the porch. Apparently needing the solace they offered, he knelt to pat them.

Justin and Amanda walked into the office to fax the forms over to the high school guidance office. "Congratulations on getting him signed up for classes," Justin said, preparing a copy for Mitzy and social services, too.

Amanda hadn't done it alone; they both knew that. She punched in the number on the machine. "I just wish he were happier about it."

Justin gave her a commiserating glance. "At the moment, I think this is the most we can expect."

Amanda knew that, too. She just wished she felt happier about *that*.

Luckily, for all their sakes, Lamar's mood improved dramatically as soon as they started working on the bunkhouse. It lifted even more when Granddad arrived to take over, while Justin and Amanda led the KTLZ producer on a tour of the facilities.

The fortysomething brunette was blunt-spoken and energetic. "I think the two of you are everything we're looking for in our Local Heroes series. Helping kids is going to resonate with viewers of all ages. And, of course, it doesn't hurt that we've got a picturesque ranch setting with two beautiful young people—the local golden boy and the former bad girl—joining forces to lead the program."

Amanda flushed self-consciously. She knew it was part of her appeal and the reason she'd been asked to lead the boys ranch, but she hated being known as a former delinquent. It was just so embarrassing when she was paired with a true role model like Justin.

He brushed off the melodramatic description, and interjected with a calm smile, "Anything you can do to help us raise more funds would be deeply appreciated."

The KTLZ producer smiled back at him. "I'd be glad to help." She slid her cell phone into her pocket. "There's only one hitch. We would need to film ten days from now, and we want everything ready for the boys a couple of days before that."

Amanda did some quick calculations. "So we'd have a week." And she'd thought her agenda was impossible before!

"You seem to be doing okay."

Justin looked up to see Amanda's grandfather framed in the office doorway. He stood to welcome A.B. "And Amanda's not." Even though, for the past three days, he and Amanda had done nothing but work toward their respective goals. To the point where she had begged off spending time with him in the evenings and headed straight for her shower and bed.

Justin had let her go because he could see she was physically and emotionally exhausted, and he didn't want to deprive her of whatever personal space she needed. But there was no doubt he had missed their evenings together. Missed spending intimate time with her. Missed having the opportunity to make love to her again and solidify them as a couple.

A.B. took a seat in front of Justin's desk, his concern evident. "She has always worried she'll be rejected if everything is less than perfect."

That, Justin thought, was obvious. He went to the minifridge in the corner, got out two bottles of water, and handed one to his guest. "She didn't get that from you."

A.B. gave a long-suffering sigh. "Her parents required perfection of everything—and everyone—in their lives."

That couldn't have been a fun way to live. Justin took a long thirsty drink. "Does Amanda ever see them?"

"My wife and I arranged it, several times, after Amanda came to live with us, but her folks always came up with excuses and never showed up. Eventually, we just stopped trying to effect any kind of reconciliation. It seemed less hurtful."

Justin capped his bottle. "Where are they now?"

"Last I heard, her dad had married his fourth wife and was managing a big hotel on Maui," A.B. admitted. "Her mom—my daughter—is in California, weathering a sixth divorce."

"And you don't see them, either," Justin guessed.

"No."

Justin thought about how different that was from his

own family, who, even when they disagreed with each other, still managed to work out their problems. "I'm sorry to hear that."

A.B. shook his head. "It is what it is. Wishing otherwise won't change that."

Justin rocked back in his chair, glad the older man had stopped by his office to chat before going to the bunkhouse to help Amanda and Lamar. "What will make Amanda feel better?"

"Zooming through the to-do lists. Achieving your goals. The big work party you've put together for tomorrow should go a long way toward accomplishing that."

Justin hoped so. Thanks to all the calls he'd made, they had plenty of people coming to assist. He had hoped Amanda would feel more confident as a result. She wasn't. Maybe because she hadn't ever seen what the people of Laramie County could do when they came together in a common cause.

Her grandfather obviously didn't share the same concerns. "You don't seem all that worried about her," Justin remarked.

"Normally, I would be." A.B. drained his bottle and screwed the cap back on. "Normally, this is the kind of situation that has her running as fast and far away as she can get. Instead—" the older gentleman smiled and inclined his head in the direction of the bunkhouse "—she's working harder and seems more committed to the cause than ever."

Justin knew that to be true. He smiled back. "We both are."

"Then take comfort in the fact that she's settling in instead of trying to move on." A.B. rose. "It's only when she has one foot out the door that you should start to worry."

* * *

But Amanda did have one foot out the door, Justin thought the following morning, as the board members and various friends and family—including his parents—arrived to help. It was evident in the fact she hadn't yet moved to her assigned quarters in the lodge, but insisted on staying in her trailer in the campground several miles away.

It was also evident in the way she managed to keep her physical and emotional distance from him while helping to organize and oversee the work.

By the time night fell, all the cabinetry had been finished, and three thousand square feet of unfinished wood flooring had been put in. The walls and trim were all painted. The entire crowd had been thanked and fed.

"We've made arrangements with a company in Dallas to provide the bunkhouse furniture," his mom had told him upon arrival.

His dad looked Justin in the eye. "I know there have been times in the past few months when your mother and I have both had our doubts, son, but that's over. Amanda helped us see how committed you are to the cause." Wade's voice caught. He gave Justin a hug, then pushed on, eyes glistening, "We're very proud of you, son."

It wasn't often his dad became emotional. Justin choked up, too. "Thank you both," he told his parents thickly as his mom hugged him, too. "This means a lot."

Meanwhile, nearby, Amanda's grandfather was deep in conversation with Miss Mim. Justin overheard her say, "Laramie Gardens is a wonderful senior-living village." Eventually, she convinced A.B. to give it a try.

"You're going to stay there tonight?" Amanda asked her granddad in disbelief.

"Laramie Gardens has rooms for prospective residents for a nominal fee. If I stay there, I'll be able to eat breakfast in the dining room and take the full tour tomorrow." A.B. seemed truly enthusiastic.

Amanda studied him in shock. "You would really consider leaving San Angelo and moving here?"

She didn't seem as happy to hear that as Justin would have expected, although she could just be attached to that home.

A.B. wrapped an affectionate arm around his granddaughter. "I want to be close to you, honey. And your future is here."

As the picnic dinner for all the helpers commenced, Libby remarked to Amanda, "Speaking of futures. When are you going to move into the lodge full-time?"

"Actually, I've been too busy trying to finish up the bunkhouse to think about it." Amanda stood up to get more iced tea. She brought the pitcher back to the folding banquet tables they had lined up across the yard. Then she made her way down the table, topping off glasses as she went.

Always thinking ahead, Mitzy added, "I think it should probably be done before the KTLZ crew arrives to film the segment on the ranch, don't you?"

Amanda smiled as if it were no big deal, when Justin knew that, to her, it was a very big deal. "I probably should."

"Do you want any help with that?" Justin's dad asked, misreading the reason behind Amanda's delay.

Justin jumped in, "We've got it covered, Dad."

At least, he hoped they did.

"So when did you want to move into the lodge?" Justin asked Amanda after all their guests had left. It was nearly midnight, and the two of them and the dogs were sitting, exhausted, on the front porch of the lodge enjoying the warm, starlit night.

Amanda brought her knees up to her chest and wrapped her arms around her legs. "I still have another four days."

Which meant she'd be waiting until the very last second before filming began, he realized. "We could do it tomorrow instead," Justin suggested mildly.

Amanda shook her head, stubborn as ever. "I want to stain the floors in the bunkhouse tomorrow, and when that dries put the first of three coats of sealant on."

Justin figured it would be unwise to push. She'd probably had enough of that at the dinner, anyway. He exhaled. "Okay."

She gave him a sidelong look. "You think I'm procrastinating."

Since she had opened the door to the next question, he returned her sidelong glance. "Are you?"

Amanda chewed on her lower lip. "Maybe."

His gaze traveled over her silky calves and bare arms. Reminded how beautiful her body was all over, he asked, "Any particular reason why?"

"One." She sighed wistfully. "You."

Was this going where he hoped it was? He sure as heck hoped his patience was about to be rewarded. His body hard and ready for action, he echoed softly, "Me." He needed and wanted her to spell out whatever she was thinking and feeling.

The corners of her lips turned up in a soft smile. "In case you hadn't noticed, it's difficult for the two of us to be alone together without making love. So, that being the case, maybe it would be best if we waited until the last minute for me to actually move in here. That way, when I do, we'll have a lot of built-in chaperones who can help us stay on the straight and narrow."

Knowing she needed a life of her own as much as he did, he pointed out casually, "Even after you move in, we'll still get time off to do whatever we please." Although they had to be mindful of their responsibilities, and the accompanying restrictions, working at the boys ranch didn't mean they forfeited a private life entirely.

She sighed wistfully, abruptly seeming miles away from him. "I know."

He waited until she met his eyes again, then said, "We'll still want each other."

She hesitated. "At least for a while."

Ah. So this was the real problem. One he could easily solve. "Not 'for a while,' Amanda," he corrected, taking her by the hand and drawing her to her feet. He slid his arms around her waist and brought her snug against him so she could feel how much he wanted—and needed—her to be his. He lifted a strand of hair from her cheek and tucked it behind her ear. "*Forever.* I'm not the kind of guy who changes my mind about that, Amanda. Once I commit to someone, I'm in it for the long haul."

The pulse in her neck was throbbing as she lifted her face to his. She gazed up at him, conceding softly, "And you're into me for the long haul."

He smiled and kissed her again, feeling victorious. "I'm talking absolute exclusivity."

Amanda wound her arms about his neck and kissed him back. "So," she said tenderly, "am I."

* * *

Amanda hadn't planned to invite Justin back to her trailer that evening, but once he kissed her there was no going back. No pretending she wasn't falling head over heels in love with him. No pretending she wanted him anywhere other than with her, in her bed. That night, and every other.

They undressed the moment they entered her trailer and fell onto her bed, senses in an uproar. And from there it only got hotter as he drew her flush against him, letting her feel his hardness, kissing her without restraint.

Draping a leg over her legs, he continued caressing her breasts, ribs and thighs with his fingertips, before sliding lower to explore the most intimate part of her. And still he couldn't get enough of her, or she him. Desire exploded in liquid heat.

She arched blissfully, never more aware of the power one woman and one man could feel. Never wanting anything to endure more.

He moaned at the trail of kisses. "Amanda…"

"Let me love you."

He surrendered until he could bear it no more. Then rolled her over, captured her wrists and pinned them on either side of her head. Kisses followed. Slowly at first, then hotter, harder, deeper.

Amanda whimpered, opening her mouth to the pressure of his, stroking her tongue with his. She rocked against him, kissing him back, urging him on, until there was no doubt about what she wanted, what they both wanted. Tingly heat spread. Her feelings intensified as he slid his hands beneath her hips and lifted her to him. He entered with excruciating slowness, taking command in a proprietary way that electrified her.

Amanda cried out softly, pushing her fingers through his hair, smoothing her palms over his powerful shoulders and down his back, wanting him never, ever to stop.

And he didn't. Not until they both reveled in the erotic feelings, the sweet hot need, the sheer pleasure of being together. Pausing and withdrawing, going deeper every time until there was no controlling that, either. She was his…he was hers. For now, and forever.

Chapter 13

Justin and Lamar were in the kitchen one morning later that week, wondering where Amanda was.

"It's nine-thirty," Lamar said. "Shouldn't she be here by now?"

Justin knew better than anyone just how early Amanda got up. This morning, they'd awakened at five o'clock and made the kind of love that just seemed to get better every time they were together. He'd left her heading for her tiny shower, come back to the ranch, taken care of the dogs and gotten a head start on his day.

Now, three hours later, still no Amanda.

"Should we go looking for her?" Lamar asked, his face pinched with worry.

"Go looking for whom?"

Justin and Lamar turned.

Amanda staggered toward them, buried under the

weight of all she had slung over her shoulders and clasped in her arms.

Both guys quickly rushed to help. Justin took the heavy stand mixer with the stainless-steel mixing bowl and the cloth bag of perishable groceries. Lamar grabbed two big bags of assorted cooking utensils, gadgets and various baking sheets, which left Amanda with an over-size plastic clothes basket full of other food items and a cardboard box that had *food processor* scrawled across the side.

It looked, Justin noted joyfully, as if she was finally moving in.

"Why did you carry it all at once?" he asked.

"I didn't." Amanda announced cheerfully. She set the basket on the floor and unloaded her belongings onto the stainless-steel island in the center of the over-size kitchen. "There's more in my truck. So if you fellas are so inclined…"

Smiling, Justin and Lamar headed for the door.

"And don't forget the plants!" Amanda called after them.

Fifteen minutes later, they had unpacked everything. "What's this?" Lamar asked, holding up what looked like a three-foot wooden baseball bat that was narrower on each end. "Some kind of sports equipment?"

That would have been Justin's guess.

Amanda made a face. "No, silly. It's a French rolling pin."

"Ahh," both guys said at once.

Amanda took the pin and tapped Lamar playfully on his shoulder. "We're going to use it to make lunch today."

The teen quickly evidenced the panic Justin felt. What did either of them know about French pastry?

"What about the bunkhouse floor?" Lamar asked quickly.

"It only requires one more coat of sealant and that can't go on until about one o'clock this afternoon. We have to make sure the previous coat is really dry before we apply the last one."

Lamar's face fell, the way it always did when he had failed to get out of something he really wanted to avoid. "Oh."

Justin lifted his hands, already backing away. "Don't look at me. Much as I'd love to join you two chefs, I have to put the finishing touches on the big grant application for the Lone Star United Foundation. It has to be mailed today."

Amanda was glad she wasn't the one slaving over that huge stack of paperwork. "Well, good luck with that."

Grinning with relief, Justin disappeared.

Amanda turned back to her charge. Lamar was still looking at the long wooden rolling pin Amanda had inherited from her grandmother. He sighed. "I don't know about this...."

Amanda clapped a hand on his shoulder. "We had fun cooking before, didn't we?"

Another sigh. "Well, yeah, but..."

"And cooking is a skill you're going to need in life, isn't it?"

Lamar frowned. "I suppose."

"So I'm going to teach you how to use a recipe, because if you can follow instructions, you can cook practically anything with a little practice." She smiled. "And mark my words…you are going to be surprised at how easy it is to make pizza from scratch."

At the word *pizza,* his eyes lit up.

Giving him no more time to fret, Amanda dove in. She lined up the cup and spoon measures, brought out a packet of yeast, the flour, salt, sugar and thermometer.

Briefly, she went through what everything was, then handed him a glass cup. "This is a one-cup liquid measure," she said. "See how it's marked off?"

Lamar nodded, his expression serious.

"Run the tap water to warm, and then fill it to the red line on top."

He did as required, then brought it back to her. "Let's see how hot it is. We want it to be between 105 and 115 degrees." They put the thermometer in, waited. Amanda smiled as the thermometer registered 107 degrees. "Perfect! Now we open up the packet and take a teaspoon of yeast, sprinkle it over the water and stir to mix." She watched as he carefully complied, then gave him another reassuring glance. "Good. We'll set this aside and wait for the yeast to activate—which will take about ten minutes."

They went on to measure the flour, salt and sugar into the mixing bowl. Amanda showed Lamar how to check the yeast for bubbles, then slowly add olive oil, and the yeast-and-water mixture to the bowl. When it was all blended, Amanda sprinkled flour on the counter and dumped the dough onto it.

Justin walked in. He had a huge stack of papers. Amanda immediately recognized the big grant application. There were sticky notes protruding everywhere. "I've marked everywhere you have to sign and date," he said. "So if you want to do this now…"

Amanda looked at her hands, which were covered with flour. "Can it wait?"

Justin frowned, impatient in a way he usually wasn't. "This really needs to go out."

"If you put it on my desk, I'll get to it as soon as I'm done here."

He slid her a long look. "It has to be mailed today."

"I'm headed into town later to pick up the window blinds for the bunkhouse. I can do it then."

"By five?" he prodded.

Trying not to be annoyed by his unusually intense level of micromanagement, she nodded. "I promise. Okay?"

"I'll leave the mailing envelope and everything with it front and center on your desk."

"Thank you." Justin still seemed less than pleased by her response. Luckily, the tension was cut by the roar of what sounded like a tractor-trailer coming up the drive. She shot a look at Justin. "Are you expecting anyone?"

"Not today." Justin paced to the front door, looked outside and groaned.

Watching, Amanda called from the kitchen doorway. "What is it?"

Justin swore. "The bunkhouse furniture."

"Justin sure is grouchy," Lamar noted several hours later.

"That's because it has been one of those days where everything that could go wrong has gone wrong," Amanda reassured him.

The bunkhouse furniture had been prematurely delivered, which meant it had to either be stored in the lodge or sent back to the Dallas warehouse and they'd have to wait another two weeks for redelivery. Sending the furniture back wasn't an option since the KLTZ crew was due to film their Local Heroes piece on Friday. While they were attempting to make room for the furniture, the state auditor had arrived to take a look at the ranch's books.

Justin had no sooner gotten the auditor situated in a room apart from his cluttered office than the architect had arrived—along with a surveyor—to decide the best place to situate the woodworking shop. The two men had driven in from Fort Worth and hadn't had time to stop for a meal en route. So Lamar and Amanda had ended up making more pizza and a huge salad, and inviting everyone—including the truck driver and his unloading partner—to stay for an impromptu lunch amid all the chaos.

"Everybody liked our pizza, though, didn't they?" Lamar remarked as they finished the last of the dishes.

Amanda smiled. Lamar was really getting the hang of thinking on his feet in stressful situations. "They really did." And with good reason. The meal had been excellent. No doubt about it. Lamar had an innate talent for cooking as well as carpentry.

"Are you going to teach all the kids that come here to cook?"

Amanda wiped down the kitchen counters. "I was thinking about it. What do you think?"

Lamar took care of the table. "They'd probably like it, too, although I don't know about all that recipe stuff."

She had noticed he'd seemed more confused than comforted by the written instructions. But then, she supposed that was normal for someone with zero experience in the kitchen. "You'll get the hang of it." Amanda paused to add a little water to the herb pots she'd situated along the windowsill.

"Maybe," Lamar looked doubtful. "But I like doing stuff that's easy to memorize."

Amanda walked outside with Lamar. They stopped at the shed to pick up the gear they needed before proceeding to the bunkhouse. "Are you ready to put the final coat of sealant on the floors?" Amanda checked to make sure all the windows were open, to ensure maximum ventilation and quicker drying time.

Nodding, Lamar picked up a can of polyurethane, a brush for the corners and tight areas, drip pan, and mop-style applicator. "You want to do it the same way we did it yesterday?"

"You start in the corner of each of the bedrooms, and work your way to the door. I'll do the kitchen and dining room and we'll meet up in the living room."

They worked well in tandem. By four o'clock they were outside, starting the cleanup, when her cell phone rang. Able to see from the caller ID that it was the chairwoman of the board of directors, Amanda stripped off her gloves and answered. "Hey, Libby. What's up?"

"Hi, Amanda. I was just talking with a friend of mine, who's overseeing the grant applications at the Lone Star United Foundation. He said ours hadn't been received yet. I wanted to make sure it was in the mail, since it has to be postmarked today to be considered."

Oh, no. Amanda blew out a breath. "Justin finished it this morning." Somehow, she managed to sound a lot more with-it than she was. "I'm on my way to the post office right now." Or she would be, Amanda amended silently, as soon as she dashed inside the lodge to get it.

"Great," Libby enthused. "The post office in town closes promptly at five, you know."

Amanda tried not to panic. "Yes. Justin mentioned that." Her heart pounding, Amanda thanked Libby for the reminder and ended the call. She turned to Lamar. "I've got to go into town to mail something that's got to go out today. Will you be okay finishing the cleanup on your own?"

"Sure."

Amanda hesitated.

"I remember what we did yesterday," Lamar promised.

She knew he had an excellent memory. Far better than most kids his age. "Okay, but just to be sure..." She reached into her pocket for the small notepad and pen she habitually carried to mark down measurements. "I'm going to write out everything you need to do— in order. And don't forget, the rags and the used roller sponges should be left outside in the empty paint trays to dry. Everything else should be put in the shed with the door closed."

"No problem."

Amanda tore off the paper and handed it to him. Her pulse racing, she ran toward the lodge, dashed inside, slowing to a deceptively casual walk as she passed the room where Justin was hunched over a desk with the auditor, and then hurried into her office. She grabbed the huge stack of papers from the desk, a pen and the mailing envelope, then headed quickly back out again, aware she now had only forty-one minutes to get to the post office. And she hadn't even signed anything yet!

Racing against time, Amanda drove toward Laramie. Halfway there, she came across a small traffic jam, caused by a wide-bodied tractor mowing the berm. It cost her a good ten minutes. Shortly after that, several volunteer fire department vehicles, including a fire truck, passed her, sirens blazing.

Giving a silent prayer that whoever needed EMS was going to be okay, Amanda turned her attention back to driving and the directions on her dash-mounted GPS.

Unfortunately, she was so rattled she got turned around once she hit the historic downtown area, where she encountered another traffic jam caused by the usual early-evening rush.

Finally, she located the post office, a small square building with an empty flag pole in front of it, and no other cars in the lot. She parked her truck, just as her phone rang.

Justin.

Figuring it best not to talk with him until she had completed her mailing, she got out of the car and sprinted toward the door. And found, not surprisingly, that it was locked, since it was now 5:10. No reason to panic. She would just find another post office that stayed open later.

Amanda went back to her truck and consulted the internet via her phone. To her relief, she saw the main post office in the next county was open until seven. GPS directions estimated it to be about an hour away from her current location.

No problem. She would just go there.

Amanda started the ignition and headed out.

She was fifteen minutes outside the Laramie city limits when Justin called again. Figuring he probably wanted to know if she had indeed gotten the grant application mailed, she again decided not to pick up. Better to talk with him after she had completed the task as promised.

Unfortunately, he called her again two minutes later. And again, three minutes after that. Beginning to think something was wrong besides her bad memory, Amanda took the call. "Hey," she said, as if everything was fine with her.

Only to hear him sounding frantic on the other end.

"Amanda, thank God I reached you! I'm with Lamar at the Laramie Community Hospital E.R."

Her heart sank. "My God! What happened?"

"I'll explain when we see you," Justin promised in a low, clipped tone.

And Amanda knew, even without him saying, that whatever had happened was all her fault.

Justin had never been one to hover. He was hovering now, like the worst helicopter parent, and he didn't care. With the foster parents and Amanda still en route to the hospital, he was all the kid had. Justin was determined not to let him down.

Lamar teared up as he eased himself into a sitting position on the stretcher. His face smudged with soot, he looked incredibly young and vulnerable in the hospital gown. "Amanda's going to be mad at me."

Seeing Lamar so distraught made Justin want to lose it, too. He fought to remain as calm as the kid needed him to be. "No, she's not," he said soothingly. Glad a little dirt was all they worried about, he forced Lamar to lie back against the pillows. "And put your oxygen mask back on."

The exam room door swung open. Amanda rushed in. She was a mess. Justin had never been simultaneously so angry and so glad to see someone in his life. What had she been thinking, leaving Lamar to his own devices? Without even letting Justin know she was headed for town? Did she really think he cared more about the grant application than the teenager in their charge?

Oblivious to Justin's tumultuous emotions, she stared at Lamar, as if unable to take it all in, then rushed to hug the teen like he were her long-lost child. "Oh, Lamar!" She released him slowly and pivoted to Justin. *"What happened?"*

What happened, Justin seethed, was that Amanda had been incredibly irresponsible! Struggling with a burst of temper that he knew had as much to do with relief as it did anger, Justin snapped, "He put paint-thinner-soaked rags in the shed and shut the door. The combination of closed air and extreme summer heat caused them to ignite within, oh, say five minutes…."

Amanda clapped a hand over her mouth. More tears welled. "Oh, my God."

Lamar shook his head and started to cry in earnest, too. He shifted his mask again. "She told me not to do that, Justin. It's not her fault—it's mine. Look!" Coughing, he reached into his pocket and pulled out a crumpled paper as proof. "She wrote everything down for me."

Justin studied the familiar writing. Sure enough, the instructions she'd left were detailed and clear as day. *Air-dry the rags and paint rollers in the paint trays. Do not put in shed.* Beneath that, underlined, was, *Important—to prevent spontaneous combustion.*

"Why didn't you follow her instructions?" he asked Lamar, looking frustrated with both of them. "Espe-

cially if you had gone through this exact same proce-
dure yesterday?"

Lamar looked even more frightened and on edge.
"Because I... I..."

Sure the kid was hiding something, as well as doing
all he could to protect the woman he adored, Justin unleashed his anger on Amanda. "You realize we could
be denied our license because of this?" If they weren't,
it would be a damn miracle!

Amanda turned ashen. She looked confused, upset,
humiliated, all of which made Justin feel worse.

"I—" Trembling, she choked back a sob. "I'm sorry."
Trying to pull herself together, she finally looked from
one to the other. "Is Lamar going to be all right?"

Thanking heaven for that, Justin nodded grimly.

Lamar nodded, too. "It's just smoke inhalation,"
he explained through his oxygen mask. "Because I
smelled something burning and opened the shed...
and...breathed in..."

Distraught, Amanda sank down into a chair. Completely overwhelmed, she buried her head in her hands.

Silence fell.

Justin stared at the crumpled notepaper, knowing
instinctively there was more to this, something Lamar
had yet to reveal. He turned to his young charge, wanting to help, knowing he would never be able to unless
the teen was straight with him. "I know you have this
thing about not following instructions," he drawled.

His efforts to prod the truth out of Lamar worked.
The boy's jaw set. "It wasn't that."

"Then *what was it?*"

Lamar glared back at him. "You really want to know?"

Justin nodded and pushed even harder. "After what

happened this afternoon, I think the least you owe us
is an explanation!"

Tears sprang to Lamar's eyes. He threw up his arms,
shouting belligerently, "I can't read, okay? I. Can't.
Read. Anything! Got it?" Coughing, Lamar ripped off
his mask and tried to swing his legs off the gurney.

Amanda leaped up, tears streaming down her face.
She caught Lamar by the shoulders, just the way a loving mother would, and held him in place. She replaced
his oxygen mask. "What do you mean, you can't read?"
she asked gently, searching his eyes, sharing his pain.

Misery engulfed Lamar. "I just can't," he declared
haltingly. "I never could."

"Which is why you hate school," Amanda said, with
all the empathy a child could ever want or need. "Why
you refuse to do your assignments. Why you skip class
and didn't want to go back."

"Yes." Lamar broke down completely and thrust
himself all the way into Amanda's arms. She held him
tight. Eventually, Justin joined in. And that was the way
the medical staff found them, clinging together, comforting, consoling, like the family they had become.

Chapter 14

"Amanda knows we have a television crew coming first thing tomorrow to do the story on the ranch?" Libby asked at noon on Friday.

Justin looked at his longtime friend. "She's aware." *Very much aware, as a matter of fact.*

Libby watched him use a dolly to roll the last of the furniture down to the bunkhouse. Clearly frustrated with all the recent setbacks that threatened to derail the project they'd all worked so hard on, she asked, "Then, where is Amanda?"

Wasn't that the question of the day! Justin shrugged and headed back to the lodge to get the table lamps he'd already unpacked and assembled. "I don't know where she is. I haven't seen her since she left the hospital last night, after Lamar's foster parents showed up to take him home."

"Did she say where she was going?" Her low voice radiated with concern.

Justin exhaled. "She said something about finishing up a few errands, that she'd see me at some point after that."

"But Amanda didn't come back to the ranch last night."

"No," Justin replied tersely. "She didn't." Neither had she been at her trailer. He knew, because he'd gone back and forth between the two locations all night long and this morning, looking for any sign of her. There had been none.

Libby frowned. "Have you spoken to her grandfather?"

Justin nodded. "A.B. is in San Angelo. He said he hadn't seen her, either, but told me not to worry." *Like that was even possible.* "He thinks she'll show up eventually."

"I hope so." Libby checked her phone for messages. "Do you want me to call some of the other board members, help you finish setting up the bunkhouse?"

All Justin wanted at the moment was to be alone, to try to process everything that had happened. Irritated with himself for not having seen this coming, even though all the signs had been there, clear as day, he replied curtly, "I've got it. Thanks."

Libby touched his arm. Happily married herself, she wanted the same for him. Everyone on the board did. "Please call me if you need me."

He nodded, promising that he would.

After she left, Justin went back to carrying lamps. He was about ready to start setting up bunkhouse beds when the dogs jumped up and ran to the door. He walked outside and saw Amanda getting out of her truck.

She looked like she had showered and washed her hair since he had last seen her, but her face was pale and drawn, and she was wearing the same clothes she'd had on the day before. Where had she been?

She came toward him, an envelope in her hand. Her amber eyes glistened with a mixture of sorrow and regret, and suddenly he only wanted to know one thing. He caught her by the shoulders. "Are you okay?"

She nodded, then took a step back. "Can we talk?"

Aware they should have done this yesterday, before they left the hospital, Justin reached for her hand. She resisted his touch. Realizing she needed her physical space, he reluctantly drew away.

She crossed the yard to the lodge. Her shoulders taut, she moved gracefully up the steps and sat down on the front porch.

The afternoon was blisteringly hot, but she did not appear to want to go inside the air-conditioned comfort of the lodge.

He followed her gaze to the burned-out shell of the shed.

Her lower lip trembled and tears filled her eyes. "It's ruined."

Justin settled opposite her. Still wishing she would let him hold her, he leaned against the rail, hands braced on either side of him. "Things can be replaced."

Amanda drew another breath, more shaky than before. "Sometimes they can," she agreed, sounding a bit stronger now. She paused, looking him right in the eye. "But sometimes mistakes can't be undone." Her jaw set. "I didn't get the grant application in on time yesterday."

She tensed, forcing herself to go on, "The truth is, I got so busy I forgot all about it."

Justin had already ascertained as much. The application was the least of his worries when the woman he wanted more than anything seemed poised to storm out of his life as swiftly and unexpectedly as she had stormed in.

Amanda shook her head in mute regret. "The fact is, if Libby hadn't called me yesterday afternoon to inquire about it, I would have let the deadline come and go. But once she reminded me about it, I grabbed the grant application, left Lamar with instructions and ran off to the Laramie post office to mail it."

Justin could understand all that. He would have done the same thing. With one exception. "Why didn't you tell me where you were going?"

Her fingers tightened on the envelope in her lap. "Because I didn't want you to know I had come so close to failing the ranch." She scoffed in self-contempt, then continued softly. "I thought I could get there in time and make the deadline without you ever knowing I had screwed up."

Abruptly, Amanda got up, set the envelope aside and paced the length of the porch while Justin and the dogs watched in concern.

"But of course," she said, throwing up her hands, "the post office was closed by the time I got there." She finished recounting her story. "But, despite everything, I was determined to turn this debacle around. So after I left the hospital last night, I drove to Dallas, checked into a hotel and went to the Lone Star United Foundation offices first thing this morning to hand over the big grant application in person."

Impressed she had done all that instead of just throwing in the towel, Justin asked curiously, "Did they accept it?"

Amanda hung her head in shame. "No. Apparently, a deadline is a deadline. We're welcome to try again next year, of course, but that won't help us in the meantime…which is why," she went back to get her envelope and handed it over, "I'm resigning."

Justin took the letter only because he didn't want to tussle with her. Refusing to open it, he said, "You don't have to do that."

Amanda dug in her heels. "You spent weeks working on that grant application."

"There will be others." The stunning truth was, he meant it. He knew he could always find a way to fundraise for the ranch. However, he couldn't replace the woman standing before him, the woman who had come to mean so much to him, the woman who had lit up his life like nothing that had ever come before.

"There shouldn't have to be other grants," Amanda lamented. She raked her hands through her butterscotch-blond hair. "The truth is, I never should have taken this job."

He set the envelope aside and stepped closer, still hoping to talk sense into her. He caught her by the shoulders again, holding her when she would have run. "Then why did you?" he asked quietly.

Tears spilled out of her eyes. "Because, Justin, I thought I could help kids who had been as unfortunate as I had been growing up. Make them feel cared for and valued, the way Granddad and Gran made me feel."

"Lamar felt—feels—that way, Amanda, and all because of you."

"And you."

An awkward silence fell.

"Face it, Justin, because I have. Lamar could have died because I didn't realize he couldn't read. When I think back on all the times I should have noticed…but I didn't even once suspect it!"

"You weren't alone in that."

She stepped closer, vibrating with emotion. "The point is, you didn't just accept his recalcitrance as par for the course the way I did. You asked the questions that led to his confession."

"It could just as easily have been you." And would have been, Justin knew, given a little more time.

Amanda sighed with palpable guilt and shook her head. "I don't think so." The dogs moved closer, trying to comfort her. She refused their loyalty and affection, too.

Once again, she turned her attention to the burned-out shed that was set to be removed in its entirety later in the day. "And let's not forget that I am the one who put Lamar in danger, too, by leaving him to finish up and clean those brushes alone."

Justin wasn't about to cast the first stone. "So you learned a valuable lesson," he said, more than ready to forgive and forget.

She swung around to face him, planting her hands on her hips. "Like where I belong and where I don't."

Justin tried another way to reach her. "I understand what it is to fail a kid you want to help. To be so ticked off at yourself you want nothing more than to run away. I felt the same way when Billy Scalia died. But eventually I came to my senses, just as I am asking you to do now, and realized that blaming myself accomplished nothing."

"I disagree. It led you to move on, to where you belong, just as I intend to do."

That had an ominous ring. "You belong on this ranch, Amanda."

"No, I don't, Justin." More tears spilled. "I know what everyone thought, but they're wrong. I'm not a local hero. I'm not the role model the kids who come here are going to need. You are."

Her declaration hit him like a sledgehammer to the chest. And suddenly, Justin knew. "You were never going to stay, were you? Never going to leave behind your nomadic ways and move into the lodge for good." He regarded her with deep disappointment. "You were always going to leave." He had just been too foolishly hung up on her to see the truth. "It was just a matter of when." Bitterly, he walked away from her.

She followed, hands outstretched, wanting his forgiveness if nothing else. "That's not true," she protested.

"Isn't it? This whole time you've had one foot out the door. It's why you're rushing to get out now."

Silence fell. She wanted to deny it. In the end, he noted sadly, she couldn't.

"We can still see each other—from time to time."

Her offer was a pale imitation of what they could have had. He shook his head, his mood every bit as melancholy as hers. "No, Amanda, we can't do things halfway. You're either in this all the way, or you're out."

"You don't mean that."

The hell he didn't.

He set his jaw. "If you walk out on this ranch now, it's the same as walking out on me." The one thing he wouldn't—couldn't—tolerate was another woman who put her own needs or wants above their relationship.

"Then I'm out," Amanda said sadly, her heart every bit as trampled as his. "Don't you see?" She covered her eyes and walked away. "I have no choice."

One week later, Amanda sat in front of the television in her granddad's home, watching—and rewatching—the KTLZ segment on the soon-to-open Laramie Boys Ranch.

There was no doubt about it—Justin was amazing. Everything the kids would need in a mentor. Plus, incredibly well-suited to run the ranch. The board members were also interviewed in the segment, but it was Justin's vision, drive and energy that stole the day.

And had stolen her heart.

Amanda sighed. If only she hadn't let him down. Let everyone down. But she had, and there was no going back. No use in her ineptitude dragging everyone else down.

The doorbell rang. Irritated—because the last thing she felt like was talking to anyone—Amanda paused the recording and went to answer.

Libby, Miss Mim and Mitzy stood on the front porch. "A.B. said we would find you here," Libby said.

Amanda wasn't surprised they'd had no trouble tracking her down. A.B. had been spending a lot of time in Laramie courting Miss Mim. Whereas Amanda had needed time alone. Out of politeness, she ushered them into her granddad's small, neat, one-story home.

She shut the door behind them, and mindful of Miss Mim's age, guided them into the sitting area so the older woman could sit comfortably. "If you're here to dress me down for botching up the big grant application, there's no need. I take full responsibility for not getting it in on time, and I feel absolutely terrible."

"It's not an apology we need," Mitzy said, taking a seat on the sofa, looking as much social worker as friend.

Libby sank into an armchair with her usual elegance. Miss Mim took the other. All noticed the freeze-frame of Justin and the boys ranch on the TV screen.

Amanda flushed and hastily switched it off before sitting beside Miss Mim on the sofa.

All eyes swung back to her. "We're here because we need you to come back, Amanda," Libby said.

Mitzy added, "Justin and Lamar most of all."

The notion that she might be missed as much as she missed the two of them hit Amanda square in the heart.

She swallowed. "I'm sure my leaving left a temporary gap in how things were running," she acknowledged reluctantly. For one thing, she had been doing most of the meal planning and cooking. "But I assure you, Justin is more than capable of picking up the slack."

Attempting to ease the tension in the room, she shook her head ruefully and said, "Just don't hire him to do any carpentry. That is definitely not in his skill set. The same way administrative duties are not in mine." He was better at rescuing homeless dogs and kids, and even women—like her—who had never experienced true, romantic love....

Libby sobered. "We realize now that we threw too much at you at once and have accepted your resignation in the spirit in which it was given. Justin has been appointed ranch director."

Something was finally as it should be. "That's good news," Amanda said with relief. At least she hadn't messed that up for Justin. Especially since he had more than deserved to have the job all along. She leaned forward. "How is Lamar doing?" She knew he had completely recovered from smoke inhalation, but other than that...

"Justin arranged to have Lamar tested last week, and we discovered he has dyslexia."

Amanda paused to absorb that. "So, since no one helped him with his disability, he's had great difficulty learning to read."

Mitzy nodded. "Now that we understand what the problem is, we can bring special teachers to the ranch to help him instead of putting Lamar back into the high school, where he could not possibly succeed at this time."

No wonder he hadn't wanted to sign up for classes at LHS. Amanda felt a twinge of guilt for having forced the issue without delving more deeply into the real reason behind Lamar's truancy.

"At Justin's urging, we've also decided to focus on students with learning disorders such as dyslexia or dysgraphia," Libby said happily. "Grouping them together that way will help the kids realize they are not alone."

"That certainly makes the selection process easier," Amanda said.

Miss Mim sighed. "Sadly, there are far too many kids who need this kind of help. Which is why we want to continue our efforts to quickly expand the funding and the facilities at the boys ranch. And we need your help to do that. Both as the head of the carpentry vocational program and as assistant ranch director."

Amanda wanted to help, more than they knew. She had only been there a month, but the ranch still felt like home to her in a way no other place ever had. Which, maybe, was what scared her. The idea that she would come to rely on being there, only to be booted out, the way she had been by her oft-divorcing parents when she was a kid.

Nevertheless, even though she was tempted to jump at the chance to go back, she felt obligated to remind them, "I not only failed in my previous employment there, but failed badly." To the point she'd had no choice but to quit in disgrace, lest she drag Justin—and the ranch—down with her.

Kindness radiated from her visitors.

"We all make mistakes," Mitzy said. "What's important is showing the kids that when you fall down, you pick yourself up, dust yourself off and keep going."

"What's that saying? 'You learn more from any failure than you ever do from any success,'" Libby quoted from memory.

Miss Mim leaned over and patted Amanda's hand. "Lamar is counting on you to help him through the tough months ahead, to provide the emotional support and understanding only you can give. You can't let him down."

Suddenly, Amanda was near tears. But she blinked them back, refusing to let herself hope until she knew. "What does Justin think about this?" she asked.

The three ladies knew the answer to her question. That was clear from the way they looked at each other as they stood and prepared to leave.

Miss Mim regarded her with a poker face. "That, you will have to ask Justin yourself."

"Got a minute?"

Justin turned to see A. B. Johnson framed in the door of his office. For a brief moment, he hoped that

Amanda had come with her grandfather, but A.B. was alone. Justin rose and the two men shook hands. "What can I do for you?" he asked cordially.

"You can hear an old man out."

Appreciating A.B.'s efforts to do right by his beloved granddaughter, Justin gestured for the older gentleman to have a seat and waited.

A.B. cleared his throat. "Years ago, when Amanda's parents started having problems, I did my best to stay out of it. In retrospect, I wish I had interfered. Because if I had sat them both down and talked to them about the importance of taking the time to work things out, instead of just getting divorced, maybe everything would have turned out differently."

Justin paused. "You think her parents are still in love with each other?"

A.B. shook his head. "I think they never had a chance to find out what true, lasting love is, because they didn't hang in there long enough to find out. Instead, they became fixated on the infatuation stage of a relationship, where everything is easy and great, and never learned what it is to work through your problems with the person you love, difficult as that may sometimes be."

Justin wished it were that simple. "That's not the case with Amanda and me."

The older man watched him skeptically. "You're saying you were never infatuated with each other?"

Justin scoffed. "We were plenty attracted." To the point he figured he would never get over her.

A.B. pressed on, "You were never friends, then."

Justin wished everyone weren't so interested in sizing up his emotional state—and offering ways to fix his problems with Amanda. "Amanda and I had the potential to be great friends."

"But anything permanent wasn't in the cards for you."

Justin made no effort to hide his growing frustration. "We never got that far." Although there had been a brief time when he'd dreamed of just that.

"Exactly my point." A.B. smiled.

"I appreciate you stopping by and trying to help…" Justin rose to his feet.

A.B. remained seated. "But?"

Justin sighed and sat back down again. "All my life I was taught that I could achieve anything I set my mind to, if I just wanted it bad enough. And worked hard enough." He swallowed around the clenched feeling in his throat. "I thought the same thing applied to my relationship with Amanda."

A.B. nodded compassionately. "Until she quit her job here and took off."

Exactly. "I can't make her want to be here. That has to come from inside." He pointed to the center of his chest, wishing he did have Amanda's heart. "And I sure as heck am not going to be with someone who doesn't value our relationship above all else." He had done that before. He wasn't doing it again.

"I see your point."

"You just don't approve."

A.B. stood up and moved slowly toward the door. "I think you're taking an easy out."

Justin stopped Amanda's granddad before he could leave. "In what way?"

Their eyes met, man to man. "In accepting her declaration that everything—her relationship with you, her taking a job here, even her getting involved and mentoring Lamar—was all a terrible mistake."

He *had* tried to talk sense into her! Only to have her head for the hills, anyway. "What would you have me do?" Justin lamented.

A.B. clapped a paternal hand on Justin's shoulder. "Fight for her as hard as you fought for this ranch. Let her know that you accept there will be setbacks and you're okay with that." He paused. "Because what you *will* have together, if you both take that big leap of faith, will surely be worth it."

Justin thought about everything Amanda's grandfather had said, and he was still thinking about it when he went out to take care of the new ranch sign. He parked beneath the archway over the entrance, grabbed his toolbox and hopped up into the bed of his truck.

He was just trying to figure out how to unfasten the wooden Lost Pines Ranch sign from the metal arch when a familiar red truck pulled up behind him.

Amanda got out, her straw hat with the sassy rolled brim pulled low over the sunglasses shading her eyes. Wearing the same short denim skirt, layered tank tops and flip-flops she'd had on the first time they'd met, she sashayed toward him. "Hey there, fella," she said.

He tried not to get too excited as he surveyed every gorgeous inch of her. "Hey there, yourself," he returned softly, getting down from the bed of the truck. Did her sudden appearance mean what he hoped?

She studied the lopsided sign above them, shook her head and heaved a dramatic sigh. "I heard you were going to attempt this yourself," she drawled.

"I can handle it."

Amanda strode toward him, her beautiful blond hair glinting in the sunshine. As she neared, he couldn't help but inhale the citrus scent of her perfume.

"I'm sure you can." Amanda stepped closer to inspect the rusty screws bolting the weathered wood to the old iron frame. She took off her sunglasses and hooked them in the neckline of her tank top. "The thing is, you shouldn't have to." A pulse worked in her neck as she swept off her hat and set it aside. "At times like this," she declared, "a man needs a partner." Her voice caught and she pushed on hoarsely. "The kind of mate who can be counted on to be there through thick and thin." She paused again, moisture glinting in her pretty amber eyes. "The kind of partner my gran and granddad had in each other."

Now they were getting somewhere. Justin fitted his hands around her waist and brought her even closer. "You're talking marriage?"

For the first time since she had arrived, she hesitated. "Longevity."

He chuckled. "What's the difference?"

She tipped her head up. "I don't know," she challenged. "You tell me."

He wanted her, but needed a real future with her and hoped that she realized that, too. "Longevity could just mean living a long time," he pointed out.

She splayed both hands affectionately against his chest. "Nothing wrong with that."

Justin threaded his hands through her hair and searched her face, still hardly able to believe she was here. Softly, he warned, "I'm not going to be content with an affair, even a long-term one. I want rock-solid commitment. Marriage." *With you, damn it all.*

His throat closing, his voice rusty, he pushed on. "I want to be with someone who isn't afraid to commit to me and our union for the rest of her life. Someone who wants to work by my side during the day and sleep in my arms at night. Someone who is ready and willing to take care of this ranch and all the kids who come to it... and maybe even have a baby or two of our own with me."

Her eyes glistened with heartfelt emotion. "That's a tall order," she allowed finally.

He gave in to the desire assailing him, lifted her face up and brushed his lips across the softness of hers. "Made for a tall woman."

She moaned with a mixture of humor and pent-up passion. "Are you making fun of my height?"

Knowing no other woman had ever made him this happy, or ever would, he shook his head. He kissed the top of her head. "Your height is one of the things I love best about you."

She let out a contented mewl and curled against him. "You know, if we did ever have kids they'd likely end up being seven feet tall."

He stroked his hand through her hair. He had missed her so much. "Then I guess we'd be looking up at them."

"We might have to raise a ceiling or two."

"Or just build the ceilings extra tall to begin with," he joked.

Amanda drew a breath and stepped back, as if needing distance to say what she had to. She flashed a wobbly yet sincere smile. "Before we get too sidetracked... the way you and I always tend to do... I want you to know something." She paused, her gaze roving his face as if memorizing it for all time. "I came here, first and foremost, to apologize with all my heart."

"For?"

She met his level look. "Walking out on you and letting you and the ranch and everyone associated with it down."

He would have forgiven her for that, even without the formal mea culpa. He nodded, hoping this wasn't the beginning of another kiss-off. "Apology accepted."

Amanda knitted her hands together. "I also came here hoping you'd take me back."

Personally? Professionally? Her wary expression gave no clue. "As assistant director?" He tried to keep the question offhand.

Amanda nodded confirmation. She rushed on while his heart was still turning over in his chest. "And girlfriend, and friend, and potential life mate or wife. However you want to say it." She lifted a staying palm. "I don't care. I just want to know that we can start over."

He liked the sound of that. Justin tugged her against him, chest to chest, thigh to thigh. He buried his face in the fragrant silk of her hair. "Or pick up where we left off."

Amanda clung to him, all artifice gone. She kissed him breathlessly. "And know that we'll be here for each other, through all the ups and downs of life."

What do you know? That was exactly what he wanted. Justin smiled. "I think we can handle that." They indulged in a leisurely kiss. "You know why?"

Her eyes were misty with happiness as she shook her head.

"Because we're meant to be together." Knowing it was time to let the rest of the barriers go, he regarded her seriously and confessed all he'd held back. "And because I love you, Amanda, and always will."

Amanda went up on tiptoe and kissed him. Hotly. Eagerly. "Oh, Justin," she whispered, trembling all the more, "I love you, too, so very much."

He pressed his lips to her temple, aware he had everything he had ever wanted, at long last. "So, it's a deal?"

Amanda looked deep into his eyes. "Absolutely, we have a deal! I'm yours. And you're mine. From here on out..."

Epilogue

Fifteen months later...

"Do you want to choose what's for dinner, or shall I?" Amanda asked her husband as they walked into the kitchen of the cozy cottage built just for them.

Justin met her at the refrigerator to survey the contents. "Depends on what we've got planned for later," he teased, appreciating—as did she—the intimacy their new living arrangement offered.

Amanda slid her arms around his neck. "Same thing as always, I expect." She nestled closer.

Justin grinned and bent his head to demonstrate. "A little kissing."

Amanda tenderly kissed him back. "A lot of cuddling."

They sighed in unison. "And everything in between."

They made out a little more, then, still tingling with anticipation, Amanda shook her head. "I can't believe it's December of our second school year already!"

Justin shook his head in wonder. "Or that you and I've been married nearly six months." He paused, reflecting. "The past sixteen months have been quite a ride, haven't they?"

Yes, they had, from the very beginning. The boys ranch had opened a year ago August, right on schedule, with Lamar, seven other boys and two house parents settling into Bunkhouse One. Amanda, Justin and a teacher specializing in learning disorders had bunked in the lodge.

The carpentry building had been completed in late fall of the initial term. And by spring they'd had the funds to add another bunkhouse, eight more kids, another set of house parents and two more full-time teachers. Now, they were planning a third bunkhouse.

"Your granddad has had a lot of great changes, too." A.B. had sold his business and his home in San Angelo, and relocated to a condo in the Laramie Gardens senior-living center.

Amanda smiled. "Can you believe he and Miss Mim are getting married on New Year's Eve?"

Justin sat down on a chair and pulled her down onto his lap. "I knew something was up when they both started volunteering at the ranch so much." Granddad had helped out, teaching carpentry to the boys. Miss Mim had set up a ranch library, complete with Dewey decimal system and online catalogue.

"And let's not forget Lamar." Amanda's heart brimmed with affection. "Not only has he learned to read, he's become quite the leader."

Justin agreed with paternal pride. "There's no one better when it comes to showing the new kids the ropes."

Amanda splayed her hands across his chest. "It helps a lot, having specialized teachers and a curriculum designed specifically for dyslexics."

In fact, they had been so successful the county was talking about starting up a day program for kids with learning disabilities from stable homes, to be paid for by the school district and held in classrooms out at the ranch.

Reveling in the warmth and strength of her handsome husband, Amanda continued, "It also helps to have such a visionary at the helm of the entire ranch."

Justin stroked a hand through her hair. "And his trusty assistant director and carpentry and culinary whiz…"

They kissed again, even more tenderly. She'd always known she loved working with her hands. Helping kids. But… "I never thought I'd enjoy being a sidekick quite so much." She chuckled as they broke apart. "But maybe that's because you do all the paperwork."

Justin's eyes gleamed with satisfaction. "We do make a good team."

"One," Amanda added mysteriously, her heart beginning to race with excitement, "that may be ready for expansion."

Justin studied her as the wonder of her words sunk in. "You're…?"

"Almost three months along," she admitted, thrilling at the contentment in his blue eyes. "I found out when I went to the doctor today. I wanted to wait until we were alone to tell you."

Justin threw back his head and laughed in triumph.

He brought her close for another heartfelt hug. "This is glorious news, Mrs. McCabe."

Amanda couldn't stop smiling. "I think so, too."

Happiness engulfed them as their fondest dreams began to take shape. "So what do you think?" Justin brushed the hair from her face and tucked it behind her ear. "Girl or boy?"

Amanda rested a palm on the gentle slope of her tummy. "I don't know about this one," she enthused with a playful wink. "But I imagine before we're done we'll have both a son and a daughter." At least she hoped.

Justin thought of his own family. "Or five sons."

Not to be outdone, Amanda exclaimed, "Or five daughters!"

They stared at each other and laughed. All Amanda knew for sure was that the ranch was a roaring success. She was going to have Justin's baby. And she had never been happier.

Justin shifted her off his lap, swung her up in his arms and strode toward the rear of the house. "Where are we going?"

"Exactly where you think." He paused and kissed her, the love flowing freely between them. "To celebrate."

* * * * *